CRIME £3
23
H

D0179022

GALLOWS COURT

Martin Edwards has won the Edgar,
Agatha, H.R.F. Keating, Macavity, Poirot
and Dagger awards as well as being shortlisted for
the Theakston's Prize. He is President
of the Detection Club, Chair of the CWA
and consultant to the British Library's
bestselling crime classics series.

In 2020, he was awarded the
CWA Diamond Dagger, the highest
honour in British crime writing.

MARTIN EDWARDS:
WINNER OF THE CWA DIAMOND DAGGER 2020

'Martin knows more about crime fiction than anyone else working in the field today. He's always been a fan of the genre and his passion shines through in his work: the fiction, the non-fiction and the short stories. In his editing, he's brought new writers and forgotten favourites to discerning readers. I'm delighted his work is being recognised in this way.'

Ann Cleeves

'Martin's fiction alone makes him a truly worthy winner of the Diamond Dagger. His editorial excellence, his erudition, his enthusiasm for and contributions to the genre, his support of other writers, and his warm-hearted friendship are the icing on the cake.'

Lee Child

'Martin Edwards is a thoroughly deserved winner of this prized award. He has contributed so much to the genre, not only through the impressive canon of his own wonderfully written novels, but through his tireless work for crime writing in the UK.'

Peter James

'Martin Edwards is a wonderful choice to receive the Diamond Dagger. He's a very fine writer but has also devoted huge energy to both the CWA and Detection Club – all done quietly and companionably, which is a rare thing. I love a man who takes care of archives. I am delighted for him, but as we always say: it's for lifetime achievement – but please don't stop what you do so well!'

Lindsey Davis

'Martin is not only one of the finest crime writers of his generation. He is the heir to Julian Symons and H.R.F. Keating as the leading authority on our genre, fostering and promoting it with unflagging enthusiasm, to the benefit of us all. I'm delighted that our community can show its gratitude by honouring him in this way.'

Peter Lovesey

'Martin Edwards is not only a fine writer but he is also ridiculously knowledgeable about the field of crime and suspense fiction. He wears his learning lightly and is always the most congenial company. He is also a great champion of crime writing and crime writers. His novels feature an acute sense of place as well as deep psychological insights. As a solicitor, he knows the legal world more intimately than most of his fellow novelists. He is a fitting winner of the Diamond Dagger.'

Ian Rankin

BY MARTIN EDWARDS

The Lake District Mysteries

The Coffin Trail
The Cipher Garden
The Arsenic Labyrinth
The Serpent Pool
The Hanging Wood
The Frozen Shroud
The Dungeon House

The Harry Devlin Series

All the Lonely People
Suspicious Minds
I Remember You
Yesterday's Papers
Eve of Destruction
The Devil in Disguise
First Cut is the Deepest
Waterloo Sunset

Fiction

Take My Breath Away
Dancing for the Hangman
Gallows Court
Mortmain Hall

Non-Fiction

Catching Killers
Truly Criminal
The Golden Age of Murder
The Story of Classic Crime in 100 Books

GALLOWS COURT

MARTIN EDWARDS

HEAD
ZEUS

First published in the UK in 2018 by Head of Zeus Ltd
This paperback edition first published in 2020 by Head of Zeus Ltd

Copyright © Martin Edwards, 2018

The moral right of Martin Edwards to be identified as the author of
this work has been asserted in accordance with the
Copyright, Designs and Patents Act of 1988.

All rights reserved. No part of this publication may be reproduced,
stored in a retrieval system, or transmitted in any form or by any
means, electronic, mechanical, photocopying, recording, or
otherwise, without the prior permission of both the copyright
owner and the above publisher of this book.

This is a work of fiction. All characters, organizations,
and events portrayed in this novel are either products of
the author's imagination or are used fictitiously.

9 7 5 3 2 4 6 8

A catalogue record for this book is available from
the British Library.

ISBN (PB): 9781800241121
ISBN (E): 9781788546065

Typeset by Divaddict Publishing Solutions Ltd.

Printed and bound in Great Britain by
CPI Group (UK) Ltd, Croydon CR0 4YY

MIX
Paper from
responsible sources
FSC® C013604

Head of Zeus Ltd
First Floor East
5–8 Hardwick Street
London EC1R 4RG

WWW.HEADOFZEUS.COM

To Jonathan and Catherine

Juliet Brentano's Journal

30 January 1919

My parents died yesterday.

Henrietta has just broken the news. Tears filled her eyes, and she put a hand on my arm. I didn't speak, and I didn't cry. The gale sweeping over the island from the Irish Sea howled for me.

Henrietta says Harold Brown sent Judge Savernake a telegram from London. My parents caught the Spanish flu, he said, like thousands before them. It was all over very quickly, and they passed away peacefully in each other's arms.

It's a fairy story. The emptiness in her voice told me she doesn't believe a word of it.

Neither do I. My mother and father were murdered, I'm sure of it.

And Rachel Savernake is responsible.

I

'Jacob Flint is watching the house again.' The housekeeper's voice rose. 'Do you think he knows about…?'

'How could he?' Rachel Savernake said. 'Don't worry, I'll deal with him.'

'You can't!' the older woman protested. 'You don't have time.'

Rachel adjusted her cloche hat in front of the looking glass. A demure face returned her gaze. Nobody would guess her nerve-ends were tingling. Was this how the Judge felt, when he put on his black cap?

'There's time enough. The car isn't due for five minutes.'

She slid on her evening gloves. Mrs Trueman handed her the bag, and opened the front door. A voice crooned from the drawing room. Martha was listening to the Dorsey Brothers on the new automatic gramophone. Rachel danced down the short flight of steps in her Pompadour heels, humming Cole Porter's song, 'Let's Do It'.

Fog was slithering over the square, and cold January air nibbled her cheeks. She was glad of her sable coat. The lamp-lights tinged the dirty greyness with an eerie yellow hue. Long years spent on a small island had accustomed her to sea frets. She felt a strange affection for the winter mists drifting in from the water, rippling like gauze curtains, draping the damp landscape. A London particular was a different beast – sooty, sulphurous, and malign, as capable of choking you as a Limehouse ruffian. The greasy air made her eyes smart, and its acrid taste burned her throat. Yet the foul and muddy swirl troubled her no more than pitch darkness frightens a blind man. Tonight she felt invincible.

A figure detached itself from the shadows. Peering through the gloom, she made out a tall, skinny man in coat and trilby. A long woollen scarf, loosely tied, hung from his shoulders. His gait was energetic yet awkward. She guessed he'd been plucking up courage to ring the doorbell.

'Miss Savernake! Sorry to bother you on a Sunday evening!' He sounded young, eager, and utterly unapologetic. 'My name is—'

'I know who you are.'

'But we haven't been introduced.' Unruly strands of fair hair sneaked from under the trilby, and a pompous clearing of the throat couldn't disguise his *gaucherie*. At twenty-four, he had the fresh, scrubbed features of a schoolboy. 'I happen to be—'

'Jacob Flint, a reporter with the *Clarion*. You must know that I never speak to the press.'

'I've done my homework.' He glanced to left and right. 'What I do know is that it's unsafe for a lady to be out while a brutal killer prowls the London streets.'

'Perhaps I'm not really a lady.'

His eyes fastened on the diamond clip in her hat. 'You look every inch—'

4

'Appearances can be deceptive.'

He leaned towards her. His skin smelled of coal-tar soap. 'If you're not really a lady, all the more reason for you to take care.'

'It is unwise to threaten me, Mr Flint.'

He took a step back. 'I'm desperate to talk to you. You recall the note I left with your housekeeper?'

Of course she did. She'd watched from the window as he delivered it. He'd fiddled nervously with his tie while waiting on the step. Surely he wasn't stupid enough to believe she'd answer the door herself?

'My car will arrive presently, and I don't intend to conduct an interview anywhere, let alone on a pavement in the fog.'

'You can trust me, Miss Savernake.'

'Don't be absurd. You're a journalist.'

'Honestly, we have something in common.'

'What, exactly?' She ticked points off on her gloved hand. 'You learned your trade as a reporter in Yorkshire before arriving in London last autumn. You lodge in Amwell Street, and you worry that your landlady's daughter seeks to trade her body for marriage. Ambition drove you to join the muckrakers on the *Clarion* rather than a respectable newspaper. The editor admires your persistence, but frets about your rashness.'

He gulped. 'How…?'

'You have a morbid interest in crime, and regard Thomas Betts' recent accident as both a misfortune and an opportunity. With the *Clarion*'s chief crime reporter on his death bed, you scent a chance to make your name.' She took a breath. 'Be careful what you wish for. If Wall Street can crumble, so can anything. How unfortunate if your promising career were cut short, like his.'

5

He flinched, as if she'd slapped his face. When he spoke, his voice was hoarse.

'No wonder you solved the Chorus Girl Murder. You're quite a detective; you put the boys in blue to shame.'

'When you sent me a note, did you expect me to do nothing?'

'I'm flattered that you took the trouble to investigate me.' He ventured a grin, showing crooked teeth. 'Or are you brilliant enough to deduce all that from the careless knotting of my scarf, and the fact my shoes need a shine?'

'Find someone else to write about, Mr Flint.'

'My editor would be shocked to hear us described as muck-rakers.' He'd recovered his composure as quickly as he'd lost it. 'The *Clarion* gives the common folk a voice. It's our latest slogan. *Our readers need to know.*'

'Not about me.'

'If you leave money out of it, you and I aren't so very different.' He grinned. 'Both new to London, inquisitive, and stubborn as mules. I notice you don't deny solving the Chorus Girl case. So what do you make of the latest sensation, this butchering of poor Mary-Jane Hayes in Covent Garden?'

He paused, but she didn't fill the silence.

'Mary-Jane Hayes' remains were found in a sack, and her head was missing.' He breathed out. 'The details were too foul to print. She was a decent woman – that's what keeps our readers awake at night. Not someone who got what she deserved.'

Rachel Savernake's face resembled a porcelain mask. 'Do women ever get what they deserve?'

'This madman won't stop at one. They never do. Before any more women are harmed, he must be brought to justice.'

She considered him. 'So you believe in justice?'

The sleek contours of a Rolls-Royce Phantom loomed through the dirty yellow fog, and the young man skipped out of its path to avoid being crushed. It drew up by Rachel's side.

'Time to go, Mr Flint.'

A broad-shouldered man, six feet four if an inch, climbed out of the car. As he opened the rear door, Rachel handed him her bag. Jacob Flint gave the fellow a wary glance. He looked as if he'd be more at home in a heavyweight boxer's dressing gown than in a chauffeur's livery. His buttons gleamed like warning lights.

Jacob gave a little bow. 'It never does to hide from the press, Miss Savernake. If I don't tell your story, someone less scrupulous will do the job. Let me have a scoop, and you won't regret it.'

Rachel seized hold of the loose ends of his scarf, and pulled the knot tight against his neck. Startled, he let out a gasp.

'I never waste time on regrets, Mr Flint,' she whispered.

Releasing the scarf, she took the bag from Trueman, and settled herself in the back of the Phantom. As the car glided away into the night, she was conscious of Jacob Flint rubbing his neck as he watched her disappear. Might he prove useful? To give him the story he craved would be risky, but she'd never been afraid to gamble. It was in her blood.

'Did the boy make trouble?' Trueman asked through the speaking tube.

'No, if he knew anything, he'd have let it slip.'

On the back seat beside her lay a parcel wrapped in tissue paper to protect the burgundy velvet upholstery. She ripped away the tissue to reveal a service revolver. She'd taught herself enough about firearms to recognise a Webley .455 Mark

VI. The chequered grips and nickel plating were distinctive, but she didn't need to ask whether it was untraceable. Trueman thought of everything. Opening the alligator-skin bag, she slipped the gun inside.

As they drove towards Euston, she saw more uniformed policemen on the pavements than passers-by. Not a single woman had ventured out on foot. With the Covent Garden murderer on the loose, nobody would stroll around central London in the murk without good cause. The air was rank with fear.

The Doric Arch reared up out in front of them, a grotesque monument to a dead civilisation. She checked her watch. Ten minutes to six. Despite the fog, they had made good time.

'Stop here.'

Jumping out of the car, heels clicking on the cobblestones, she hurried into the station. People were milling around in the bright blue light of the refreshment room. Rachel strode towards the luggage office. An elderly man who bore a startling resemblance to Stanley Baldwin was complaining loudly to nobody in particular, while waving his walking stick at the message in black capitals on a large piece of cardboard.

CLOSED UNTIL FURTHER NOTICE

She halted beneath a yellow film poster advertising Alfred Hitchcock's *Blackmail*. All she had to do was wait, an elegant spider anticipating the arrival of a hapless fly.

Lawrence Pardoe came into view at precisely one minute before six. A small, portly man in a cashmere overcoat and bowler hat, he was carrying a cheap plywood case so gingerly it might have been crammed with Dresden china. His eyes kept darting around, as if he expected a thief to cosh him.

She watched him approach the luggage office. Only when he was two yards away did he notice the cardboard sign. The sight of it knocked the breath out of him. Putting the case on the floor, he pulled a handkerchief from his pocket and mopped his brow. A burly police constable materialised out of the crowd, and marched towards him. Rachel took a step forward, and saw the policeman mutter into Pardoe's ear.

Pardoe contrived a bilious smile, seeming to insist that he was quite all right, officer, and no, thank you, he didn't need any help. With a parting glance at the plywood case, the constable gave a cheerful nod, and turned away. Pardoe sagged in relief.

Would panic make him cut and run? He was a sick man: he might keel over from a heart attack.

But no. After a moment's hesitation, he picked the case up again, and plodded towards the exit. This was her cue to retrace her steps, moving twice as fast.

Outside the station, the fog was thickening, but the Rolls-Royce's outlines were unmistakeable. Trueman opened the rear door, and she climbed in. Peering through the window, she spotted Pardoe stumbling through the grey night, weighed down by his burden, searching for a maroon Phantom with black wings.

Without a word, Trueman strode forward. He seized hold of the plywood case, hoisted it into the motoring trunk, and motioned Pardoe inside the car.

The door had closed on Pardoe before he noticed her. Sweat smeared his forehead, and his breathing rasped. His complexion was the colour of an over-ripe plum. He was a man of fifty, unaccustomed to exercise; people had always fetched and carried for him. Rachel smiled sweetly, hoping he wouldn't die before the time was right.

'Good evening, Mr Pardoe.'

'Good… good evening.' He scanned her features, screwing up his eyes as if trying to decipher a cryptograph. 'It's not… Miss Savernake?'

'You detect a family resemblance?'

'Yes, yes. Faint, of course, but… remarkable man, your late father.' He fished for a silk handkerchief, and wiped his damp forehead. 'Judge Savernake was… a very great loss.'

'You seem distressed.'

He coughed. 'My apologies, Miss Savernake, but I have had… a rather trying time.'

His brow contracted. Was he trying to read her mind? A hopeless task. He couldn't possibly guess his fate.

Trueman started the engine, and Rachel laid one hand upon her bag. The Phantom's engine was so quiet that she could almost hear the clank and grind of Pardoe's brain.

As they turned into Tottenham Court Road, he said, 'Where are we going?'

'To South Audley Street.'

'Not my house?' He was bewildered.

'Your house, yes. You did as you were told, I hope, and instructed your staff that their presence wasn't required this evening?'

'I received a message from a trusted friend, asking me to come to Euston Station and leave… something at the luggage office. I was told this car would collect me, and that I'd meet a young lady – I didn't realise it would be you, Miss Savernake – who would take me to see my friend. He didn't explain why he wanted me to clear everyone out of the house…'

'Forgive me,' Rachel said. 'I sent the message.'

Terror flared in his eyes. 'Impossible!'

'Nothing is impossible,' she said quietly. 'You must believe that, if it's the last thing you do.'

'I don't understand.'

She took the revolver from her bag, and pushed it against his ribs. 'You don't need to. Hush, now.'

A sour tang of wood polish hung in the air of Pardoe's study. The room had a single door, but no window. The only light was cast by a candle in a gold stick; the ticking of a grandmother clock seemed unnaturally loud. Pardoe bent over his roll-top desk, hands trembling as if he suffered from palsy. On the desk were a pen, several blank sheets of foolscap, two envelopes, and a bottle of Indian ink.

Trueman sat in a leather wingback armchair. His right hand held a gun, his left a butcher's knife with a gleaming blade. At his feet lay a Kodak Brownie camera. A brown bearskin rug was spread out on the floor. In the middle stood the plywood trunk Pardoe had carried inside at the point of Rachel's gun.

Rachel delved into her handbag, and brought out a chess piece. A black pawn. Pardoe gave a low moan. She walked towards the desk, and placed the pawn next to the inkwell, before picking up a sheet of foolscap and an envelope, and putting them into her bag.

'Why are you doing this?' Pardoe blinked away a tear. 'There's a Milner safe next door. The combination...'

'Why would I steal your valuables? I have more money than I know what to do with.'

'Then... what do you want?'

'I want you to write a confession to murder,' Rachel said. 'Don't worry about the phrasing. I shall dictate every word.'

The last vestiges of colour drained from the plump cheeks. 'Confess to murder? Have you lost your mind?'

Trueman leaned forward in his chair, a movement pregnant with menace. Rachel pointed her gun at Pardoe's chest.

'Please.' Pardoe made a gurgling noise. 'Your father would not wish…'

'The Judge is dead.' She smiled. 'But I inherited a taste for melodrama.'

'I… I have been the most loyal—'

'Once you blot your signature, we shall leave the room, and you will lock the door. Leave the key in the lock. In the bottom drawer of your desk – you will find the fastening broken – is a pistol loaded with one bullet. Place it to your temple, or inside your mouth. You are free to choose. It will be a quick end, far preferable to the alternative.'

He twitched like a guinea pig confronted by a vivisectionist. 'You cannot order me to kill myself!'

'It's for the best,' she said. 'You are already under sentence of death. How long did your friend in Harley Street give you? Six months at the outside?'

Astonishment made him blink. 'You can't know that! I told nobody, and Sir Eustace would never…'

'Remember Sir Eustace's prognosis. This is your chance to escape the drawn-out agony he foresaw. Don't waste that single shot.'

'But… why?'

'Do you know what happened to Juliet Brentano?'

'What are you talking about?' Pardoe screwed his eyes shut. 'I don't understand.'

'You're right,' she said. 'You'll go to your grave not under-standing.' She gestured to Trueman, who pointed his knife at the older man's throat.

'Don't dwell on what you have to do,' she said. 'A swift end is a mercy. Sixty seconds, that's all you have from the moment we are outside the room. No longer.'

Pardoe looked into her eyes. What he saw there made him flinch.

After a long pause, he said hoarsely, 'Very well.'

'Fill your pen with ink.'

Slowly, Pardoe did as he was told.

'Write this.' She spoke slowly, burying each word in his brain like a soft-nosed bullet. '*I strangled Mary-Jane Hayes with her own scarf, and then dismembered her with a hacksaw. I acted alone...*'

2

Jacob Flint walked home. Exercise helped him to order his thoughts. The long-awaited conversation with Rachel Savernake had left him grappling with fresh questions, when he'd yearned for answers.

Disappointment weighed him down, heavy as a boulder on his back. He prided himself on his ability as an interviewer, and he often pored over copies of *Notable British Trials*, studying techniques of cross-examination. This afternoon, he'd rehearsed in front of the mirror in his bedroom. Yet preparation counted for nothing once he came face to face with the woman. He felt hot and stupid at the memory of her cool, concentrated gaze reducing his questions to babble.

What had he learned? About the murder of Mary-Jane Hayes, nothing. A copper he knew was part of the hunt for the man depraved enough to strangle a woman, and then decapitate her, and conceal the head. His tame constable, Stan Thurlow, had let slip that Scotland Yard expected Rachel Savernake to take an interest in the Covent Garden murder. If she'd formed a theory about the latest murder, she'd given him no clues. The scoop he dreamed of remained as distant as the moon.

As he turned into Amwell Street, he told himself that he'd not wasted his time. At the cost of fleeting embarrassment, he'd discovered that Rachel Savernake's thoroughness knew no bounds. The note he'd sent her, which he'd worded with as much care as if writing a leader for *The Times*, had provoked her into checking into him. For heaven's sake, she'd even found out that Elaine Dowd wanted to marry him.

Why take such pains, when she could simply refuse to say a word? As he passed the cavernous post office building at Mount Pleasant, the answer struck him, clear as a torch beam slicing through darkness.

It was a sign of a guilty conscience. Rachel Savernake had something to hide.

His landlady refused to refer to her home by its street number. Mrs Dowd had christened it Edgar House, in memory of her husband. A bomb dropped by one of the Zeppelins during the Silent Raid had killed Edgar Dowd. A prosperous accountant, he'd left his widow and young daughter comfortably provided for, but Mrs Dowd's capital had diminished with the passage of time, a process speeded by her fondness for French couture and London gin. She took in lodgers to make ends meet.

Oliver McAlinden, a former tenant, and a colleague of Jacob's at the *Clarion*, had recommended Edgar House as convenient for Fleet Street and surprisingly cheap. Mrs Dowd offered a generous discount to young men she regarded as a 'good let'. The price Jacob paid was putting up with her incessant chatter and unsubtle matchmaking.

Despite the low rent, he was her only paying guest, and she'd taken to inviting him to join her and Elaine for supper. Jacob gathered that she'd spent years encouraging her daughter to fraternise with the pimpled son of a wealthy local draper, with scant success. She'd fared no better with Oily McAlinden, whose tastes didn't seem to include the opposite sex. Elaine had refused to introduce her mother to her most recent beau. Jacob suspected the fellow was married, and she'd needed to be devious. All she'd let slip was that she'd ended the relationship shortly before Jacob's arrival in London; he guessed she'd tired of waiting for the fellow to leave his wife. Perhaps she'd decided her mother was right, and that it was time to settle down. But the horizons of a young journalist wanting to make his way in the world lay far beyond a pipe-and-slippers existence in Amwell Street.

He meant to dash up to his eyrie on the second floor, but was thwarted by the opening of the kitchen door. The smell of frying sausages wafted out, swiftly followed by Mrs Dowd. Once, perhaps, she'd been voluptuous; now she was merely large and billowing, her chiffon dress displaying décolletage as impressive as it was unexpected in a landlady cooking an evening meal.

'There you are, Jacob! What a dreadful night! Will you join us for a bite to eat? Keep out the cold?'

Jacob wavered. The aroma was tempting. 'That's kind of you, Mrs Dowd.'

She wagged a fleshy finger. 'How many times must I tell you? My name is Patience, even if it's never been my nature.'

Jacob's stomach was rumbling, and he surrendered. Besides, Elaine was always good company. She might even find a way of taking his mind off Rachel Savernake.

'So how did you get on with your lady friend?' Elaine asked, warming her hands in front of the fire.

'She refused to talk to me.'

'Go on! Nice-looking chap like you, what can she be thinking of?'

They were alone in the parlour, a tiny room brightened by hyacinths Elaine had brought from the florist's where she worked. Mrs Dowd, with elephantine tact, had withdrawn to her spick and span kitchen. She'd left her late husband – stern, with an abundant moustache – to keep an eye on them from the mantelpiece, where his framed photograph occupied pride of place, flanked by small ornaments supplying colourful reminders of long-ago holidays in Deal and Westcliff. Jacob sipped at his tea, wishing he'd not spoken so freely to Elaine about his work. An easy mistake to make. Since coming to London, he'd thrown himself into his new job, body and soul. He wrote long if infrequent letters to his widowed mother in Armley, but had little time to spare for seeking out new friends as he strove to make himself indispensable to the *Clarion*.

Elaine was flame-haired, freckled, and flirtatious. The pleasantries the two of them exchanged had ripened into friendship, and one day she'd announced that a customer at the shop, knowing her love of a show, had presented her with two unwanted tickets for the Inanity. She and Jacob had sung along with Sinbad and his Sisters, held their breath at the high-wire antics of the Flying Finnegans, and gasped at the illusions performed by Nefertiti, the Nubian Queen of Magic and Mystery. Nefertiti was beautiful, but even as he was enraptured by her sinuous movements on the stage, Jacob felt

Elaine's firm body pressing against his in an unambiguous manner that he found equally exciting.

Subsequently, he'd taken her to the Regent Theatre to see Edgar Wallace's *The Squeaker* (when she'd insisted on waiting at the stage door to add Bernard Lee's autograph to those she'd collected from Sinbad and Nefertiti) and twice to the pictures. Her interest in him and his work was so flattering that the other night, after Mrs Dowd had gone to bed, he'd confided his hope that a scoop about Rachel Savernake would make his name as an investigative journalist. She'd returned his kisses with an ardour that gave him the giddy sensation she'd mistaken him for her hero, Ivor Novello. Her married admirer had obviously taught her a thing or two. Elaine's healthy English looks might lack the sleek sophistication of Nefertiti's wonderfully sculpted features, but her curves were full of promise. She loved his north-country accent, and said it made her heart skip a beat.

He doubted she'd insist on having a ring on her finger before giving herself to him, but he was terrified of getting her pregnant, and finding himself honour-bound to propose marriage. Her mother kept hinting that, at the ripe old age of twenty-three, a woman was ready to become a wife and mother. Jacob's frisson of anxiety matured into alarm following an arch remark, accompanied by an appallingly ostentatious wink, about having a journalist in the family. The prospect of domestic bliss in Edgar House struck Jacob as more like a form of life imprisonment. Better that they remain Just Good Friends.

'Hard to believe, I agree.'

Laughing, Elaine joined him on the settee. An inch of no-man's-land separated them. 'Spoken for, is she?'

'Not as far as I know.'

'Call yourself a news hound? I bet she loves pretending to be a woman of mystery.'

'I don't think she's pretending.'

'Sounds like a witch who's cast a spell on you. Come on. If I've got a rival, I want to hear all about her!'

He spread his arms in an admission of defeat. 'I don't know much. Nobody does.'

'Don't try being evasive with me, Jacob Flint. I'm not stupid. Spill the beans!'

Jacob suppressed a sigh. It was true: Elaine was far from stupid. Nor did she give up easily. He'd blundered by piquing her interest in Rachel Savernake.

'I first heard her name mentioned by a constable I know. A few drinks one night loosened Stan Thurlow's tongue, while we were discussing the Chorus Girl Murder.'

Elaine frowned. She often said she'd stopped reading the newspapers, because they were too depressing. The Wall Street crash, the threatened slump, the world was going mad, and ordinary folk couldn't do a blind thing about any of it.

'Was that the poor girl who…?'

'Dolly Benson, yes. She was suffocated and… violated. When I said I'd heard that the killer had committed suicide, he told me the story. A woman called Rachel Savernake had turned up out of the blue at Scotland Yard, and announced she knew the killer's name. They'd already arrested Dolly's former fiancé, and charged him with murder. Rachel Savernake is the daughter of a prominent judge, otherwise she'd never have got past the door. An amateur sleuth who happens to be a young woman. Why would self-respecting policemen take her seriously?'

Elaine stroked his arm. 'Never underestimate a woman.'

'Rachel Savernake begged them to trace Claude Linacre's movements on the night of the murder. Linacre was a rich dilettante, younger brother of a cabinet minister, and fancied himself as an artist. He admired the work of Walter Sickert, and shared his interest in the macabre, but not his talent. He'd joined the board of the theatre where Dolly worked, and knew her personally. Dolly gave her boyfriend the heave-ho, and boasted to friends she'd taken up with a millionaire. Rachel said that Linacre was Dolly's lover. Her theory was that he'd turned violent because Dolly was expecting a baby.'

'And was she?'

'Yes, Dolly was pregnant, though the police never made that information public. Even so, Rachel's claims seemed like wild speculation. She claimed to have a passion for detective work, but the powers-that-be at the Yard suspected her of bearing a grudge against Linacre. Perhaps he'd rebuffed her, and she wanted revenge. Perhaps she was simply a nosey parker with too much time on her hands. They thanked her politely for her interest, and sent her away. Twenty-four hours later, Linacre took strychnine. Enough to kill a horse, let alone a man.'

'Dear God.' Elaine shivered. 'Did he leave a confession?'

'No, but the police found incriminating evidence at his home in Chelsea. Half a dozen locks cut from the dead woman's hair were tucked into his cigarette case. In his studio was a half-finished painting of Dolly in the nude, over which he'd scrawled obscenities.'

'So your friend Rachel was right?'

'She's not my friend. The police also discovered a telegram she'd sent to Linacre. The message referred to a conversation they'd had on the telephone, and said she planned to call at his home.'

Elaine's eyes opened very wide. 'It sounds as if he killed himself because he thought the game was up.'

'Who knows? Rachel wasn't called to give evidence at the inquest. The medical evidence suggested insanity, and the verdict was suicide. Linacre's brother managed to hush up the whole business. The man charged with murdering Dolly Benson was released from custody, and the investigation quietly wound up. After pumping Thurlow, I asked Tom Betts about the case, and—'

'Tom Betts is the chap who was run over the other day?'

'Yes, poor devil. Our chief crime reporter. What I told him didn't come as a surprise. He'd heard whispers about Rachel Savernake accusing Linacre of the murder, but nobody would talk to him on the record. Linacre's brother is the Prime Minister's right-hand man. He wields a good deal of power.'

'So other journalists won't risk printing the story?'

'Even if they hear the same whispers, yes. But Rachel intrigued Tom. Why did she want to play detective, and what led her to suspect Linacre? She collects modern art, which may be how she heard rumours about him. He was notoriously boastful. Probably he gave himself away.'

'Ah.' Elaine smirked. 'So Rachel Savernake isn't really such a brilliant sleuth?'

'If criminals never made mistakes, the prisons would be empty. The fact is that Rachel was right, and the Yard was wrong. Imagine what an exclusive that would make for the *Clarion*. But she ignored Tom's requests for an interview. We didn't even have a photograph of her. So he encouraged me to write a paragraph for our gossip column, dropping her name. He was desperate to draw her out, but it was a very long shot, and nothing came of it. He was still digging away when he was run over. With another woman savagely murdered in central London, I wondered if Rachel Savernake would involve herself. So did the Yard, according to my pal Thurlow.'

She shot him a glance. 'Surely the cases aren't connected?'

'How could they be? But if crime fascinates her... well, with Tom in such a bad way, I wanted to talk to her.'

'Only to be sent away with a flea in your ear? Serves you right for bothering the poor woman on the Sabbath.' Elaine giggled. 'Is she beautiful?'

'I suppose,' Jacob said cautiously, 'that depends on one's taste.'

'A man's way of admitting that he's smitten.' Elaine gave a histrionic sigh. 'Go on, then. I know you can't resist a pretty face. Remember how you swooned over Queen Nefertiti?'

'I certainly didn't swoon!'

'Get away with you. Anyhow, I want to hear all about this siren. What is she like?'

'If women were allowed to sit as judges, she'd reduce any wretch in the dock to a jelly.'

'But is she pretty?'

Jacob dodged the question like a footballer swerving past a fullback's tackle. 'At least she hasn't inherited the Savernake nose. When the Judge was on the bench, *Punch* printed a cartoon of him, making a joke about beaks.'

'Never heard of him.'

'Savernake of the Scaffold, people called him. He was notoriously harsh. His wife died before the war, and his mind began to give way. His behaviour in court became erratic, his sentencing ever more brutal. In the end, there was a scandal. He slashed his own wrist during an adjournment at the Old Bailey.'

'Good grief!'

Elaine shuddered, and Jacob slid his arm around her, his sleeve just grazing her breast. 'He didn't die, but they made him retire from the judiciary. So he went back to Savernake Hall. The family home, on an island called Gaunt.'

Her breath was warm on his cheek. 'Where's that?'

'Out in the Irish Sea, off the west coast of Cumberland. Remote spot, by all accounts. At low tide, you can reach the mainland by a rough causeway. Otherwise you need to go by boat, but the current's treacherous. Rachel grew up there, with a demented father and a handful of retainers for company.'

Elaine shuddered again. 'Sounds worse than being stuck inside Pentonville.'

'Since her father died last year, she's made a new life for herself. Her house overlooks one of London's finest squares. The last owner was a company promoter. Within the past eighteen months, he fitted it out with every modern convenience, from a gymnasium and a darkroom in the basement to a swimming pool on the top floor.'

'Why on earth did he sell it?'

Jacob laughed. 'The money he spent on it wasn't his. He was found guilty of fraud, and sentenced to ten years in prison. Two of them with hard labour. Rachel bought the place from the trustee in bankruptcy, and named it Gaunt House.'

Elaine pressed her warm leg against his. He inhaled her lavender scent. 'Why on earth would she want to be reminded of being cut off from civilisation on a horrid, lonely island in the middle of nowhere?'

'For all I know, it's idyllic.'

'Idyllic, my eye!' She heaved a sigh. 'You know, I'm not sure I'm jealous of her anymore.'

He grinned. 'You'll change your tune when I tell you her Rolls-Royce was custom-built, and her furniture is designed to order by Ruhlmann of Paris. She buys lurid modern art for prices that would make your eyes water. Her only other interest seems to be amateur detection. She shuns high society, and hates the press.'

'Can you blame her?' Elaine retorted. 'Not everyone wants their face plastered all over the *Clarion*. I suppose if I was filthy rich, I wouldn't want a nosey parker like you prying into how I spent my money.'

'Something else intrigues me. She keeps astonishingly few servants. Only a married couple, and a housemaid. A craving for privacy, I understand. But why be so frugal about help in the house?' He closed his eyes for a moment. 'There's a story to be told about the woman, and I want to tell it.'

'I can see the headline now,' Elaine breathed. '*The Garbo of Detection.*'

He laughed with delight. 'Excellent! I might steal that. If you're ever sacked by the shop, a glittering future awaits you as a subeditor.'

'I'll take that as a compliment.' She snuggled up even closer, and Jacob slid his free hand inside her pink cardigan.

A furious knocking on the front door stopped his wandering fingers in their tracks. Mrs Dowd's footsteps pounded along the hall, and she made a noisy performance of unlocking the door, before giving a low exclamation.

Moments later, with Elaine smoothing the tangles in her hair, the landlady marched into the parlour, clutching a sealed envelope. It bore Jacob's name in an elegant hand.

'Someone left a note for you. In this weather, too! I looked to see who it was, but they'd vanished into the fog.'

He tore the envelope open.

'Who is it from?' Elaine demanded.

Jacob stared at the message, before glancing up at Mrs Dowd.

'No signature.'

'Anonymous!' The landlady was agog. 'Not a poison-pen letter, I hope?'

'No, no...'

'You look hot and bothered, dear.' Mrs Dowd's blue eyes sparkled with excitement. 'Don't keep us in suspense! What does the note say?'

Groaning inwardly, he asked himself why he'd ever talked to his landlady and her daughter about his job. But there was nothing for it. He cleared his throat.

'*Find your scoop at 199 South Audley Street. Nine o'clock sharp.*'

A burly young policeman with a broken nose blocked the pavement as effectively as a brick wall. He raised a shovel-like hand. 'Sorry, sir, you can't go through.'

Jacob climbed off his bicycle. The road was cordoned off, and through the fog, he could make out three police cars, and an ambulance. The door of one of the grand houses was open, with uniformed police officers and men in plain clothes bustling in and out. Windows of the neighbouring houses were lit. Curtains twitched as people tried to make out what the fuss was about.

'Don't you recognise me, Stan? The fog may be thick, but surely you've not forgotten my ugly mug?'

'Flinty?' A note of wonder entered the officer's voice. 'How the blazes did you get wind of this so quick?'

'Get wind of what?'

'Don't give me that sad puppy look, my lad. Your flannel may work a treat with the ladies, but you can't butter me up, not when I'm on duty. A budding crime reporter doesn't stumble across something like this by accident.'

'Something like what?'

Detective Constable Stanley Thurlow frowned. 'Are you denying that you know what's happened?'

Jacob bent his head towards the policeman's cauliflower ear. 'I'll be straight with you. I was tipped off that something was up, but I haven't the faintest clue what it might be.'

'Who told you? Come on, Flinty, spill the beans. It'll do me a power of good with Superintendent Chadwick if I can give him some inside information. I need to keep him sweet.'

'Sorry. I can't say. Even if I wanted to, I'd have to keep my mouth shut. You know a journalist never reveals his sources. The tip-off was anonymous.'

Thurlow scowled. 'Expect me to believe that?'

'Why not? It's the truth.'

'And my name's Ramsay MacDonald.'

Stung, Jacob dug into the pocket of his coat, and brought out the note with a flourish. Taking a pace forward, Thurlow peered at the crumpled notepaper under the lamplight.

'You see?' Jacob demanded. 'Even if I tried to guess who sent me here, chances are I'd be wide of the mark.'

'Posh handwriting. Not like a man's.' Surliness gave way to a touch of swagger. 'One of your fancy women, Flinty? Truth to tell, it makes no difference to us. We're not looking for anyone else in connection with this case.'

In silence they watched two ambulance men manoeuvring a laden stretcher out of the house. A sheet covered the body from head to toe.

Jacob exhaled. 'Dead?'

'As a doornail.' Thurlow lowered his voice. 'Between you, me and the gatepost, it's the bloke who lives here. Name of Pardoe.'

'Murder, accident, or suicide?' Jacob hesitated. 'If you're not looking for anyone else, I suppose he topped himself.'

'Got it in one.' The policeman jerked a thumb towards the house. 'You'd better have a word with the inspector when he's finished in there.'

'You're sure nobody gave him a helping hand?'

'Out of the question. He locked himself into his study, and shot himself at close range after writing a detailed note. Saved us a hell of a lot of trouble.'

'How do you mean?'

'He left a confession, saying he killed that woman in Covent Garden.'

Jacob's throat constricted, as it had when Rachel knotted his scarf around his windpipe. 'Who is this man? He might be deranged. How can you be sure he's telling the truth?'

Thurlow chuckled. 'No mistake, Flinty, scout's honour. You didn't hear this from me, right? Let the boss tell you himself, if he's of a mind to do so.'

'Of course,' Jacob whispered.

'The proof is what you might call conclusive. Looking us straight in the eye when we broke in to the locked room.'

'How do you mean?'

'Staring out of a plywood trunk was the poor woman's head.'

3

'Satisfied?' Mrs Trueman demanded.

Rachel Savernake looked up from her armchair, putting aside the final edition of the *Clarion*, and Jacob Flint's breathless exclusive. Night lawyers had seasoned the report with an *allegedly* in every other sentence, but no caveats could blunt the sensational suicide and confession to murder of a prominent banker with a reputation as a philanthropist. The young reporter had bagged his scoop.

'Satisfied?' She gave a wry smile. 'I've barely started.'

The housekeeper shook her head. 'Last night, everything went perfectly. None of Pardoe's staff sneaked back unexpectedly. The left-luggage attendant took his bribe, and closed his office down. Pardoe realised that if he didn't kill himself, Trueman's photograph of him holding the woman's head like a trophy would destroy him. We won't always be so lucky.'

'Lucky?' Rachel pointed to the story. 'We make our own luck. Our tame journalist has done our work for us. Did you notice his final paragraph?'

Mrs Trueman leaned over her shoulder, and read aloud.

'*The deceased was renowned for unstinting generosity towards good causes. His personal fortune came from the family bank which bears his name. Over the years he acted as personal banker to a uniquely distinguished list of clients. His circle included members of the aristocracy, politicians, and such distinguished figures in public life as the late Mr Justice Savernake.*'

She hesitated. 'How did Flint find out about the Judge's connection to Pardoe?'

'He does his homework.'

'I don't like it. There was no need to mention the Judge.'

'It's a clue disguised as a space-filling irrelevance.' Rachel contemplated the blazing fire, watching the flames writhe. 'He's sending me a message, showing off what he's deduced. That I wrote the note sending him to Pardoe's house.'

'You should never have encouraged him.'

The housekeeper folded her arms, and planted herself in front of the fireplace. Her hair had turned grey during her thirties, and worry had dug deep furrows in her forehead, yet her solid frame and square-set jaw gave the impression that not even an earthquake would shake her.

Rachel yawned. 'It's done now.'

The vast sitting-room looked down on the square. The spiky branches of the oaks and elms in the central garden were bathed in pale sunlight, the fog of the previous evening barely a memory. Inside, the furniture was all delicate lines and subtle curves, with exotic wood grains embellished by ivory and sharkskin. Book-crammed shelves occupied the alcoves on either side of the fire. On the other walls hung paintings: dark, sinister, impressionistic. As Mrs Trueman cleared her throat, she glared in disapproval at a Gilman nude, sprawled over an unmade bed.

'What if he makes himself even more of a nuisance than Thomas Betts? If he finds out about Juliet Brentano...'

'He won't.' Rachel's voice was flat and uncompromising. 'She's gone. Forgotten.'

'He's bound to show your note to his friend at Scotland Yard.'

'Of course. How else can he explain his presence in South Audley Street at nine?'

'You don't sound dismayed.'

'I'm positively euphoric. Linacre and Pardoe are dead. As for Scotland Yard, it suits me to keep them guessing.'

'Wondering who is next?' The housekeeper picked up a poker. 'Jacob Flint will be next, if you ask me. He was a fool to mention the Judge's name in the same breath as Pardoe's. He might as well have tied a noose around his own neck.'

'He likes playing with fire. But then, so do I.'

The older woman stabbed the burning coals. 'One day you'll get burned.'

Rachel's eyes flicked back to the garish headline in the *Clarion*. 'HEADLESS TORSO KILLER' FOUND SHOT. *Millionaire philanthropist is suspected suicide.*

'The danger,' she said softly, 'is what makes life worth living.'

'Not bad,' Walter Gomersall said.

From the lips of the editor of the *Clarion*, this amounted to effusive praise. Gomersall's features, rugged and unyielding as the Pennine landscape of his forefathers, never gave anything away, but Jacob detected a hint of pleasure in the older man's growl. The editor loved stealing a march on the *Clarion*'s competitors.

'Thank you, sir.'

Gomersall's thumb indicated a chair. 'Take the weight off your feet, lad.'

Jacob sat, obedient as a puppy awaiting his master's instructions. Gomersall was a gruff and parochial Lancastrian, but for all the old rivalries between the Red and White Rose counties, he'd given the young man from Leeds the chance to deputise when Tom Betts' accident left him fighting for life. Betts, who hailed from Grange-over-Sands, had once told Jacob that the editor had more time for Northerners than any upstarts from London.

'A question.' Gomersall tugged at his left ear lobe. His ears were exceptionally large, and he liked to say they were the greatest asset a journalist could have. 'How did you get to the scene of the crime so fast?'

Jacob hesitated before replying, 'Information received, sir.'

A phrase favoured by every close-mouthed policeman Jacob had met. He hoped Gomersall would appreciate his wit, rather than resent the evasion.

The editor folded his arms, and Jacob caught his breath. Perhaps he'd been too cheeky.

'Fair enough. In the absence of a straight answer, here's another question. Why mention old Judge Savernake?'

Jacob's reply was ready and waiting. 'He died last year, sir. If I mentioned any of Pardoe's living friends or clients, there would be uproar. Nobody in respectable society relishes being associated with a self-confessed murderer.'

Gomersall grimaced. 'All right. Why did Pardoe do it?'

'I spoke to the inspector in charge of the case, sir, and he refused to let me see the confession, but the police assume the motive was... um, sexual in nature. Pardoe killed and

31

decapitated the woman in a frenzy, and then panicked when it came to disposing of his trophy.'

'She was a nurse by profession, supposedly respectable. He was a banker without a stain on his character, if you can imagine such a contradiction in terms. Spent his spare time, and a small fortune, Doing Good. No known history of sexual misconduct on her part, or violence on his.' Gomersall shook his head. 'Makes no sense.'

'You're absolutely right, sir.' Flattery, Tom Betts often said, was a vital weapon in the journalist's arsenal. Might even newspaper editors succumb to its seductive caress? 'Inspector Oakes seemed baffled.'

'Smart as paint, young Oakes. Unlike that old blunderer they put in charge of the Yard.' Gomersall pursed his lips. 'What if Pardoe is innocent, and this is a put-up job?'

Jacob blinked. 'He shot himself inside a locked room.'

'Never take anything at face value, lad.'

Time for a tactical retreat. 'I'm already planning how to follow up my story. I've called Scotland Yard and asked to meet Inspector Oakes. And I want to interview the dead woman's family, and someone who knew Pardoe.'

Walter Gomersall's raised eyebrows resembled hairy black caterpillars, arching their backs. 'That'll keep you out of mischief.'

'Assuming you approve, of course. We want to keep one step ahead of the *Witness*, two ahead of the *Herald*. Don't we, sir?'

'Get on with it, then. But watch your step.'

'I'll tell the truth as I find it,' Jacob said. 'Pardoe's no more of a threat than the old Judge. Neither of them can sue for libel.'

'Don't be too cocky,' Gomersall said. 'I wasn't thinking of Pardoe, or the wretched woman who lost her head. Remember what happened to Tom Betts.'

Each day Rachel Savernake devoted an hour to taking exercise, dividing the time between the gymnasium in her basement and the swimming pool on the top floor. She was working up a sweat on the wooden treadmill when she heard footsteps. Glancing over her shoulder, she watched Martha, the housemaid, coming downstairs.

'A visitor?' she asked, breathing hard.

Martha nodded. She seldom spoke when a gesture would suffice. Her figure was disguised by a starchy grey uniform, her luxuriant chestnut hair crammed beneath an unflattering cap. Anyone who glimpsed her right profile would be captivated by her beauty, but it was her habit to avoid catching anyone's eye. She dreaded seeing revulsion in those who saw, for the first time, the puckered flesh of her ruined left cheek.

Rachel halted the treadmill. 'Not Gabriel Hannaway?'

A brisk nod.

'Quick off the mark for an old man.' Rachel mopped her brow. 'Offer him whisky while he waits for me. He'll need a stiff drink to calm his nerves.'

Walter Gomersall's parting remark echoed in Jacob's mind as he returned to the cramped and noisy junior reporters' office. The editor measured his words with the care of a pharmacist dispensing henbane to a discontented spouse. Did he suspect that Betts had been the target of a deliberate attack?

Betts' career as a crime reporter stretched back twenty-five years. Long ago, he'd attended the trials of Crippen and the Seddons, and had a ringside seat when George Joseph Smith was found guilty of killing the Brides in the Bath. In childhood, polio had left Betts with a withered leg precluding military service. The same cussedness that helped him to overcome infantile paralysis was responsible for a chronic inability to respect authority. Time and again he'd resigned from good jobs to forestall dismissal after provoking his superiors beyond endurance. He sniffed out scoops where most reporters smelled nothing, but neither Beaverbrook nor Northcliffe could stomach him, and the trade union barons who held the purse strings at the *Herald* found his unwillingness to toe the party line equally intolerable. Gomersall, determined to build circulation come what may, had given him a last chance in Fleet Street, and although the pair came close to blows more than once, Betts had earned his place on the payroll.

Taciturn and short-tempered, he was never afraid to make himself unpopular, but he'd taught Jacob the value of persistence. After hearing from his sources at the Yard that the enigmatic Rachel Savernake had somehow identified Linacre as the Chorus Girl Murderer, Betts was like a dog with a bone. He'd wanted to find out the full story, and then tell it to the *Clarion*'s readers. But then he was hit by a passing car in a side street off Pall Mall, and left for dead by the roadside.

The accident occurred on a foggy evening, and was witnessed by a young Welsh crossing sweeper. When an ambulance and the police arrived, he said he'd seen Betts miss his footing, and stumble under the wheels of a motor car as it turned into the street, knocking him to the ground. The car had been moving slowly, given the poor visibility, but the driver had failed to stop. In such a pea-souper, the Welshman couldn't swear that the driver would realise he'd hit a man rather than some minor obstacle. The vehicle might be a Ford, but the lad hadn't noticed the registration plate when rushing over to tend to the injured man. At first, he'd thought Betts was a goner. As well as smashing both elbows, the journalist had cracked his head open, losing a great deal of blood. Although he'd not died on the spot, his internal injuries were severe, and the prognosis was bleak.

Jacob needed to interview the crossing sweeper. Such creatures belonged, in his mind, to a Dickensian past, when the poor earned a few coins by dusting dirty urban streets for the benefit of well-to-do passers-by, but a few still plied their trade in the capital. The account of the accident carried the ring of truth. Betts' disability sometimes caused him to lose his balance, and in the darkness and the fog, it would be easy to slip in a puddle or on a patch of mud, and fall under the wheels of a passing motor car. But what if the Welshman was wrong? Or lying?

'Forgive me for calling upon you unannounced, my dear,' Gabriel Hannaway said in a croaky wheeze. 'I have business in the vicinity, and the thought of you cooped up here on your own pricked my conscience. I have been remiss. I owe it to your late father to make sure that, after so many years cut off from the world on Gaunt, you are settling happily into London life.'

Rachel smiled, entertained by the notion that Gabriel Hannaway possessed a conscience.

'You are very kind,' she murmured. 'But I enjoy my own company, and the Truemans and Martha cater to all my needs.'

Hannaway had been the Judge's confidant and personal legal adviser. She'd first met him on one of his rare visits to Gaunt, a shrivelled little man who might have worn the same black frock coat for the past forty years. Advancing years and the ravages of emphysema had done nothing to enhance his charms. His skin, a shade not quite yellow and yet not quite brown, had been leathery and wrinkled for as long as she could remember. His small black eyes danced around as if in constant search of means of escape – or legal loopholes. He reminded her of a malevolent reptile, a sharp-toothed iguana that skulked in cracks under desert boulders, tiny snout sniffing the air to seek out prey before it pounced.

'A fine-looking young lady like you deserves better than the company of servants.' His false teeth clicked in disapproval. 'I reproach myself for having seen you only once since your arrival in the city, but my failure is not for want of trying.'

'Sorry, I'm irredeemably unsociable. I'm happiest when solving an acrostic, or doing battle with Torquemada's fiendish crosswords, with the latest gramophone record for company. I'm especially fond of the modern American music.' She gave an innocent smile. 'Do you care for "Makin' Whoopee"?'

Hannaway snorted. 'Jazz, is it? Whatever that word means. Utter tripe, my dear!'

Rachel's eyes narrowed, and for a moment, the lawyer faltered. 'Really... puzzle games and recorded music are all very well for the halt and the lame, but we cannot have you mouldering away with such solitary pastimes. May I repeat the invitation to come and dine with Vincent and me?'

He paused, but Rachel said nothing. 'The two of you will get along famously. Who knows where such a friendship might lead? My son certainly admires a woman with spirit.'

'How very civil of him.'

'A rich young girl, recently arrived in an unfamiliar city, is easy prey for adventurers seeking to take advantage of her trusting nature. It is always wise to grasp a helping hand proffered by a trusted friend.'

'On Gaunt, I learned to look after myself,' she said. 'I'm not entirely feeble.'

The iguana eyes flickered. 'Please do not take offence, my dear. I suppose I am getting ahead of myself. Another reminder that it is time for me to pass on the role of your trusted adviser to a younger and fitter man. Vincent is as capable a solicitor as you will find in London, and his gifts are not confined to skilful draughtsmanship and tenacity in litigation. His judgement is impeccable. You may repose complete confidence in him.'

'I'm overjoyed to hear it. However, I have no pressing need for his wise counsel at present. As you will recall, under the terms of the Judge's will, I gained control of my inheritance on my twenty-fifth birthday.'

'Indeed!' Hannaway was struggling for breath. 'I was alarmed that you withdrew your funds from Pardoe's Bank with your father still barely cold in the grave. You have led such a sheltered life...'

'You think so?' Rachel asked.

'Gaunt was no place for a child to grow up. It's as isolated as anywhere in the kingdom.' He flapped one of his claws. 'We live in desperate economic times. Should our government be so feckless as to desert the Gold Standard... suffice to say that, had you cared to discuss your intentions, I could have suggested suitably discreet and rewarding havens for your fortune.'

Rachel bared her teeth. 'After last night's events, I wondered if you'd called to congratulate me on my foresight.'

The wizened features crinkled. 'Really, my dear! Pardoe's Bank remains in the best hands, despite the... tragic demise of its chairman. Vincent and I happen to be members of the board, and the other directors are equally well-versed in matters financial. The chairman's death will not provoke a run on the bank. Investors in Pardoe's are a select band, shrewd enough to resist any foolish impulse to panic.'

'Perish the thought.'

'I was also distressed to learn that you have liquidated your equity holdings. Forgive my bluntness, but it takes time for a young woman, however confident and independently minded, to become wise to the ways of the world.'

'Are men really more reliable?' She took another sip of Darjeeling. 'Every morning I read news of the latest stockbroker to swallow cyanide or be thrown into Pentonville.'

'Your father knew his own mind too,' Hannaway murmured. 'Though I dare not speculate what the Judge would say about your taste for investing in all this fancy French furniture, and… supposed works of art.'

He glared at a Sickert with vivid splashes of black, gold, and pink. A voluptuous courtesan, admiring her fleshy reflection in a gilt-framed mirror.

'Given the calamities befalling the markets, he might be impressed by my eye for a good investment. The pleasure I derive from Ruhlmann's designs and the artists' insight into human nature is an agreeable dividend.' Rachel waved a slim hand at the Sickert. 'Didn't Claude Linacre persuade you of the virtues of the Camden Town Group?'

'Virtues?' Hannaway coughed. 'Hardly the word I'd choose. Young Linacre was feckless. Rumour had it that he was addicted to drugs.'

'Perhaps we will find that Lawrence Pardoe was equally… weak.'

Hannaway swallowed. 'Stuff and nonsense! Lawrence Pardoe, a murderer and suicide?'

'Possibly he succumbed to a severe temporary derangement. The moment he came to his senses, he was overcome by the horror of his crime, and took the honourable way out.'

A phlegmy sigh. 'The whole business is appalling. Not least the report in that vile rag, the *Clarion*. When I rose this morning, and heard the news, I studied a report written by the man who was first on the scene.'

'Oh yes?'

The iguana eyes fixed on her. 'What struck me was his unexpected mention of your late father.'

'The Judge made a great impression on everyone he met.'

'The reporter is your age,' Hannaway hissed. 'He never met the Judge, nor saw him in court. I fear he will make trouble for… everyone.'

He struggled to his feet, striving to conquer yet another spluttering cough. Rachel wondered if Sir Eustace Leivers of Harley Street was any more optimistic in his prognosis than he had been with Lawrence Pardoe. It seemed unlikely. She watched Hannaway's gaze roam around the room until it fell on the far corner, and a chess board inlaid on an exquisitely carved mahogany table. Shuffling towards it, he bent over the board, and peered at the arrangement of the pieces.

'Chess problems are another of my solitary pastimes,' she said. 'You play the game, don't you? I'm sure you recognise Taverner's famous puzzle. Fascinating, don't you agree? Such beautiful cruelty.'

The old lawyer's mottled complexion turned grey.

Rachel pointed at the board. 'What happens next creates *zugzwang*. Black is compelled to move, yet whatever he does inevitably puts him in greater danger.'

As if by accident, the sleeve of Hannaway's frock coat caught the white queen, and sent it tumbling to the floor.

'Whatever game you are playing, my dear, don't make the mistake of playing alone.'

'The crossing sweeper's name was Sear,' George Poyser, the news editor, told Jacob. A seasoned journalist renowned for his memory for detail, he'd made sure he was first on the scene once the *Clarion* learned that one of its reporters had suffered a potentially fatal accident.

'You met him?'

'Slipped him a few bob as a thank-you. Decent young chap. But for him, Tom might not even have made it as far as a hospital bed.'

'According to his story.'

Poyser's nickname was Pop-Eye, thanks to the protuberant eyes forever blinking behind huge horn-rimmed spectacles. He was portly and bald, and his unprepossessing appearance made him the butt of many a joke, but those pop-eyes didn't miss much.

'Are you suggesting that he exaggerated? You think he wanted to make himself out a hero?'

'Just checking.' Jacob didn't want to start a fluttering in the dovecote. 'I'm going to visit Tom in the Middlesex, and I'm sure he'd like to know more about the lad who helped to save his bacon.'

Poyser wrinkled his snub nose. 'Don't hope for too much. I saw Tom the day before yesterday. If he's going to make it, then I'm a Dutchman.'

'Do you have Sear's full name and address?'

'Bear with me.' Poyser burrowed in the drawer of a desk overflowing with galley sheets, and retrieved a dog-eared notebook. 'There you are. A place for everything, and everything in its place, see? Iorwerth Sear, yes, that's him. Number twenty-nine, Balaclava Mews, Kilburn.'

Thirty minutes later, the story of the accident had unravelled. Jacob could find no trace of anyone called Iorwerth Sear in London. There was no Balaclava Mews in Kilburn, or anywhere else in the city. A young man who earned a crust as a crossing sweeper might have his own reasons for concealing his identity from the authorities and the press. But what if he'd been paid to lie about what had happened to Tom Betts?

Rachel Savernake's cool words echoed inside Jacob's head.

'How unfortunate if your promising career were cut short, just like your predecessor's.'

Juliet Brentano's Journal

30 January 1919 (later)

After Henrietta told me about my parents, I ran up to my room. I've stayed here all evening, listening as the wind and rain pound this bleak lump of rock in the sea. I won't go down to dinner. I never want to eat anything again.

On the stairs, I passed Rachel. Neither of us uttered a word, but she knows exactly what has happened, I can tell. Excitement shone in her eyes. She is triumphant, and sees no need to hide it.

She's despised me from the moment my mother and I arrived, when my father went off to fight in the war. Because Rachel and I were born a matter of weeks apart, my father thought the two of us would become fast friends. Her mother had died, and the Judge was sick and solitary. Father said she must be lonely on Gaunt. He didn't know her.

Rachel has no use for friendship. She regards herself as queen of this godforsaken island. She hates sharing it with another girl. Once she learned my parents weren't married, she taunted me for being a bastard.

Now she has what she wanted. And with my mother and father dead, I am at her mercy.

4

'You still want to visit the art gallery?' Trueman asked.

Rachel picked up the chess piece that the old solicitor had knocked over, and squeezed it in her palm. 'Certainly.'

'Pardoe's associates will cluster round you like moths to a flame.'

'Performing fleas would be nearer the mark. If only their attentions were due to my delightful personality, it might turn my head. As it is…'

'Yes?'

'I expect some unpleasantness.'

Trueman shrugged. 'If you're determined to go ahead…'

'Oh yes,' Rachel said. 'I am determined.'

Flinging open the door to the sitting room, Mrs Trueman bustled in. 'Levi Shoemaker is here. I asked him to wait downstairs while I see if you're available.'

'What does he want?' her husband asked.

'To tender his resignation,' Rachel said. 'Pardoe's death will be the straw that broke the camel's back.'

'You're willing to see him?'

45

'Why not?'

The Truemans left without another word. A minute later, the housekeeper ushered in a middle-sized man with wispy, greying hair. He had a sallow complexion, small, deep-set eyes, and an air of gentle melancholy, as if he'd peered inside too many unhappy lives. He might have been any age between fifty and sixty-five, and nothing in his cast of features suggested his racial origins. His only distinguishing feature was an unceasing watchfulness.

'This is an unexpected pleasure, Mr Shoemaker. May I offer you afternoon tea?'

'Thank you, no. I shan't detain you for long.'

Rachel felt his hand tremble as she shook it. She found his nervousness strangely thrilling. Levi Shoemaker was made of sterner stuff than most men. He'd worked for the police in Kiev prior to being dismissed in a purge of Jews. His wife and brother had been burned to death during a pogrom, and he'd suffered torture before escaping to England. In London, he'd set up as a private investigator, and his single-minded zeal meant his reputation soon became as formidable as his fees. Yet he lived in a modest manner, charging heavily simply because it enabled him to pick and choose assignments.

'You have read the news,' she said.

'Concerning last night's events in South Audley Street?' His hand fumbled in a coat pocket, and he pulled out a copy of the *Clarion*. 'Given my enquiries on your behalf concerning the late Lawrence Pardoe, I was intrigued to learn of his sudden death. Also to see the name of the first reporter to arrive at the scene. Young Flint's story has prompted me to come to a decision.'

'You wish to terminate our retainer?'

'You make a good detective, Miss Savernake. Always one step ahead.' His English was careful, but almost accentless; he weighed his words like a lawyer. 'Yes, I am here to end our relationship. In fact, I am retiring from business altogether. This time next week I shall be overseas. Warmer climes will be good for my health in more ways than one.'

Rachel raised her eyebrows. 'All because a banker blows out his brains?'

The enquiry agent shook his head. 'I have been followed several times. A nuisance, nothing more, but I prefer to be the watcher rather than the watched.'

'Did you recognise the person who followed you?'

'Three different men are involved, and I have yet to identify them. My working hypothesis is that their activities are connected with my work for you.'

'What makes you think that?' Rachel snapped.

Shoemaker lifted one arm, as if to ward off an imaginary blow. 'Please, Miss Savernake. Don't let my honesty rile you. My duties for you were all-consuming, and I have turned away all other prospective clients – a duchess and a bishop among them, I should say. There is no other reason why my activities should suddenly attract attention from someone rich enough to hire a team of men to shadow me. You said at the outset that your enquiries would prove complex and sensitive. Was that a euphemism for life-threatening?'

Rachel's dark eyes glittered. 'You never struck me as a coward.'

'The horrors I witnessed in the Ukraine hardened my soul, Miss Savernake. That said, I prefer not to meet my Maker before reaching my allotted span. Call it cowardice if you will, but Thomas Betts has already paid the price for finding out too much. A similar fate presumably lies in store for his young henchman, Flint.' Shoemaker jabbed his forefinger at the front page of the newspaper. 'Did you send him to South Audley Street last night, and if so, why?'

She ignored the question. 'Has anyone threatened you?'

'Nobody has said a word to me. I find that oddly intimidating. I'm too old to swim in such shark-infested waters. It's dawned on me lately that I am drifting out of my depth.' He waved the inky sheets of newsprint in her face. 'Young Flint's story proves it.'

'In that case, I shall waste no more of your time.'

He considered her. 'You never made a secret of the fact that, in addition to hiring my services, you engaged others to pursue enquiries on your behalf. No doubt they can assist you in the future.'

'Quite.' She gave a curt nod. 'It only remains for me to thank you for your help, and to urge you to take care. Distance yourself from me now by all means. But it may already be too late.'

Lydia Betts was a small, colourless woman who had lived in her husband's angular shadow for twenty years. Even her Yorkshire accent was barely discernible, one more aspect of her personality she'd learned to suppress. She greeted Jacob politely when he turned up unannounced on the doorstep of her flat, on the ground floor of a small block close to Farringdon Road, and insisted on offering him a cup of weak tea and digestive biscuits. Yet he could tell her mind was elsewhere, at her husband's bedside in the Middlesex Hospital.

'Mr Gomersall has been ever so kind,' she said, ushering him inside. 'The *Clarion* is covering all the costs of Tom's treatment, and more besides. Heaven only knows how I'd manage without the money.'

She led him to a sitting room that was spick and span, yet made dingy and dismal by an inescapable mood of despair. On the sideboard stood a framed picture of Tom and Lydia Betts on their wedding day, smart and smiling and scarcely recognisable to Jacob. A palm drooped in one corner, next to a shelf occupied by half a dozen books. An old family Bible, a complete Shakespeare, *David Copperfield* and *Great Expectations*, Poe's *Tales of Mystery and Imagination*, and a well-thumbed copy of Mrs Beeton's *Book of Household Management*.

Jacob murmured platitudes, recalling Tom Betts' advice about putting nervous witnesses at ease. Neither of them had envisaged that one day Jacob would be seeking clues from Betts' wife about an attempt to murder her husband.

'I tried to get in touch with him,' she said when Jacob mentioned Iorwerth Sear. 'He'd been so kind to Tom, tried to save his life. A poor fellow like that, a crossing sweeper – it just goes to show, doesn't it? But the police took down the wrong address. The house doesn't exist. Nor the street. There must have been some mistake – it's easily done. I checked on places with a similar name, but I had no joy. Such a pity.'

'Was young Sear the first on the scene?'

'Oh yes. He was sweeping that side of the street, I understand. Though it's a busy area, and even in the fog, several people were milling about at that time of evening.'

This solved one puzzle vexing Jacob. If Sear was in the pay of someone who wished Betts harm, why not finish the job the car driver had started? With a man lying injured on the ground, a few well-directed kicks would do the trick. Perhaps his instructions were simply to tell a good story when help came, putting the blame for the incident squarely on Betts and his gammy leg, rather than on the driver who failed to stop. One fact was certain. If Sear was lying, the car in question would not have been a Ford.

'Do you know where Tom was going that night?'

Lydia Betts shook her head. 'It was about this story he was working on. A big story, that's all I know.'

'About Rachel Savernake? Did he discuss her with you?'

She shook her head. 'He kept his own counsel, did Tom. Leastways, when it came to his work. I sometimes wished… he would confide more in me. I always tried to show an interest.'

She was already talking about her husband in the past tense. Her subconscious protecting her, Jacob thought, accustoming her to what lay ahead.

He bit into a biscuit. 'I ought to follow up the story.'

'About this Savernake woman?'

'Yes. If only,' Jacob said, hating himself for his mendacity, 'as a way of paying tribute to Tom. Of course, we all long for the day when he's back in harness, but in the meantime…'

'Tom will never be back,' his wife said. 'The doctors are close to giving up. He's so very poorly. It would be kinder… to let him go.'

Jacob laid his hand on Lydia Betts' spindly arm. 'Hush. You mustn't talk like that.'

Her pinched features were a portrait of defeat. All the life had been sucked out of her. She even lacked the energy to answer.

An idea struck him. 'Did Tom keep any notes here about stories he was working on?'

'No. You know how untidy he was. If he'd treated our home as an office, we'd have drowned in scraps of paper.'

Untidy, Jacob thought, was an understatement. In Clarion House, Tom's fondness for clutter was legendary. 'So you didn't know anything about those stories?'

'He used to joke that London needed a better class of criminal. Just before the accident, he was down in the mouth. He said a villain he'd met had been murdered by his gang. The man had wanted to sell him a story but he'd asked for far too much money. Tom was upset he'd missed the chance to find out more. More than that, I don't know.'

'This wasn't Harold Coleman?'

Coleman was associated with the Rotherhithe Razors, whose members menaced London's racetracks. Six years ago, he'd been jailed for the manslaughter of a bookmaker who wouldn't pay for protection. Late last year, he'd escaped from Wormwood Scrubs, and gone on the run – until finally, his past caught up with him. A courting couple had found what was left of his body nestling under a hedge. Tom Betts had reported his murder in the *Clarion*, and written a couple of follow-ups. Such crimes were commonplace among members of London's gangs, even if few were marked by such savagery. Jacob thought it no bad thing if villains wiped each other out, and Tom's interest in the killing had puzzled him.

'Sorry, I'm not sure he mentioned a name,' she said. 'He was very preoccupied in the days leading up to the accident. I suppose that's why he got run over. He wasn't looking where he was going.'

She was right about Tom's distracted state, Jacob thought, but what was the cause of it? Crime reporters saw the seamy side of life every day. However gruesome the case, it was water off a duck's back. Otherwise, how could you survive?

'He never said anything else?'

'All I can tell you is this.' Her voice dropped to a whisper. 'One night – it must only have been a day or two before the accident – he had a bad dream. He woke me up, talking in his sleep.'

Jacob's spine tingled. 'Did he speak about Rachel Savernake?'

'No.' Lydia Betts' eyes were moist with distress. 'He simply mentioned a place. Nowhere I'd heard of, but he kept repeating its name.'

'Which place, what name?'

'*Gallows Court.*'

Four vast oil paintings by Cayley Robinson dominated the entrance hall of Middlesex Hospital. *Acts of Mercy*, commissioned by a wealthy benefactor, depicted the care given to the sick and needy, delicate orphan girls and wounded soldiers returning from the battlefield. The aim was to symbolise the triumph of human spirit in the face of adversity, but the paintings had haunted Jacob ever since his last visit. The orphans seemed serene if pensive, forming an orderly queue in their pleated white bonnets to collect their bowls of nutritious milk. Yet one of the children stared out of the canvas at him, as if appealing for him to do something impossible – cure terminal illness. The yearning in her eyes revealed her fear that nobody would ever be able to help.

Jacob hated hospitals. The whiff of ether and surgical spirit always made him feel sick. His conscience was pricking because he'd visited Tom Betts only once since the accident. It wasn't the enigmatic murals that had kept him away. The sight of his colleague's grey face, straggly hair, and scrawny, diminished body had been more than he could bear. Huddled up in bed, Tom seemed to be waiting for the end to come.

'Any improvement?' he asked the sister, a plump Geordie whose beam was as warm as a fleecy blanket.

'Ah, now you're asking. Once or twice he's come round briefly. He's even murmured a few words, but we couldn't make head nor tail of what he said. At other times...'

'I see.' While there was life, there was supposed to be hope, but even Lydia Betts was reconciled to the inevitable.

'I've just come from seeing Mrs Betts.'

'Ah, poor lass, she... finds it very difficult.'

The sister pulled a chair up to the bed. Betts was breathing loudly, and she murmured that he might be coming to again. But the rasping sound made Jacob think of a drowning man, who bobs up and down above the waves before the sea finally claims him.

The stench of disinfectant and the coarse noise from the bed made Jacob's flesh crawl. Not for the first time, he felt pangs of self-disgust. A man who had, in his no-nonsense way, been generous to him was close to death. Yet here he was, averting his eyes, holding his nose, struggling in vain to overcome revulsion. He uttered a silent, selfish prayer that Betts would not die while he sat by his bedside. How could he console the widow if the worst happened? It would seem like his fault.

The sister left to tend to others in her care, and Jacob moved close to the figure under the bedclothes. 'Tom, are you awake? Can you hear me? It's Jacob, Jacob Flint. I talked to Rachel Savernake.'

Was he imagining it, or did the sick man's eyelids flutter? The racket of wheezing was almost unbearable.

'She's mixed up in another murder.'

Jacob shifted closer, gripping the edge of the iron bedstead as the sick man's eyes opened a fraction. Under the lids, the whites were bloodshot. His gaze was unfocused, yet Jacob thought that Betts was making a superhuman effort to communicate. His own throat was dry. He dare not imagine how much pain the man was in, how much these questions were making him suffer. Could he find one key that might unlock the door?

'Tom, tell me this. Where is Gallows Court?'

Betts' lips began to move, without making a sound. Jacob's head moved until it was almost touching the older man's cheek. Finally he heard a few words, so faint as to be almost inaudible.

'*Coleman said he knew her secret.*'

'Whose secret, Tom? Who are you talking about?'

Betts' eyelids flickered, and there was a long pause before the older man forced out the name.

'*Rachel Savernake.*'

The telephone shrilled as Rachel solved the final clue in her crossword. Moments later, Mrs Trueman put her head round the door.

'Flint wants to speak to you.'

'Shoemaker warned me he was persistent.'

'He's calling from Middlesex Hospital. Betts is still alive, and he's paid him a visit. He sounds excited, as though he's onto something.'

'We were told Betts wasn't expected to regain consciousness. Perhaps the doctors underestimated his resilience.'

'Shall I say you're busy?'

Rachel looked out across the square. Even on this fine, crisp afternoon, there was nobody about. Tucked between the tall trees and evergreen shrubs was a single wrought-iron bench, but she'd never seen anybody sit on it. One neighbouring building, separated from Gaunt House by a narrow passageway, was owned by an august but inactive literary and philosophical society, while the elderly couple who lived next door were wintering in Cap d'Antibes. At the heart of the capital of the British Empire, the square was an oasis of quiet.

'No, I'll talk to him.'

The housekeeper grimaced. 'Best not to encourage him.'

'Refusing to talk to Betts didn't put him off.' Rachel folded *The Times*. 'Would you mind tidying the chess set away? The Taverner problem has served its purpose.'

She strode out onto the spacious landing. A telephone stood on a table beneath a tall window. It commanded a view of a large garden to the rear of the house, crowded with lush evergreens, and surrounded by a wall topped with railings spiked to deter even the boldest intruder.

She picked up the receiver. 'Yes, Mr Flint?'

'Miss Savernake?' The journalist sounded as if he'd run a sprint.

'Didn't I make myself clear last night? I never speak to the press.'

'I wanted to thank you,' he said. 'For the note. You gave me the finest scoop of my career.'

'The note?'

'You sent me a message, telling me to go to Lawrence Pardoe's address in South Audley Street, not two hours after you'd talked about my yearning for a scoop. Even if for some strange reason you don't want to admit it, I'm extremely grateful.'

Her lavish sigh was worthy of a schoolmistress driven to distraction by a pupil's stupidity. 'Mr Flint...'

'You took the trouble to find out everything about me. I can't believe that you haven't seen the *Clarion* today.'

'I have an appointment shortly,' she said. 'Now, if you'll excuse me—'

'Wait! Please. I need to ask you something. Are you familiar with Gallows Court?'

Softly, she said, 'I can't help you, Mr Flint.'

'Tom Betts was onto something, wasn't he? He was curious about the murder of a man called Coleman. About what happened at Gallows Court.' Excitement rose in his voice. 'Is that why someone ran Tom over? What do you know about his so-called accident?'

Rachel squeezed the receiver until her palm hurt.

'I told you last night not to threaten me, Mr Flint. You should heed my advice. There are worse fates than the misfortune that befell Thomas Betts.'

5

'Damned good work.'

Light from a low sun filtered through the narrow windows of the assistant commissioner's room, streaking the
newspapers piled high on his writing table. New Scotland
Yard was a honeycomb of claustrophobic offices and granite
staircases, but the Office of Works had done Sir Godfrey
Mulhearn proud. Comfortably upholstered armchairs and a
turkey carpet supplied a hint of luxury, and there was even
a miniature telephone exchange, with private wires to the
principal branches of government.

Sir Godfrey folded his arms, as if daring his companion
to contradict him, but there was no danger of that.
Superintendent Arthur Chadwick had not risen through the
ranks of the CID by antagonising his superiors, or by failing
to take credit when it was his due.

'Absolutely, sir.'

Sir Godfrey stroked his moustache, a favourite gesture. A
former soldier, he was the very model of a modern assistant
commissioner, tall and bronzed, with a square jaw and

steel-grey hair. 'Pardoe was a pillar of respectability. Spent half the family fortune on doing good. No criminal record, obviously. Any suspicion of financial malpractice?'

Chadwick's head, bald and shaped like a bullet, shook with regret. 'Bankers are never as pure as the driven snow. But Pardoe belonged to the old school, like his father and grandfather before him. His list of clients reads like an extract from *Who's Who*. None are fools easily parted from their money by a scoundrel.'

Sir Godfrey gave a man-of-the-world cough. 'Nothing... untoward in his private life?'

'Not that Inspector Oakes has found, sir. Pardoe was a widower, and there is no indication that he spent heavily – except on worthy causes. He didn't gamble at the races or on the tables. Despite being a generous donor to numerous charities, he didn't crave the limelight. Less than twelve months ago, he lost his second wife, and since then he's lived very quietly.'

'Any suspicious circumstances surrounding her death?'

'She died in childbirth, sir.'

The reply was a cue for further moustache-stroking. 'Unusual for a crime as shocking as the Covent Garden case to occur... out of the blue. You're satisfied that this man did murder the Hayes woman? And that he committed suicide? There's no question of his being killed by a third party?'

Puffing for breath, Chadwick pulled out his notebook. A hefty man, in his youth he'd won trophies as an amateur boxer. Nowadays his girth was a tribute to his wife's cooking, and it was hard to believe he'd ever been nimble in the ring. For years, he had been office-bound, but he'd given evidence in the Old Bailey enough times to know that a fact was not a fact unless and until recorded in writing.

'None whatsoever, sir, we have it on the highest authority. I sent word that Mr Rufus Paul must be called in at once, and he conducted a thorough examination of the body in situ.'

Sir Godfrey nodded. 'Very wise. There's no one better.'

'Indeed, sir. The door was locked from the inside, with the key left in place. There are no windows, or means of access to the study from above or below. Pardoe's fingerprints are on the gun, and the confession is certainly in his own hand. The style of calligraphy is difficult to forge, and his confidential secretary is in no doubt that Pardoe wrote the note. The weapon is a distinctive example of a well-known model, although we haven't traced where he obtained it. Our theory is that it was an heirloom. We also found the saw he used to decapitate the woman in the basement of his house. He'd washed it, but not thoroughly enough to remove all traces of her blood.'

'A bad business.'

Sir Godfrey's fondness for platitudes led many people in Whitehall, let alone in Fleet Street, to believe he was stupid. A generously minded minority argued that it suited him to be underestimated, and to wear his bluff military manner as a form of disguise.

'Quite so, sir.'

'One good thing about a suicide.' Sir Godfrey tapped his blotting pad with a pen. 'It saves everyone a great deal of time and bother. What was his state of health?'

'He suffered from a malignant tumour, diagnosed by Sir Eustace Leivers of Harley Street. Apparently he confided in no one else. Sir Eustace confirms that he expected Pardoe would be dead within months. He'd felt it his duty to warn Pardoe that the final stages would not be pleasant. Pardoe's confession mentions that he had little time left, and that too confirms its authenticity.'

'And the plywood trunk?'

'We've traced the shop that sold it to him. Pardoe's idea of concealing his identity was to wear a shabby old Ulster, with a peaked cap pulled low over his eyes, and adopt an old Etonian's version of an Irish accent.'

'Can we be sure it *was* Pardoe?'

'The shopkeeper has been shown his photograph, and can't swear to the identification. He realised the fellow was up to something rummy, but of course didn't guess why he wanted the case.'

'I presume Pardoe cleared his staff out last night so that he could do the deed in peace and quiet?'

'Exactly, sir.' Chadwick puffed on his pipe. 'His secretary thought he seemed agitated yesterday. So did the butler.'

'Yet you've uncovered no history of mental instability?'

'Nothing known, sir, though Sir Eustace said Pardoe took the diagnosis badly. Evidently he'd disposed of a good deal of paperwork, burning it page by page. Whether he destroyed compromising material of some sort, we'll never know. The confession is the work of a man overwhelmed by guilt and shame.'

Sir Godfrey tutted. 'Better late than never, I suppose. What else do we know about his private life?'

Chadwick consulted his notes. 'His first wife succumbed to consumption, and there was no issue. Three years ago, he remarried. His second wife was less than half his age, sir, described to us by the cook as a flighty piece, and by the secretary as rather common. She was a theatrical. After losing her and their baby, it looks as if he lost his mind.'

'Suicide fits,' Sir Godfrey said. 'Why else would a respectable banker behave like the worst kind of animal?'

'Indeed, sir.'

'Tell me about this young journalist. Extraordinary that he arrived outside Pardoe's home within minutes of the body being found.'

A hint of reluctant admiration entered Sir Godfrey's voice. His own career was testament to a gift for exquisite timing worthy of a test match batsman. Having acquired more medals than wounds during the Great War, he had left the army before the ink was dry on the armistice, and secured a post as assistant commissioner at a time when active-service counterparts of similar rank were too weary or flu-ridden to contemplate peacetime. When the A.C. in charge of the Criminal Investigation Department had retired twelve months earlier, Sir Godfrey's seniority had made him the natural choice as replacement. But becoming the public face of the CID presented more testing challenges than overseeing traffic and lost property.

'Name of Flint.' Chadwick jabbed a forefinger at the newspaper on top of the General's pile. 'The lad came down from Leeds to join the *Clarion*.'

'Worst of the "Pennies", if you ask me.' Sir Godfrey's nose wrinkled with disdain. The *Clarion*'s withering leader about CID's inefficient handling of the Chorus Girl Murder had blamed the man in charge.

The superintendent, who had profited many times from the *Clarion*'s racing tips, and found the paper's more sober-minded rivals dull, kept his mouth shut. 'You may be aware that Betts, their chief crime correspondent, was run over recently?'

'Stepped into the gutter once too often, I expect.'

'I hear the doctors are fighting a losing battle. Flint is wet behind the ears, but is said to be ambitious.'

'Why would anyone tip him the wink about Pardoe?'

'Oakes talked to him last night, sir. Shall I call him in?'

Chadwick pushed the button on the house telephone, and refilled his pipe. Within a minute, the pair were joined by a thin, sharp-chinned man twenty years their junior. Inspector Philip Oakes was a rarity, a product of Repton and Caius who had opted to join the police, and apply his intellect to detective work. An expensive education was not a recipe for easy popularity among fellow police officers, and Chadwick shared the widespread scepticism about the youthful graduate, with his wide vocabulary and civilised table manners. Whether Oakes' success in clambering up the greasy pole was due to brains and hard work, or mainly to luck and knowing the right people, was hotly debated within the Police Federation.

'Flint claimed not to know who advised him to turn up at Pardoe's place,' Oakes said.

Sir Godfrey pursed fleshy lips. 'You believed him?'

'I never believe anything a newspaperman tells me, sir,' Oakes replied. 'Flint showed me the note that was delivered to his lodgings. I said I'd like to test it for fingerprints, and he made only a token protest.'

'Presumably he anticipated that the only prints on the note would be his?' Chadwick said.

'Quite, sir. And so it proved.'

'You don't think he wrote the note himself?'

'His landlady confirms that the note was delivered to her house yesterday evening, when Flint was talking to her daughter. Of course, he might have arranged it himself.'

'That would be bizarre,' the assistant commissioner said.

'What really is bizarre, Sir Godfrey, is where the notepaper came from. It doesn't bear an address, but it's an exact match for Pardoe's personal stationery. We found a supply in the room where he shot himself.'

'Good Lord!'

'We checked with the stationer's, a high quality firm in Bond Street. They haven't sold that brand of paper for eighteen months. One of the last customers for it was Lawrence Pardoe. That doesn't prove that the sheet came from Pardoe's stock, but if it didn't, the coincidence is breathtaking.'

'You think Pardoe sent the note to Flint?'

'I can't imagine why he would, sir, but it's one of three possibilities. Another is that Flint sent the message to himself. Or else a third party did so.'

'A third party? Someone in whom Pardoe confided?'

'Or someone who knew he was about to kill himself.'

Chadwick scowled. 'One of his servants? His secretary?'

'Alternatively, an outsider.'

'Who have you got in mind, Oakes?' Sir Godfrey demanded. 'Spit it out, man.'

'I put a name to Jacob Flint,' Oakes said. 'He wouldn't confirm that I'd scored a hit, but since his face turned beetroot red, I drew my own conclusions.'

'Which were?'

'In my judgement, he believes the note came from Miss Rachel Savernake.'

Sir Godfrey swivelled in his chair. 'What do you make of that, Chadwick? Might she be involved?'

'Impossible to say, sir.' Another secret of the superintendent's success was an ability to avoid committing himself to controversial opinions. 'Frankly, it seems a long shot. And it doesn't explain how she laid her hands on the notepaper.'

'What makes Flint think she knew Pardoe murdered Mary-Jane Hayes? Let alone that he was about to commit suicide?'

'Journalistic speculation,' Oakes suggested. 'He's learned of her connection with the Dolly Benson case. The Covent

63

Garden killing has been all over the press. If he suspects she's acquired a taste for looking into notorious crimes...'

'You're not convinced, Chadwick?'

The bullet head lifted. 'Ask yourself why she accused that swine Linacre of butchering Dolly Benson, sir. I reckon she was paying off a private score.'

'And made a lucky guess?' Oakes asked quietly.

'What else could it be? Brilliant amateurs belong to the story books. Sleuthing is no game for a lady. Feminine intuition is scarcely a substitute for meticulous detective work. At most, the Linacre case was an exception proving the rule. A pure fluke.'

'What do you say, Oakes?'

'For the past forty-eight hours, the newspapers have salivated over Mary-Jane Hayes' murder, and the fact her head was cut off. Crime evidently fascinates Miss Savernake. It would be astounding if she wasn't tempted to play the detective again. If anyone is shrewd enough to have got onto Pardoe's trail, I'd put my money on her.'

Chadwick twisted his pipe cleaner into the shape of a triangle. 'And how do you suppose she pinned the crime on Pardoe?'

'There you have me, sir,' Oakes said pleasantly. 'But assume she let Pardoe know she was on his track. She may have foreseen that he'd kill himself rather than face due process of law, just as Linacre did. Hence the note to Flint.'

'Why contact him rather than us?' Sir Godfrey demanded.

'Perhaps our response last time disappointed her.'

Chadwick grunted. 'Far-fetched.'

'True, sir. But with respect, it's in keeping with Miss Savernake's modus operandi. She moves in mysterious ways.'

Sir Godfrey nodded. 'After Linacre killed himself, there was no question of her seeking to embarrass us or hog the limelight. I must say I liked that. Discretion is a fine quality in a woman.'

'Why did she approach Linacre?' Chadwick demanded. 'Candidly, gentlemen, I wouldn't trust that woman an inch. If she wasn't well-born and handsome, we'd regard her behaviour as deeply suspicious.'

The assistant commissioner frowned. Chadwick seldom spoke so bluntly, and had never before hinted at class consciousness. Surely the fellow didn't still have a chip on his shoulder because his father was a drayman from Shoreditch?

'Even if I'm right,' Oakes said, 'there is a second riddle. If Rachel Savernake suspected Pardoe was a murderer, and planned to kill himself – why tell Flint rather than one of the established crime correspondents?'

'Perhaps,' Sir Godfrey mused, 'she reasoned that an ambitious young journalist would be content to break an exclusive story without asking too many questions about where his tip-off came from.'

'There's another possibility,' Oakes said. 'I keep my eye on what the papers say, and I've been looking out for Rachel Savernake's name. She's young, attractive, and unmarried, and not afraid to spend her considerable wealth. In a word, she is newsworthy, yet her name is curiously absent from the cheap prints. Recently, however, the *Clarion* ran a gossipy paragraph about her. Trivial nonsense, but it described her as enigmatic, and mentioned that she enjoyed solving fiendish puzzles. Crosswords, acrostics, chess problems, you name it. Reading between the lines, you might detect a coded hint at the part she played in the Linacre case. I wonder if Flint wrote that piece. Does he suspect there's more to Miss Savernake than meets the eye?'

Sir Godfrey picked up his paper cutter, and stabbed the blotting pad with it. 'Something discreditable?'

'Frankly, sir, I can't answer that. Why should a young woman with money to burn interest herself in murder?'

'At all events, it's hardly our concern. Pardoe is dead, and the Covent Garden case is solved.' Sir Godfrey smiled. 'All's well that ends well. Congratulations.'

'Thank you, sir.'

'Well, Chadwick? You're grimacing when you ought to be cock-a-hoop.'

'Forgive me, Sir Godfrey.' The superintendent rose. 'Of course, I'm delighted to put a tricky case to bed. Now, sir, if you'll excuse me…'

'One small point does remain unresolved,' Oakes said.

'Namely?' Sir Godfrey demanded.

'A chessman was found next to Pardoe's inkwell. A black pawn.'

'What of it?'

'The curious thing is this, sir. We found no chess set in the house.'

6

'An exquisite corpse,' Rachel Savernake took a sip from her glass. Vintage burgundy, the colour of blood.

Her companion hesitated before responding with a well-practised smile. A tall, dark Catalan, whose sharply tailored suit was as elegant as his manners, he had greeted Rachel Savernake as if she were a princess. She was the patron – he deplored the word customer – whose purchases ensured the prosperity of the Galeria Garcia at a time when most rich art-lovers were shell-shocked by the carnage on the markets. The gallery was a dense fug of people and cigar smoke, but Rachel guessed the other guests were keener to relish the fruits of Javier Garcia's wine cellar than to squander their money on modern art.

'Ah yes,' Garcia said. '*Cadavre exquis*. I have an example next door from Barcelona. You might care to...'

'Cadaver?' murmured a voice behind them, barely audible in the hubbub. 'That's my line of country. At a private view, I'd hoped to escape them for an evening.'

Garcia spun on his heels. 'My good sir, your sense of humour is as acute as ever. Excuse me, have you met

Miss Rachel Savernake? Dear lady, this is Mr Rufus Paul, the...'

'The forensic pathologist.' Rachel gave an ingénue's sweet smile. 'Of course I am familiar with your name.'

Rufus Paul, portly and red-cheeked, had once been described by Thomas Betts in the *Clarion*, in an account of a trial where his testimony sent a wife-murderer to the gallows, as looking like a village butcher. If so, he was a butcher of the highest class. His flair for conjuring a capital case for the Crown out of the most microscopic human remains was uncanny, while his evidence as an expert witness had more than once saved defendants with deep pockets from the scaffold.

Rachel gripped his beefy hand, and imagined it wielding a cleaver. She noticed his gaze slide downwards. Most men would enjoy examining her figure, clad in a silk dress designed by Sonia Delaunay, but Paul's professionally curious demeanour suggested he was checking how much flesh she had on her bones.

'Honour to meet you, Miss Savernake,' he said, as Garcia slipped away to court more guests. 'As a young fellow, I testified before your late father at the Old Bailey. An experience I shall never forget.'

'As disconcerting as my enthusiasm for cadavers, no doubt. Javier and I were talking about the surrealists, and I mentioned the notion of the exquisite corpse.'

'Alas,' Paul said. 'I'm a humble *Hay Wain* man. For me, the real world is challenge enough. No corpse I've ever seen has been in the least exquisite.'

'Exquisite corpses?' An elderly man with a patrician air joined them. 'Parlour game, y'know. People pass notes around, each adding a word or two at random, waiting to see what strange hybrid phrase results. Once, so the story goes, the upshot was: *the exquisite corpse will drink the young wine.* Inspired the surrealists to all kinds of visual experiments, drawing bodies in collaboration, made up of seemingly ill-matched parts. Their work isn't to my personal taste, frankly, but *chacun à son goût*. Forgive me, I shouldn't get carried away. Am I right in presuming that I have the pleasure of addressing Miss Rachel Savernake?'

'You know Sir Eustace Leivers?' Paul said to Rachel. 'My dear Miss Savernake, may I introduce the doyen of Harley Street? Between us, he and I care for both the living and the dead. Of course, his work is far more important than mine. Should the King fall ill, be assured the Palace will send for Leivers. Not content with being London's pre-eminent doctor, he's a walking encyclopaedia on pretty much any subject you care to name.'

Sir Eustace's gracious bow indicated that he took flattery as his due. Rachel said it was an enormous pleasure to be in such company, and asked the men for their opinion of a drawing by Duchamp. As Leivers and Paul pontificated, her gaze drifted across the gallery. Only a handful of the guests were women, all expensively dressed, and none under forty. She spotted the austere features of Alfred Linacre, brother of Dolly Benson's murderer. He was deep in conversation with two other men instantly recognisable by anyone who ever opened a newspaper. One was William Keary, the Irish actor, the other a thickset man called Heslop, the trade union leader widely credited with the abandonment of the General Strike after only nine days. As she watched, Linacre murmured to his companions, and all three men glanced over in her direction. Demure as a nun, she looked away.

The door at the far end of the gallery swung open, and in strolled a tall, confident man, immaculately pin-striped.

He accepted a glass from a hovering waiter, even as his eyes shifted around the room. When he caught sight of Rachel, he gave a nod of satisfaction, as a sportsman might do on a grouse shoot, the moment he spotted his quarry.

He advanced towards her. 'Miss Rachel Savernake, I presume? My name is Vincent Hannaway. I've been waiting to meet you for such a very long time.'

'I suppose,' Inspector Oakes said disarmingly, 'that I'll be wasting my time if I repeat the question you dodged last night. How did you come to be present outside the home of Lawrence Pardoe within moments of our own arrival?'

'You suppose correctly,' Jacob replied. 'I told you everything I know.'

This wasn't true. He was certain that Gallows Court meant something to Rachel Savernake. In their brief conversation, he'd dented Rachel's cool self-assurance enough for her to bang the telephone down on him.

He and Oakes were sipping strong tea in a windowless office down in the bowels of Scotland Yard. Jacob still couldn't quite believe his luck. Senior policemen seldom granted young journalists the time of day, far less summoned them to a private, off the record tête-à-tête. Oakes was one of a new breed of police officer, well-educated and sophisticated, very different from the hard-bitten sceptics who regarded newspapermen as the spawn of the devil. Rumour had it that he was destined for the top of the tree, and no doubt he'd prove more effective than that superannuated old soldier Sir Godfrey Mulhearn. Oakes could become an invaluable contact for years to come, Jacob thought. The trick was to develop the right kind of professional relationship from the start. Cordial but not too chummy, discreet yet down-to-earth.

The inspector leaned back in his chair, and put his hands behind his head. 'So what do you make of this business?'

'You're the policeman,' Jacob said. 'You tell me.'

His impudence was met with a bleak smile. 'It's because I'm a police officer that I'm asking the questions.'

'On the face of matters, Pardoe saved you a deal of trouble.' Jacob put down his cup. 'Might I see his suicide note?'

'That is asking too much, Mr Flint.' Oakes seemed amused by Jacob's cheek. 'I can assure you that the gist is unremarkable. He indicates that he'd come across Mary-Jane Hayes – he doesn't say how – and fell for her. When she failed to reciprocate his interest, he... took it amiss. He briefly describes strangling her and cutting off her head, in a way that precisely corresponds with the evidence. There's no doubt about the authenticity of his confession.'

'The world is full of spurned lovers, but when a woman rejects one's overtures, it's unusual to retaliate by decapitating her.'

Oakes shrugged. 'Despair does strange things to a man, or so they tell me.'

Jacob guessed that Oakes had never been troubled by self-doubt, let alone despair. Newspaper cuttings recorded a serene and pre-ordained progress through life. He was the fifth son of a baronet, and his family owned an extensive estate in the Home Counties. Remarkably, all his older brothers had survived the war, and he would never inherit the baronetcy, but he'd been a popular head boy at school, an oarsman good enough to win a blue, and was now the youngest inspector at the Yard. Small wonder that he exuded confidence as well as authority.

'Mary-Jane Hayes' torso was found in an alleyway in Covent Garden early in the morning, by a fellow on his way to work at the market,' Jacob said. 'Pardoe must have killed and dismembered her in the vicinity. Did he explain where he did the deed?'

'There's an unoccupied but well-furnished house in a mews a short distance from the market. The title deeds are in the name of a company personally owned by Pardoe. We suspect he lured the woman there on a pretext, and that's where she died.'

'Not McAlinden Mews by any chance?' Jacob asked, borrowing the name of a colleague in a shameless subterfuge.

Oakes was far too experienced to fall into such a trap. 'Sorry, Mr Flint, I'm not disclosing the address. We don't want the place to become some kind of macabre shrine. Suffice to say that Pardoe cleaned up after himself, but imperfectly. He left traces of blood and tissue. As you know, he put her body in one sack, and her clothes and bag in another, before abandoning both nearby. The head he kept in his possession. Presumably he regarded it as some ghastly form of trophy.'

'Pardoe baffles me, Inspector. Homicidal mania is one of the few sins nobody has attributed to financiers until now. Had he been issuing fraudulent stocks?'

'His solicitor, a fellow called Hannaway, assures us that Pardoe's financial dealings were beyond reproach. As a director of Pardoe's Bank, Hannaway has a vested interest in damping down speculation, but we've found no indications that Pardoe was either dishonest or unsuccessful.'

Jacob drank the rest of his tea. 'Might he have committed other crimes that nobody ever linked to him?'

'If so, he didn't confess to them,' Oakes said. 'He describes what he did as a moment of madness.'

'Such brutal violence surely doesn't come out of the blue?'

Oakes shrugged. 'My name isn't Sigmund Freud, Mr Flint. Perhaps Pardoe was unkind to animals, who knows? Nobody seems to have spotted his fatal flaw. He must have been lonely after the death of his wife and unborn child, and he was seriously ill. That may be as close to an explanation for his crime as we'll find. His solicitor has already disclosed that Pardoe's very substantial estate is willed, apart from a few minor bequests, to a range of good causes. It all fits with his reputation for philanthropy. Thank the Lord someone will benefit from this foul business, eh?'

'Then Scotland Yard is satisfied?'

'Absolutely.' Oakes permitted himself the glimmer of a smile. 'There will be an inquest, of course, but do not expect startling revelations. Fleet Street has treated us roughly of late. My superiors welcome a respite.'

'And Inspector Oakes?' Jacob persisted. 'Is he content?'

Oakes shrugged. 'The case does present eccentric features.'

'Such as?'

'Like you, we were tipped off about the death. Someone telephoned Scotland Yard. In a hoarse whisper, they told us we'd find a corpse in a locked room in South Audley Street. The caller didn't give a name.' He paused. 'We do not even know if it was a man or a woman.'

Jacob considered. 'Perhaps the same person sent me the note.'

'You still have no idea who gave you such a helping hand?'

'I'm as much in the dark as you.'

'Curious.'

Jacob nodded. 'And how do you intend to satisfy your curiosity?'

Oakes gave a wry smile. 'The demands on us are many and pressing. Superintendent Chadwick is a highly experienced officer, and he regards Pardoe's confession as conclusive. I can't justify any significant expenditure of time on the matter. It's rare for us to be presented with a solution to a crime, and left with no loose ends to tie. Without wishing to be crude, why look a gift horse in the mouth?'

Jacob grinned. 'My editor, on the other hand, is willing to allow me considerable licence.'

The two men's eyes met. 'How fortunate, Mr Flint. If you do come across any information that might interest me, please get in touch.'

'You can be sure of it.' Jacob stood up, and they shook hands.

'May I offer one word of advice before you leave?'

Jacob stopped at the door. 'Please.'

'Look both ways when crossing busy roads.'

'Your father didn't mention your love of modern art,' Rachel said.

'The old man's a Philistine,' Vincent Hannaway said. 'He's convinced nobody has painted anything worthwhile since *The Monarch of the Glen*. I'm no expert as far as these modern chaps are concerned, but I pride myself on being broad-minded.'

'I'm sure you do,' she said.

He'd manoeuvred her away from Leivers and Paul, and into a corner of the room. Six inches taller than his father, he had fair hair and blue eyes, presumably inherited from his mother. After bearing a son, Ethel Hannaway's mind had given way, and twelve months later, she'd died in a lunatic asylum. She'd served her purpose.

As a waiter strolled by, bearing drinks, Hannaway plucked another burgundy from the tray, presenting it to Rachel in exchange for her empty glass.

'Decent vintage,' he pronounced. 'Even if one isn't tempted to buy any of the daubs, there's ample compensation from Garcia's cellars, to say nothing of your company. Perhaps the wine's going to my head. I feel an irresistible impulse to let you into a little secret.'

His voice purred with condescension. Was it a family trait to patronise women, she wondered, or simply something lawyers couldn't help? Perhaps it was impossible, when one's advice cost so much and was treated as gospel, not to believe in one's innate superiority.

'I'm agog,' she said.

His smile showed a lot of teeth. They resembled small, sharp tombstones.

'You're the reason I came along tonight.'

'You flatter me, Mr Hannaway.'

'Please, call me Vincent. We may never have clapped eyes on each other before, but I feel I've known you all my life. You see, Rachel – if I may be so bold – safeguarding the Savernake family's interests has always been of paramount importance to my father. Our parents held each other in the highest esteem. I can't help but feel a similar regard for you.'

'Really, Vincent, I'm lost for words. Perhaps it's better to remain silent. Otherwise I'm bound to disappoint your high expectations.'

He gulped down the rest of his wine. 'I hear that your sense of humour is laced with irony. Excellent. I like…'

'A woman with spirit?' Rachel pursed her lips. 'One who yearns for a female equivalent of droit de seigneur?'

He took refuge in an uneasy laugh. 'Now you're mocking me. And my pater, too. You'll have gathered that he doesn't understand any woman under the age of fifty. He still maintains it was a grievous error to give you the vote. Though when you look at the shower we have in government at present, Alfred Linacre excepted, I can't believe we'd do worse if the entire electorate wore petticoats. One thing he and I do have in common. I'm equally anxious to be of service to you.'

'Thank you kindly, but I have no desire to buy another house, and I'm too young to make a will.'

'I'm afraid I can't agree,' he said suavely. 'A woman in your position should make a will. One can never foresee what the future may hold. Tragedies befall even the healthiest of us.'

'I suppose you're right.' She looked him in the eye. 'The last time I came to this gallery, I spoke to Claude Linacre. Who could have predicted his fall from grace? Strychnine: wasn't that his chosen means of self-destruction?'

Hannaway's features froze. 'I hear he'd persuaded his doctor that he needed a stimulant. Dreadful blow to his brother, but thank goodness he's rallied. We need men like Alfred in such uncertain times as these.'

'He's here tonight, I see.'

'A few of us are old friends, and we enjoy spending time together.' The mask dissolved into a fond smile. 'Your own father is often in our thoughts. A good companion, and a leader among men.'

'The Judge was very discreet,' Rachel said. 'Even with his only child. Though towards the end… he did talk more freely about his life in London. Unquestionably, his friends meant the world to him.'

Hannaway gave an appreciative nod, like a connoisseur scenting a fine wine. 'The Judge, you will know, was a champion at chess. We still enjoy an occasional game.'

'How cosy.' Rachel ran her finger around the rim of her wine glass, as if in aid to thought. 'And I'm sure you and your friends still like to… play fair?'

He flinched, but didn't answer. She knew he must be thinking fast.

Smiling sweetly, she said, 'You don't by any chance tolerate the possibility of allowing mere females to take part?'

Slowly, he said, 'Nothing stays the same forever.'

'How very true.'

He seemed to come to a decision. 'How fitting that the Judge's daughter should join our company.'

'Marvellous!' she exclaimed softly. 'I was afraid you might decline such a… bold gambit.'

'Now you're teasing me.' Hannaway's eyes glinted. 'After all, our little fellowship was founded by your father and mine. It seems you already have an inkling of how much we enjoy our games.'

Rachel inclined her head, and smiled. 'Let me sound a cautionary note before you elect me to the brotherhood.'

'I promise you,' Hannaway said. 'I will not stand in your path.'

'When I play,' – her smile faded – 'I play to win.'

7

Jacob quickened his stride as the unmistakable landmark of Clarion House loomed out of the gaslit darkness of Fleet Street. The newspaper's majestic home bristled with tall, soot-blackened chimneys, and an observation tower from which Gomersall enjoyed glowering down at the competition. Had Rennie Mackintosh been hallucinating when he'd conceived the original design? The building's wild extravagance made the home he'd created for the *Glasgow Herald* seem like a model of architectural restraint.

Jacob headed for the newsroom, and asked Pop-Eye Poyser if the name Gallows Court meant anything to him.

'Oh yes. Five minutes away from here, if that.'

'What? Where is it, for heaven's sake?'

'Unfrequented corner at the back of Lincoln's Inn. Only one way in, and one way out. Miserable little apology for a courtyard, as I recall.' Poyser whipped off his spectacles, and subjected Jacob to myopic scrutiny. 'Why do you ask? Not in trouble with m'learned friends, I trust? Promise me you haven't libelled someone rich and famous.'

'Not knowingly,' Jacob said.

'Intention is no defence to a claim of libel,' Poyser said mournfully. 'If you want to know why Walter Gomersall has dark shadows under his eyes, blame the fear of defamation claims. It induces insomnia in every editor on this street of shame. If you've anything to confess to him, better get it off your chest right now.'

Jacob shook his head. 'It's just a lead I picked up. Thanks for your help.'

The pop-eyes blinked furiously. 'You were asking about Tom before. Is this connected with his accident?'

'That would be telling.'

Five minutes later, he was trawling through a directory listing lawyers who practised in the environs of the Inns of Court. An entry for Gallows Court jumped out from the page, as vivid as if scrawled in blood.

Hannaway & Hannaway, Solicitors.

Inspector Oakes had mentioned that name earlier in the day. Lawrence Pardoe's solicitor was called Hannaway. So there was a connection between the dead man and Gallows Court. But what did the place mean to Thomas Betts?

'Don't hog the loveliest lady in the room to yourself all evening, Hannaway!'

The voice, Irish and musical, belonged to William Keary. He clapped the solicitor on the back, but his eyes locked on Rachel. Hannaway effected the introductions, and was drawn aside by Garcia and Heslop.

'Such an honour to meet you at last, Miss Savernake.' A swooning critic had once compared listening to Keary's mellifluous tones to bathing in honey. 'Your father was a truly great man.'

Charm oozed out of him like sweat from a lesser man's pores. His boyish habit of running one hand through thick and curly dark hair was engaging, although Rachel was sure it was a cultivated mannerism. At first glance, William Keary was the very picture of sincerity, but he was also the most versatile stage performer of his generation.

'I never met anyone like him,' Rachel said.

Keary considered her for a moment before breaking into a smile. The famously irresistible William Keary smile, the smile that set a thousand female hearts aflutter.

'Delicately put, Miss Savernake. I can imagine that as a parent, he might have been... a taskmaster. As my lawyer, I found him tenacious and single-minded. As my friend, he epitomised ferocious loyalty.'

In his youth, Keary had made his name as a singer and dancer with a gift for impersonation, 'the Man of a Hundred Voices', signing a contract to perform exclusively for the New Moorish Theatre. When the management of the Inanity offered to triple his earnings, he defected, only to receive a writ from his former employers demanding colossal damages. Once he instructed Lionel Savernake K.C. to represent him, the litigation came to a rapid end on agreed terms, leaving Keary free to pursue his new career. Within weeks, he was being feted by audiences at the Inanity, while his lawyer was elevated to the judiciary. Now the Judge was dead, and Keary owned both the Inanity and one of the country's leading agencies for theatrical performers.

'Did you keep in touch with him?'

'Until he moved back to Gaunt. Afterwards, it became... difficult. Although he was a private man who seldom spoke of personal matters, it was clear you were the apple of his eye.' Keary paused. 'I remember him describing you, when you were a small child, as very highly strung. How gratified he'd be to see you today. So svelte, so self-possessed.'

'And so impervious to soft soap.'

Rachel's smile did not rob her words of their sting, but the famous smile danced again on those full, sensuous lips.

'You've made yourself at home in London. Garcia says you are his favourite customer.'

'Only because my purchases keep him out of Queer Street.'

'I'm sure you always invest shrewdly, Rachel. You're not offended if I call you by your Christian name? I've never been a stickler for formality.' He lowered his voice. 'Hannaway disapproves of my louche ways. He'd be furious if he knew I was inviting you to lunch à deux.'

'And are you?'

'Most certainly. Would tomorrow suit? The Restaurant Ragusa is my favourite. I can recommend it.'

'How generous. Doesn't lunch at the Ragusa cost as much as a working man earns in a month?'

'Thankfully,' he smiled, 'I'm not really a working man. For me, acting is pure joy. I'd gladly fool around on the stage for nothing. Don't tell my fellow shareholders at the Inanity, will you?'

'Your backers are an illustrious bunch, I hear,' she said. 'An eclectic mix, too. Heslop, the trade unionist, and the Bishop of Hampstead, to say nothing of Rufus Paul. Several are here tonight, I see.'

'You're very well informed, Rachel.' Keary paused. 'Salt of the earth, all of them. Heslop's a sound man, whatever political colours you fly. Knows where the workers' interests lie. Without him, the strike could have brought down the government.'

'Goodness me,' she said. 'That would never do.'

'I wonder,' he said slowly, 'what's in your mind?'

She swallowed the last of her wine. 'Ah, William. You gentlemen must permit a lady to preserve a little of her mystery.'

'You'll become famous if you carry on like this,' Mrs Dowd announced as she served Jacob with his favourite among her culinary specialities, piping hot shepherd's pie.

He fell upon it like a starved man. Elation had yielded to exhaustion, and instead of exulting over his scoop, he'd felt an unexpected sense of emptiness.

The sight of his name emblazoned across the *Clarion*'s front page captivated both his landlady and her daughter. Elaine, whose rather tight black cardigan contrasted with her exuberant red hair, was in coquettish mood. She gave a tinkly laugh.

'He won't want anything to do with us soon, Mother. Mixing with the hoi-polloi will be beneath the great reporter's dignity. We'll have to make do with gathering round the wireless, and admiring his broadcasts to the nation. Best BBC pronunciation, posher than Monsignor Knox! Oh no, not a soul will ever guess he came from darkest Yorkshire. I wouldn't be surprised if he takes up with someone famous, like Nefertiti, the Nubian Queen. His eyes were out on stalks that night when she waltzed onto the stage. I'd better get him to give me his autograph, before he starts charging a shilling for the privilege.'

'You will have your little joke, Elaine.' Mrs Dowd became sombre. 'It's a terrible business, all the same. That poor, defenceless creature. I don't hold with those who say it was her own fault, because she was no better than she ought to be. You can't blame women simply because they've suffered bad luck. I suppose she fell on hard times and started walking the streets?'

'The papers said she was a nurse,' Elaine said. 'Isn't that right, Jake?'

'Correct,' he mumbled with his mouth full.

'How can it have happened? This chap Pardoe was a respectable widower, wasn't he? Gave generously to charities.'

'Plenty of so-called respectable men,' her mother said darkly, 'are nothing of the kind. You only have to read the *News of the World* to know that.'

'Why pick on an innocent nurse?' Elaine persisted. 'Jake, I bet you know more than you're letting on. What does Scotland Yard have to say for itself? What are your own theories? Help yourself to that last slice of pie while you bare your soul.'

He piled more meat onto his plate. 'Even the boys in blue don't know the full story. Not that they're losing any sleep. They've got their man, and we can't keep berating them for failing to protect the city's womenfolk. Pardoe's done their job for them. The crime is solved, and the culprit is dead. That's all the high-ups at Scotland Yard care about. Psychology they leave to the Freudians. As for the press, we can grub around for titbits about Pardoe and his poor victim if we choose. Our wonderful police will devote themselves to making sure the streets are safe for decent God-fearing Londoners.'

'Don't you care for the police?' Mrs Dowd was open-mouthed at this hint of Bolshevism. 'The constable who came here to ask about the note you were sent was very well-mannered.'

'They're human, like the rest of us.'

'Who sent you the note, do you know?'

'As you saw, it was anonymous.'

'Very mysterious,' Mrs Dowd said.

'What will you do?' Elaine demanded. 'Grub around yourself, until you find out the full story?'

'Depend upon it.' He put down his knife and fork. 'You're right. There's more to this crime than meets the eye. I want to find out the truth.'

The young woman's eyes shone. 'You'll do it!'

Murmuring something about rhubarb crumble, Mrs Dowd retreated to the kitchen. As the door closed behind her, Elaine placed her hand on Jacob's thigh. He enjoyed the touch of her slim, warm fingers, but when they became bolder, he eased away.

'I'd better have an early night. Pity about the crumble, but I hardly got any sleep last night, and I'm dead on my feet.'

She pouted. 'You're getting bored with me.'

'No, no,' he said hastily. 'Not at all.'

'You are!'

The hint of neediness troubled him. Was this why her affair with the married man had fallen apart? He dreaded the thought of upsetting her.

'It's just that I've got an early start tomorrow. I'm off to Southend. Mary-Jane's married sister lives there. She may be able to give me a lead.'

'Lucky you – a trip to the seaside!'

'In the freezing cold. I'll take my warmest scarf.'

'I was only joking.' Her tone softened, as if she regretted her outburst. 'Your job can't be easy. Interrogating people during the darkest days of their lives. When Ollie McAlinden was lodging here, I asked him how he could bear it.'

Jacob bit his tongue. He couldn't imagine his ambitious colleague at the *Clarion* ever suffering from prickles of conscience. And why should he? A journalist's job was to ferret out the truth.

'I bet it keeps you awake at night, worrying that you might hurt them.'

He pecked her on the cheek, reflecting that his work had never cost him a moment's sleep. Yet after an hour in bed, he was still wide awake, restless thoughts making his head ache. Once or twice lately, he'd drifted off with memories of Nefertiti, the Nubian Queen of Magic and Mystery, floating through his brain. Tonight, the image of a different woman filled his mind. Her cold eyes stared at him through the fog, while he recalled Tom Betts' hoarse whisper.

Rachel Savernake.

Trueman, clad in chauffeur's cap and a greatcoat, was waiting for Rachel when she slipped out of the gallery. He'd parked the Phantom in a side street five minutes away. He was carrying an umbrella, but didn't unfurl it despite the drizzle. They walked side by side, Rachel humming 'Singin' in the Rain'. The moon was skulking behind a cloud. As they turned the final corner, Rachel slowed almost to a standstill, straining her eyes in the darkness.

The street was narrow and poorly lit. One side housed a row of small, shuttered shops, the other a disused box factory. There was nobody in sight, just a mangy cat prowling in search of scraps. The Phantom was fifty yards away.

Ahead of them, barely visible in the gloom, a squat shape emerged from the shadows. A stocky man in cap and muffler, clutching something that might be a weapon. Trueman lengthened his stride, but in a whirl of movement, the man lunged forward, and Trueman seemed to lose his balance, as he struggled to ward off the attack.

Behind Rachel, someone stepped out of the warehouse doorway, and clamped an arm around her shoulder. The man was taller than her, and his grip was powerful. She felt his breath, a smell of stale beer and onions, warm and sticky against her skin. His knee pressed on her spine. His other hand brought a knife up against her neck. The blade pricked her skin.

'Lie down!' the other man growled. He and Trueman crouched in front of each other on the cobbles, each waiting to pounce. The man brandished a jagged piece of broken pipe. 'Else we slit her throat.'

Rachel squealed. 'Help! I am just a poor, defenceless woman!'

A sudden flick of the knife sliced through her necklace of pearls. Trueman uttered a low, agonised groan.

'Not really so poor, are you?' her assailant hissed. 'I bet them pearls are real.'

As he spoke, Trueman thrust forward with his umbrella. A long steel point ripped through the squat man's midriff, as Rachel seized her attacker's wrist, jerking it in a smooth, violent movement. She heard a crack of snapping bone, and the knife fell from his hand.

Yelping in pain, he slipped on the rain-slicked cobbles, and sank to his knees. She swung her leg, and raked a pointed heel across his face. He screamed and clutched at his damaged eyes as Trueman seized his companion's neck in a chokehold, and began to bang the man's head against the cobbles. Once, twice, three times.

Taking a gun from her coat pocket, Rachel pointed it at the man who had assaulted her. Blood streamed from the gash on his face. He uttered a gurgle of self-pity and pain.

'Not so defenceless, either,' she said.

Juliet Brentano's Journal

31 January 1919

I keep my door locked. Supposedly, I am free to come and go as I please, but really I'm trapped. Trapped forever, whether or not the weather worsens, and the island is cut off from the mainland for days on end. Bolts and chains may not shackle me, but I'm still a prisoner, on my own at the top of this rambling old house. Like a Princess in the Tower.

Except that I am not a princess.

Why lock myself in? It's hard to explain, even to myself. The Judge could not climb the winding flight of eighty-five steep steps that leads to my door. The exertion would kill him.

Rachel never comes here. She prefers to give me a wide berth, terrified that I might infect her. Mother taught me long ago that with a single cough, I could rid myself of her hateful presence. From the moment we arrived on Gaunt, she made her hostility towards me plain. Yet it took time for me to realise how cruel she is.

Whenever servants annoyed her, she took revenge by poisoning the Judge's mind against them. Invariably, they were dismissed without a character. The last governess the Judge employed, a fat spinster called Miss Donachie, was devoted to a silly Pekinese almost as plump as herself. Six months ago the dog disappeared. Twenty-four hours earlier, Miss Donachie had finally lost patience, and chastised Rachel in my hearing for dumb insolence. When she realised her pet had vanished, the governess was beside herself.

Rachel couldn't contain her glee. Eventually, she announced she'd found the dog's collar, while clambering over an outcrop of rocks on the north shore. She pointed out a smear of blood on it. But the poor creature was never found.

Nobody doubted who was responsible. Everyone knew that, if Rachel was in a temper, someone or something must suffer. Miss Donachie departed at the next low tide, and three maids and the cook followed her across the causeway, never to return.

Rachel was jubilant. 'See?' she hissed at me. 'That's how you kill two birds with one stone.'

Of course, the Judge didn't punish her. He blamed the servants, and said they were envious of his beloved daughter. In an outpouring of senseless rage, he dismissed those who remained. Subsequently, Henrietta came to work here. She's a woman of thirty, pleasant in appearance, but unmarried. She was engaged to a sheep farmer who got himself blown to bits at Ypres, and since then she's scraped a living to care for two ailing parents. Their medical bills are ruinous, and she's desperate for money. The Judge has to pay through the nose to bring anyone in. Even so, Henrietta says she wouldn't stick it but for me and my mother.

A man called Cliff agreed to help with labouring jobs around the Hall. He was invalided out of the army with shell shock, and needs to earn enough to look after himself, his young sister, and their widowed mother. Finally, Harold Brown turned up, claiming to have worked in a great house *as a butler. A likely story. Henrietta caught him eyeing the Judge's gold candlesticks.*

Mother liked Henrietta. She'd never found anyone to confide in before. Apart from me, and I'm sure she sheltered me from a great deal. She took care to avoid talking about the Judge or his daughter, but one day, I overhead her talking to Henrietta.

'If you ask me,' she said, 'Rachel Savernake is as mad as the old brute who fathered her.'

'My only regret is that the wicked creature took the coward's way out.' Agnes Dyson's eyes glistened as she turned away from Jacob to stare at the waves leaping beyond the promenade. Were the blustery conditions making her eyes water, or was she fighting back tears? 'I'd gladly have hanged him myself, after what he did to my poor sister. May he rot in hell!'

She twisted her woollen gloves in her bare hands, as if rehearsing how to make the punishment fit the crime. Jacob couldn't find it in his heart to blame her, for all his nagging doubts about judicial execution. Cases like Edith Thompson's troubled him. Had she really deserved to have her neck broken because her young lover had murdered her husband?

'It must be hard for you.' He imagined himself as a priest with a distressed parishioner. 'I gather you and Mary-Jane were very close.'

'We were sisters.' Agnes' tone softened. 'There were eleven years between us – we had a brother, but he died in infancy, poor lamb – but we never lost touch, even when our paths wound in different directions. She was a good-hearted woman, was Mary-Jane. Never a bad word to say for anyone. Lovely to look at, too, quite beautiful in her younger days. Always respectable, mark my words. Nobody ever got up to any funny business with her, whatever tittle-tattle you hear from people with minds like sewers.'

After a stiff wind had blown him from the station to her boarding house, he'd agreed to Agnes' proposal of a walk while the rain held off. Out of season, Bella Vista was quiet, and he guessed she didn't want the girl clearing up the breakfast things to eavesdrop.

Mary-Jane Hayes had been identified from the personal possessions bagged up and left a few feet from her decap itated corpse. Her purse was full of money; the motive for the murder had not been theft. The newspapers had skirted around the false rumours that Mary-Jane was a prostitute, but the killer's butchery of the corpse invited comparisons to the Whitechapel murders, as did the police's inability to turn up any clues to the crime. The Great British Public could be relied upon to put two and two together and make five, assuming the worst of the victim as well as of her nemesis.

'So I gather.' He gave an embarrassed cough. 'To be candid with you, Mrs Dyson, my own newspaper wasn't blameless. Our chief crime correspondent is in hospital, and the story was covered by other people who aren't... well, all I can say is thank goodness for the stroke of luck which meant I could break the story of Pardoe's confession and suicide.'

'You're young,' she said. 'How do I know I can trust you? After what happened to Mary-Jane, I've been pestered by reporters from dawn till dusk. They all promise to tell the truth, and none of them do. They only want a good story.'

'I happen to believe that the truth *is* a good story.' The phrase sprang to his lips from nowhere, and pleased him. 'You must decide whether you can trust me.'

They trudged on in silence. Agnes Dyson was sturdily built, with thick greying hair which flew about in the wind. Large brown eyes and high cheekbones were her most attractive physical features, and judging by photographs he'd seen of her late sister, they ran in the family. Mary-Jane had been the beauty, but for all the ferocity of her rhetoric, Agnes Dyson was hardly the forbidding seaside landlady of caricature. But the brutality of murder brought out the worst in everyone, not just journalists.

'Shall we walk onto the pier?' he suggested. 'We needn't go right to the end. I hear it's the longest in the country.'

'In the world, never mind the blessed country,' she assured him. 'Last year, they made it even longer, and Prince George came for the official opening. The electric railway is being extended, too, but I'd rather exercise my legs. Twenty-five years of cooking for other folk doesn't do your figure any good at all.'

'Good heavens, Mrs Dyson, don't be so modest!' he said with cheerful gallantry.

She laughed, and he rejoiced inwardly. 'It's as well you've wrapped up warm. The sea breezes are sharp at this time of year.'

'My parents used to take me to Bridlington in all weathers. Bracing, they call it, when the wind blows in, a euphemism for freezing cold. The climate here is positively tropical compared to East Yorkshire.'

She proceeded to explain to him exactly why Southend-on-Sea was the finest resort in Britain. Quite apart from its never-ending pier, trippers could pick and choose between such attractions as the Hippodrome, the Victoria Arcade, and the Wall of Death at the Kursaal Amusement Park. As if all that were not enough, a new boating lake on the front and an art gallery were both in prospect.

'I've seen the advertising posters at Tube stations,' he said. 'I'll have to come back when it's warmer. We can't change what happened to your sister, more's the pity, but I'd like to make sure that we print the truth, not distorted rubbish.'

She sniffed noisily, and turned her head away from him. 'If you can pull that off, Mr Flint, I'd be eternally grateful.'

'Please, call me Jacob.'

'You remind me of my own son. He's a rating in the Royal Navy. Always loved boats and sailing, ever since he was little. Poor Mary-Jane never knew the joy of motherhood. Or the worry of it, I might add.'

'She never married, did she?'

'A lovely fellow with a baker's shop in Chalkwell courted her for years, but he had his leg blown off in France. They fitted him up with an artificial replacement, but he was in terrible pain, and shot himself a week after we signed the armistice. My son was already at school when war broke out. She doted on him, but really she always wanted children of her own. The snag was, she was getting on for thirty, and there weren't many men around. She used to joke about it. "You know what I am? A superfluous woman."'

'A horrid term. Nobody is superfluous.'

'But some people feel they are surplus to requirements, Jacob. Because she looked so lovely, chaps kept asking her out, but all she said to me was that the spark was lacking.

It didn't help that she was shy. I was always the chatty one in the family. Once she'd lost her Mr Right, she never found anyone to match him. As time passed, she devoted herself to her work. There wasn't a more dedicated nurse in Essex, I promise you.'

'She moved to London seven years ago?'

'It was time to spread her wings, she said. She saw an advertisement for a job at Great Ormond Street, and applied on the spur of the moment. When they offered her the position, she leapt at it.'

'You saw less of her after that?'

'Yes. I wrote to her regularly at first, but she was never much of a correspondent, Mary-Jane. She and I were both busy with our lives, and it didn't…'

She bent her head, and Jacob put his hand on her shoulder. 'You imagined you had all the time in the world to see each other in future.'

Agnes Dyson looked up at him. 'That's right,' she said in a muffled voice. 'When… anyway, no use crying over spilt milk, eh?'

'Why did she leave London?'

'A job was going at an Orphans' Home on the outskirts of Oxford. Deputy matron, with a view to taking overall charge. The matron was getting on – she'd had the job for thirty years – and wanted to call it a day. It was a big step up, very well paid, but with much more responsibility. She sent me a postcard, saying it was the chance of a lifetime.'

'Yet she didn't stay there long?'

'No, it came as a shock when she dropped me a line to say she'd left.'

'Do you know why she resigned?'

'No, she never explained. I can't believe there was any unpleasantness. She wasn't the argumentative sort, wasn't Mary-Jane. I suppose she found that being in charge isn't all it's cracked up to be. Less time with the children, more time with paperwork. She never had my head for business, and perhaps she couldn't face the prospect of becoming matron. So she went back to London, and rented a flat in the building where she'd lived before, in Mecklenburgh Square. She was wondering whether to go cap in hand to Great Ormond Street, and ask for her old job back.'

'Did she ever mention Lawrence Pardoe to you?'

'Not once.' She mustered a mirthless smile. 'Mary-Jane didn't confide in me about men. I suppose the age difference...' A gull squawked overhead.

'I see.'

Agnes Dyson gazed across the estuary towards the distant shores of Kent. 'I never knew Mary-Jane play a mean trick in her life. She cared about her patients, and loved the little ones. To think that beast destroyed her so callously makes my blood boil. All I can do now is make sure she's remembered for the right reasons. Will you help me do that, Jacob?'

'Yes,' he said, startling himself with the fervour of his reply. 'You can depend on me.'

'You risked your lives,' Mrs Trueman said, pouring coffee from a silver pot. 'And for what?'

Rachel yawned. 'We were never in danger. The ruffians would have come to grief even if they'd taken us by surprise. Those hours of training in ju-jitsu with Trueman were well spent. No wonder the Suffragettes' Bodyguard proved so formidable.'

'But did you learn anything to make the whole affair worthwhile? Or did you just want to prove yourself in a tussle with a man?'

'Admittedly, they knew precious little.' Rachel tasted her drink. 'Even when they were begging for their lives, they told us nothing of interest. Scarcely worth the sacrifice of a fake pearl necklace. A go-between hired them, a publican from Shadwell. He said his principals didn't want us dead. Just warned off. If I wasn't on the train back to Cumberland within forty-eight hours, they'd find me again. And next time, they'd throw acid in my face.'

The housekeeper shuddered. 'Like poor Martha.'

'They won't hurt anyone else.'

'Plenty more roughnecks where they came from.'

'Last night proved that I've made my mark. Nobody mourned Claude Linacre, but Pardoe meant something. There's a stench of panic in the air.'

The telephone rang, a rare enough occurrence in this household for the women to exchange glances. Within moments, Martha appeared in the doorway.

'Inspector Oakes of Scotland Yard,' she said. 'He wants to come here this afternoon.'

The moment he arrived back in Fleet Street, Jacob despatched a telegram to the matron of the Oxford Orphans' Home, asking if he could meet her the following day. Nothing ventured, nothing gained. His next move was to invade the smoke-filled fortress of the *Clarion*'s City editor.

William Plenderleith was a morose sceptic whose excoriations of capitalism stemmed from a strict Calvinist faith rather than from adherence to the teachings of Marx. Jacob had scant understanding of the arcane mysteries of high finance, but on the rare occasions when he read Plenderleith's columns, he realised how they suited the *Clarion*'s readership. Even those who cared nothing for the subtleties of the stock market could thrill to Plenderleith's thundering denunciations of incompetence and corruption. He was not so much a commentator as a hellfire preacher.

'Lawrence Pardoe.' Plenderleith rolled the syllables around on his tongue, his expression making clear that they tasted bitter. 'Made Midas look like a pauper. Inherited a fortune, and unlike most sons similarly blessed, he didn't fritter it away, but devoted himself to increasing his wealth.'

The reek of tobacco made Jacob's sinuses sting. 'How much was Pardoe worth?'

Plenderleith stubbed out his Woodbine, and immediately lit another. A tall, skeletal man of forty, he was painfully thin, and it was rumoured that each day he smoked more cigarettes than he consumed calories.

'Not the faintest idea, laddie. If I were a guessing man, three million would be a conservative estimate, but I leave guesswork to the politicians elected to determine our miserable destinies.'

Jacob whistled. 'I wonder he bothered to work at all.'

'Money begets money. And the begetting becomes addictive, laddie.'

Like smoking, Jacob almost said, but he stopped himself just in time.

'The Good Book says it all: *lay not up for yourselves treasures upon earth, where moth and rust doth corrupt.* Be thankful you're spared the nightmare of worrying about punitive taxation and death duties.'

'I'll console myself with that next time I pay my rent. Did you ever meet Pardoe?'

'Once or twice, but we only exchanged a few words. He was aware of my reputation, and gave me a wide berth. In that, of course, he was not alone.'

'Was he honest?'

'Lord, no, laddie. You can't handle so much money and remain unbesmirched. Even if you salve your conscience through acts of benevolence. If you're asking whether I expected him to slaughter a defenceless woman, the answer is no, but that is simply proof of my tendency to be over-generous. Where rich financiers are concerned, one should always assume the worst. I can't claim to have discovered any shocking examples of infamy on his part. But they'll be lurking somewhere in the tangled undergrowth of his financial affairs, depend upon it.'

'He wasn't ostentatious, and doesn't seem to have had expensive hobbies. Was there no gossip about him?'

'He kept himself to himself. By the dismal standards of rich men, he seemed not to make many enemies.'

'So despite his prominence in the world of finance, you never found out much about him?'

Plenderleith bridled, and Jacob felt a buzz of satisfaction: the shot had hit its target. 'Very little, laddie. As you know, I write nothing that is not supported by verifiable fact. I never rely upon unsubstantiated hearsay.'

'So you did hear something?'

'Tittle-tattle, nothing more.'

'I'd be really grateful...'

'I didn't tell you this.' The older man glared. 'Mind, if anything comes of it, I expect a promise of due acknowledgement.'

'Of course,' Jacob said meekly. 'Cross my heart and hope to die.'

With exaggerated caution, Plenderleith folded his lean body over the desk, and breathed in Jacob's ear. 'Not long ago, I heard a whisper that someone was asking about Pardoe. A private detective was covertly making extensive inquiries about his activities. I couldn't ascertain why someone would be so interested in Pardoe. A disappointed investor might have an axe to grind, but Pardoe didn't indulge in extravagant schemes destined to make paupers of participants with more money than sense. But whoever instructed the investigations must have been serious. You need deep pockets to engage this fellow. He's said to be the smartest enquiry agent in London, and by far the most expensive.'

'What's his name?'

Plenderleith's mirthless smile gave a glimpse of nicotine-yellowed teeth. 'Leviticus Shoemaker.'

9

'Kind of you to see me,' Inspector Oakes said, as Mrs Trueman served Darjeeling and scones. 'I'm sure you have many calls on your time.'

'Dear me, no. I lead an uneventful life.' Rachel gave a nod of thanks as the housekeeper left them. 'To spend tea time with the coming man at Scotland Yard is a novelty.'

'You grew up on a small island, I hear.'

'Yes, Gaunt's a wild place. Given to some long-forgotten Savernake many years ago by a grateful monarch. The establishment has never been afraid to reward loyalty and discretion.' She smiled. 'Though a bleak rock isn't much of a prize. As I grew up, the fishermen's cottages in the village at the far end of the causeway seemed like the last word in sophistication. Places where families talked to each other, and laughed and cried together.'

'It must have been lonely for you, as an only child. Your mother had died, and your father... wasn't well.'

Rachel shrugged. 'For a time, a distant cousin lived there too. We were much the same age, but... she died. I must confess, I didn't miss her. I had the sea to swim in, the rocks to climb, and books to learn from. Even in winter, when we were cut off for days on end, there was always the joy of escape... into my imagination.'

Oakes shifted in his chair. Something in her tone made him feel ill at ease. 'London must seem very strange too you.'

'Didn't someone once describe it as a great cesspool into which all the idlers of the Empire are irresistibly drained?' The gleam in Oakes' eye told her that he recognised the allusion. 'I plead guilty to being an idler. Quiet pleasures amuse me. Word games. Chess problems.'

Oakes followed her gaze to the inlaid chess table. 'I admired this house the last time I came, but it's all the more appealing now it bears... your hallmark.'

Rachel smiled. 'You called on the previous owner in a professional capacity, I believe?'

'You're very well informed. Yes, I arrested Crossan. He relished showing off the swimming pool and underground gymnasium, even though he couldn't swim and was morbidly obese. He liked owning things beyond the reach of ordinary mortals. Such as police inspectors.' Oakes buttered a scone. 'His boastfulness destroyed him.'

'A cautionary tale. More tea?'

'Thank you, but no. I remember Crossan's horde of flunkeys, dancing attendance on him. How different he must find his new life behind bars. You, on the other hand, evidently prefer to rely on... a skeleton staff.'

'My wants are simple, Inspector. I don't require a large entourage to cater to them.'

'Your modesty does you credit.'

'I'm lucky. My servants are exceptionally capable.'

He gave her a curious glance. 'You seem to treat them almost on equal terms.'

'Remiss of me.' She smiled. 'Sometimes, I wonder who is really in charge. Me – or them.'

He cleared his throat. 'Forgive my asking, but your house-maid, who showed me in...'

'You're curious about her disfigurement?'

'Her looks are very striking,' Oakes said. 'Before her face was damaged, she must have been...'

'A beauty?' Rachel said. 'In my opinion, she still is, but her looks were a curse. She attracted the attention of a wicked man, who was driven to fury when she resisted his crude advances.'

'Acid?' She nodded. 'I've seen such injuries before, on poor girls in the East End. Vitriolage, they call it. I hope to blazes the blighter who ruined her looks was caught.'

'Rest assured,' Rachel said. 'He received his just deserts.'

Oakes seemed about to ask something else, but Rachel's expression made him change his mind. 'Another development since my last visit is that your windows now have steel shutters. Even on the upper floors.' He indicated the window overlooking the square. 'The lock on the front door impressed me as well. One of those new-fangled American jobs. And I see you've invested in the latest Rely-a-Bell alarm. I've never seen a private home so well protected. You must feel as secure as the Bank of England.'

'You're observant, Inspector.' Rachel returned his smile. 'You'll, therefore, have noticed my taste for works of art. They were not inexpensive, and I mean to keep them safe. Burglars can look elsewhere.'

His crisp nod reminded her of a fencer saluting an opponent who has parried a sabre thrust. 'Very wise.'

'Now, do enlighten me. What brings such a busy man to my door?'

He finished his scone. 'You've read the newspaper reports about the death of Lawrence Pardoe?'

'It's impossible to escape the story in the press today.'

'On the face of things, his case bears curious similarities to that of Claude Linacre.'

'Really? Linacre suffocated Dolly, whereas Pardoe used a scarf to strangle Mary-Jane, and then decapitated her. The homicidal equivalent of chalk and cheese.' She lowered her eyelashes. 'I'm sorry. Does my tasteless turn of phrase distress you?'

'I'm not talking about how the murders were committed,' he retorted. 'Linacre and Pardoe belonged to the same circle. The artist banked with Pardoe's, and both of them had a stake in the theatre where Dolly Benson sang in the chorus. Both crimes suggest perverted passion. Each of the victims was an attractive woman...'

'Yet Mary-Jane Hayes was twice the age of the Benson girl, and Pardoe was twenty years older than Claude Linacre,' Rachel interrupted. 'As for the social connection between the murderers, wouldn't it be more startling if two rich Londoners were *not* acquainted with each other?'

'I hadn't taken you for a believer in coincidence, Miss Savernake.'

'Didn't you attend the same great university as both murderers? I wouldn't be astounded to learn your family has entrusted its money to Pardoe's Bank for the past half century. The world of privilege and power is small and incestuous, Inspector.'

A pink tinge coloured his cheeks. 'You sound like someone preaching socialism at Hyde Park Corner.'

'My point is not political. I merely suggest that anyone seeking to link the two crimes needs to present a compelling case.'

'You interested yourself in the Chorus Girl murder. What about the death of Mary-Jane Hayes? Did that arouse your curiosity, too?'

'What makes you ask, when Pardoe is dead, and news of his confession is splashed across every front page?' She folded her arms. 'It's not as if Scotland Yard took any notice when I told you who murdered Dolly Benson.'

'Granted, Miss Savernake. In our defence, for a young lady to accuse a cabinet minister's brother of a grotesque crime is… unorthodox. Scepticism was inevitable. What the newspapers haven't printed is that this time, we were alerted to Pardoe's death by an anonymous telephone call. You didn't make it, by any chance?'

She looked him in the eye. 'No.'

Oakes put down his cup. 'Are you sure, Miss Savernake?'

'I'm not accustomed to having my word doubted, Inspector.' She stood up, and pressed a bell on the wall. 'It was bad enough when my attempt to help Scotland Yard was rebuffed. If that is all…'

He rose. 'I must apologise if I have offended you. I didn't mean…'

The door swung open, and the maid with the spoiled cheek came in. 'Inspector Oakes is leaving, Martha,' Rachel said. 'Please don't let him forget his hat and coat.'

Awkwardly, Oakes held out his hand. 'Thank you for sparing me a few minutes, Miss Savernake. I hope our paths will cross again.'

Rachel's expression gave nothing away. 'Stranger things have happened, Inspector. For now, goodbye.'

On leaving the City editor, Jacob returned to his desk. A telegram had arrived from Mrs Elvira Mundy, matron of the Oxford Orphans' Home. She was willing to see him at half past ten the next morning. She proposed a cup of tea at Fuller's in Cornmarket.

Jubilant, he confirmed his agreement by return, and was still congratulating himself when a message came from Peggy, the permanently bored young woman who guarded the *Clarion*'s staff from unwelcome visitors.

'Lady to see you.' Peggy sighed, irritated at being disturbed in her enjoyment of a magazine. 'Name of Delamere.'

'Never heard of her. What does she want?'

'Said needs to speak to you urgently.'

'What is so urgent? Can't it wait until tomorrow?'

'Dunno,' she yawned. 'I'll tell her you've gone home for the day, shall I?'

'Surely she explained what she wants to see me about?'

'Not really. Only that it's about someone called Rachel Savernake.'

*

'Well?' Trueman demanded, ten minutes after the Scotland Yard man had left Gaunt House.

'Levi Shoemaker was right,' Rachel said. 'Oakes is a good detective, and he noticed the shutters, even if he hasn't grasped the full scale of our renovations. He suspects me of something, but doesn't know what.'

Trueman took a seat. The leather armchair seemed inadequate for his immense physique. 'You sent him off with his tail between his legs, Martha tells me.'

'He's had a civilised upbringing, and possesses excellent manners. A wretched handicap for a detective. He asked if I'd called the Yard about Pardoe's death, and when he challenged my denial, I brimmed over with righteous indignation. He was too embarrassed to think of asking if someone else telephoned the police on my behalf. Such a well turned-out, capable fellow. I loved making him blush.'

Trueman laughed, a raucous, discordant sound. 'Remember what else Shoemaker said. Oakes' greatest failing is the same as Flint's. They've been educated to respect wealth and social position, but what really makes them go weak at the knees is a pretty face.'

'Let's not speak too soon. We've not heard the last of the good inspector. Superintendent Chadwick is a crafty old fox. He'll give me a wide berth, but I'm sure Oakes will be back.'

'He'll still be putty in your hands.'

'You exaggerate my powers.'

'On the contrary.' Trueman bared his teeth. 'The poor swine hasn't a clue what he's dealing with. But remember, Keary's made of stronger stuff. This lunch isn't a good idea. You can still change your mind and cancel.'

'And miss a chance to sample the culinary wonders of Restaurant Ragusa?' She shook her head. 'I won't become a prisoner in a gilded cage. You can drop me outside the front door, and pick me up there after I've said goodbye to William Keary. I'm looking forward to the lunch. It's a chance in a lifetime.'

'Do you recognise me?'

The woman's voice was soft, as if she didn't want Peggy to overhear.

Nonplussed, Jacob put out his hand. He was incapable of correctly estimating the age of any woman, and sensible enough not to try, but he guessed she might be a year or two his senior. Slender, with short mousy hair in a bob, she had pale eyes and pleasant features that seemed stretched by tension. No rings adorned her fingers, nor was there so much as a freckle on her face to remember her by. It would be easy to walk past her in a crowd. He had no recollection of ever meeting her before.

'I'm very sorry, but…'

'To be honest,' she said, gripping his hand, 'I would be rather disappointed if you did realise who I am.'

Her smile was tinged with gentle mockery. Jacob stared at her in bewilderment.

'My name is Sara Delamere,' she said. 'You know me better as Nefertiti, Nubian Queen of Magic and Mystery.'

10

'*Nefertiti?*' Jacob stretched out each syllable in a hapless attempt to cover his confusion.

'Believe it or not.'

He clapped his hand to his head. Behind her desk, Peggy was sufficiently intrigued to have abandoned *Film Fun*. She craned her neck in the hope of eavesdropping on a juicy nugget of scandal.

A memory came back to Jacob of that final act in the show he and Elaine had enjoyed at the Inanity. Nefertiti, performing the cremation of Anubis. Was this the woman who had entranced him that night? With elaborate make-up and an exotic Egyptian costume, he supposed anything was possible. Nefertiti's lithe body seemed immeasurably more provocative than Sara Delamere's boyish figure. He'd never have imagined that this slight woman could command a stage as the mistress of illusion, let alone haunt his thoughts as an unattainable figure of seductive beauty.

'We spoke at the stage door – was it a fortnight ago?' Her

carefully modulated vowels did not quite disguise cockney origins. 'Your companion collected my autograph.'

Good Lord, she remembered him! At Elaine's insistence, they'd queued so that she could add Nefertiti's dashing scrawl to her collection of signatures of the stars.

'Elaine, my landlady's daughter.' He felt compelled to add, 'She's just a pal.'

Sara Delamere smiled. 'I noticed a look of ownership in her eye when she put her arm in yours. I bet she thinks of you as more than just a friend. She struck me as a very nice young lady. And such gorgeous red hair. You're lucky, Mr Flint.'

'She's... well, it doesn't matter.' Feeling inept, he asked, 'So you are really Queen Nefertiti?'

'*Really*, as I said, I'm Sara Delamere. But yes, I am an illusionist, and yes, my stage name is Nefertiti.'

'You've certainly knocked the wind out of my sails. I'd never have guessed.'

'In real life, I'm nobody's idea of a Nubian beauty.' She sighed. 'I enjoy playing a part, but I keep my true self separate. I don't want to lose it altogether.'

'I'm sure there's no danger of that,' he said. 'I'm flabbergasted you recall signing that autograph. You must be constantly besieged by fans.'

Again the teasing smile. 'Perhaps you should be flattered, rather than astonished.'

To cover his confusion, he stammered, 'But... how do you know my name, and where I work?'

'Your lady friend introduced you, surely you've not forgotten? She was obviously very proud of your work as a reporter. Somehow or other, you... stuck in my mind.'

'You have quite a memory, Miss Delamere. So what can I do for you? Of course I'd love to help, if I can.'

'You're good at asking questions, Mr Flint. Answering them may take a little time.' She glanced at Peggy, whose mouth had dropped open as she listened shamelessly. 'Is there somewhere private we could talk? It won't take long. Tonight I'm performing at the Inanity as usual, and I daren't be late. To tell you the truth, I shouldn't be here at all.'

A tremble had come into her voice. What was she afraid of?

'We can go across the road, and have a drink in the Wig and—'

'No, please.' She breathed out, visibly striving to calm herself. 'Do not take this amiss, but we must not be seen in public together.'

'But a private club...?'

'No.' Incredibly, she was pleading with him. 'It is not... safe.'

He thought quickly. 'There's an empty office at the back of this building. Nobody will disturb us there.'

'Thank you, Mr Flint... May I call you Jacob?'

'Please.'

'And I'm Sara. Oh, I'm so grateful to you, Jacob. I had to talk to someone, and I couldn't think of anyone else. Your report in this morning's paper spurred me. I felt I could rely on you.'

Sara might have the jitters, but he found it hard not to swagger as he led her down the narrow corridor which ended at Tom Betts' door. The office remained as Tom had left it, a jumble of papers, books, and chewed pencils. This chaotic haven was his refuge from the austere tidiness of the flat off Farringdon Road. On the cluttered desk, tucked under the typewriter and barely visible, was a dusty photograph. Jacob tugged it free, and found himself looking at Lydia Betts perhaps fifteen years earlier, smiling shyly at the camera.

Sara Delamere wriggled out of her coat, and he hung it up on the door. She wore a striking gown of gold tissue, furred at the neck and wrists with long-haired, creamy fox. An outfit more in keeping with his idea of an actress's clothes, if hardly as daring as Queen Nefertiti's stage costume. He pulled up a chair for her, and settled himself behind the desk. It felt almost indecent to take the place of a man hovering between life and death, but Betts himself had said that no journalist could afford to be sentimental.

'You have a story to share, Miss Delamere.' Having recovered his composure, he bestowed an encouraging smile. 'Please tell it in your own way and your own time.'

She cleared her throat. 'It's funny, you know. On a stage, I can lose myself in the performance. Talking to you is different, somehow.'

He felt himself colouring again. 'Well, I don't bite.'

She cast him a shy glance. 'My upbringing wasn't easy, but I set my heart on going on the stage. As a child, I found stories about witches and wizards, and the spells they cast, entrancing. I became fascinated by magic. John Nevil Maskelyne was my hero. Eventually, William Keary heard that I was a half-decent conjuror. You must know of him.'

Jacob nodded. 'They say he's the most versatile performer in the West End. Also the richest. Owns the Inanity, doesn't he? With a finger in plenty of other pies.'

'Mr Keary – William – gave me my break. Over time, I climbed up the bill. Eventually I dreamed up Queen Nefertiti. By then, though I say it myself as shouldn't, I'd become adept as a magician. I adored ambitious illusions. Levitation, bringing automata to life...'

'Elaine and I enjoyed your finale, the cremation trick,' Jacob said. 'How you did it, I'll never know.'

She gave a little giggle. 'I'm afraid that must remain my little secret, Mr Flint, but thank you kindly. William showed faith in me, and I'll always be grateful, but...'

'But?'

'I don't care for the company he keeps.' She swallowed. 'There were two men in particular who had a stake in the theatre. One was Claude Linacre.'

Jacob sat up straight. 'The man who murdered Dolly Benson?'

'That's right.' Sara shivered. 'I detested him. For all his wealth and education, his behaviour was disgraceful. Called himself an artist, and one day he asked if I'd like to be his muse – sauce! I told him where he could stick his paintbrush. He took a shine to Dolly, but of course, I never imagined he'd kill her when she spurned his advances. You may recall her fiancé, George Barnes, works as a stagehand at the theatre. He's a hot-tempered fellow, and the police thought he'd suffocated Dolly in a fit of rage after she broke off their engagement. If I'd spoken out sooner, he would have been spared the misery...'

'You mustn't blame yourself. You're speaking out now.'

Her smile shone with gratitude. 'Then there was Mr Pardoe, the banker. He was another I never cared for. Careless about where he put his hands whenever he talked to any of the girls in the show.'

'What about Pardoe?'

'I heard him talking to William the day before that poor woman was butchered in Covent Garden. That's why I've come to see you. I read your article in the *Clarion*. You were there when Pardoe's body was found. And your report mentioned Judge Savernake.'

'That's right.'

'Pardoe talked about a woman called Rachel Savernake. He became very heated and loud, that's how I happened to overhear. It was just before the show was due to start, and I was in my dressing room. William's room is next door. You know which part he plays?'

Jacob shook his head. 'His name wasn't in the programme. Elaine was disappointed not to see him.'

'It amuses William to keep it a secret, but he's Nefertiti's foil at the climax of the show. You remember Anubis?'

'The god of death, with the jackal's head,' Jacob said. 'The creature Nefertiti destroys, only to bring him back to life.'

'Exactly. Well, I heard Pardoe demanding whether William knew what this woman was up to. William must have said no, because Pardoe started yelling. He said Rachel Savernake should stop prying into other people's business, or she'd pay for it. If he didn't deal with her, others would. William tried to pacify him, but Pardoe ranted like a madman, it was horrible. In the end, William told him to leave. The show was due to begin, but I could see he was distressed. When we were alone, I asked what was wrong, but he brushed it off, and said he'd never felt better.'

'You didn't mention what you'd heard?'

'Absolutely not!' Her face creased in horror. 'I'd hate him to think I was a nosey parker. I worried myself sick, trying to decide what to do. And then I read your report, and discovered that Pardoe was a murderer. The beast who killed that poor woman in Covent Garden.'

'Was William Keary on good terms with Pardoe?'

'William is the life and soul of any party. Five minutes after you meet him for the first time, it's as if he was a lifelong friend. Pardoe was a dull dog, and slimy with it. They had nothing in common.'

'Except money.'

She sniffed. 'I suppose so.'

'I'm still not clear why you came to see me.'

'Because I'm afraid for this woman, Rachel Savernake. I can't pretend to understand what I heard, but Pardoe was a murderer, and so was Linacre. I believe there's a threat to her life, even though Pardoe is dead. He was in cahoots with some vicious folk.'

'Have you considered going to the police?'

She put her hand to her mouth. 'Out of the question!'

'Because of your loyalty to your employer?'

Her slender body was shaking. 'You don't understand, Jacob. All I will say is that, by giving me a chance at the Inanity, William Keary rescued me from... personal humiliation. I am forever in his debt.'

'You're right, I don't quite...'

She lowered her eyes. 'When I was younger, to my eternal shame, I did certain things that were... well, it's impossible for me to contemplate approaching the police. I feel sick in my stomach every time I pass a constable patrolling the streets.'

He didn't know what to say. 'I'm sorry that...'

'No, I'm sorry. Coming here was a mistake. I presumed too much on the slenderest acquaintance.' She sprang to her feet. 'Thank you for listening to me, Mr Flint. I apologise for disturbing you. Please forget this conversation ever took place.'

As she opened the door, he said, 'Wait a moment!'

She turned to face him. Tears filled her eyes.

'I'd like to help you. I simply don't know what you want.'

'I'm not sure I know myself. It was stupid of me to come here. Too much of a risk. I should keep my nose out of other people's business. Goodbye, Mr Flint.'

She trotted out into the corridor, but he raced after her, and caught up before they reached the entrance lobby. 'Please,' he panted. 'Just tell me – what you want me to do.'

Her face crumpled, and he felt sick in his stomach. Could this fragile, frightened woman really be the Egyptian Queen of Magic and Mystery, who strode around the stage with panache, holding audiences in the palm of her hand with her dazzling blend of prestidigitation and showmanship?

'I'm all of a muddle, Mr Flint. How can I tell whether what I overheard meant something or nothing? Pardoe's death may have finished the whole rotten business. I'm probably torturing myself for no good reason.'

'You don't really believe that.'

'No.' She closed her eyes. 'I suppose I don't.'

'Then – what?'

Her voice shook. 'Remember what happened to Dolly Benson and Mary-Jane Hayes. I'm sure Rachel Savernake will be next.'

Juliet Brentano's Journal

1 February 1919

Henrietta is my only visitor. She's kindness itself, and knows better than to mither me about keeping the room clean and tidy. It's not as if she hasn't enough on her plate. In the village, people despise the Judge. Anyone who works for him risks being treated as an outcast. That is why, when he tried to hire a butler, he finished up with Brown, the coarsest man I have ever met. I don't believe Brown is really a butler at all. I saw the way he looked at my mother, and even at the odd-job man's sister, whenever she was dragooned into lending Henrietta a hand.

It's hard to believe that barely a week has passed since my father rejoined us after his long absence. He looked twice as old as the boisterous soldier who said the fighting would be over by Christmas, and promised us escape from the city while he taught the Hun a thing or two.

I'd never met the Judge before I came to the island in 1914. Nor had Mother. We didn't belong in decent society, though I never realised until Rachel told me so.

The night before my parents disappeared, I overheard them talking as they shared a bottle of wine. My father said how bitterly he regretted sending us to Gaunt. He'd just had his first glimpse of Rachel's true nature.

'The little minx claimed she felt a burning pain close to her heart, and pleaded with me to... examine her. When I declined, and said we must call a doctor, she flew into a vicious fury. I said I'd tell the Judge how she behaved.'

'A waste of time,' Mother said wearily. 'The old man's brain is mush, and she twists him around her little finger. I never knew a child so intent upon controlling people, like marionettes in a puppet show. She hoped to lure you into an indiscretion, so she could blackmail you into doing her bidding. That's how she enslaved that vile beast Harold Brown.'

'I must take you both away from here.'

'At low tide tomorrow, please. There's no time to lose. If you have rebuffed Rachel, she will not take it kindly.'

My father snorted. 'What can a child do?'

I could understand his scorn. He'd survived the war; what threat could be posed by a fourteen-year-old girl?

But the next morning, Henrietta told me my parents were missing.

II

William Keary held Rachel's hand for five seconds longer than politeness between strangers customarily allowed. She guessed he'd intended to bestow a kiss, before thinking better of it. Such restraint was not in his nature, but not even he would take liberties with a Savernake.

A fragrant young waiter had ushered Rachel to her host's table, discreetly situated in a corner at the rear of the Restaurant Ragusa. Taking their places in the opposite corner were members of a classical trio. The hanging silk balloon lights, lush vermilion carpet, and patterned yellow brocade curtains created a mood of luxurious self-indulgence if not outright decadence, while the display of a massive bottle of 1860 liqueur brandy emphasised that the glories of the Restaurant Ragusa encompassed alcohol of rare distinction as well as the most lavish and expensive fare in London.

'You enjoyed your visit to the gallery?' he asked.

'It was… memorable.'

'Perhaps one day you will grant me the privilege of taking a look at your… works of art.'

Rachel smiled. 'Equally, I'd love to attend one of your performances at the Inanity.'

'You shall have the finest seat in the house! A marvellous show is running at present. My role is rather... untypical. A welcome respite from sketches and song-and-dance routines.'

'Did I hear that you're collaborating with a female illusionist?'

'Nefertiti, yes – the dear girl is wonderfully gifted. Capable of making any man believe in magic. Her speciality is making automata behave like human beings that live and breathe. Together we offer an even more dazzling spectacle.' He leaned across the table, and dropped his voice to a sombre whisper. 'I play Anubis, God of Death and the Afterlife. Nefertiti cremates me... and then she gives me the gift of life again.'

'How marvellous,' she whispered, 'to possess such power over life and death.'

Holding her gaze, he picked up the menu. 'May I recommend the Dalmatian curry? An unlikely confection of onions, tomatoes, and fruit, with eggs mixed in at the end of the cooking, and rather splendid. In either case, I'm tempted to suggest chestnut chocolate Ragusa as a suitably sinful dark dessert.'

At the snap of his beautifully manicured fingers, the waiter materialised, a genie summoned from a bottle. A hint of musky perfume clung to the boy's skin. High cheekbones attested to Slavic origins, and Rachel noticed that his colleagues were all cast from the same mould. Slender, pretty, and not a day over twenty-one. As the boy disappeared into the kitchen with their order, Keary confided that the esoteric tastes of the proprietor, an exile from the Balkans, were by no means confined to food and drink.

'Luko is a born artist. One deduces as much from his choice of decor, even if one is not by nature inclined to play the detective.' He threw a glance at her. 'Speaking of which, a little bird told me that you interested yourself in the dreadful tragedy that befell us at the Inanity.'

'I have a lifelong interest in crime. Perhaps I should blame heredity.'

'The Judge owned the finest private library in Britain, did he not? His collection of books about crime and criminals was his pride and joy.' Keary chuckled. 'During those long winter nights on that lonely island, I suppose you spent many hours browsing among the titles.'

'You suppose correctly,' she said. 'Almost everything I know, I owe to that library. I devoured any book I could lay my hands on, from Blackstone to Sir Richard Burton, from Defoe to Dumas. Only lately have I developed a taste for Mr Austin Freeman and Miss Sayers.'

The classical musicians started to play, and Keary tapped his fingers on the table. 'Do you care for Schubert?'

She smiled. 'I prefer Rudy Vallee.'

The waiter arrived with their meals, and fluttered long lashes at Keary as he poured the wine for tasting. The Irishman sniffed thoughtfully before granting approval with a grin as warm as a furnace. The curry was hot and sweet, and Rachel savoured each mouthful. At length, Keary pushed his plate to one side.

'You were so shocked to hear about poor Dolly's murder that you set about finding the man responsible?'

'I never met her,' Rachel said, 'but such savagery cannot be allowed to escape unpunished. Did you know Dolly well?'

'No better than any other member of the chorus. Girls come and go all the time, as you can imagine. When Dolly vanished, we assumed she'd run off with an admirer. She was lovely, but had a name for being wilful, and perhaps a little foolish.'

'Didn't someone once say that's the best thing a girl can be in this world, a beautiful little fool?'

Keary shifted in his chair. 'Nobody suspected anything untoward.'

'Yet she abruptly ended her engagement.'

'Poor George Barnes,' he said with a heavy sigh. 'Decent enough fellow, and an accomplished craftsman. He was older than Dolly, and took the whole business very hard. It seemed she'd met some rich fellow who had spirited her away. The other girls said she'd become secretive, and they suspected her of dallying with someone more exciting than Barnes. The only question was whether she'd gone forever, or would come creeping back after her new boyfriend found fresh fields to conquer. When her body was found, we were all stunned. Especially when Barnes was arrested.'

'He was a scapegoat.'

'I can't find it in my heart to blame the police. The case against Barnes was that Dolly had made him jealous, and so he resorted to violence. He has a fiery temper, and once broke the arm of a colleague who made an improper suggestion to Dolly. I smoothed over that little contretemps, but after Dolly's death, the police soon came to hear of it.'

'You didn't believe Barnes was a murderer?'

'I felt duty-bound to look after him. He was a loyal servant of the Inanity. Of course, I paid for him to have legal representation.'

'I heard whispers of that, despite your efforts to keep your generosity secret,' Rachel said. 'A kind gesture.'

He waved away the compliment. 'I hated the thought of a man who worked for me facing the gallows. Yet the law must take its course.'

'You doubted his innocence?'

He closed his eyes. 'All the evidence pointed in his direction.'

'That evidence was circumstantial.'

'But convincing.' Keary leaned back in his chair as the desserts arrived. 'Rufus Paul, no less, examined the body, and found a thread of clothing in the poor girl's hair which matched a jersey in Barnes' wardrobe.'

'Barnes was Dolly Benson's lover. An innocent explanation for Rufus Paul's discovery was entirely possible. Under cross-examination, Mr Paul would have been bound to concede that the stray thread proved nothing.'

'Even so, things looked black for poor Barnes.' He shook his head. 'Presumably you hired an agent to make enquiries into the case?'

'I made sure I was fully informed, yes. I came across Claude Linacre on my first visit to the Galeria Garcia.'

'And you deduced that he was a murderer? Or did you rely on intuition?'

Rachel pursed her lips. 'Linacre frequented the Inanity, and more than one young woman there had caught his eye, only to become repelled by his bizarre tastes. He paid handsomely for the pleasure of inflicting grievous wounds on at least two of them. Did you not hear rumours?'

'Certainly he was known to be fond of girls of... shall we say, the commoner classes. But he seemed harmless enough. If every selfish libertine resorted to homicide, the population would be decimated.' Keary's easy grin remained in place, but she noticed his brow tightening. 'Do let me into the secret. What led you to accuse young Claude Linacre of murder?

And what was so compelling about the case you made that he felt driven to take poison?'

The young waiter arrived with the coffee. He seemed sulky, perhaps because Keary only had eyes for Rachel.

'All I shall say is that his death mirrored his life. He was a coward.'

Keary placed a sinewy hand upon hers. 'I've met few women capable of such discretion,' he murmured. 'And what of the latest outrage? Dare I ask if you played any part in... securing justice for Lawrence Pardoe's victim?'

Rachel withdrew her hand. 'My understanding is that he killed himself inside a locked room, after writing out a detailed confession.'

'As a keen student of criminology, you'll know that confessions are often unreliable.'

She opened her eyes wide. 'I forgot! Wasn't Pardoe connected with the Inanity too? Perhaps you know something I don't?'

He flinched, as if bitten by a trusted pet. 'Sadly, no. Pardoe was an odd fellow. Between us, I never cared too much for either him or Linacre. Although I never dreamed they were capable of murder, their attitudes struck me as... rather sordid.'

'Very perceptive of you.'

'I have an instinct about people sometimes. As I do about you. I won't beat about the bush. I find you utterly fascinating.'

'How flattering.' Rachel moved her chair back, as if preparing to leave. 'Truly, I'm thrilled by the prospect of seeing you at the Inanity.'

He leaned across the table. 'Come to the theatre right now, and I'll conduct you on a personal tour backstage.'

'I'm not sure the Widow Bianchi would approve,' Rachel said lightly.

He blinked. 'Chiara and I aren't married, you know. We merely have… an understanding.'

'I'm sure she is very understanding,' Rachel smiled. 'I'm afraid my chauffeur is waiting.'

'What a pity. Then perhaps after the show?'

'Perhaps.' Rising to her feet, she extended her hand. 'If you are free to see me.'

He studied her calm features, and for a moment his composure wavered. Swallowing, he said, 'You know, Rachel, you definitely remind me of your father.'

'I am very different from the Judge,' she said. 'But I do believe in justice.'

12

'How good of you to see me at short notice,' Jacob said, as Mrs Mundy lifted the white cup – stamped in red with Fuller's name – to her thin lips.

Squeezing the lemon into his tea, he gave an ingratiating smile which she failed to return. His head hurt, and he doubted a cup of Earl Grey would improve it. After oversleeping, he'd caught the train to Oxford by the skin of his teeth.

He and Elaine had stayed up late following after a trip to see *Bitter Sweet*, the perfect antidote to an overdose of murder, mystery, and magicians. Afterwards, they'd drunk a few cocktails in an excitingly seedy bar in Long Acre, and ended up singing 'I'll See You Again' all the way back to Amwell Street. Once home, Elaine had poured them each a generous measure of her mother's gin, and they'd indulged in some woozy fumbling on the sofa before she'd disentangled herself, and announced she was going to bed. Jacob hadn't been quite drunk enough to suggest that he accompany her.

After waking with a hangover, he'd foregone his usual hearty breakfast, and now his stomach was rumbling. He cast a covetous glance at the next table, and an elderly couple tucking into fat slices of walnut cake, complete with frosted icing. Unfortunately, Mrs Mundy had ordered for them both before his arrival. Presumably she was accustomed to making decisions for others.

She'd waited for him at the table nearest the window, looking out at the students striding along Cornmarket as though they owned not only the street but the whole world. She was knitting a child's scarf from bright green wool. Small, with silver hair in a bob and a wiry frame snugly fitted in an ankle-length grey fox-fur coat, she was a woman of few words. When she did speak, she did so with a pronounced Scottish accent, and in a brisk, no-nonsense manner that must have stood her in good stead over the past thirty years.

Jacob tried again. 'I'm sure your work at the Orphans' Home keeps you extremely busy.'

'I needed to call in at the bank, so meeting you here was convenient. You will understand that I prefer not to entertain a newspaperman at the home.'

'Have you been disturbed by the press?' Jacob's expression was a study in sympathetic concern.

'Very severely, Mr Flint.' A knitting needle tapped the table for emphasis. 'An institution such as ours depends on maintaining a settled routine in order to function efficiently. This whole affair has been shockingly disruptive. Poor Miss Hayes worked at the home for less than six months, but your colleagues from Fleet Street descended like vultures as soon as it was known that we'd employed her.'

'How upsetting. A crime of this sort has untold ramifications. I travelled to Southend yesterday to meet her sister. She's naturally anxious that our readers understand that Mary-Jane was a thoroughly decent woman.'

'Indeed she was. The whole business distresses me so much that I cannot bear to read about it. Goodness only knows how her kith and kin must feel.'

'Quite so, Mrs Mundy.'

'Very well, what do you want from me? A taxi is due to collect me, so I can get back to my desk. Five minutes should be ample. I doubt I can tell you anything that isn't already in the public domain.'

'Why did Mary-Jane leave the home? It seems odd. She didn't have another job to go to, yet she left Oxford, and returned to London.'

Mrs Mundy sighed. 'We had such high hopes of her. Her curriculum vitae was first class, and when she was interviewed by myself and the former chair of trustees, we were impressed. The position she applied for was new. I hope to retire before long, and we regarded the role of deputy matron as a stepping stone. Mary-Jane seemed to have the credentials to make an ideal successor. Unfortunately, she'd under-estimated the gulf between her former duties and the diverse responsibilities of deputy matron, and she found it difficult to adjust.'

'She told you this?'

'Oh yes, she was honest to a fault. I did my utmost to encourage her. Coping with promotion is never as easy as it seems. She had a dreadful inferiority complex. Each time she told me that she couldn't possibly cope with the role of matron, I told her bluntly she was talking through her hat. I felt equally uncertain many years ago, when I took charge of the home.'

Jacob found it hard to imagine that this small, forceful woman was ever uncertain about anything. 'She wasn't reassured?'

'Thirty years ago, she said, the home was smaller, and its ambitions more limited. She'd been happy working as a nurse. Looking after the complicated financial arrangements of a charitable institution, dealing with trustees, and supervising all the staff, all that was foreign to her.'

'So she walked out?'

'Her terms of employment required a month's notice, but she was so downhearted and anxious to leave that I agreed – with the trustees' reluctant consent – to waive that obligation.' Mrs Mundy sniffed her Earl Grey, and duly satisfied, took a sip. 'As a result, I am back to square one, still in search of someone to take over so that I can enjoy a peaceful retirement in St Andrews, knowing the home is in safe hands.'

'Did she ever mention the name of Lawrence Pardoe?'

'The man who committed the atrocity?' Mrs Mundy's eyebrows shot up. 'You're suggesting a prior acquaintance between them?'

'It does seem that Pardoe knew her, yes.'

Her small eyes subjected him to piercing scrutiny. 'I can honestly say that she never discussed him with me.'

'Are you sure about that, Mrs Mundy?'

'Really, Mr Flint!' Her disdain cut like a whip. 'I had hoped you were a different class of person from the other reporters who have besieged our home, trying to fashion a scandal out of thin air, and making it more difficult for us to carry out our vital work in caring for girls who begin their lives with unenviable disadvantages. I am disappointed to find I am mistaken.'

'I'm sorry.' Jacob was instantly abashed. 'I really did not mean—'

'I have honoured my promise, and given you five minutes. I must bid you good morning.'

Picking up her knitting bag, she jumped to her feet. Jacob half rose and held out his hand, but she ignored him, and walked swiftly out into the hubbub of Cornmarket. He made no attempt to follow her. He'd mishandled the conversation, and needed to console himself with a slab of the mouth-watering walnut cake.

While exchanging idle banter with a young waitress, pert and neat in her black uniform and white pinafore, he wondered if he'd learned more than he'd realised. Mrs Mundy's assertion that Mary-Jane had never discussed Pardoe struck him as credible, but she'd chosen her words with care. On reflection, her reply resembled a lawyer's quibble.

As he savoured the crushed walnuts, he decided that the matron had failed to tell him the whole truth, seeking to distract him with a show of synthetic outrage. Instinct told him that not only did Mary-Jane know Pardoe, but Mrs Mundy was well aware of it.

As the train rattled through the countryside on its way back to Paddington, Jacob found himself assailed by second thoughts. Even if Mrs Mundy's reply had been disingenuous, she probably felt justified in prevaricating with a journalist. He'd questioned her word, no doubt a rare occurrence during her three decades as matron of the Orphans' Home. Hostility was inevitable.

Mrs Mundy, like Agnes Dyson, attributed Mary-Jane's departure from Oxford to an inability to cope with extra responsibility. Plausible, but Jacob wondered if Mary-Jane had been romantically involved with Pardoe at some stage in her life. Perhaps they had encountered each other in London, only for Mary-Jane's ambition to lead her to end the liaison, and move to Oxford. Supposing Pardoe had pursued her, he might have persuaded her to give up her new job at the home, and return to the capital. Pardoe's vast wealth meant she was under no immediate pressure to find work, while she deliberated about their future together. If she'd finally decided against committing herself to him, his anger...

Perhaps. Supposing. Might. If.

Jacob looked out of the window of his carriage, frightening a flock of sheep with his frustrated glare. Why deceive himself? He was none the wiser about Mary-Jane's murder, just as he was no closer to ferreting out the truth about Rachel Savernake.

Immediately after speaking to Sara Delamere, he'd despatched a telegram to Rachel, pleading for another meeting. As soon as he walked through the front door of Clarion House, he demanded to know whether a message had arrived for him. Peggy broke off from reading about Harold Lloyd's first talkie to announce that someone – she didn't know who it was – had handed in a cheap envelope bearing his name. Ripping it open, he found an anonymous note which simply said, *Meet me at the Essex Head at one.*

He recognised the careful but unsophisticated hand. Stanley Thurlow, the detective constable he'd encountered outside Pardoe's home, must have a titbit for him. Their regular meeting place was a public house on the corner of Essex Street and the Strand. Thurlow was fond of a drink, as well as the occasional flutter on the horses, but his young bride had recently given birth to their first child, and money was tight. In return for dribs and drabs of police gossip, Jacob was happy to stand a few rounds, and give his friend a present in cash 'to buy something for the baby'. There was no harm in it. You scratch my back, I'll scratch yours.

'I brought fresh towels,' Mrs Trueman said.

She stood at the top of the stairs leading onto the roof of the house. Stretching in front of her lay a kidney-shaped swimming pool. Three-quarters of the roof had been glassed in to form a vast conservatory; the rest of it formed a roof garden with seats and plant tubs, edged by a knee-high wall and overlooking the rear of the property and the shed and garden far below. There was space in the conservatory for a large sitting area, as well as a gramophone at the far end, and an area for dancing under the stars. The heating system ensured that even on a crisp London morning, the temperature was closer to that of Cannes or Monte Carlo.

Rachel loved the water. On Gaunt, swimming offered the fantasy of escape. In London, a mansion with a rooftop pool was a suitably extravagant way of spending a slice of the Savernake fortune. She hauled herself out, the red and kelly-green striped maillot clinging to her body. Pulling off her rubber swim cap, she shook her dark hair.

'Fancy a dip?'

Mrs Trueman scowled at the maillot's plunging neckline. 'Some of us have work to do.'

Rachel reached for one of the Turkish towels, and started drying herself. 'Your hands are red raw. I'll find you extra help if you need it.'

The older woman shook her head. 'You're not suggesting we hire someone recommended by the Orphans' Home?'

Rachel gave a wicked smile. 'Is it such an insane idea?'

'For goodness' sake! You've such a peculiar sense of humour, I never know whether you're joking or not.'

'You don't need to do this,' Rachel said. 'You don't need to stay here. With the money you two have put away in the bank...'

'Don't twist what I say. You know you can depend on us.'

'Yes,' Rachel said. 'I know.'

Jacob made sure that two foaming pints of beer were standing on the counter by the time Thurlow marched into the saloon bar. Today he looked bleary-eyed, and he apologised in case he fell asleep over his beer. The baby was teething, and had kept both parents up all night.

'Here's to domestic bliss,' Jacob said, as they clinked glasses.

'Cheers, Flinty.' Thurlow grinned. 'Might be drinking to something else before long,'

'Your good lady isn't expecting again?'

'Bloody hell, no. At least if she is, she hasn't dared to break the news yet.' The grin broadened. 'Keep it under your hat, but soon you'll need to show me a bit of respect. I've been tipped the wink that I'll be a detective sergeant by Christmas.'

Jacob slapped him on the back. 'Congratulations, Stan.'

'Shouldn't count my chickens, but I've booked a week in Brighton to celebrate. The weather will be foul, but who cares? Not that I'm the only one with something to brag about. Read your piece about that carry-on in South Audley Street.' He laid a beefy paw on Jacob's arm. 'Couldn't believe my bloody eyes when you showed up. Figured out who tipped you off?'

The smoky air was as noxious as a pea-souper, and Jacob indulged in a diversionary coughing fit. 'Who knows? I don't suppose it matters. I gather Scotland Yard considers the case closed.'

'Yes, well. Superintendent Chadwick is a good bloke, all for a quiet life, while old Mulhearn is as happy as a dog with two whatsits. Funny thing is, Oakes is all on edge. Doesn't seem convinced that Pardoe simply sent his staff away, then topped himself.'

'Why not?'

'According to him, it's too neat. But life doesn't always have to be a shambles, does it? We're all entitled to a spot of luck, once in a while.'

'A smart fellow like Oakes must have something to go on.'

Thurlow drained his glass, and Jacob signalled to the barman for a refill.

'Cheers, Flinty. I'm betting you're spot on.'

'Is that why you wanted to see me?'

'There is something.' Thurlow gulped down his beer. 'Seems like nothing to me, but it bothers Oakes.'

'Go on.' Jacob fished a banknote out of his jacket, and slid it into the policeman's vast palm. 'Find a babysitter, and treat Mrs T to a slap-up meal with my best regards.'

'You're a pal, Flinty.'

Jacob could smell the beer fumes on Thurlow's breath. 'So what is on Oakes' mind?'

'We found a chess piece next to the packing case where Pardoe hid Mary-Jane Hayes' head. A black pawn.'

'What do you make of that?'

'Pardoe didn't play chess, if his confidential secretary is to be believed. That fellow is a keen 'un, plays in tournaments and captains the Kilburn Chess Club, but he claims Pardoe had no interest in the game.'

'What's so unusual about that?'

'Turns out that Pardoe was a member of a chess club.'

'Surely the secretary knew that?'

'No, that's the weird thing. When we told him, he was flabbergasted.'

'Maybe Pardoe simply didn't want to play chess with him. Didn't want to risk losing to a servant.'

'We searched the house from attic to cellar, but there wasn't a chess set or board to be found. Let alone a set minus a pawn.'

Thurlow sank the rest of his drink with a flourish. Jacob nodded at the empty glass. 'Sounds like a three-pint problem.'

'Eh?' Thurlow consulted a gold pocket watch. 'Sorry, mate. Best be getting back.'

'How do you know that Pardoe really was a member of a chess club?'

Thurlow lowered his voice. 'Because he mentioned it in his will.'

'In his will?' The cacophony made by fellow drinkers meant that Jacob had to crane his neck to hear. 'I don't understand.'

'He left a small fortune to be used...' Thurlow cleared his throat, and mimicked the sonorous tone of a dusty old lawyer, *'at the discretion of the board of trustees for the benefit of my friends and fellow chess players in the Gambit Club.'*

13

Jacob's next stop was Whitechapel. He wanted to talk to Levi Shoemaker. His previous experience of private enquiry agents was limited and depressing. In Leeds, he'd encountered a handful of grubby individuals who helped their clients to gather – or falsify – evidence for divorce proceedings, or to collect debts owed by people with no means to pay. Everything he'd managed to find out about Shoemaker suggested a very different breed of detective.

Shoemaker's name never appeared in the *Clarion*, or any other newspaper for that matter. He didn't advertise his services: discreet recommendations from satisfied clients kept him busy. Jacob had never known the grapevine so kind to a private investigator.

The memory of his encounter with Mrs Mundy in Oxford itched like a flea bite. If he'd managed to infuriate an old lady who had spent a lifetime caring for orphans, prising information out of a professional oyster was likely to prove an insuperable challenge. Shoemaker was no Stanley Thurlow, and Jacob had nothing to offer in the hope of loosening the man's tongue. He could scarcely out-bid Rachel Savernake.

Cycling through a fierce downpour, he pondered how to gain Shoemaker's confidence. Assuming he found him, that was. He'd decided not to invite a rebuff by trying to arrange an appointment. Rain had emptied the drab thoroughfares. He slowed down, peering through the gloom, searching for his destination.

This was the street, with a shuttered pie house (*Hot Stewed Eels & Mashed Potatoes Always Ready*) on the corner. A weary old man with a battered felt hat was getting drenched to the skin as he trudged home. Jacob deduced that he was not Shoemaker, given that he was carrying an ancient concertina under his arm. He stopped outside a double-fronted coffee shop and dining rooms (*Haddocks, Bloaters, Kippers, and Saltfish Our Specialities – Quality, Civility and Cleanliness Guaranteed*), and jumped off his bicycle. Fifty yards further on, a hunched, solitary figure, wearing an overcoat and carrying a walking stick, was fumbling with a bunch of keys. Jacob broke into a run, and the skid and clatter of his footsteps on the wet cobbles caused the man to glance round.

His face was swollen, and bandaged above the left eye, and dark red bruises disfigured his cheeks. Even before he uttered a word, it was plain that he recognised Jacob, and that he was dismayed to see him.

'Flint!'

'Mr Shoemaker?'

The detective winced with pain. 'What are you doing here?'

'I was hoping for a private word.'

The age-spotted hand holding the keys was shaking. 'Go away. I have no wish to speak with you.'

'You've had a nasty accident.' Jacob gripped the other man's bony shoulder. 'What can I do to help?'

Breathing noisily, Shoemaker wriggled free. 'The last person I need help from is you.'

'You identified me straight away, yet we've never met. I'm not in the least famous, so I ought to be flattered. Instead, I'm very curious.'

As Shoemaker struggled to fit a key into the lock of his door, the silky scorn in Rachel Savernake's voice echoed in Jacob's mind.

'*You lodge in Amwell Street, and you worry that your landlady's daughter seeks to trade her body for marriage. Ambition drove you to join the muckrakers on the* Clarion *rather than a respectable newspaper. The editor admires your persistence, but frets about your rashness.*'

'I suppose you fashioned those arrows for Rachel Savernake to fire at me? I thought she was too harsh about my juvenile poetry.'

Gasping for breath, Shoemaker bent over, supporting himself on the stick. 'Go,' he whispered. 'Please. It's for your own good.'

'You're really not well. You ought to go to hospital.'

'No... no hospital.' The stick slipped, and Shoemaker lost his balance. Jacob caught hold of his arm, to save him from collapsing in a heap on the ground, and dragged him to his feet.

'You need to rest, for *your* own good. Back into your office?'

Unable to speak, Shoemaker nodded.

Shoemaker's office was on the first floor, above a workmen's cafeteria that had shut up shop for the day. The old man felt like a dead weight as Jacob helped him up the stairs.

When they reached the landing, the detective indicated the key for the door to his office, and they entered a dusty L-shaped room with a desk and three chairs. A connecting door led to an inner room, sparsely furnished with two large cabinets and a folded bed, and a small bathroom whose cracked tiles were streaked with blood. Here Shoemaker had bandaged his head: a box of first aid supplies was lying open on the floor, and the air had a salty whiff of iodine.

'Get your breath back,' Jacob said. 'Then we can talk.'

While he waited, he studied his surroundings. Whatever Shoemaker spent his fee income on, it did not include interior decoration. The rooms were as scruffy as the rat-holes inhabited by the brutal debt-collectors of Leeds.

'Feeling better?' Shoemaker nodded. 'Good. Let's move next door.'

Wrapping his arm round the other man's shoulder, Jacob led him back to the office, and helped him into his chair. 'Nice place you've got here.'

In a thin, wheezing voice, Shoemaker said, 'Doesn't pay to have swanky premises. Clients with an ounce of intelligence realise they foot the bill.'

'What happened to you?'

'I tripped and hit my head on the pavement.'

Jacob made a derisive noise. 'Accidents don't happen to successful detectives. You're a careful fellow, Mr Shoemaker. Everything I've learned makes that clear. Somebody roughed you up.'

'You've been checking on me?'

'Sauce for the goose.' Jacob grinned. 'Rachel Savernake hired you to investigate my background. I'm honoured that she thinks I'm fascinating enough to justify your fees. Naturally, I'm keen to know why she bothered.'

'I never discuss my work.'

Jacob pouted. 'For a moment, I hoped you might actually co-operate. Is there a file about me in one of your cabinets? Do you mind if I take a peek?'

'I've emptied them already. Leave now, Mr Flint. For your own safety.'

'What happened? Did someone try to kill you?'

Shoemaker chewed his lower lip. 'Two fellows set upon me at Aldgate East. They looked like working men, a joiner and his apprentice. Nobody else was on the platform. I must be getting careless in my old age. I should never have exposed myself to such danger.'

'They tried to throw you onto the live rail or under a train?'

'No, no. If they'd wanted me dead, they'd have made no mistake.' Gingerly, Shoemaker rubbed his damaged face. Tomorrow he would have a spectacular black eye. 'The attack was a message, masquerading as a random act of brutality committed by two fascist hooligans on an elderly Jew.'

'What sort of message?'

'The same as I'm giving you. Drop this, Mr Flint, while you still have the chance. You've had your scoop. I am sure you couldn't believe your luck, eh? Now go back to the *Clarion*, and write about something else.'

Jacob reached out, and touched the bandage with the tip of his index finger. On the way here, he'd never dreamed that the detective might resemble a chewed rag. Energy surged through him like an electric current. He had youth and confidence, and he meant to press his advantage home.

'Did Rachel Savernake hire thugs to beat you? Have you outlived your usefulness? Is she trying to cover her tracks? Why did she ask you to investigate Lawrence Pardoe?'

'You ask far too many questions.'

'It's my job.'

'You're not a fool,' Shoemaker muttered, 'but too often you talk and behave with idiotic bravado. Take my advice, Mr Flint. If you want to live to a ripe old age, this particular game is not worth the candle. I intend to heed the message those ruffians delivered. This time next week I'll be far away.'

Physically weak as the man was, there was something oddly majestic about him. Quietness and dignity were not qualities Jacob associated with private detectives. Shoemaker might be wrong, but he believed what he was saying; Jacob would stake a year's wages on it.

'I'd like to help you, Mr Shoemaker, and I wish you would give me a hand in return. You'll have your reasons for discouraging me, but I can't walk away from this, even if you can. Won't you at least give me a start? A hint, a clue. Rachel Savernake…'

'Rachel Savernake is the most dangerous woman in England.'

Jacob laughed. 'Really?'

'You have no conception of what you are dealing with. Linacre died in convulsions of agony. Pardoe's face was blown off, and his brains splashed around his study.'

'You're not saying their deaths were her doing?'

'I've said more than enough.' Shoemaker hauled himself to his feet. 'Now, if you'll excuse me, I need to get home. Tomorrow I leave London for good.'

Jacob stood up. 'There's nothing more you are prepared to tell me?'

Shoemaker hesitated. 'In you, I see a shadow of my young self, determined never to take no for an answer. Whilst I was enquiring into your antecedents, I came to feel a ridiculous sense of kinship with you. The final proof that I've grown soft in my old age. Wait a moment.'

He opened a drawer in the desk, and pulled out a pen, notepad, and envelope. Tearing off a sheet, he scribbled rapidly on it, before sealing it inside the envelope.

'Make me a promise,' he said. 'If I give this to you, will you swear not to open it, unless and until something happens to me?'

Jacob was amused. 'What if you live to a ripe old age?'

'Then my note will be irrelevant.'

'Very well.'

'You swear?'

'I swear.'

Shoemaker gave him a quizzical glance, as if regretting his impulse, before handing the envelope to Jacob.

'Shall I accompany you to your train?' Jacob asked.

'Thank you, but no. We mustn't be seen together. That was why I tried to shoo you away when you first accosted me. The damage has been done. We must leave separately.'

'Are we being watched?'

'Humour me, Mr Flint. Will you leave by the fire ladder, rather than the front door?'

Jacob thrust the envelope into his pocket. 'If you insist.'

'This way.'

Shoemaker hobbled out onto the landing, and managed to unlock a door that gave on to an open iron ladder. The rain had eased off, but there was no light, and the steps were greasy. In the event of a fire, Jacob thought, the escape route would prove as hazardous as gambling with the flames.

The cobbles, eerie in the glow of a gas lamp, seemed a long way down. He looked away again quickly, but he didn't want the old man to think him a coward. He couldn't resist giving a little bow.

'Till we meet again, Mr Shoemaker.'

The detective grunted, but said nothing. As he swivelled before commencing the treacherous descent, Jacob glimpsed in the older man's eyes an expression of utter desolation. It chilled him more than the cold night air.

Two minutes later, Shoemaker was speaking urgently on the telephone.

'His name is Jacob Flint. He works for the *Clarion*.'

A woman's voice at the other end of the line said, 'A newspaper reporter?'

'That's right. Don't—' He was interrupted by a commotion downstairs at the front of the building. 'I'm sorry. I must go.'

He put the receiver down. Someone was banging on the door to the street. Within moments, the door was being kicked. The scream of wood splintering set his teeth on edge.

He stepped outside. Clinging to the door handle, he inched onto the top rung of the iron ladder. His shoes slid underneath him, and he came close to letting go of the handle, and plunging to oblivion. Dizzying vertigo made his head swim. He wanted to be sick.

The ladder offered no escape, only the certainty of a smashed skull and spine. His only hope was to talk his way out of trouble. Over the years, he'd done so time without number, but tonight felt different. Fear smothered him.

He heard the door to the street giving way. If he barricaded himself into his office, what purpose would that serve? The ruffians had destroyed one door. They could break down another. His stomach was churning, but he must show no weakness. He'd explain he was leaving England, perhaps offer a bargain. If he was still in the country in twenty-four hours, let them do their worst.

Shuffling into his office, he heard heavy boots clattering up the stairs. The men were young, strong, and cruel; that he already knew. Might they be susceptible to reason? He offered up a silent prayer.

When they burst into his office, he was sitting behind the desk. One man, broad-shouldered and unshaven, carried a large canvas holdall. His gaze reminded Shoemaker of a dead fish. His colleague had a broken nose, pockmarked cheeks, and a squint.

'Where's your chum, Ikey?'

'I told him to leave by the fire ladder. Better than getting mixed up in something that isn't his concern.'

'He's already mixed up in it. What did you tell him?'

'Nothing. He helped me up here against my protests.'

The man grabbed Shoemaker's arm, and twisted it. 'You were warned what'd happen if you breathed a word to anyone.'

'He came looking for me. I told him to go away, but he didn't listen.'

The man released his grip, and jerked a thumb towards his silent partner. 'See Joe, here? Used to be a carpenter. Doesn't say much, doesn't Joe. Reckons actions speak louder than words.'

'There is no need for any difficulty between us.' Sweat dribbled down Shoemaker's pallid cheeks. 'I'm leaving Britain for good. Tomorrow I'll be far away, on other side of the Channel.'

'Out of harm's way, eh?'

'No one has anything to fear from me, I swear it.'

'You know what I think? I think you're a lying old Jew.'

The man yanked Shoemaker's tie, and the knot against his windpipe made the old man gasp.

'Please! I didn't tell him anything. I don't know—'

'Enough!' The man gestured towards the canvas bag. 'All right, Joe. Take out your tools.'

Juliet Brentano's Journal

1 February 1919 (later)

Henrietta doesn't linger when she brings a tray of food and drink. She wants to help, but is powerless. I am grateful that she leaves me to cope with my grief as best I can. Outwardly, she's respectful of the Judge and Rachel, but she's on my side, I know it. At least there is one person still alive whom I can trust.

I haven't pressed her for details about my parents' deaths. She doesn't know the truth anyway. Is there to be a funeral? I don't know, and I don't care. I shall remember them in my own way.

Am I right to suspect Rachel of orchestrating their murder? I was filled with foreboding from the moment Henrietta said there was no sign of them, or of Harold Brown, anywhere on the island. I became so desperate that in the end I went to the Judge's study. Forbidden territory, but I marched in without knocking.

He was dozing in his favourite chair, a leather-bound book in his lap. Even in repose, his sharp features reminded me of a bird of prey, waiting to swoop on an unsuspecting victim. I coughed noisily, and his eyes opened.

'What do you mean by this intrusion, miss?'

His tone was severe, as always, yet for once his face wasn't puce with rage. A faint smile played on his lips. Something amused him, and I found that more frightening than the most violent outburst of temper.

'Where are they?'

'Your mother and father?' He grunted. 'Called away to attend to urgent business in London. Brown has accompanied them.'

'It's impossible! My mother hates the man!'

A chill entered his voice, and the smile was gone. 'Remember what I have said before. Children should be seen and not heard. Never interrupt me when I am at work. Now be off with you, before I reach for my strap.'

As I fled from the study in tears, I caught sight of Rachel, staring at me from the staircase. Our eyes met, and she smirked.

I believe she told the Judge some wicked story about my father, and persuaded him to have my parents killed in retaliation. Not on Gaunt; that would be too obvious. Brown spirited them away – probably he'd drugged their wine, so there was no fear of resistance – and had them dealt with in London.

How long before Rachel disposes of me too? To her, I'm no more deserving of life than the governess's Pekinese.

14

'Shoemaker is dead,' Trueman announced as he strode into the gymnasium the next morning.

Rachel was absorbed in her work on the rowing machine. She did not spare him a glance. For a full minute he waited as she exercised. Finally she halted the machine, and wiped the sweat off her brow.

'He didn't seem in the best of health when he came here.'

Trueman exhaled. 'His body was fished out of the Thames. What was left of it, that is. Before his death, he'd undergone crude surgery. They must have tried to force him to talk.'

Her mouth tightened. 'Prolonging his agony was futile. He'd grown careless, but he couldn't have told them anything they don't already know.'

'At least he was wise enough not to ask you questions.'

She folded lean, sinewy arms. 'His death alters nothing.'

'What's wrong, Flint? You look like you've just read your own obituary.'

Walter Gomersall's habit was to wander round the office first thing in the morning, prior to his meeting with senior journalists to discuss which stories to concentrate upon for the day. His tone was jocular, but his expression suspicious.

Jacob put down his copy of the *Clarion*.

'Not my obituary,' he said thickly.

'Whose, then?'

Jacob pointed to a paragraph at the bottom of page two. *Body Dragged from Thames*. The story warranted neither the front page prominence of Pardoe's suicide nor extensive reporting. Corpses were dredged out of the river almost as often as Wellington boots. This story would barely have merited a line had it not been for the identity of the corpse.

'Leviticus Shoemaker's.'

He almost choked on the name. The previous day they had been together, and now the old man's remains were being poked over in some mortuary. The thought sickened him.

'You knew Shoemaker?'

'I talked to him yesterday.'

Gomersall blinked. 'And a few hours later he finished up in the Thames? Good God, Flint, you're developing an uncanny nose for a story. First Pardoe, now this.'

Bile rose in Jacob's throat. He breathed deeply, desperate not to disgrace himself in front of his editor. 'It's the same story.'

Gomersall scowled. 'Riddles are all very well for our readers, but I can't abide them. Be in my office in five minutes, with your thoughts straightened out, so you can explain yourself. In words of one syllable, mind. I'm a simple man.'

Jacob nodded, not trusting himself to speak, and broke into a run on his way to the cloakroom. By the time he presented himself in the editor's lair, he had regained a semblance of composure, despite the aching void inside him.

Spread out on Gomersall's desk was the latest *Clarion*. Beside it were two steaming mugs of tea. The editor motioned Jacob to take one. 'Nowt better for helping a man get a grip of himself after a shock. Now then, lad, what is all this? Begin at the beginning.'

'Thank you, sir.' Jacob drank some tea. 'The lead came from Mr Plenderleith. He mentioned rumours that Shoemaker had been asking questions about Lawrence Pardoe.'

'So you decided to question Shoemaker? Despite his reputation for being close-mouthed?' Jacob nodded. 'Ah, the optimism of youth.'

'When I met him, he was injured. His face was a mess, and he could hardly put one foot in front of the other. He told me two ruffians had set upon him at the Tube station.'

'He's Jewish,' Gomersall said. 'These things are happening more and more, especially in the East End. Once the economy falters, folk cast round for someone to blame, someone different from them. I don't like it, but it's the way of the world.'

'He said they warned him off. That is, to drop his investigations.'

'Pardoe is dead. There is nothing more to investigate.'

'I'm not so sure.' Jacob's spirits were recovering. 'Shoemaker took them seriously. He told me he was about to leave the country.'

Gomersall shrugged. 'Getting on in years, wasn't he? He must have made his pile. Probably he was ready to retire, and put his feet up in warmer climes.'

'He was frightened, and even insisted I shouldn't leave by the main door to the building. I shinned down the fire ladder, nearly breaking my neck on the way. By the time I reached the ground, I was cursing him for an excess of imagination.'

'You're a fine one to talk,' Gomersall said. 'Notice any hooligans lurking nearby?'

'No, sir. It was dark, and I was more than ready to get home. I thought Shoemaker was exaggerating when he suggested he and I were in danger. Now I'm...'

'He said you were at risk? What reason did he give?'

'It must be the Pardoe case. Nothing else makes sense. Someone doesn't want the truth about that business to come to light.'

'We know the truth. Pardoe indulged a barbaric murderous fantasy after learning he hadn't long to live. You're not saying he didn't kill Mary-Jane Hayes?'

'I simply don't know.'

Removing a pencil from behind his ear, Gomersall drew a circle around the paragraph reporting the fire. 'This is Oliver McAlinden's story. Maybe he has more background that the subs cut out. Shoemaker may have been drunk, and fallen into the river by accident.'

'Too much of a coincidence.'

The editor harrumphed. 'Come back to me when you have a properly sourced story to run, and not before. And one more thing.'

Jacob gritted his teeth. 'Yes, Mr Gomersall?'

'Wipe that sulky look off your face.'

Oliver McAlinden, three years Jacob's senior, was as sleek as a Whitehall mandarin. The resemblance was inherited; his father was a permanent secretary in the Home Office. In the presence of his superiors, McAlinden's manner was as oily as his hair and complexion, but he had a habit of mocking colleagues behind their backs, and his mimicry of Gomersall's northern vowels was amusing in small doses.

Early in their acquaintance, he'd told Jacob he was moving out of his lodgings at Edgar House, and recommended Mrs Dowd as a landlady whose charges were modest and cooking excellent. This act of kindness made Jacob think they would become good friends, but one evening after work, Oily McAlinden had invited him along to an ill-lit casino and club in Wardour Street, where men held hands and occasionally kissed each other, even if they didn't have the excuse of winning at roulette. One grey-haired man in a velvet smoking jacket had even blown Jacob a kiss, much to McAlinden's amusement.

'Your luck's in, my boy. I happen to know that fellow is worth upwards of a million, even in these troubled times.'

'I think I'd better say goodnight.'

'Quite right. You go and amuse yourself with him,' McAlinden said, putting a finger to his lips. 'Mum's the word, eh?'

'No.' Jacob felt like a bewildered child. 'I'm going straight back to Edgar House.'

'Nothing like this in darkest Dewsbury, eh?' McAlinden demanded in a passable Yorkshire accent. 'I bet there is, you know. It's just a question of knowing where to look.'

After that night, Jacob became wary of McAlinden. Live and let live was his creed. He didn't care what other people got up to in their own lives, but he was dubious about his colleague's motives. McAlinden's prose was pedestrian, but he fizzed with ambition. Unfair it might be, but Jacob had a sneaking fear that McAlinden was capable of seeking to lure him into an indiscretion, with a view to exploiting it for his own benefit.

'Sorry,' McAlinden said with patent insincerity when Jacob bumped into him coming out of Tom Betts' office, and asked what else he knew about Shoemaker's death. 'Can't tell you any more than I put in my paragraph. A Jewish private detective, eh, what next? Nothing more than a glorified debt collector, I expect. The only surprise is that he lived to such a ripe old age. I wager a box of cigars to a burnt match that he was done in by someone with a grudge. Ever meet a truly popular Jew? No, it's a contradiction in terms. So why are you interested in this Shylock Holmes?'

Sickened, Jacob didn't want to talk about it. 'Long story,' he mumbled.

McAlinden yawned. 'Save it for some other time, there's a good chap. I have to cover a meeting where Mosley is due to speak. Funny cove, but not to be written off. I have a saving bet on his becoming our next Prime Minister if some misfortune befalls Alfred Linacre.'

As soon as McAlinden disappeared from sight, Jacob sneaked into Betts' office. Nobody had attempted to impose order upon the mess of papers and litter during Betts' absence, and Jacob hoped for clues to Tom's investigation into Rachel Savernake. He pored over a handful of buff document files, looking for mention of her, or of Gallows Court. His quest yielded several old pieces of orange peel and the disgusting remains of a banana skin.

He found only one reference to Rachel. Her name, and the telephone number of Gaunt House, were scribbled on the carbon copy of Tom's story about the killing of the escaped prisoner, Harold Coleman. After ten minutes, he abandoned his search, and returned to his own desk. Still no word from

Rachel. After his encounter with McAlinden, Jacob's temper was fraying, and he started to draft another telegram.

After discarding several versions, he settled for brevity. *I talked to Shoemaker shortly before he was murdered.* Cryptic enough to be impossible to ignore? Surely the woman must wonder if her tame investigator had given her game away? Whatever her game was.

As soon as he'd sent the telegram, he attempted to secure an appointment with Vincent Hannaway, but was told by a clerk as condescending as Oily McAlinden that Mr Hannaway was out of the office, attending upon clients, and would not be back until later in the afternoon, in time to sign his post. His diary was full for the next few days, but if Mr Flint cared to submit an enquiry in writing, and perhaps a letter of introduction…

Jacob rang off, and tried his luck with Scotland Yard. Inspector Oakes' minions also did their utmost to fob him off, until Jacob said that he was calling about a murder. Finally he was put through to the man himself.

'When I asked you to keep in touch,' Oakes said, a sliver of wry humour robbing his words of their sting, 'I didn't contemplate a daily briefing.'

'You know Levi Shoemaker is dead?'

'Of course.'

'I believe he was murdered.'

A long pause followed. 'I shall need a break for lunch. Meet me at the Earl of Chatham at one o'clock.'

Shoemaker's note was burning a hole in his pocket. Jacob's moral dilemma about whether or not to take a peek had been resolved, more quickly and more dreadfully than either of them could have imagined. *If I give this to you, will you swear not to open it, unless and until something happens to me?* That condition had been fulfilled within hours.

On second thoughts, Shoemaker *had* imagined it. It could only have been because he expected to die in the near future that he'd entrusted confidential information to a young reporter he'd only just met.

Almost certainly, Shoemaker had been killed by the two men who had attacked him shortly before Jacob's arrival. They'd kept an eye on him when he left Aldgate East, and after seeing him accompanied by a journalist to his office, they'd silenced him. Jacob guessed they were acting on instructions. Who had ordered them to kill Shoemaker?

Shoemaker had worked for Rachel Savernake. Had he outlived his usefulness to her, and become a threat because he knew too much? Over the years Shoemaker must have found himself in many a tight corner, yet terror had shone in his eyes as he ushered Jacob to the fire ladder. He knew what she was capable of.

Rachel Savernake is the most dangerous woman in England.

Jacob shivered. Was he the next target? Surely nobody would risk trying to kill him. Betts' accident wasn't being treated as suspicious, but if something happened to a second *Clarion* reporter interested in Rachel Savernake, Gomersall would not let it rest. Nor, he thought, would Inspector Oakes.

The office was thick with cigarette smoke, and Jacob needed air in his lungs. He hurried downstairs, and out of the building. Furtive as a sneak thief, he slipped into a narrow alleyway. Nobody was watching him, as far as he knew, but he was not in the mood to take chances. When he was satisfied that not even a casual passer-by could see him, he took out the envelope and ripped it open.

The old man's hasty scrawl was hard to read, and he seemed to have written his message in a crude form of code.

CGCGCG91192PIRVYBC

Jacob could make nothing of it. He stuffed the sheet back into his pocket, and made his way back to the office. If only Levi Shoemaker had written a last message both lucid and newsworthy.

'Sounds like Shoemaker told you next to nothing,' Oakes said, munching the last of his bread and cheese.

The Earl of Chatham was crowded with sober-suited civil servants, and loud, hefty young men who, Jacob presumed, were numbered among Scotland Yard's finest. On the principle of hiding a leaf in a forest, it seemed reasonable to have a confidential conversation in a place so noisy that nobody could overhear anything. For all Jacob knew, the government officials at the nearest table were spies trading state secrets. But Oakes was taking no chances. He'd chosen a nook sheltered by a snob-screen of frosted glass. It might have been designed to protect well-to-do customers from the scrutiny of the lower orders, but it was perfect for people wanting to have a discreet conversation about murder.

'Not as much as I'd hoped, no.'

Jacob felt a pinprick of disappointment. He'd expected to startle Oakes with his claim that Levi Shoemaker had been killed by thugs, but the inspector seemed unimpressed.

Oakes wiped his mouth, and lit a cigarette. He offered one to Jacob, who shook his head. 'I spoke to my colleague, Inspector Batty, who is in charge of the investigation into the death. He's ahead of you. His working hypothesis is that Shoemaker was thrown in the Thames, perhaps by someone he'd worked for or investigated. It seems that… parts of his body had been amputated before he died.'

Jacob's gorge rose. 'Wicked.'

'Very.' Oakes' expression was as dark as the wood panelling all around them.

'I thought he was making a fuss when he insisted I leave by the fire ladder,' Jacob said, trying to suppress his vivid imagination. The last thing he wanted was to picture the agony of the detective's dying moments. 'In fact, he knew we were in mortal danger. Levi Shoemaker saved my life.'

'Don't be too quick to make him out to be a hero,' Oakes said. 'The culprit or culprits were probably after money, or information. I doubt they had any interest in you.'

'I wish I could be so sure.'

'Shoemaker was an enquiry agent. That's a dirty game, however cleanly you try to play. He'll have made enemies.'

Jacob took a swig of bitter. On the way here, he'd wrestled with the question of how much to divulge. Oakes was approachable, but he and Jacob served different masters. Oakes would keep information back without compunction if it suited his purposes; equally, Jacob had no intention of blurting out everything he knew or suspected. As regards Shoemaker's curious scribbled message, he needed to make sense of it before deciding whether to share it with the police.

'I never met him,' Oakes said, 'but he was renowned for being tight-lipped. That's why the rich and famous flocked to his door, when they needed help we were unable to give. Still, it's a pity you couldn't prise anything out of him that might identify his attackers, or anyone who hired them.'

'He didn't say a word.' The scribbled note did not count, Jacob told himself. 'I came away no wiser.'

'Ah, well. So what do you plan to do next?'

'I intend to call on Vincent Hannaway, solicitor to the late Lawrence Pardoe.'

Oakes' eyebrows lifted. 'And what do you hope to glean from him?'

'I'm planning to write an article about Pardoe. Our readers have been denied a trial that would have kept them entertained, but I won't let the story drop. Anything you can tell me about Hannaway?'

'His firm is old-established, eminently respectable. Founded by his grandfather, I believe. His father is getting on, and has taken a back seat. They handle business and trust work, hence the connection with Pardoe. We never come across them in our line of business. They don't conduct criminal cases, so there aren't any thieves and vagabonds among their clients.'

'Not counting bankers, and the better class of murderer?'

Oakes laughed. 'Surely you don't expect Hannaway to talk freely? Why would a solicitor give the time of day to the young whippersnapper who trumpeted news of his client's suicide on the front page of the *Clarion*?'

'Nothing ventured, nothing gained.'

'I admire your optimism, Mr Flint. Do you intend to call on Hannaway today?'

'Yes, his chambers are only moments from Fleet Street.'

'Gallows Court, that's right.' Oakes allowed himself the glimmer of a smile. 'Once upon a time, it was a place of execution. Watch out if Hannaway gives you plenty of rope. Chances are, he'll try to hang you.'

15

'Jacob Flint is losing patience.' Rachel held her hand out for the telegram. As she read it, a faint smile crept across her face. 'Now he wants me to know he chatted with Shoemaker before he died. Presumably he expects me to panic.'

'He'll wait a long time for that,' Mrs Trueman said. 'I sometimes wonder if you were born without a nerve in your body. What are you going to do?'

'Flint's like a boisterous terrier, constantly demanding attention,' Rachel said. 'It's time to throw him another bone.'

She was writing in her study when Trueman rapped on the door, and marched in without waiting for a reply. She blotted the sheet of notepaper, and slid it into an envelope.

'You spoke to our friend from the Inanity?'

'Yes,' he said, 'we met in a public house in Battersea.'

'Any sign that he's having second thoughts?'

Trueman shrugged his brawny shoulders. 'Nothing is certain in this life, we both know that. However, he swears he's determined to see it through to the bitter end. Not long ago, he was on the verge of swallowing poison. Now he has a purpose.'

'Excellent. I feel quite altruistic.' Rachel picked up the envelope. 'Would you take this to Jacob Flint? I'm inviting him along this evening.'

'You're confident he'll accept?'

'He's desperate to find out what I'm up to. Why would he decline?'

'People blow with the wind.'

'Not us.' Rachel handed Trueman the envelope. 'The choice is Flint's. Turn me down, and he misses the story of a lifetime.'

CGCGCG91192PIRVYBC

Having memorised Shoemaker's cryptic message, Jacob found it impossible to get the string of letters and numbers out of his head. As he walked along the Strand, the characters jigged around in his brain, tantalising and provocative as cancan dancers. His love of mystery meant he was attracted to codes and ciphers. He'd read spellbinding tales about the cryptanalysts who had worked in Room 40 at the Admiralty during the Great War. Yet he could never have held down such a job. A teacher's long-ago jibe that he had a butterfly mind had come uncomfortably close to the truth. He was the last person to pore over a set of meaningless squiggles day after day, week after week. Left to him, the Zimmerman Telegram would never have been cracked, and the United States might never have declared war on Germany.

On his arrival at Clarion House, Peggy on the front desk condescended to hand him an envelope. 'Bloke came in not five minutes ago,' she said. 'Said to give you this, the instant you walked through the door.'

Jacob tore it open. The message said simply, *Finsbury Town Hall at seven tonight*. The note was unsigned, but the handwriting bore a strong resemblance to the summons to South Audley Street on the night of Pardoe's death.

'This bloke, what did he look like?'

'Big chap, ugly-looking blighter,' she sneered. 'Friend of yours, is he?'

The next task on his list was to pay a surprise visit to Gallows Court, and Lawrence Pardoe's solicitor. There was just enough time to squeeze in a visit before racing back to Edgar House, and apologising to Elaine for cancelling their date, in favour of an assignation at Finsbury Town Hall with – he presumed – Rachel Savernake.

Gallows Court was tucked away in an unfrequented corner at the back of Lincoln's Inn, a tiny rectangular cul-de-sac squeezed between New Square Passage and Carey Street. A quartet of tall brick buildings loomed over a cobbled courtyard reached by a dank alleyway no wider than an arm's stretch. A scaffold had once stood here, although the last public execution, of a woman convicted of stealing from a shop, dated back two hundred years. Standing on the spot where she had been strangled to death in the name of justice, Jacob supposed that Gallows Court had become an unpopular venue for entertainment, far too cramped for spectators to gain a good view of the death throes. Even on a summer's day, when fingers of sunlight might probe between the chimneys, the oppressive atmosphere would induce claustrophobia in the hardiest soul. In the gathering dusk, with gas lamps casting a murky yellow glow over the cobblestones, Gallows Court struck him as worse than sinister. Its eeriness was frightening.

He walked round the courtyard, and saw that three of the buildings were occupied by barristers' chambers. A discreet brass plate on the railings outside the fourth bore the name *Hannaway & Hannaway*. Jacob ran up the short flight of steps to the entrance, and pushed the bell. His plan was to catch the lawyer at the end of the working day, with no clients left in the waiting room to provide an excuse for refusing to see him. The flaw in his scheme, he realised, was that the well of solicitors' excuses never runs dry.

The heavy oak door creaked open, and a painfully thin man of about sixty, clad in a dusty suit and wearing pince-nez, peered out at him. He resembled a cadaver who had stepped out of a coffin, and who was inclined, having seen Jacob, to return there in disgust.

'The office is closed for business. If you desire an appointment, come back again at nine o'clock tomorrow.'

Jacob put his foot in the door to ensure that the cadaver didn't slam it shut. 'Mr Hannaway?'

'Certainly not. I am his chief clerk.' An edge of contempt emphasised the absurdity of the firm's proprietor opening his own front door to unexpected callers. 'Moreover, I should add that Mr Hannaway does not see clients other than those who come with a letter of introduction.'

'I'm not a prospective client.' Jacob saw no point in beating about the bush. With a member of the legal profession, that was a game he could never win. 'I wish to speak to Mr Hannaway about the late Lawrence Pardoe.'

The cadaver glared. 'Out of the question. Mr Hannaway would never discuss a client with third parties.'

'I'm not a prying member of the public.' Jacob flourished his card. 'I'd be obliged if you would take this to Mr Hannaway without further prevarication.'

In the corridor behind the cadaver, a door opened, and a brisk voice demanded, 'What is it, Broadis?'

'Mr Hannaway?' Jacob called out. 'I'm only asking for a moment of your time.'

The cadaver glanced over his skinny shoulder. His master waved him aside, and walked briskly forward to snatch the card from Jacob's hand. Vincent Hannaway was far from the elderly, dessicated creature of Jacob's imagination. With wavy black hair, and an unexpectedly sensuous mouth, he might almost have been described as handsome. His lips pursed as he read the name on the card.

'The *Clarion*, eh?'

'I wrote a report—'

'Yes. I do not make a habit of reading your newspaper, but your story was drawn to my attention following Mr Pardoe's death. Why are you here?'

'I'm working on a related article. Lawrence Pardoe was a successful man, with no history of violence. The case is not only horrific but also psychologically compelling. My readers would love to know the background to... what occurred.'

'If they desire entertainment, let them go to the circus.'

'They desire knowledge and understanding.' Jacob enjoyed pretending to be pompous. 'Stories about real life.'

'My client's affairs are confidential.'

'Your client is dead, Mr Hannaway.'

'Nevertheless, my professional obligations endure. I am the executor of his estate.'

'You and Lawrence Pardoe shared business interests as well.'

Hannaway considered him. 'Do you know how much I charge for an hour of my time, Mr Flint?'

'More than many of our readers earn in a month, I expect. Luckily, I'm not calling on you for paid advice. May I come in?'

Broadis took a step forward, as if itching to slam the door in Jacob's face, but Hannaway halted him with a movement of the hand. 'Five minutes, not a second longer. I have an appointment at the theatre this evening, and I do not intend to be late. Follow me.'

Jacob trotted after him down the corridor, passing open doors which gave on to the waiting room and a cubbyhole with desks for Broadis and a secretary, before reaching Hannaway's private office. Bookshelves filled with fat volumes of law reports took up most of the wall space, together with professional certificates and a framed cartoon of bewigged lawyers milking the cow of Litigation. A gold clock ticked on the top of an oak cabinet which, Jacob presumed, held client files. Hannaway settled himself behind a vast desk, and motioned Jacob into a deep-cushioned chair. Presumably a solicitor who charged by the hour had every incentive to encourage his clients to linger in comfort.

'Very well, Mr Flint. You arrived at my client's house moments after the police were called. What took you there?'

'You'll have to allow me more than five minutes if you start asking questions,' Jacob said. 'Like you, I am bound by obligations of confidentiality. Now, I gather from the police that Lawrence Pardoe left the bulk of his estate to a deserving cause. Such generosity seems hardly the act of a monstrous sadist.'

Hannaway studied Jacob, as if memorising every freckle on his face. 'I can only tell you this. In my dealings with Lawrence Pardoe over many years, I found him trustworthy and honourable.'

'You never dreamed he might be capable of...'

'Forgive me, but I'm neither a mind-reader nor a psychiatrist, merely a humble solicitor.' Jacob had seldom seen anyone less humble, but he let it pass. 'I cannot tell you what any of my clients might be capable of. It is not my job.'

'You were much more than Pardoe's solicitor, Mr Hannaway. More than his business colleague. You were his friend.'

Hannaway's expression did not flicker. 'A solicitor works with many people, Mr Flint. I presume you desire to quote me in your newspaper? Very well, I am prepared to say this: *I am shocked by the news concerning Lawrence Pardoe. It came as a bolt from the blue.*'

'Do you suspect that the so-called suicide note was forged?'

'Beyond what I have already said, I can volunteer no comment.'

'Pardoe and Mary-Jane Hayes knew each other prior to the murder.'

'Did they?'

'I believe so. Didn't he speak of her to you?'

The solicitor raised his hand. 'Enough, Mr Flint.'

'I need to ask you about Pardoe's will.'

Hannaway considered the clock on the cabinet. 'I am sorry, Mr Flint, your time is almost up.'

'Can you at least confirm the names of the good causes that will benefit from Lawrence Pardoe's largesse?'

The solicitor waved towards the door, a lord of the manor dismissing a serf. 'Broadis will see you out.'

Jacob made as if to leave before turning to ask the one question that mattered. 'Why did he leave so much money to a chess club, when he didn't even play the game?'

He exulted silently as Hannaway's expression flickered, and disdain gave way – only for an instant, but Jacob's eyes were sharp – to an expression of cold fury.

'How can I help being jealous?' Elaine demanded, as Jacob reached for his overcoat. 'You're obviously very smitten by this Rachel Savernake. How can a simple girl who works in a flower shop in Exmouth Market compete against a smouldering beauty with untold riches?'

'Rachel Savernake is just a story to me.' It was almost true, he told himself. 'As for smouldering, she's more like a Snow Queen. I've pestered her for an interview for ages, and finally she's agreed, so I need to seize the moment before she changes her mind.'

'I suppose I understand.' Her frown suggested otherwise. 'It's just such a shame that we're missing the play. I was so looking forward to it.'

He'd promised to take her to Frank Vosper's *Murder on the Second Floor*. For compensation, he'd brought her a box of Belgian chocolates, but he knew it wasn't enough.

'I'm sorry, Elaine. We'll go another time. Even though I'm as jealous of Frank Vosper as you are of Miss Savernake.'

She giggled. 'He's a real heartthrob. And so clever. When did your Rachel Savernake ever write a play? Let alone act in it and direct it.'

'I'd really better go. I daren't miss her.'

A heavy sigh. 'I won't still be up, you know, if you're back late.'

He pecked her on the cheek. She smelled of the liver and onions that her mother had rustled up on learning that their date had been cancelled.

'I'm sorry about letting you down,' he said. 'I'll make it up to you.'

'You'd better.' She forced a smile. 'Be good.'

He was unlikely to have a chance to be bad, he reflected, as he turned into the street. It took only him five minutes to reach Finsbury Town Hall, an unexpectedly imposing red brick edifice with art nouveau trimmings. Rain began to fall as he reached his destination, and he sheltered under the glass and wrought-iron canopy outside the main entrance. On the way, he'd tried to fit together the fragments of information he'd collected since his first encounter with Rachel Savernake, but he could not form anything resembling a full picture. Rachel worked to her own script. Unlike Frank Vosper, she chose to lurk in the shadows. He could only hope she was ready to take him into her confidence.

As he checked the time to make sure he wasn't late, a memory hit him like a blow to the solar plexus. In the Essex Head, Stanley Thurlow had produced a gold pocket watch to make sure he wasn't late back for work. Jacob had never seen the watch before, but remembered a previous occasion when Thurlow had consulted a battered old service watch, which he said once belonged to his late father. If the service watch broke, perhaps he'd buy a replacement. But how could a young detective constable with a small child, and a wife who did not work, a man who often complained of being short of money, afford something so expensive?

A host of possible explanations sprang to mind. Perhaps it was a Thurlow family heirloom, or simply not genuine. Or, just possibly, someone with deeper pockets than Jacob was supplementing Thurlow's income. Had they also paid for his forthcoming holiday in Brighton?

Jacob shuddered at the thought. But was he a hypocrite? After all, he was happy enough to slip Stan a few bob in return for information. But the payments were modest, and hardly compromised the forces of law and order. That sort of thing made the world go round. Oiling the wheels was one thing, though. Bribery was quite another.

Suddenly he was aware of a car drawing up beside him. A silver Rolls-Royce Phantom, the car that had collected Rachel Savernake from Gaunt House on the night of Pardoe's suicide. He peered through the windows.

Rachel was not inside.

Juliet Brentano's Journal

2 February 1919

Perhaps my room is not a prison cell but a safe haven. Henrietta, much distressed, tells me that the odd-job man has caught influenza.

It's Rachel's fault. She insisted that Cliff should drive her to collect her blue gown from the seamstress, whose cottage is on the mainland. Cliff protested, but she threatened to tell her father to dismiss him if he refused. Mother was right. I think she must be insane. Half a dozen people have died in the village since the new year. The seamstress' husband is among them, and one of her sons is laid up in bed and not expected to survive. Rachel was risking her own life, as well as Cliff's.

Cliff is very sick, Henrietta says, coughing so hard that she fears his stomach will tear. I dread the thought that she might catch the flu. If only the Judge had succumbed, instead of Cliff. He is old, and his mind is failing, but sometimes I fear he will live forever.

16

'Rachel! What a joy to see you again! Welcome to the Inanity!'

William Keary detached himself from a huddle of admirers with the ease of long practice as Rachel walked into the bar. A sweep of his hand took in the gold-leaf and glass extravagance of their surroundings. Once a poor cousin to the Palladium, the Coliseum, and the Hippodrome, the Inanity had become their formidable rival. The lavishly baroque private lounge was on the top floor, accessed by an electric lift; the hoi-polloi were confined to the cavernous public bars downstairs. Waiters scurried hither and thither, pressing cocktail glasses and canapés upon everyone in sight.

Keary bent to kiss Rachel's hand. 'My dear, you look even more ravishing than when we met at the Ragusa.'

It was true. Rather than contenting herself with a smart supper frock, Rachel had chosen to wear a full-length black gown that showed off her figure. 'You're too generous, William. I warned you that I'm not a sociable woman. I feel most at home with one or two of those closest to me.'

'Your guest hasn't arrived?'

'Not yet,' Rachel said.

Keary offered her one of his Tunisian cigarettes, which she declined. Turning, he beckoned to a waiter bearing a silver salver crowded with cocktails.

'Here's to an evening to remember.' Rachel lifted her glass. 'You are still intending to perform tonight?'

'Oh, yes, but not till later. That's the joy of owning your own theatre – you can always make sure that you top the bill! Before each show, I love to circulate among our Very Important Guests.' His white teeth sparkled. 'Especially on a night like this, when we are honoured by your presence. Rest assured, you have the best seats in the house. I've fobbed off the head of the civil service, an eminent novelist, and a rear admiral with inferior views of the stage.'

'I'm sure I don't deserve such generosity.'

'Nonsense, dear Rachel. It's a privilege to extend hospitality to a great man's daughter.' He gazed into her eyes, as if hoping to hypnotise her. 'Which reminds me. There is something I'd like to discuss with you after the show. It concerns… your father's legacy.'

'I'm intrigued,' Rachel said. 'But please, don't let me monopolise you. I'd hate to keep you from looking after all your other guests.'

'Even a good host is entitled to have his favourites.' Keary laughed. 'I hope very much to enjoy your company later tonight. Perhaps we could dine together, once you've said goodbye to your guest.'

'You're most generous.'

'Delighted you think so. In the meantime, I do hope you enjoy our little show.'

'I'm looking forward to it.' Rachel finished her cocktail. 'I've waited for this for a very long time.'

'Where are we going?' Jacob asked, as the car turned into Shaftesbury Avenue.

'Don't waste your breath on questions,' the chauffeur said. 'You'll find out soon enough.'

His accent had a blunt north-country edge. He didn't sound like a Yorkshireman, and Jacob guessed that he came from the other side of the Pennines. Despite the spaciousness of the Phantom's interior, his gigantic frame seemed too big for the driving seat. Peggy had been unkind in describing him as an ugly looking blighter; his dark eyes were too thoughtful for a mere bruiser. But his demeanour was as intimidating as his physical bulk. Jacob's experience of chauffeurs was negligible, but he'd anticipated a touch of courtesy, if not deference. This fellow's brusqueness perplexed him.

Where was he being taken? This well-heated car was the most comfortable he'd ever travelled in, but his spine was touched by a sudden chill. Had Rachel Savernake sent the message to lure him to a quiet spot where the chauffeur could torture and kill him just as someone had snuffed out Levi Shoemaker? Jacob was fit and young, but he knew in his heart he'd be no match for the chauffeur.

Before he'd fretted long enough to become queasy, the car pulled up in Shaftesbury Avenue, next to the squat columns guarding the entrance to the Inanity. Extraordinary! He'd never guessed his destination would be that palace of popular entertainment, the vast Edwardian theatre where Sara

Delamere wove her magic in the guise of an Egyptian queen, and where poor Dolly Benson had once flaunted herself in the chorus line.

The chauffeur got out, and opened the door for him. His expression was unreadable.

'In you go.'

Relief prompted an impudent grin. 'Sorry, I didn't bring any change, or I'd give you a tip.'

The chauffeur gave him a hard stare, and the smile died on Jacob's lips.

'Is – is Rachel here?'

'Miss Savernake to you.' A massive thumb jerked in the direction of a uniformed flunkey at the door. 'Give her name to the boy, and he'll escort you.'

Jacob did as he was told, and was whisked upstairs in the lift. Standing at the door of the lounge bar, he scanned the crowd, increasingly conscious that he was the least smartly dressed man in the room. It was just as well that working as a journalist had thickened his skin.

At last he caught sight of Rachel, and moved swiftly to her side. 'Good evening, Miss Savernake.'

'Ah, there you are! Trueman timed your arrival to perfection. The curtain will be up in five minutes.'

'I wasn't expecting—'

'A pleasant evening at the theatre? Ah, Mr Flint, I'm full of surprises.'

He considered her. 'You never spoke a truer word.'

'We have a box to ourselves,' Rachel said. 'Just the two of us. Such a generous gesture on the part of William Keary.'

'I'm honoured,' Jacob said. 'Keary is a friend of yours?'

'Of my late father, to be precise,' Rachel said coolly. 'Let's go in.'

They took their places at the front of the bow-fronted box. The plush upholstery and the lampshades on gilt brackets were the colour of ripening plums; the enclosed space reeked of decadence masquerading as luxury. Marble cherubs and nymphs adorned the vast proscenium arch below. Peering at them through a pair of opera glasses, Jacob fancied that the sculptor had captured a mischievous look in their eyes. As the lights dimmed, Jacob seized the chance to whisper in Rachel's ear.

'Can we talk in private?'

'Not now, and there is no interval in this performance. Let's just sit back and enjoy the entertainment. This evening should supply you with excellent copy.'

She was playing a game, but he had no idea of the rules. He found himself retorting, 'A pity I'm not a drama critic.'

In the darkness, he glimpsed her smile, and felt a tide of anger well up inside him. There was so much he wanted to know. Why had the woman invited him to the Inanity, if she didn't want to speak to him?

The musky whiff of French perfume was tantalising. He felt light-headed, as if Elaine's joke about Rachel Savernake putting a spell on him was coming true.

He glanced across at the boxes on the opposite side of the theatre. There were enough famous faces in the audience to make an autograph hunter swoon. It was almost a pity that Elaine wasn't here. He recognised a distinguished opera singer and a man who opened the batting for England, as well as Sir Godfrey Mulhearn from Scotland Yard.

A drum rolled, and the blood-red curtain rose; moments later, the orchestra was in full flow. Tap-dancers with shoes like polished mirrors twinkled around the stage, but his mind kept wandering back to his conversation with Sara Delamere. Even if Rachel knew about Pardoe's inexplicable threats, he couldn't imagine why, with Pardoe dead, she'd want to spend the evening at the Inanity.

Unless, perhaps, she was already aware that Sara had a story to tell, and intended to interrogate her after the show. This seemed plausible. Perhaps he should take Rachel at her word, and simply enjoy the performances. She'd reveal her hand when it suited her.

One of the secrets of the Inanity's success was that its programme changed each week. Jacob recalled a couple of the acts from his visit with Elaine, but parts of their routines had changed, and other artistes were new to him. A troupe of dwarf acrobats tumbled into a large triangle which collapsed as the acrobats split apart like falling cards. The Flying Finnegans from Fermanagh performed gravity-defying stunts on creaking trapezes with silvered ladders, and a fat comedian from Pudsey had the audience rolling in the red-carpeted aisles with innuendo-laden quips fired out one after the other, as fast as bullets.

Below their box, Jacob saw people all around, laughing until the tears flowed. Beside him, Rachel Savernake clapped politely, and smiled at every punchline, but her thoughts seemed elsewhere. Only when it was time for the final act of the evening did she lean forward, rapt eyes fixed upon the stage, as the curtain fell before rising again. The shifting of scene to an ancient temple, with desert sand in the background, and the arrival, to a steady drumbeat, of Nefertiti, Nubian Queen of Magic and Mystery.

'Magic fascinates me,' Rachel murmured.

'Me too,' Jacob whispered, thankful they'd found common ground, if only for a moment.

Meek, apprehensive Sara Delamere was unrecognisable as the brown-skinned, swan-necked beauty in a clinging silk gown, virginal white with a vivid red sash, and brilliant blue eyeshadow to match her tall, tapering crown. She never spoke to the audience, but danced around the stage in between performing her tricks with a histrionic flourish. A flock of doves flew out from an empty casket, and a dozen sheets of papyrus ripped from an ancient tome formed magically into a single banner bearing hieroglyphs which suddenly changed to spell *Nefertiti*. She even indulged herself in one of the oldest tricks of all, shimmying up a rope until she disappeared out of sight, only to emerge seconds later from behind a huge replica of the Sphinx.

As the applause died down, the orchestra launched into a sombre theme pregnant with menace, and Anubis emerged from the far wing. He had a black jackal's head, with long, pointed ears and a tapering muzzle, and the lean, bronzed body of a man. He wore nothing but a yellow loincloth and, on his left index finger a jade scarab ring. Nefertiti feigned shock at his arrival, and the Sphinx rolled away to reveal, in front of a pyramid, a large stone sarcophagus raised above the ground by four low pillars.

The Queen and the Death God danced in an exotic courtship ritual; one moment she cowered from him in fear, the next she became coquettish and coy. As the music became deafening, Anubis strove to seize hold of her, but each time he was thwarted as she slipped from his grasp. Finally, she stood her ground, and faced him down with a broad smile. Bowing in triumph, she mouthed a few words, and the jackal head nodded. A wager had been struck in mime.

Suddenly, she produced from nowhere a steel chain, and neatly snapped it around his wrists like a pair of handcuffs.

The music died away as, for the benefit of the audience, she took hold of a ring on the top of the sarcophagus. With one strong pull, she'd lifted the heavy lid, and with it, the top half of the side of the sarcophagus. While Anubis struggled in vain to free himself, she directed the audience's attention to a tiny opening in the lower part of the side of the sarcophagus.

At the snap of her fingers, two boys in Egyptian costume ran onto the stage. One handed to Nefertiti four pieces of firewood, the other a burning touch. Nefertiti hurled the wood into the sarcophagus, before goading Anubis towards it with the torch. She drove him to wriggle his way up and into the stone coffin. Once the whole of his body was inside, she pulled down the lid, and the music built as she danced ecstatically with the torch of flame.

Jacob and Elaine had found the cremation illusion breathtaking, and he marvelled all over again, even though he knew what came next. Nefertiti would push her torch through the opening in the side of the sarcophagus to start a fire inside it. While members of the audience held their breath, she'd lift the lid to admire her handiwork. A skeleton would be revealed, with a burning jackal's head and a jade scarab ring on its left index finger. And then Anubis would stride out from the shadows at the rear of the stage, and tear off his chain, ready to take his conquest into the desert. Familiarity with the trick didn't breed contempt. Jacob tensed as Nefertiti waved the burning torch, before sliding it through the side of the sarcophagus.

Next to him, Rachel exhaled. She closed her eyes, as if uttering a silent prayer.

Everyone in the theatre could see underneath the sarcophagus, as well as all around it. The flames were so fierce that they burst out from beneath the lid. The audience gasped.

Anybody inside must be burned to ashes. How could Anubis possibly escape? Jacob couldn't work out the secret of the trick. For all her modesty, Sara Delamere was a gifted illusionist.

'Amazing,' he murmured in Rachel's ear.

'Unforgettable,' she breathed.

Cymbals clashed, and Nefertiti raised the stone lid of the sarcophagus. Jacob recalled that last time, the skeleton had sat up for a moment, a jade scarab ring glinting on one of its bony fingers. Horror had rippled through the shocked onlookers.

Tonight, something was different. Despite the heat from the dying flames, Nefertiti had frozen. She was staring down into the sarcophagus. This time the skeleton did not sit up. The music stuttered, and then the orchestra fell silent.

Everyone was leaning forward in their seats, waiting to see what came next. Several women gasped, and the cherubs on the proscenium arch grinned down at the stage with malevolent delight. Only Rachel Savernake was unmoved.

Rachel knows, Jacob thought. *She was expecting this, like an enchantress waiting for her prophecy to come true.*

And was his imagination working overtime, or was there wafting up towards them the smell of charred flesh?

Nefertiti screamed, and he had his answer.

17

'Are you absolutely certain that William Keary was deliberately murdered?' Sir Godfrey Mulhearn tugged at his moustache, as if ripping it off his upper lip might somehow solve the mystery. He prided himself on being able to pass for fifty, but a disrupted night had left him with the haggard look of a man who had spent every day of his sixty-two years in backbreaking toil.

'Not a shadow of doubt, sir.' Superintendent Chadwick lowered himself into a chair on the other side of the desk with elephantine care. His very ponderousness was reassuring. 'Oakes and his men are tidying things up as we speak. There is still work to be done, but the essentials are clear. Keary was killed in the most vicious manner possible, and the culprit was one of his own stagehands.'

'This man Barnes? The fellow who wanted to marry that poor wretch Dolly Benson?'

'And whom we arrested prior to Linacre's suicide,' Chadwick said, his grammar as punctilious as his demeanour. 'I always fancied he was a bad lot.'

'Was there any talk of ill will between him and Keary?'

'Not a whisper, that's the strangest feature of the whole business. Keary's treatment of Barnes was exemplary. Far from sacking the fellow when he was suspected of killing his young lady, he paid for Barnes to be legally represented. And that was certainly not out of character. Keary had a reputation as a first-rate employer.'

Sir Godfrey indulged in a further bout of moustache-torturing. 'Barnes must have gone mad. Losing the woman he loved, coupled with the distress of being suspected – even if only for a short time – of having killed her, that would be enough to turn any man's mind.'

'Possibly, sir.' Chadwick sounded unconvinced.

'I mean, dash it all.' Sir Godfrey banged his fist on the desk. 'Look at the method he used to murder Keary. Burning the fellow to death when his hands were chained, and he was trapped on stage in a stone tomb. Absolutely barbarous. No sane Englishman could contemplate such a crime.'

'I understand the argument, sir.' Chadwick was a seasoned diplomat. 'Yet the case has curious features. Barnes clearly planned his actions in detail. Not only the crime, but his means of escape. For a madman, he seems to have been exceptionally well organised.'

'Even a maniac can display low cunning,' Sir Godfrey grunted. 'Have you established precisely how he committed the murder?'

'I take it you understand how the illusion is performed, sir?'

'I presume the girl who plays the part of Nefertiti isn't actually capable of performing miracles,' came the testy reply, 'but no, I don't know the secret of the cremation shenanigans.'

'Let me explain.' Chadwick settled back in his chair, like a grandfather telling a fairy story to a child. 'Cremation illusions come, I'm led to believe, in various forms. This one is tailored to the Egyptian theme. At the rear of the sarcophagus is a panel which can be moved from inside.'

'Ah!' Sir Godfrey's eyes narrowed.

'Once Keary, playing the part of Anubis, God of Death,' – here, Chadwick coughed to convey his opinion of such ill-judged frivolity – 'slid into the container, he shifted the panel. In effect, it's a trapdoor. His collaborator, the woman pretending to be Queen Nefertiti, gives him all the time he needs by prancing around the stage with her burning torch. This distracts the audience. They can't see what else is happening behind her, because the bulk of the sarcophagus conceals everything. A stagehand concealed in the fake pyramid to the rear of the stage runs out a ladder which connects with the opening in the sarcophagus. The sarcophagus is elevated from the ground, so people can see by looking underneath it and towards the pyramid – but there's a blind spot. Keary squeezes through the opening at the back of the sarcophagus, and the stagehand pulls back the ladder, conveying Keary into the pyramid, and safety. Crucially, the illusionist is at the front of the stage, distracting the audience. She is a very handsome woman. People can't take their eyes off her.'

'Indeed. Her costume was... scanty. Not indecent, mind you, nothing to agitate the Lord Chamberlain. But rather suggestive.' Sir Godfrey coughed. 'How can she make sure that her accomplice is safe?'

'Good question, sir. The moment Keary reaches the pyramid, the stagehand presses a button which releases a puff of smoke into the air. It means nothing to the audience, but Nefertiti is waiting for the signal.'

'And did Barnes give the signal last night?'

Chadwick nodded. 'We're not merely relying on the woman's word. Two other stagehands waiting in the wings confirm it. Unfortunately, their positions meant they could not see that Keary had failed to make his escape. She had every reason to believe it was safe to thrust the burning torch into the sarcophagus.'

'Poor creature.'

'She is quite demented. Gabbling wildly, and blaming herself. In my judgement, however, she was an innocent dupe.'

'Really?'

'Yes, sir. When we pieced together her story, it made perfect sense. She believed Keary was strolling round to the back of the auditorium, as usual, ready to make a dramatic reappearance on the stage while the spectators were still awestruck by the sight of the skeleton in flames inside the sarcophagus.'

'Tell me about the skeleton,' Sir Godfrey demanded.

'The skeleton is a stage prop, sir. In the lid of the sarcophagus is a hidden compartment. Inside is a skeleton dressed in a tattered version of the Anubis costume – complete with jackal head and duplicate jade scarab ring. The stagehand presses a lever concealed within the pyramid which releases the door of the compartment, and activates the skeleton, which has a mechanism enabling it to sit up in order to horrify the audience.'

Sir Godfrey blinked. 'Quite clever, I suppose.'

'Barnes' scheme was simple. He fixed the sliding panel in the rear of the sarcophagus so that Keary could not shift it an inch. It's meant to move at a touch. The lid is close-fitting and heavy, and although it's hinged, so that the woman can open it without undue difficulty, there is no means of opening it from within. Keary's hands were chained, and although you can do some jiggery-pokery with the chain to release yourself, it would take Keary, with all his experience, at least half a minute. But the task would become impossible for a man sick with terror and pain as the fire took hold.'

'He must have screamed in agony.'

'I'm sure he did, sir, but the music was reaching a crescendo.'

Sir Godfrey winced. 'So while we watched, it drowned out his cries.'

'Quite so. Barnes made sure that Keary was burned to a crisp, and then calmly walked away. I gather pandemonium broke out when the girl – Delamere – opened the lid and realised that Keary was inside.'

Sir Godfrey sighed. 'When I made my way down to the stage, the stench was indescribable. Everyone was in a blue funk. Nobody could understand what had happened.'

'As you know, it took a few minutes for Barnes to be missed. He'd made his way to the back of the building, and left via the stage door. In the uproar, nobody paid any attention.'

'This car he had waiting close to the theatre. Did it belong to him?'

'We've established that he bought the vehicle forty-eight hours ago. An Invicta, sir, a very natty sports car. The salesman couldn't believe his luck. Barnes struck him as a rough diamond, but when it became clear he had the money to buy outright, the chap bit his hand off.'

'I wonder,' Sir Godfrey said. 'Did Barnes drop any hint about his intentions?'

'He certainly failed to mention that he was planning to murder his employer in the most dreadful way imaginable, sir.' Sir Godfrey glared, but the superintendent's rugged features betrayed no trace of sarcasm. 'What he did say was that he planned to go touring. Witnesses tell us that the Invicta was parked a hundred yards away from the Inanity, and it appears that he set off at a cracking speed, on his way to Croydon.'

'Rather late for a flight, surely?'

'A plane had been chartered specially to take him to Beauvais in France. We're looking into who made the arrangements – Barnes, or an accomplice.'

'You think that he cooked this up with someone else? Surely that blows a hole in the theory that he killed Keary in a fit of insane rage?'

'Barnes obviously planned his actions with care. Whether he had help from a third party is uncertain. On the surface, it's highly doubtful, but we are sure he couldn't have afforded to buy an Invicta. Keary was a generous employer, but the wages of a stagehand at the Inanity don't go so far.'

'Damned peculiar. Could he have stolen the money?'

'Quite possibly. We are also trying to ascertain if somehow he persuaded Keary himself to advance him the cash.'

'Macabre thought,' Sir Godfrey muttered. 'How did we get onto him so quickly last night? Once I realised Keary was dead, I called a taxi for my wife, and then reported to the Home Secretary. At the time I left, the whole place was in uproar.'

'Once it became clear that there'd been monkey business with the sarcophagus, and that Barnes was missing, we knew who to look for. A report came in of an Invicta being driven fast and erratically, five miles short of the airport. One of our chaps gave chase on a motorcycle, and the rest you know.'

Sir Godfrey contemplated his fingernails. Barnes had put his foot down, and soon lost his pursuer, but also lost control of the car. Taking a bend too fast, he'd wrapped the Invicta round an elm tree, breaking his neck in the process.

'Saved the hangman a job,' Chadwick said sourly. 'The only pity is, we never had the chance to discover what led him to murder Keary. We've questioned the staff at the theatre, but nobody is aware of any quarrel between the two men. Everyone is in a state of shock. Barnes was an awkward cuss, but good at his job. People say he'd seemed depressed of late, but nobody can believe he hated Keary enough to want to kill him in such a brutal fashion.'

'What do we know about the woman who set fire to him?'

'Queen Nefertiti? Her real name is Sara Delamere; at least that's what she goes by. One of the dancers – a spiteful little minx – said that in the past, Keary had taken advantage of the girl.'

'Really?' Sir Godfrey was startled. 'Might she have been his mistress?'

'If so, he was a busy man. He lived with a widowed Italian woman. I gather they hadn't made the union legal, but you know how these theatricals behave. They're a law unto themselves.'

'If Keary dallied with the Delamere girl, and then abandoned her, she might have thirsted for revenge. Could she have put Barnes up to it, provided the wherewithal to buy the car?'

'We never rule anything out, sir, but it seems unlikely. All the signs are that she and Keary remained genuinely fond of each other, up to and including last night.'

'Even so,' Sir Godfrey mused. 'Hell hath no fury, and so on.'

'Given the exceptional circumstances, I took it upon myself to talk to her. She's very different in real life to the character she portrays on the stage, but all I can say is that if her distress was feigned, Mary Pickford should look to her laurels. She must be the finest actress of her generation.'

'An appalling crime, Chadwick.'

The superintendent pursed his lips. 'You must have found it shocking yourself, sir. Out for an evening's relaxation in the company of Lady Mulhearn, only to watch a man fried to death.'

'I witnessed plenty of ghastly sights during the war, Chadwick, but a soldier expects such things.' Sir Godfrey's voice was hollow. 'Last night was uniquely vile.'

'You weren't the only notable witness,' Chadwick said. 'Seen this morning's *Clarion*?'

'Frankly, I've only had time to glance at the serious newspapers. I suppose the others are swarming over the story like wasps round a jam pot.'

'Jacob Flint has written an eyewitness account of events at the Inanity.'

'The young fellow who turned up in South Audley Street, the night Pardoe died?'

'That's him. Like you, he was watching the show last night.'

'Dammit, that's an astonishing coincidence!'

Chadwick's face made clear his opinion of coincidence. 'He was a guest in the box of Miss Rachel Savernake.'

'Congratulations, young man.' Walter Gomersall gestured to the front page of the *Clarion* on his desk. 'Not a bad piece.'

Jacob nodded his thanks. Lack of sleep would hit him eventually, but for now he was thriving on adrenaline. Never in his life had he experienced anything to compare with the previous evening. To spend so long sitting next to a beautiful woman was memorable in itself, but the drama that had followed Nefertiti's piercing scream he'd never forget.

At first, some members of the audience had presumed that her shrieking horror was all part of the performance. A handful of people actually laughed, but Jacob realised at once that something had gone badly wrong. The audience's enjoyment turned to stunned disbelief as the boys in Egyptian costume ran on to douse the remains of the fire, and haul the charred remains of William Keary out of the sarcophagus.

Yet Rachel had remained utterly serene. Jacob stammered that he'd meant to pass on a warning from the actress who played Queen Nefertiti, but she'd cut him off in mid-stream, saying that surely he should go downstairs and find out what had happened. He'd hesitated before hastening down towards the stage. Chaos reigned, but within minutes, he had the makings of an exclusive.

'I was lucky,' he admitted.

'Very.' Gomersall put his hands behind his head, a familiar pose when he was in reflective mood. 'Twice in a matter of days, you've been on the spot to report a major murder story. That sort of good fortune, any journalist would kill for.'

Jacob wasn't ready to admit that Rachel had invited him to the Inanity. First, he needed to understand what she was up to. With a cautious nod of the head, he said, 'Quite a coincidence.'

'I'll say.' Gomersall screwed up his eyes, as if trying to see through his young reporter. 'Sure you've not entered into some kind of Faustian pact? Not sold your soul to old Nick in return for a couple of banner headlines?'

Jacob laughed. 'I'd put a higher price on my soul, sir.'

'Glad to hear it.' Gomersall didn't laugh with him. 'Well done, lad. Nobody could fail to hit the bull's eye with such a sensational story, but you've written it up with flair. I'm impressed, but I'm also worried.'

'Worried, sir?'

'Yes.' The editor shook his head. 'Good luck always runs out. Watch it doesn't turn to bad.'

'Where did Barnes find the money to buy the Invicta?' Chadwick demanded.

'He paid in cash, and it didn't go through his bank account.' Inspector Oakes stifled a yawn. His eyes were duller than usual, and he hadn't shaved with his customary precision. 'Was it the proceeds of a crime we haven't discovered? Nobody knows. He had few friends, and didn't confide in anyone.'

'Is it possible that he was a blackmailer?' Chadwick sounded doubtful, an unimaginative man venturing into the twilight world of ifs and maybes. 'That would explain the secret hoard. Did he have some hold over Keary, who then threatened Barnes with exposure?'

'Conceivably, sir. The only other plausible explanation is that he blamed Keary for the girl's death, which seems ridiculous. There can't be any doubt that Linacre was guilty of the crime. Keary showed Barnes nothing but kindness, yet the fellow repaid it by inflicting on his benefactor the most agonising death.'

'Utter madness,' Chadwick said.

'Perhaps.'

'At least Barnes is dead.' Chadwick thrust out his lower lip. 'Let's be thankful for small mercies.'

'That he escaped justice?'

'Depends on your notion of justice,' Chadwick said heavily. 'It was a stroke of luck that Sir Godfrey was present, and quick to raise the alarm. We'd have stopped his plane from flying to France even if he'd made it to Croydon alive. I suppose we shouldn't worry about the odd loose end. It's still a neat outcome.'

'Neat as the Pardoe case, sir?'

Chadwick glowered at his subordinate. 'Let's not confuse the issue.'

'Jacob Flint was spotted by young Thurlow shortly after Pardoe died. What if he hadn't just arrived, as he told Thurlow, but was present at the time Pardoe killed himself?'

'What are you suggesting?'

'Nothing, sir, just thinking aloud. Last night, Flint watched Keary's death from the comfort of a luxurious box in the company of Miss Rachel Savernake. I'm left wondering why a wealthy young woman would invite a junior reporter along to the Inanity.'

'Some sort of romantic tryst?'

Oakes sighed. 'If so, it took an unusual form. Our men were at the scene within minutes of Keary's death, and they took the names and addresses of everyone there, including Flint. But there was no sign of Rachel Savernake.'

Jacob made himself a cup of strong, sweet tea, and retreated to Tom Betts' old room to straighten the tangles in his brain. When he'd run down to join the mêlée on the stage last night, his overriding instinct had been to discover what had happened, and turn it into copy. The smell turned his stomach, and the commotion hurt his ears. Women were wailing, members of the audience and the cast alike, while police officers kept shouting for calm.

A weeping Sara Delamere, still unrecognisable in her guise as Nefertiti, had been shepherded away by the police, and his attempt to beg an interview met with a stern but inevitable rebuff. When he looked up at the box, Rachel had vanished. He made a token effort to look for her, but soon abandoned the search to devote himself to writing and filing his sensational story.

A fresh burst of tea-fuelled energy prompted him to telephone the Inanity, and ask for Sara Delamere.

'She ain't here,' an adenoidal voice informed him.

'Can you give her a message?'

'Who's speaking?'

'I'm a journalist with—'

The phone went dead. He decided to try his luck with Rachel's house. His call was answered by the housekeeper, who told him that Miss Savernake was not at home. He doubted it was true, but he'd gain nothing from calling the woman a liar.

'Would you be good enough to tell Miss Savernake that I called? I'm anxious to speak to her as a matter of urgency.'

'I'll pass the message on, sir. Good day.'

She rang off, leaving him to scowl at the silent receiver. Prising information out of Rachel Savernake was like squeezing juice out of granite. He took his cup back to the smelly, claustrophobic kitchen used by the junior staff writers, and bumped into Oily McAlinden.

The kindness Oily had shown him in recommending him to Edgar House had later given way to ill-concealed professional jealousy. His brief words of praise for Jacob's front-page story were conspicuous for their insincerity.

'You're becoming quite the star reporter,' he sneered. 'Ready to step into Tom Betts' shoes, I shouldn't wonder. You've heard, I suppose?'

Jacob's heart sank. 'Heard what?'

McAlinden grinned. He always seemed to take pleasure in being first to break bad news. 'Old Gomersall's calling a meeting in half an hour to make a formal announcement. The hospital has been in touch. Betts kicked the bucket early this morning.'

18

'Barnes was killed outright,' Trueman announced as he walked into the sitting room. 'He was flying along at sixty miles an hour when he smashed into that tree.'

Rachel was idly picking out 'Tiptoe Through the Tulips' on the Steinway as Martha served coffee. Trueman threw his coat over the back of the sofa. He'd spent half the morning digging out information about the circumstances of George Barnes' death.

'A blessing, if you ask me.' Mrs Trueman folded her arms, daring her husband to contradict her. 'Didn't Barnes tell you that his life ended the day Dolly Benson died? He'd never have settled in France. What sort of miserable existence is it, forever looking over your shoulder, trying desperately to convince yourself that you're out of harm's way?'

'Not so very different from our lives.' Rachel gave a cynical smile. 'But I'm not in the least miserable. It's simply a matter of attitude.'

'Barnes was never beholden to anyone.' Trueman shrugged.

'I don't say he rammed his car into that old elm on purpose, but he was past caring what happened.'

'Poor soul,' his wife said. 'At least you needn't worry he'll betray you.'

'I was never worried.'

'If the police had made him talk...'

'He'd never have breathed a word,' Trueman said. 'Depend on it. I can judge a man's character better than most. Even if they'd got him in the cells, and roughed him up, he'd have kept his trap shut.'

Mrs Trueman turned to Rachel. 'I suppose you'll say nobody's to be trusted.'

'You're both right.' Rachel abandoned the piano stool to warm her hands in front of the fire. 'Trusting Barnes was a gamble, yes, but worth taking. Everything worked out perfectly.'

'Except for Barnes,' Mrs Trueman said.

Walter Gomersall took Jacob aside two minutes before he was due to address the staff meeting. 'You've heard the news?'

'About Tom? Yes, it's awful.'

'God knows how that poor woman will cope on her own.' Jacob had never seen Gomersall look so grim. 'Betts was everything to Lydia. We'll do what we can for her, but not even the *Clarion* can give someone a reason to live.'

Jacob blurted out, 'I called on her the other day.'

'You did?' The thick black eyebrows jumped. 'Paying your respects, or ferreting out information?'

'Bit of both, sir.' Jacob flushed. 'I wanted to know if... if she could tell me anything that could cast light on what happened to Tom.'

'No need to go beetroot red, lad. You can be a human being and a reporter at the same time. Remember that. You'll be tested by worse folk than me.'

Jacob's smile was uneasy. He didn't know what to say.

'Just to give you advance warning. I'll be announcing the name of our new crime correspondent shortly. Congratulations, you've earned it.'

Gomersall pumped his hand. Jacob stammered, 'You mean I'm...'

'Tom's successor, yes. It's what he wanted, just ten bloody years too soon. You'll do all right. Call in the office in half an hour, and we'll talk about pay. Just don't go buying your ladyfriend a mink coat to celebrate. We're not made of money.'

'Thank you, sir.' The words seemed inadequate.

'Don't thank me, thank Tom. Last time I sat by his bedside, the only thing he said that made any sense was to give you his job.'

'Jacob Flint telephoned,' Mrs Trueman told Rachel, after her husband left the sitting room. 'Wanted to speak to you. Says there's something he can't understand.'

Rachel laughed. 'Bewilderment is his natural state; it has a certain sweet charm. The urge to ruffle his hair, give him sixpence, and tell him to go off and play is overwhelming.'

'Get away with your bother. What did he say last night?'

'Only that he'd had a conversation with Sara Delamere. She told him she'd heard Pardoe and Keary talking, and what Pardoe said made her fear for my life.'

'And why she didn't approach you herself?'

'Because of her dubious past.'

The older woman snorted. 'Are you going to talk to Flint?'

'When the time is right.'

'He's in danger, isn't he? He's made himself a target.'

'He only has himself to blame. All our actions have consequences, you and I both know that.'

'You like him, though.' The housekeeper peered at her over her spectacles, a prosecuting counsel cross-examining an unscrupulous witness.

'His innocence entertains me. But I can't save him from himself.'

Jacob was still reeling from the twin shocks of Tom Betts' death and his sudden elevation to the *Clarion*'s hierarchy when the shrilling telephone jerked him out of a daze of conflicting emotions.

'Inspector Oakes for you,' Peggy announced.

An icy voice murmured, 'You ought to be re-christened Johnny on the Spot, Mr Flint.'

Jacob began to mutter a vague reply, but the detective cut him short. 'Are you free for another of our little chats?'

'I did give a statement to one of your officers before I left the Inanity to file my story.'

'I've read it. Naturally, the constable you spoke to wasn't aware of the full background. Can we meet?'

'Very well.' Jacob paused. 'Tom Betts is dead.'

'My condolences.'

'The editor has promoted me. I suppose you'll say every cloud has a silver lining, but I'm sure Betts didn't have an accident. He was murdered.'

'Why do you think so?'

'He was asking questions about Rachel Savernake.'

'Are you suggesting she arranged for him to be run over?'

'I'm not... look here, we shouldn't discuss this on the telephone.'

'Let's meet at the Lyons Corner House on the Strand.' Oakes spoke curtly, with no hint of his habitual dry humour. 'Be in the Mirror Hall in half an hour.'

'I'll be there.'

'And Flint.'

'Yes?'

'This is just between you and me, understand? Don't breathe a word to anyone else.'

Jacob hurried down the steps to the Mirror Hall, and spotted Oakes waiting for him at a table crammed next to an elegant looking glass. A band called The Dixieland Entertainers was playing Scott Joplin's 'The Easy Winners', and the smell of pastry and freshly baked bread wafted through the air. This working-class Versailles was one of the capital's most popular haunts, with hardly a spare seat to be found. He pushed his way through the maze of tables, and had to apologise to a wide-hipped nippy for knocking her tray, and almost sending a teapot and crockery flying over a pair of smart young chaps whose lamb cutlets lay untouched on their plates. The men were so engrossed in their conversation that they didn't even notice that they'd almost been drenched in scalding hot tea. The nippy gave Jacob a cheeky wink, and he couldn't help blushing.

Since coming to London, he'd heard talk that the vast corner houses here and in Piccadilly Circus were haunts favoured by men of Oliver McAlinden's persuasion. The waitresses often took pity on them, guiding fellows towards tables occupied by other single men, so they had the chance to strike up conversation in the most innocent fashion. Jacob glanced round, wondering if anybody would think he and Oakes were playing that game. Would the inspector rather be presumed to be looking out for male company than exchanging information with the *Clarion*'s newly anointed chief crime correspondent? Surely not, judging by Stan Thurlow's lurid accounts of the savage treatment meted out in police prison cells to those suspected of unnatural practices.

Oakes stubbed out his cigarette, and put down the menu he'd pretended to study, but made no attempt to shake hands. 'I ordered tomato soup and a bread roll for both of us,' he said brusquely. 'No point in wasting time.'

'Why all the secrecy? There's no shame in meeting a journalist, you know. Police officers often talk to the press.'

'You're no ordinary member of the press, Mr Flint. I never knew a reporter with such an uncanny gift for sniffing out a story.' There was no mirth in Oakes' smile. 'Three times in a week, you've been at the scene when a man has died.'

'Hope you don't find that suspicious, Inspector?' Jacob's genial tone disguised anxiety. Oakes' manner today was distinctly less cordial. 'Pardoe's body was being taken to the morgue by the time I arrived at South Audley Street. Shoemaker bundled me out of his office before he was attacked. I was one of a large audience which witnessed the horror of Keary's death.'

'You were sitting in the most luxurious box in the house, right next to Miss Rachel Savernake.'

'What of it? She was Keary's guest, and she invited me along.'

'Why?'

'To be honest, I've no idea. I hoped to speak to her after the show, but Keary's death put paid to that. As for the three deaths, you're well aware that I had nothing to do with any of them. Pardoe shot himself in a locked room, Shoemaker was attacked by brutes, and Keary's murderer died while fleeing from justice. Speaking of Barnes, what in heaven's name was his motive?'

Oakes fiddled with his napkin. 'We can't ask him for an explanation. Perhaps even he couldn't explain himself. And I doubt he could cast light on the connection between Miss Savernake and Keary. I'm hoping you can help me fill in the gaps.'

'The message from Rachel Savernake making the appointment came out of the blue. I'd been trying in vain to talk to her.'

'What about?'

Behind Oakes' head was a large mirror, and Jacob checked to make sure that his expression betrayed no lack of candour. He'd resolved to keep quiet about his meeting with Sara Delamere. She'd dreaded talking to the police even before the horror of becoming an unwitting accomplice in the murder of William Keary.

'I want to write about her.' It was the truth, if far from the whole truth. 'Our readers would love a story about a well-born lady playing the detective game. To my amazement, her chauffeur picked me up and took me to the Inanity.'

'How did Rachel Savernake behave when it became clear the final illusion had turned into a tragedy?'

'She... said next to nothing.'

'Surely she was shocked? Upset?'

An obscure instinct warned Jacob to choose his words with care. 'I really can't tell you anything more.'

Oakes scowled as a ginger-haired nippy, resplendent in black alpaca dress, white apron, and starched hat, arrived with their soup. The success of the corner houses was built upon inexpensive but wholesome fare, and neither man spoke again until their bowls were empty, and the band had launched into the 'Maple Leaf Rag'.

'I suppose there is one thing.' Jacob wiped his mouth with a paper napkin. 'When... when the illusion went wrong, everyone else was panicking, but Miss Savernake's calm was uncanny. If it wasn't absurd, I could almost believe she was expecting something horrific to happen.'

'As you say,' Oakes muttered, 'that would be absurd.'

'Flinty?'

After returning to Clarion House, Jacob scarcely expected a further call from Scotland Yard, but Stanley Thurlow's voice was unmistakable, even when he spoke in a hoarse whisper.

'I need to talk to you.'

'What's up?'

Thurlow cleared his throat so noisily he might have been preparing to make a speech at Hyde Park Corner, but when he spoke, it was sotto voce.

'It's like this, Flinty. I've... I've got myself into a spot of bother.'

Jacob caught his breath. So he'd been right.

'Sorry to hear that, Stan. What's the problem?'

'It's... well, it's a real pickle, Flinty. Bloody awful, actually. For you, too. You already know too much. Can't talk over the phone. I'm at the Yard right now, and someone might walk in.'

'Shall we meet?'

'Yes.' Thurlow coughed. 'Yes, please.'

'Usual place?'

'No, Flinty. It needs to be somewhere different, out of town. If I'm followed, I'll have to shake them off. Besides, they know about the Essex Head.'

'Who are they?' Jacob asked. 'You sound windy, Stan. What's eating you?'

There was a long pause. 'I don't mind admitting, Flinty, I've got the heebie-jeebies, good and proper. I'm in over my head. I'd never have dragged you into this mess otherwise.'

Jacob dug his nails into his palms. 'What do you want?'

'Are you free tonight? Lily's brother has a bungalow out in Benfleet, an hour from London. Quiet spot, and he's away at the moment. We ought to go separately. You take the train from Fenchurch Street, and I'll drive.'

'Never knew you had a car, Stan.'

'Ford Roadster. Lovely motor, Flinty, rumble seat and all. Cost a few bob, but worth every penny.' Thurlow's voice brightened, before fading in a heartbeat. 'S'pose I got carried away.'

'Where is this bungalow?'

'Creek Lane. Stone's throw from the station, you can't miss it. Eight thirty?'

'I'll be there.'

'Thanks, Flinty, you're a pal.' Thurlow hesitated. 'One other thing.'

'Tell me.'

'For God's sake, make sure nobody follows you.'

19

Jacob's phone rang again the moment he replaced the receiver. A lady, he was told, calling on behalf of Miss Rachel Savernake.

'Put her through.'

Mrs Trueman didn't believe in wasting time on niceties. 'Miss Savernake can see you this evening. Nine o'clock sharp. She says—'

'I'm sorry,' Jacob interrupted. 'It's very good of her, but unfortunately this evening is impossible. I'm committed to another pressing engagement.'

In the silence that followed, Jacob exulted. The callow cub reporter had become chief crime correspondent for the *Clarion*. Scotland Yard inspectors consulted him, erring detective constables begged for his support. Rachel Savernake must take her turn in the queue.

'Cancel it.'

Had he over-reached himself? He was desperate to discover what Rachel was up to. Her behaviour at the Inanity seemed intensely suspicious, even if he didn't know what to suspect her of. Yet letting Thurlow down was unthinkable. If the woman wanted to speak to him, she'd try again. He wasn't her poodle.

'Out of the question, I'm afraid. I've promised to keep the appointment. Is Miss Savernake free tomorrow?'

The phone went dead.

'*You already know too much.*'

If only Thurlow were right, Jacob reflected, pulling his coat off the hook. This evening, by rights, he ought to be out celebrating his elevation to Tom Betts' old role, but he had too much on his plate. For a newly promoted (and thus, by definition, successful) journalist, the scale of his ignorance was hard to exaggerate. Rachel Savernake's behaviour became more mysterious by the day. He could only hope she'd still talk to him tomorrow.

As he strode down the corridor, colleagues kept stopping him to congratulate him on the new job. Their generosity humbled him. Oily McAlinden, he noticed, had made himself scarce. Consumed by jealousy? Jacob didn't care. All that mattered was making sense of what he knew.

On impulse he decided that, rather than going straight back to Amwell Street, he would make a detour. Outside Clarion House, he turned in the direction of Lincoln's Inn, and headed for Gallows Court. Darkness had fallen, and the cold night air needled his skin. Halting at the end of the dank passageway, he peered through the gloom for any sign of Hannaway or his cadaverous minion. The lamps shed a sulky yellow glow over the silent yard. Not a soul was to be seen. People only visited this place if they had no choice, and they fled the instant their business was done.

Jacob scampered across the cobbles to the doorway to Hannaway's chambers. Apprehension made his neck prickle. Did burglars feel so nakedly conspicuous, dreading a policeman's whistle, and the grip of a hand like a vice?

An inconspicuous plate beside the front door bore the name *Gaunt Chambers*. Judge Savernake must have worked here during his years at the Bar. The names of organisations registered at this building were painted in neat black italics on a long, white vertical board, the same kind which elsewhere in the Inn listed members of a set of barristers. He scanned the list, and found himself rejoicing. The vague memory of his previous visit, the obscure instinct that had drawn him back to Gallows Court, had been founded in fact. Names jumped out.

Inanity Theatre Limited, The William Keary Talent Agency, Pardoe Properties, The Oxford Orphans' Trust, Linacre Investments.

Some were new to him: *Harley Street Holdings, The Amalgamated Workers' Union Welfare Fund, The Soho Land Acquisitions Company, The Gambit Club.*

Cog wheels clicked in his brain. *Pardoe Properties* – hadn't Oakes told him that Mary-Jane Hayes had met her end in a house owned by a company controlled by the banker?

Click, click, click.

The Gambit Club, Gaunt Chambers, Gallows Court.

GC, GC, GC.

Or alternatively, *CGCGCG* in reverse. Had Levi Shoemaker intended his cipher to lead Jacob here?

Jacob scuttled out of Gallows Court. Logic told him that the cipher must be straightforward. Shoemaker had barely hesitated before writing it out. He must have made it up on the spur of the moment. Surely that must mean the code was really very simple.

CGCGCG91192PIRVYBC

A newspaper vendor made a fruitless attempt to sell him a copy of the *Evening News*. From habit, Jacob glanced at the front page. What struck him was not the bold headline about the tragedy at the Inanity, but the date above it. An idea sprang into his mind.

If Shoemaker meant the cipher to be read backwards, might the numbers represent 29 January 1919? He couldn't imagine why Shoemaker would be concerned about anything dating back more than a decade. But the unravelling process had to start somewhere. The letters were a puzzle, but it occurred to him that RIP might stand for *Requiescat In Pace*. Had Shoemaker meant to alert him to the death of someone with the initials CBYV?

Returning to Clarion House, he decided to test his theory, and sought out Trithemius, an exceptionally fat man seldom seen without a cake or a bun in his hand. His real name was Toseland, and he was the *Clarion*'s puzzle specialist, a compiler of crosswords, acrostics, and assorted brain-teasers designed to take readers' mind off everyday woes such as whether they were about to be cast into the dole queue. The pseudonym came from a fifteenth-century German abbot with a penchant for cryptography.

'Little conundrum for you,' Jacob said, handing Toseland the scrap of paper on which Shoemaker had jotted down his code. 'I have a theory about what it means, but I'd like to test it out.'

Toseland swallowed what remained of a chocolate eclair, and glanced at the cipher. 'Any clues?'

'I'm sure the message isn't complex. The man who wrote this made it up on the spur of the moment.' Jacob debated how much to reveal. 'Your clue is Gallows Court.'

'That dingy hole in Lincoln's Inn?' Toseland was as well informed as Poyser.

'Spot on.'

'Leave it with me.' Toseland wiped chocolate from his chin with the back of his sleeve. 'I'm up to my eyes with our next bumper puzzle book, but I'll get round to it tomorrow.'

Jacob thanked him, and headed home. The previous night, having filed his story about Keary's death, he'd returned to Edgar House in the small hours, tiptoeing up the stairs to avoid disturbing Mrs Dowd or Elaine, cringing at every creak and groan of the floorboards. This morning, by the time he'd hauled himself out of bed and got ready for breakfast, Elaine had already left for work. Mrs Dowd had been uncharacteristically monosyllabic. A strong smell of gin clinging to her suggested she'd spent the previous evening drinking herself into oblivion. He could have crashed a pair of cymbals all the way up to bed and still not woken her.

On arriving back at Edgar House, he popped his head into the kitchen, and was dismayed to find Mrs Dowd in a state of distress. Her pink face was tear-stained and blotchy, her thinning hair in disarray. The kitchen was, as always, clean and tidy, but she hadn't remembered to hide her glass of gin, or the half-empty bottle of Gordon's on the table.

'Anything wrong?'

'Elaine and I have fallen out. She's flounced off in a real huff.'

'Sorry to hear that.'

'You didn't…' Mrs Dowd bit her lip. 'I hate to ask, but did you and Elaine have a quarrel?'

'About the fact I couldn't take her out? Not really. I did my best to explain and apologise. Why do you ask?'

'Nothing.' Her tone was lacklustre. 'Would you like some tea?'

What on earth had Elaine said? 'I don't want to put you to any trouble.'

'Oh, it's no bother. It'll take my mind off things. How about a nice omelette?'

'That's very kind.' He hesitated. 'What did Elaine…?'

'Please, Jacob. I'm not in a fit state to be cross-examined. I've given you the wrong impression. Elaine is all right. Everything is as it should be.'

She avoided his eye, fixing her gaze on the linoleum floor, an unhappy, gin-sodden woman, to whom disappointment clung like a cheap, pungent scent.

On the way to Fenchurch Street, and even when making his purchase at the ticket office, Jacob experienced the uncomfortable, tickling sensation of being watched. Yet each time he glanced over his shoulder, nobody suspicious was taking an interest in him. Oakes and Thurlow had done more than put him on his guard, he decided; their warnings had induced a touch of paranoia.

No need to worry, he reflected, as he finally got off the train at Benfleet, venturing out of the brightly lit station, and into the darkness. The landscape was flat, and a short distance from the railway line ran a wide creek, presumably an inlet of the Thames estuary. The moon and a scattering of stars cast a glow to soften the bleak emptiness of the marshlands, but he was glad he'd taken the precaution of bringing a torch. The beam illuminated a penny-in-the-slot water pump, and a cinder track leading towards a ferryman's cottage and workings for a new bridge. Even this lonely spot would soon surrender to the march of progress. At present, there was no made-up road, just a narrow grass lane snaking away from the cinders and alongside the creek.

An owl hooted. Fancifully, he interpreted it as yet another warning. A small creature, perhaps a fox, scrabbled unseen near the water's edge. The lane was soft and muddy, and he could smell the moist earth. Just as well he'd changed his shoes for a pair of sturdy boots at Amwell Street. His torch picked out a small wooden building designed in the manner of a seaside chalet. A verandah ran along the front of the house, and a few yards away stood a large rainwater tank. The grass lane petered out at the bungalow's gate, with a sleek Ford Roadster parked next to a ragged hedge. Thurlow was right; it looked a lovely motor. But how much had it cost him?

The curtains weren't drawn. No lights shone at the windows, and Jacob couldn't even detect the flickering of a candle. There would be no gas or electricity at such a remote spot, and he supposed paraffin was used for fuel. Lengthening his stride, he approached the bungalow, but detected no sign of life. Was Thurlow so panic-stricken that he was hiding at the back of the house?

Jacob walked up to the front door, and rapped three times. When nothing happened, he lifted the letterbox flap, and called, 'Are you there?'

The door gave when he leaned against it. Jacob shone his torch on a narrow vestibule with a closed door on either side, and a third standing ajar that was evidently the way in to the kitchen.

'Stan? I'm here.' He consulted his watch. 'Bang on time.'

Nothing stirred.

He pushed open the door to his left, and shone his torch inside. The room was sparsely furnished with a small sofa, a single armchair, and a sideboard. Lying on the sofa was the body of a man. His frame was so bulky that his long legs hung over the end of the sofa, and touched the matting on the floor. Blood had spurted from a cruel wound in his stomach. Another ugly gash disfigured his neck.

Stanley Thurlow had been right to be afraid.

Shock paralysed Jacob. He didn't need to touch the corpse to see there was nothing he could do. The young constable's eyes were staring sightlessly at the ceiling.

An unpleasant odour tainted the air. It seemed familiar, yet mysteriously out of place. In his numb state, Jacob could not identify it.

The trembling of his hand made his torch beam waver. It caught a woman's pointed red shoe, peeping out from behind the sofa. Swallowing hard, he forced himself to move forward a couple of paces, so that he could see the shoe's owner.

The body sprawled on the threadbare carpet belonged to a young woman with vivid red hair. Her green silk blouse was ripped and blood-stained. Her white throat had been slashed.

But it was not merely the sight of the butchered corpse that made Jacob retch. Even worse was a sickening horror of recognition.

He was staring at the earthly remains of Elaine Dowd.

Juliet Brentano's Journal

3 February 1919

Another dreadful day. Henrietta is beside herself.

Harold Brown is back from London. He arrived in a wild and drunken state. No doubt he'd spent his thirty pieces of silver in the capital's dens of vice.

When he heard Cliff was sick, he laughed. It seemed like mere nastiness. Now it is clear why the news pleased him.

Henrietta says he hurried back across the causeway and into the village, where Cliff's sister lives with their mother. Apparently he's done something terrible to the girl.

'Where is it going to end?' Henrietta said, and burst into tears.

Poor, brave Henrietta. I have never seen her so wretched. And I too dread to think how it will end.

20

The sight of Elaine's lifeless corpse hit Jacob like a truncheon blow. Tottering, he clutched the sofa to prevent himself crumpling on the floor in a heap. Shock and disbelief made him groggy. His throat had never felt so dry. Even if he'd tried to scream, he could barely have managed a yelp of pain. A single coherent thought formed in his mind.

Keep quiet. Whoever did this is still here.

He'd trodden on something. Looking down, he saw the torch beam pick out a large carving knife. The cruel blade was dark with the blood of Thurlow and Elaine. With a jolt of recognition, he realised that the knife's badly chipped black handle was identical to one in Mrs Dowd's kitchen. It couldn't be a coincidence. His first instinct was to pick it up, but a muddled instinct for self-preservation stopped him even as he bent over. Instead he shifted his foot, and switched off his torch.

He'd seen enough.

What was that? He strained his ears. Outside the room, someone was moving. He heard soft, cautious footsteps. The murderer was wearing shoes with soles of rubber rather than leather. He was in the hall, preparing to kill for a third time.

Jacob's temples throbbed. He was crouching in the dark, with the corpses of a man and woman he'd called his friends for company. The horror of the deaths he must shove to one side. All that mattered now was life. He must survive.

He had no weapon, only his bare hands to defend himself, and he'd never been any good at fighting. Was the killer still armed, or had he only come here with the knife? Holding his breath, afraid to make a sound, he tiptoed forwards.

The door creaked.

Hypnotised, Jacob watched as slowly, slowly, it began to open. He dared not move another inch. The only light was cast by the moon, a sliver of brightness falling through the window. He caught another whiff of that strangely familiar greasy odour that he'd noticed on entering the room.

He heard the rubber soles move again. The door opened wider, and suddenly the murderer was framed in the doorway. His frightened eyes were visible in the moonlight.

Oliver McAlinden, whose hair oil gave the atmosphere its malodorous tang, was pointing a small black revolver straight at Jacob's stomach.

Vincent Hannaway was ensconced in a leather armchair in the oak-panelled members' room at the Gambit Club. After signing the last correspondence of the day in his office, he'd trotted up the members' staircase to the club's premises. In the tiny private restaurant, he'd feasted on a wonderfully tender and bloody steak, followed by floating island dessert washed down with the finest Imperial Tokay, before settling down to transact a small amount of business while enjoying a Cuban cigar. A servant had placed a telephone on the rosewood table by his side, and he spoke quietly into the receiver, so as not to disturb two distinguished colleagues who were passing the time with a game of chess prior to enjoying the more recondite privileges of club membership.

'I have no news as yet. Be patient.'

'I've always had doubts about McAlinden. He's unreliable. Like so many of his sort.'

'Watch your words. His sort, as you call them, include several distinguished members of our fraternity. And of course his father—'

'Is a fine man, goes without saying. It's simply the question of the son's reliability…'

'This is an acid test. Before tonight's out, we'll know what stuff he's made of.'

'You'll notify me as soon as you hear?'

A bookcase facing Hannaway slid to one side, revealing a well-lit corridor wallpapered in the rose and pink style of William Morris. This was one of several concealed exits from the Gambit Club's rooms. Ultimately they led, by circuitous routes, to unmarked doors opening out into Carey Street and Chancery Lane, rather than Gallows Court. A young Chinese woman, whose white satin gown contrasted with her waist-length black hair, stood in the entrance to the passageway. Her delicate red lips formed in a polite, enquiring smile, and Hannaway inclined his head.

'Let me call you later.' He frowned at the receiver. 'In the meantime, I must ask you not to telephone me here again. Please assure me that you aren't losing your nerve.'

'There's no question of that, believe me. I merely—'

'I'm glad to hear it. With so much crime about, Scotland Yard needs you to be at your sharpest.'

The hand in which McAlinden held the gun was shaking. Jacob thought: *He's almost as scared as me.*

'Lie down on the floor, and close your eyes.'

McAlinden sounded like a schoolboy actor, terrified of fluffing lines so painstakingly rehearsed.

'Oliver. What have you done?'

'What have I done?' McAlinden's voice was pitched high. 'I've earned my spurs, that's what I've done. I've committed the perfect murder. Three times.'

Jacob felt the muscles in his face tightening. 'I don't understand.'

'You stabbed Thurlow and that trollop Elaine with a knife you stole from your lodgings, then shot yourself in the mouth while suffering a fit of overdue remorse.' McAlinden giggled. 'Only your fingerprints will be found on the gun. Perfect, eh?'

Once, at school, Jacob had been lashed on his bare buttocks when a schoolmaster seized on a minor misdemeanour to gratify himself by inflicting pain. Not since that whipping had anything hurt as much as McAlinden's needling glee. It wasn't enough for McAlinden that he was to die. He was to be condemned as a cowardly murderer who committed suicide to escape the wrath of the law. A poor man's Lawrence Pardoe.

'Oliver, please.'

'Please?' McAlinden's hand had steadied. Jacob had no idea what to do, other than play for time, and hope for a miracle. 'What have you ever done for me?'

Was it possible to jump at him, and knock the gun away before he squeezed the trigger? Anything was better than tame surrender to a bullet in the mouth. To have a chance, he must edge closer to his target.

'Don't move!' McAlinden screeched.

'What on earth is all this about?' Jacob asked. 'Tell me that, at least, before you...'

A smile sidled across McAlinden's moonlit features.

'The Damnation Society, of course. Don't pretend you don't know anything about it.'

Jacob stared. He had no idea what the fellow was talking about.

McAlinden raised the gun. 'Now, lie down. If you are good, I'll settle your hash quickly. If not... I'll make a real mess of you.'

Jacob tensed, preparing to jump at his enemy.

Suddenly something happened. A loud explosion ripped the air, and McAlinden pitched forward, firing the revolver as he fell. Flinching, Jacob shut his eyes, and hurled himself to one side. Colliding with the floor jarred his shoulder, but he felt nothing else. Not the pain of a bullet tearing through his flesh, for sure. The shot had missed.

Relief surged through him like a tidal wave, but before he could wrench open his eyes, a powerful hand seized his neck. Thick fingers pressed into his windpipe, and something hard hammered against his head.

The rest was black nothingness.

'Can I get you anything else?' Mrs Trueman asked.

'That is three times you've asked in the last hour.' Rachel looked up from *The Beautiful and the Damned*. A cheerful fire warmed the sitting room while Bing Crosby crooned on the wireless. 'Stop fretting. If you persist with your embroidery, instead of breaking off every five minutes, the results will be delightful.'

'I'm a bag of nerves tonight.'

'I've noticed,' Rachel said lazily.

'I'd go to bed, but I'd not get a wink of sleep.'

'Pour yourself a glass of whisky, and the world will seem a better place.'

The older woman snorted. 'Confidence is all fine and dandy, but don't get complacent.'

'Listen.' Noting her place with a tasselled bookmark, Rachel fixed her gaze on the housekeeper. 'We agreed what must be done. There's nothing more for either of us to do, except wait.'

'How can you remain so calm?' the older woman demanded.

'You'd prefer hysterical whimpering? I've waited for years for this, don't forget. A few more hours are nothing.'

'It's not just a matter of a few more hours, is it?' Mrs Trueman's face was as bleak as winter. 'When will we see an end to it?'

'On Wednesday, actually,' Rachel said. 'Be patient. Soon it will be over. I'll have done what I set out to do.'

How long Jacob remained unconscious, he never knew. As he began to come round, he forced open his eyes, although it took a supreme effort of will. His whole body was hurting, and something strange had been done to him. Blinking, he realised he was out in the cold night air. The moon had disappeared, and he seemed to be alone. But he was helpless. He'd been draped head-first over the side of the large iron tank he'd glimpsed on his approach to the bungalow.

His head was so sore that he wanted to cry out in pain, but his mouth had been taped to prevent him making a sound. Something was cutting into his wrists and ankles, and he realised he'd been tied up with a strong cord. Even if he tried to free himself of his bonds, he'd have no chance of success. Movement carried danger. What if he fell into the rain-water tank?

The tank was ten feet deep, and the bottom third was filled with foetid water. His body was precariously balanced. If he slipped over the side of the tank, he would drown.

Gingerly, he lifted his head until he could just about peer over the edge of the tank. There was a small platform of half-bricks, on which his assailant must have stood to position him like this. Looking round, he saw the bungalow's back door, open and swinging in the night breeze.

A catarrhal snort of satisfaction came from inside. Jacob didn't know whether to be glad that he'd not been abandoned to his fate, or terrified of what lay in store. He had no idea who was in the building. It took a few moments for him to remember that Elaine and Thurlow were dead.

Oily McAlinden, of all people, was a murderer.

Or had he dreamed it all? Were his lurid mental pictures of the bloodstained corpses no more than a perverted night-mare? On such a surreal night, he could not be confident of anything.

A loud noise from inside the house shattered the quiet. A single gunshot.

Holding his breath, Jacob glimpsed a shadow in the doorway. Someone was emerging through the back door.

Jacob's helpless body tightened in a spasm of fear.

21

'Better now?' Rachel asked.

Mrs Trueman drained the tumbler of Glenlivet, and put it down on the small burled walnut table. 'You have something in common with the Judge.'

Rachel savoured her whisky. 'Really?'

'You know a fine malt when you taste one.'

Rachel gave an ironic little bow. 'You alarmed me. I thought you were suggesting that despicable old tyrant and I share the same mental kink.'

'You're as sane as me or Trueman.'

'Should I find that comforting?'

The older woman's face creased in a reluctant smile. 'Probably not.'

'How much of one's nature is formed by heredity, and how much by life's experiences?' Rachel closed her eyes. 'I wonder.'

'It's not like you to sound unsure.'

'I hoped an admission of frailty might remind you that I'm human.'

'Oh, you're human, right enough. I remember your face the night that vile man demanded money as the price for his silence about Juliet Brentano.'

Rachel opened her eyes again, but said nothing.

'White as a blessed sheet, you were. Trying to fathom how much he knew, how much he'd guessed.'

Rachel breathed out. 'He got what he deserved.'

The housekeeper nodded. 'You're decisive, I'll give you that. But even now, we can't be sure, can we? We'll never be safe. Never.'

'Fearing the worst is futile.' Rachel's voice rose. 'Remember, by Wednesday, it will be over. Look at what we've achieved already. Pardoe and Keary are dead. As for Claude Linacre...'

'And what about Betts? Or Levi Shoemaker?'

'Casualties of warfare.'

'And Barnes?'

'He – he wanted to die. Your husband told us so, remember?'

'Even so...'

Rachel's voice sharpened. 'We've always known the truth about life. Even the innocent suffer. Usually, they suffer most of all.'

Mrs Trueman shook her head. 'It's not easy to bear.'

'No.' Rachel reached for the older woman's hand, and squeezed it. 'There is nothing easy about justice.'

'That sounds like the Judge talking.'

'Some of the people he condemned to death were actually guilty.'

'What about Jacob Flint?'

'What about him?'

'He'll be no great shakes in a rough house.'

Rachel shrugged. 'I can't help that.'

'And if he dies tonight?'

Rachel didn't answer.

The man who came out from the bungalow was broad-shouldered, and over six feet tall. Dressed from head to toe in black, he wore a stocking mask with slits for his eyes and mouth. A gun nestled in his massive palm. As he marched towards the tank, he ripped off the mask.

Jacob let out a gasp, and Rachel Savernake's chauffeur scowled at him.

'Don't talk,' Trueman said. 'I'm going to lift you down. Be very careful. One sign of trouble, and into the water you go. Head-first.'

Jacob held his breath. The big man lifted him as if he were a ragdoll, and set him on the ground.

'Behave.' Trueman thrust the gun's nozzle between Jacob's ribs. 'I've used this once tonight. What difference would a second shot make? To me, nothing. To you, everything.'

They were standing on a cinder track, a quarter of a mile from the bungalow. There was no sign of the Phantom in which Trueman had taken him to the Inanity, but a rusty Bullnose Morris four-seater was parked by the hedge. Trueman's clothes were shabby. No chauffeur's livery for him tonight.

What about McAlinden? He was nowhere to be seen. Jacob couldn't help opening his mouth again.

'Why—'

'Didn't you hear?' The gun dug into Jacob's guts. '*Don't talk.*'

Jacob's head was throbbing, and the cord was still cutting his wrists. He ought to be glad to be alive, but the night's events had left him not only bewildered but sickened.

'I'll untie your hands, and shove you in the back of the car. You'll find some bits of a broken bicycle in there, push them out of your way. Get some sleep; you look as if you need it. I'll keep off the main roads, and I don't expect anyone will stop us, but if we drop unlucky, keep your mouth shut. I'll make up a story. Probably say you're drunk and incapable. Whatever I do, go along with it. I've nothing to lose. Understand?'

Jacob nodded. Incapable, yes, he certainly felt incapable.

'Don't try anything clever.' Trueman jerked a thumb in the direction of the bungalow. 'I saved your life, but remember this. What you're given can always be taken away.'

The long drive through darkness was a nightmare that Jacob thought would never end. Even seated behind a steering wheel, Trueman radiated menace. He might be heading for some other godforsaken spot, to dispose quietly of his passenger. Exhaustion and misery had mashed Jacob's brain, but he'd seen enough of Trueman to know it would be fatal to provoke him. As they bumped along endless country lanes and side roads, he obeyed the order to keep his mouth shut. Soon he was dozing fitfully, his mind infested with nauseating images of the blood-soaked corpses of the policeman he'd drunk with, and the girl he'd kissed.

Although Trueman had anticipated that they'd be stopped, nobody interrupted their journey. Eventually it came to an end in the heart of London. Trueman stopped the car outside Rachel's house in the square, and bundled him up the steps.

The front door was opened by a comfortably built woman whose expression betrayed relief, but no sign of surprise. This must be the housekeeper he'd spoken to on the telephone. She'd been expecting them.

'You look as though you could do with a nip of brandy, Mr Flint. Come inside. Miss Savernake will join you presently, once Trueman has done the necessary with the car.'

'Thank... thank you.' His voice sounded scratchy and old. He had no idea what doing the necessary entailed.

The woman led him into the drawing room, poured brandy into a tumbler, and departed. Framed paintings adorned the walls: nudes, claustrophobic interiors, and music hall scenes. Their sombre hues matched Jacob's mood. He downed the brandy without bothering to savour its tang, and poured himself another from the decanter thoughtfully left on the table.

Sipping more slowly this time, he tried to interpret his surroundings. Did they reveal anything about their owner? Not much, he concluded, only that she was very rich, and her tastes ran to art deco furniture and macabre modern art.

What had brought Trueman to Benfleet? The murders hadn't disconcerted him. Was McAlinden working for Rachel? Or did she know that McAlinden was a deranged madman, and if so, how on earth was it any business of hers? He couldn't fathom it.

Ten minutes passed before the door opened again, and Trueman strode in. He was followed by his wife, and a housemaid. None of them spoke, but the younger woman watched carefully as Jacob took in the sight of her ruined cheek. It reminded him of a girl from the slums of Leeds whose face had been destroyed by acid. He'd reported on her trial for stabbing the man who had attacked her.

He swallowed hard, sensing that he was being subjected to some kind of test. He mustn't betray emotion, not pity, nor disgust, nor even rage that anyone could have been so inhuman as to spoil the young woman's loveliness. According to Betts, Rachel only employed three servants. Were they not so much loyal retainers as conspirators in murder?

Rachel Savernake walked through the door, and gave Jacob a wry smile.

'Good evening, Mr Flint. Alive and well, I see. Congratulations. You've just committed the perfect crime.'

'I don't understand…' Jacob began.

'That's the story of your life, isn't it?' Rachel interrupted. 'You may not think so, Mr Flint, but this is your lucky day. Thanks to Trueman, you've escaped death by the skin of your teeth.'

The back of Jacob's head was throbbing. He rubbed it gingerly.

'What's more, I've decided to take you into my confidence. Against my better judgement.'

Jacob cleared his throat. 'I suppose I should be flattered.'

'There is, of course, a catch.'

'Which is?'

Rachel leaned forward in her chair. 'You will never write about what I am going to tell you. Is that agreed?'

Jacob shifted. 'I don't—'

'Let me be clear,' she said. 'This isn't a negotiation.'

'An ultimatum, then?'

She shrugged. 'Call it whatever you wish. Do I have your word?'

Trueman, sitting between his wife and the maid on the vast settee, made a scornful noise which Jacob had no difficulty in interpreting. *The word of a journalist is worth nothing.*

'I suppose so.'

'If it's any consolation, you're not making a significant concession. This story you could never publish.'

'If you say so.' Jacob was becoming mulish. He was alive, but Elaine was dead. In all his life, he'd never felt so weary and depressed.

'I do,' Rachel said. 'In fairness, I should point out that your personal situation is somewhat... compromised.'

Jacob glanced at Trueman. The big man's fists were clenched tight. His tension was palpable. He seemed to be readying himself for a fight.

'Are you threatening me?'

'How dare you be so crude?' Rachel's tone sharpened. 'You owe your life to Trueman, make no mistake. It would have been so easy for him to allow Oliver McAlinden to kill you.'

'Where is McAlinden? Is he dead?'

'He won't trouble you again.'

Jacob felt his gorge rise. He turned to Trueman. 'You murdered him.'

'McAlinden suffered the fate he'd intended for you,' Rachel said. 'Ironic, isn't it?'

'How did he know I'd be there?'

'Someone told him that Thurlow had persuaded you to come to Benfleet.'

'You mean it was a conspiracy?' Jacob's eyes widened. 'Were Thurlow and McAlinden in it together?'

'Up to their necks, but neither of them was pulling the strings. Thurlow in particular was out of his depth, and wanted to make a clean breast of things to you. I suppose he thought Elaine would help encourage you to keep his own misdemeanours quiet in return for the promise of a story. A good newspaperman always protects his sources, isn't that your motto?'

'What does Elaine…?'

'Thurlow's fatal error was to let his unhappiness become obvious to others. He'd outlived his usefulness. So had Elaine. And so had you.'

Jacob closed his eyes. 'Glad to hear I was considered useful at one time, at least.'

'Not for long. When you joined the *Clarion*, McAlinden presumed you'd be much more malleable than Betts. He took you under his wing, but quickly discovered you were determined to be your own man.'

'So he dropped me?'

'Never mind, this story has a happy ending. The police will find his corpse, together with the other two bodies, and they have a genius for drawing obvious conclusions.'

'Double murder, followed by suicide?'

'Precisely. A verdict that will, I predict, be supported by expert forensic evidence from that distinguished pathologist Mr Rufus Paul. Stanley Thurlow was having an illicit liaison with Elaine Dowd. You knew she'd recently been entangled with a married man?'

Jacob gaped at her. 'I… well, yes. But I had no idea that her lover was Stanley.'

'I suppose not. McAlinden lodged at Edgar House prior to your arrival there, didn't he?'

'As a matter of fact, he recommended the place to me.'

'Of course he did. How useful for his masters to have a promising young journalist living where Elaine could keep an eye on him.'

'You're surely not saying that Elaine was…?'

'All in good time, Mr Flint. As I say, the police can construct a plausible narrative. McAlinden carried a torch for Elaine Dowd, but she preferred to consort with a young policeman destined for a rapid rise through the ranks. After McAlinden moved out, she dallied with you to blind him to the truth, but the affair continued, and McAlinden found out. He'd kept a key to Edgar House, let himself back in secretly, and stole a knife from the kitchen, before following the couple to their trysting place in Benfleet, where he killed them in a jealous rage before shooting himself in the face. An open and shut case. No need to look for anyone else.'

Jacob took a deep breath. 'Good God.'

'Embarrassing for the *Clarion*, to have their journalists involved in an eternal triangle murder case, but their readers are famously broad-minded. Who knows? It may even benefit circulation. McAlinden himself is no loss. He lacked your talent as a journalist, and came to hate you.'

Her face was a mask, just as on the night of their first encounter. Try as he might, he could not see through it.

'Is that so?'

She sighed. 'Well, I've described one version of events in Benfleet, but it's conceivable that the authorities might come up with an alternative scenario. Would you like to hear it?'

Something in her voice reminded him of the hollowness in his stomach.

'I'm all ears.'

'Elaine Dowd was liberal with her favours. She—'

'She was convivial, warm-hearted,' Jacob interrupted. 'You shouldn't defame her, now that she's dead, and isn't able to defend her good name.'

Rachel gave him a withering look. 'She charmed you, as she'd bewitched Thurlow and McAlinden. You knew the other men, and had an uneasy relationship with both of them. Thurlow was a source of useful titbits of information, and you paid him for them. It would not be too much of a stretch to construct an unedifying story about the bond between a venal copper who lived far beyond his means and an unscrupulous reporter with overweening ambition.'

Jacob swallowed hard. 'I bought him the occasional drink, that's all.'

'A little more than that, surely? Thurlow's widow will confirm the extent of your generosity.'

'I never even met her!'

'She's even less intelligent than her husband. He told her that you funded the purchase of his new car, and a good deal else beside. The Chancellor of the Exchequer has taken an axe to the pay of policemen, yet your friend has prospered. To his wife, he portrayed his special relationship with the press as the most valuable perk of the job.'

'It isn't true!'

'Surely your years in journalism have taught you that the truth takes many forms. Reality is in the eye of the beholder.'

'Whoever greased Thurlow's palm, it wasn't me.'

'I believe you, but if the authorities are put on enquiry, they will be less sympathetic.'

'It's outrageous!' Anger choked him. 'Utterly unfair.'

Rachel shrugged. 'Life is unfair. You're old enough to have learned that. As for McAlinden, you and he were competitors, riven by ambition. It was common knowledge that you disliked each other. Quite apart from your shared admiration for Elaine.'

'McAlinden wasn't interested in women.'

'You may defame him, and claim he was a pansy. On another view, he was merely a libertine who loved to smash taboos. Perhaps he encouraged you to do likewise.'

'Preposterous!'

'How can you say so,' Rachel enquired pleasantly, 'when you and he spent an evening at the Gay Gordon Night Club in Wardour Street together? It's a notorious haunt, positively infamous. Young and new to London you may be. Even so, why on earth weren't you more circumspect?'

Jacob groaned. 'I won't ask how you know about that night.'

'It's enough that I do know. My understanding is that you didn't disgrace yourself, but I wouldn't be surprised if witnesses come forward who tell a very different story. Anyway. There is, of course, much more to be said. You could have stolen the knife as easily as McAlinden.'

'But I...'

'And when the police attend the bungalow, they'll come across fingerprints that don't belong to the three dead bodies at the scene. Naturally, they will be curious.'

Jacob pointed to Trueman. 'I wasn't the only one at the bungalow this evening.'

'You were the only one who didn't wear gloves inside the house, and the only one who left muddy footprints on the doormat. You take a size nine in shoes, don't you? Trueman checked while you were unconscious. It would have been so much wiser to enter in your stockinged feet, as he did. And a more prudent fellow might have made sure he was not observed by the railway clerk who sold him a train ticket to Benfleet. When I congratulated you on committing a perfect crime, I'm afraid my tongue was firmly in my cheek.'

There was a long pause. Jacob screwed his eyes shut, trying frantically to order his thoughts. Could he escape, Houdini-like, from the trap she'd laid? McAlinden had fired a shot the moment before Trueman knocked him unconscious. What if the police found the bullet? Would it cause them to look beyond the irrelevance? No, he told himself. They would know he was an inexperienced marksman. He might have fired wildly to frighten McAlinden before killing him.

Was there another loophole? He struggled to compose himself.

'How did I get away from Benfleet?'

'Good question.' She smiled. 'I bet you stole a bicycle. You're a fit young fellow, and an enthusiastic cyclist. You may even have tried to cover your tracks by destroying the cycle upon your return to London. Not well enough, I'm afraid. Pieces of it may be found close to your lodgings in Amwell Street.'

Oh God, those segments of a broken bicycle with which he'd shared the back seat of the Bullnose Morris!

His fingerprints were plastered over them.

'Ingenious,' Jacob muttered.

'Rudimentary, my dear Mr Flint.' There was no humour in her smile. 'But I'm afraid that our police like easy answers.'

Throat parched, he croaked, 'You're forgetting something.'

Arms folded, she leaned back in her chair. 'Surprise me.'

'I did nothing wrong.' He jerked a thumb at Trueman. 'Our friend here killed McAlinden. He saved me from being murdered, yes, but then he knocked me out, and did the deed.'

Rachel shook her head. 'Slander, Mr Flint. I advise you not to repeat that allegation outside these four walls. Trueman was here all evening; I can vouch for that. The two of us were playing bezique.'

'So who was driving your Bullnose Morris?'

'Bullnose Morris?' She made a performance of scratching her head. 'Goodness, I've never set foot inside one in my life,' she said. 'My car is a Rolls-Royce Phantom, surely you recall?'

He thrust his head into his hands, as his brain bumped into gear.

'I suppose he stole the Morris?'

'Motor cars are stolen in London all the time. Happily, they are often recovered with no damage done. Sometimes the owner isn't even aware that they have been taken for an evening.'

Jacob found the urge to burst into tears almost irresistible. Yet he must show this woman and her servants that he wasn't the limp idiot they took him for.

In a muffled voice, he said, 'You seem to have thought of everything, Miss Savernake.'

She shrugged. 'You flatter me, Mr Flint. I'm afraid there are always lacunae. An inevitable consequence of creative improvisation. It would, however, be distressing if the police cottoned on to the interpretation of events I've outlined. Don't you agree?'

'Yes,' he said through gritted teeth.

'Very well. I'm sure you understand why I'm optimistic that you'll never breathe a word about the events of tonight. Trust me, and all will be well.'

'Trust you?'

'Yes.' Her tone was harsh. 'Now, tell me about your dealings with Thurlow. Miss nothing out. That young fool may be more use dead than he ever was alive.'

When Rachel finally swept out of the room, Jacob was reminded of a boxing match he'd once watched in Bradford. The referee had called a halt to a contest between ill-matched opponents before the weaker man, his head already bruised and bloodied, suffered irreparable damage to the brain. He knew exactly how that beaten fighter felt.

Trueman and the maid followed their mistress, but the housekeeper lingered, and asked Jacob if he'd like something to eat. When he shook his head, she scolded him, saying that it would do him good after such a night.

'You need to get your strength up,' she said. 'I'll make you some nourishing soup.'

'Thank you, but no.' Even if he tried to force himself to eat something, it wouldn't stay down.

She tutted in disapproval. 'You'll be sorry later on, when your tummy starts complaining.'

He looked wildly about him. 'Later on? How long do you expect me to stay here?'

Her theatrical sigh was worthy of a mother confronted by an obtuse child. 'For tonight, certainly. After all, you're not yet ready to go back to your lodgings, and console the mother of the murdered girl. Are you?'

She was right, naturally. As he sat on his own, hunched up in the armchair, the realities of this catastrophic evening began to sink in.

Nothing would be the same again. Not in his domestic life, for a start. Elaine was dead, and Mrs Dowd would be demented with grief. Losing her husband had driven her to the bottle, and he doubted she could survive the loss of her daughter. As for what connected the landlady, her daughter, and McAlinden, he could not begin to guess.

His working life, too, was changed forever. After the pleasant shock of his promotion, he'd been present at the scene of multiple murders, a story to end all stories, and yet he had no choice but to keep quiet forever. Not for one second did he doubt that his hostess was ready, willing, and able to make him pay if he broke his word. She'd rip him up like confetti.

Even now, sitting in her luxurious residence like an honoured guest, he knew next to nothing about her. As he puzzled over the enigma, Mrs Trueman returned with a steaming cup of cocoa.

'Drink this,' she said. 'Go on. It won't kill you.'

He flinched. Was it a sign of paranoia to wonder if this comfortable woman was about to poison him?

'I don't think...'

Dawning realisation lit up the housekeeper's face.

'Worried that it might be laced with arsenic?' She chortled. 'After all you've been through tonight, I suppose anything seems possible. Go on, then, I'll have a sip myself, to set your mind at rest.'

She tasted the cocoa before passing the cup to him. Cheeks burning with humiliation, he swallowed a mouthful. It was hot and flavoursome.

'Not so terrible, is it?' Mrs Trueman demanded. 'Before she comes back, let me tell you one thing. Nobody gets the better of Rachel Savernake. Even to try is more than your life's worth. Believe me, young man, the only person capable of destroying her is... she herself.'

'Why would she destroy herself?' Jacob asked. 'What does she want?'

The woman shook her head, and stood up. 'I've said enough. Finish your drink, and I'll take your cup for washing. Are you sure I can't get you anything to eat?'

Five minutes later, Rachel Savernake rejoined him, accompanied by her three servants. They were, Jacob thought, more like partners in crime.

'Martha made up a bed in the room at the back of the second floor before you arrived,' Rachel said. 'You'll be perfectly comfortable. The pillows are filled with the finest goose down.'

Jacob yawned. He could barely keep his eyes open, yet he yearned to keep her talking. If there was a chink in her armour, he wanted to find it.

'Thanks,' he said. 'On reflection, I'll accept your kind offer of hospitality. But I'm confused about so many things. Such as what happens tomorrow.'

'You go back to work, what else?'

'The *Clarion* will be in uproar,' he said. 'There'll be absolute pandemonium the minute the news gets out. McAlinden dead, along with Elaine Dowd and a young policeman. For all I know, the editor will want me to cover the story. What do I do then?'

'It would be insensitive even by the miserable standards of Fleet Street to order a man to report on the murder of a girl he'd courted, and in whose house he'd been living.'

'You don't know Gomersall.' He mustered a humourless smile. 'What do I say about this evening? That I came here to make up a four for bridge?'

Rachel laughed. 'A pleasing idea, but not, I think, appropriate. My name mustn't cross your lips. Let's talk further tomorrow morning, over breakfast.'

He thought about protesting. Whatever alibi she proposed would be far from watertight, but he'd learned that arguing with Rachel Savernake was futile. She was a true chess player, always thinking two or three moves ahead.

He changed tack. 'How did you know I was going to Benfleet this evening?'

She breathed out. 'You'd pursued me with such vigour, plainly you had a special reason for turning down an invitation to meet this evening. I always prepare for a range of eventualities. It was a simple matter to have you watched, as well as Elaine Dowd. The bungalow in Benfleet we already knew about. Your friend Thurlow was hopeless at covering his tracks. A poor advertisement for the Metropolitan Police, I'm afraid. He was useful to his paymasters for a while, but his sheer ineptitude made him a liability.'

'His paymasters?' Jacob frowned. 'Someone outside Scotland Yard? Or on the inside?'

She gave a dismissive wave of the hand. 'Time to catch up on your beauty sleep, Mr Flint. If you'll forgive my saying so, you look rather the worse for wear.'

He took in a breath. Should he press her again about Gallows Court?

'Permit me one last question. What is the Damnation Society?'

Putting a finger to her lips, she said, 'Hush, Mr Flint. Goodnight.'

'Please. What is the Damnation Society?'

Rachel Savernake's expression hardened.

'There is no such thing as the Damnation Society.'

22

The aching of Jacob's head and shoulders provided a painful reminder of the punishment he'd sustained at Trueman's hands. Four hours' sleep, albeit in the most comfortable bed imaginable, was all he managed before the housekeeper summoned him to breakfast. It wasn't nearly long enough to freshen his mind. He needed to crank up his brain like a misfiring Model T before he could even take in Rachel's instructions.

She sat opposite him at the breakfast table, watching as Martha the maid served him in silence with a plate full of bacon, eggs, mushrooms, and fried bread. She looked immaculate in a pale-blue woollen dress emphasising her tiny waist and narrow hips. Not a hair on her head was out of place. Nobody would doubt that she'd enjoyed a virtuous night's sleep following a quiet evening playing cards with her good and faithful servant. In the unlikely event that anyone came to check on Trueman's alibi, she would supply it with absolute conviction, all sweetness and light as she spun her web of lies.

But he told lies too. Everyone did, when it suited them. When she asked what he'd told Mrs Dowd about his plans for the evening, he admitted saying that he was going out to celebrate his promotion, and expected to be back very late.

'A good enough story,' Rachel pronounced. 'You may as well stick to it. If anyone wants to know, you wandered from one drinking den to another, and passed out in a back alley. That's why you failed to return to Amwell Street last night, and why your jacket and trousers look so disreputable.'

He bit into the fried bread. 'What about the clerk at Fenchurch Street?'

'Irrelevant, unless the police become interested in your movements last night. For your sake, let's hope they concentrate on other lines of enquiry. Don't contact me, or come back here. When I'm ready to speak to you again, I will.'

'What about Amwell Street?' The way she drummed in her instructions made him feel like an incompetent apprentice. 'All my clothes are there. All my possessions.'

'Later today, you should go there, and console the grieving mother.'

'I cared for Elaine myself, you know,' he snapped.

'Yes, she made sure you would.'

'Was she... seeing Thurlow all the time?'

'Intermittently. His opportunities for slipping away to meet her at the bungalow were few and far between.'

'They used to meet in Benfleet?'

'Yes. Thurlow lied to you about the bungalow. It's one of many properties—'

'Owned by Pardoe Properties Limited?'

Her eyebrows arched. 'A deduction based on seeing the company's name on a plate at Gallows Court?'

'You know my methods,' he retorted.

'Splendid!' Rachel mimed applause. 'Presumably, I don't need to tell you anything else. You know the rest already.'

'This isn't a game.' Choking back the memory of Elaine's corpse, he pushed aside what was left of his breakfast. 'Three people are dead.'

Rachel's smile vanished. 'You think I've forgotten?'

'Elaine was—'

'Greedy. She was bribed to seduce Thurlow. And later, to lead you on. Didn't you notice that the clothes she wore last night were far more expensive than anything a girl who works in a flower shop could afford? Save your tears for someone worthy of them.' Rachel chewed her toast. 'It's not as if you were in love with her.'

He winced at her brutality. 'Not... in love, no. But I liked her. Even her mother...'

'Edgar Dowd was a rich man,' Rachel interrupted. 'His widow drank away his fortune, and when she and her daughter were offered money in return for rendering certain services, they had no qualms about taking it.'

He put his head in his hands. 'God, what a mess. What should I do?'

'Tell Patience Dowd you think you should move out. She'll beg you to stay.'

'And should I?' He hated sounding like the classroom dunce.

'Why not? You've suffered a bereavement, even if your loss is hardly as profound as Mrs Dowd's. Nothing is more terrible than the death of one's child. The consequences can be unimaginable.'

Something in her tone made him look up. To his surprise, a faint smile was playing on her lips, as if a memory amused her.

'Where's McAlinden?' Gomersall demanded.

The question provoked ill-tempered muttering from Plenderleith and other senior members of the editorial team. McAlinden's arrogance and naked ambition had made him unpopular, and Jacob suspected that the older reporters doubted he was competent enough to deserve a place on the staff, let alone the promotion he so obviously craved.

Jacob was making his first appearance at the conference which Gomersall led each morning. Half an hour was allocated for the journalists to debate the day's stories, and decide which to prioritise. Jacob lurked at the back of the room. Today of all days, he didn't want to draw attention to himself. In any case, the discussion would serve no purpose. As soon as news broke of events at Benfleet, nothing else would count for a bean.

'Forgot to set his alarm clock again,' Poyser said.

Gomersall grunted, and started talking about the political crisis. There was always a political crisis, Jacob reflected; there would be for as long as the hapless MacDonald remained in office, and probably forever and a day. As he half-listened to the journalists talking about the slump, he wondered what Rachel could possibly know about the loss of a child.

The door at the side of the room was flung open, and Maisie, who typed Gomersall's confidential correspondence, hurried into the room. From the stir around him, and the shocked look on the editor's face, Jacob gathered that this interruption amounted to an extraordinary breach of office protocol. He watched as Maisie bent to whisper something in Gomersall's ear.

He didn't need to be a lip-reader to know that the bodies in the bungalow had been discovered. Soon everyone would know why McAlinden had missed the meeting.

'My sympathies once again,' Gomersall said, an hour later. He'd summoned Jacob to his office to brief him about the tragedy at Benfleet. The police had been summoned to the bungalow after a luckless postman had found the front door swinging open in the wind, and had ventured inside to check that all was well.

'Thank you, sir. Although Elaine and I went out together a time or two, we were friends, nothing more.' He was desperate to distance himself from the deaths. 'I was one friend among many. She was a lively young woman, very gregarious.'

'That's one word for it.' Cynicism came more naturally to Gomersall than condolences. 'You knew about her and this policeman, Thurlow?'

'He and I knew each other slightly,' Jacob said, opting for vagueness. 'Of course, he was married…'

'You didn't enquire too closely, I suppose? You need to be less tactful if you want to get on in this business. And what about McAlinden? The two of you were chummy at one time, weren't you?'

'Not really, sir. Though he used to lodge with Elaine and her mother, and when he moved out, he recommended Edgar House to me.'

'Did he now?' Gomersall's thick eyebrows exercised themselves. 'I suppose he gave up his digs after quarrelling with the girl, but never managed to get over her.'

'It seems the most likely explanation, sir.'

'Jealousy, yes. Worst sin of all, if you ask me. And McAlinden was the jealous sort, God rest his soul. Mind you, I can hardly believe it. Apart from any other consideration, he never struck me as… the marrying kind.'

'Perhaps it was just his manner, sir.'

'There had been incidents in his past,' Gomersall said. 'At Harrow and Cambridge. His father disclosed them to me in the strictest confidence when he begged me to give the boy a chance to make good in Fleet Street. He said it was simply a matter of youthful high jinks, but that always sounded like wishful thinking. Between ourselves, I took the lad against my better judgement. I doubt that surprises you?'

Jacob had never seen the editor of the *Clarion* in an introspective mood before. 'Not really, sir.'

'Never does any harm to have friends in high places, but if I had my time again, I'd say no. As for his father, this business has destroyed any hope he had of becoming head of the Civil Service. None of the law-and-order crowd will countenance a fellow whose son killed a pretty girl and her lover – a policeman, to put the tin lid on it! – and then took the coward's way out by shooting himself.'

Jacob nodded, but kept quiet. It is always politic to let one's superior do most of the talking. All the more so where one has so much to hide.

Gomersall shifted some papers on his desk. 'As you know, I've asked Poyser to find someone else to cover the story. Too close to home for you, despite your recent elevation.'

'Yes, sir. Of course, I'll give him every assistance.'

'Thanks, lad. I suppose you'll want to nip off and have a word with the girl's mother.'

Jacob could think of few things he wanted to do less. 'She'll be heartbroken, sir.'

'Naturally. But our readers will want to hear her thoughts on the… sad situation. Poyser's already sent out a photographer.'

Jacob nodded grimly. In his early days as a journalist, his attitude to newsworthy tragedies had been complacent, verging on glib. All that mattered was making sure that readers' curiosity was satisfied. Now that death had touched him more closely, he wasn't quite so sure. But these weren't reservations to be shared with one's editor the day after being granted a dizzying promotion.

'Very well.' Gomersall consulted his watch, a favourite prelude to dismissing subordinates from his presence. 'On your way, then. We've both got a difficult day ahead. There's only one thing that surprises me.'

Jacob stopped on his way to the door. 'What's that, sir?'

'We talked before about your uncanny record of being in the right place at the right time.' Gomersall's wry grin signalled that the sardonic newspaperman was already reasserting himself. 'I'm almost disappointed you weren't on the scene at Benfleet. What a scoop that would've been, eh?'

The telephone was howling as Jacob returned to his room. 'There's a police officer here, wants to ask you a few questions,' Peggy said, barely able to contain her glee. 'I said you'd be down in a minute. And there's a lady on the line for you as well. Insisted on holding.'

He had a sick feeling in the pit of his stomach. Was it Mrs Dowd, desperate to cry on someone's shoulder?

'Does the lady have a name?'

'Wouldn't give it,' the girl said darkly.

'Put her through… Hello?'

'Mr Flint, is that you?'

Sara's voice, urgent yet mellifluous, he recognised at once.
'Yes, Miss Delamere. Are you all right?'

'Yes.' A pause. 'I mean, no, not really.'

'What's the matter?'

'I daren't discuss it on the telephone.' She sounded short
of breath, as though she'd been running. 'Can we meet
somewhere? A public place, I'd feel safer there.'

'Safer?' He hesitated, bothered by her desperation. 'Does
the British Museum qualify as sufficiently public?'

'Yes, all right. Not that I've ever been inside it.'

He glanced through the window. It was a crisp January
morning, and there was even a thin streak of sun. 'Let's meet
on the steps outside the main entrance. I have someone waiting
to see me right now. Would one o'clock be convenient?'

'Oh, thank you so much. You might just be able to save
my life.'

The police officer proved to be a long-jawed constable in his
fifties called Dobing, whose appearance put Jacob in mind
of a melancholy horse. He already knew that Jacob was
acquainted with all three of the people whose bodies had
been found at the bungalow. Scotland Yard had moved with
lightning speed, Jacob reflected. Hardly surprising, given that
they had lost one of their own.

He didn't need to simulate his horror about the deaths
of three people whom he'd known with varying degrees
of intimacy. His visit to Benfleet had all the qualities of an
excruciatingly vivid nightmare.

Dobing was intent on gathering, rather than imparting,
information, and he stonewalled Jacob's occasional questions
with the ease of long practice.

'How has Elaine's mother taken the news?'

'Afraid I can't say, sir. I didn't have the sad duty of informing her about her loss.'

Frustrating as Jacob found this, some of his own answers were also less than helpful. He admitted to having been a drinking chum of Thurlow's, while McAlinden was a work colleague with whom he rarely socialised ('He took me out for a few drinks after I joined the *Clarion*, but we had little in common, and that was the only time.') He denied any knowledge of a liaison between Elaine and Thurlow, which was true enough, and said he had no idea whether she and McAlinden had ever been romantically involved. ('Neither of them mentioned it, but why would they, if it was over and done with?')

Elaine, he said, had been a pleasant companion for an evening out, but although her mother occasionally teased her about settling down, their friendship was entirely platonic, and they'd never exchanged more than a chaste kiss. Dobing went so far as to raise a tufted eyebrow at this, but recorded Jacob's denial with painstaking diligence.

Jacob knew enough about police procedure to realise that Dobing's failure to challenge his account did not mean that it would be accepted without a murmur. This was merely the first stage.

His stomach clenched as he bade farewell to the policeman.

'I hope that's helpful, Constable. Let me know if I can be of any further assistance.'

Dobing's equine features gave nothing away. 'Thank you, sir. I expect we'll take you up on that kind offer.'

*

As he walked down Great Russell Street towards the British Museum, Jacob caught sight of a willowy female figure, wearing a long coat with a fur collar and a hat with an unfashionably wide brim.

'Sara!'

She spun round as if jolted by a thunderbolt. At the sight of him, she seemed to droop with relief. 'Thank you so much for coming.'

'The pleasure's mine.'

'Forgive me if I seem a little... on edge,' she murmured. 'It has been a very difficult few days since we last met.'

'Of course.' He coughed. 'I'm so sorry about what happened to William Keary.'

She bowed her head. 'It was terrifying. Unspeakable.'

He hesitated. 'Shall we go inside the museum? Or find a tea shop nearby?'

'Can we just talk as we walk? I'd rather keep on the move. You never know who might be listening.'

Her voice shook, and her hands had a nervous twitch. There wasn't a trace of colour in her cheeks. He suspected she was on the verge of collapse. The horrific finale to Nefertiti's cremation illusion was enough to shake anyone to the core.

Anyone except Rachel Savernake.

'I called the Inanity.' She looked doubtful, and he added quickly, 'Not because I wanted to interview you about... what happened, but to see how you were coping.'

It was true, he told himself. Up to a point, at least.

'How kind,' she whispered. 'Did they tell you I've thrown in my job?'

He was taken aback. 'Really?'

'I'll never play the Queen of Egypt again. Or perform another illusion. I simply couldn't face it.'

'What happened wasn't your fault,' he said. 'This man Barnes...'

'Oh yes, George made sure that William couldn't escape from his blazing tomb. But I was the one who set it on fire.'

'You'd performed the trick scores of times. How could you know that Barnes wanted to commit such an appalling crime?'

'I couldn't know, of course,' she said. 'But that's no consolation.'

'I understand.'

'Do you?'

He itched to tell her that he'd had his own shocking encounter with sudden, brutal death less than twenty-four hours earlier. But he daren't break his promise to Rachel Savernake. He squeezed her arm as they crossed the street, and went into the garden in Russell Square. They found a secluded bench, and he noticed her glance surreptitiously this way and that, as if to make sure nobody was following.

'You wanted to speak to me,' he murmured.

'Yes.' She closed her eyes, as if summoning inner reserves of strength. 'You see, I don't know who else to turn to.'

'You have your friends and colleagues at the theatre,' he said. 'I'm sure they'll be only too glad...'

'Can I trust them?' A wild look came into her eyes. 'Any of them could be my enemy, determined to do me harm.'

'I'm sure—'

'There's only one thing that *I* am sure of,' she said.

'What's that?'

'Someone wants me dead.'

23

As if ashamed of its feebleness, the pale sun slipped behind a cloud at the very moment Jacob demanded, 'Why do you think that someone wants to kill you?'

'Two attempts on my life have been made since William was murdered.' Her voice dropped, and he had to move close to her in order to hear. 'I'm scared they will be third time lucky.'

'What happened?'

Sara leaned towards him, and he caught a whiff of gardenias. 'I must tell you the whole truth. When we met last time, I hinted about my chequered past. I've done things I'm deeply ashamed of.'

He cleared his throat, hoping to give the impression of a man of the world whom nothing could shock.

'I won't give you details. That would be too humiliating. But it so happened that William and I met in the course of... a business transaction, so to speak. He was gentle when other men enjoyed inflicting pain, and he... well, he took a shine to me.'

Jacob placed his hand on hers.

She lowered her eyes. 'William had his faults, like any man. But he saw me as a person, not just as… well, a vehicle for his pleasure. He said he'd help me to enjoy a better life. It's the sort of promise many a man has made to unfortunates like me. The difference was, he kept his word. Thanks to him, I was able to leave behind the sordid life I'd led, and start again.'

'I see.'

'Do you?' She shook her head. 'I'm so afraid you'll despise me.'

'No danger of that.'

'I became William's mistress. I'm not proud to admit it. He was married, as you may know, to the daughter of a member of the House of Lords.'

Jacob nodded. He'd done his research after Keary's murder.

'His wife's mind gave way years ago, and after that she was confined to a private sanatorium. I knew William would never divorce her, even if the law allowed it, and he didn't pretend otherwise. Our liaison came to a natural end, without a hint of acrimony. On the contrary, he made sure that I wanted for nothing. I'd risen to top of the bill at the Inanity, and he installed me in a flat close to Regent's Park. He wasn't seeking favours, or buying my silence. It was a simple act of generosity, which I accepted with gratitude.'

'I see.' How naive she was, he thought.

'We remained close, and there was never a cross word between us. Not even when his wife died, and instead of coming back to me, he became enamoured of a beautiful Italian woman. Chiara Bianchi was the widow of a wealthy businessman, someone who moved with ease in high society, as I never could. But it became clear to me that he was unhappy.'

'Because of the Bianchi woman?'

'Oh, no. Some of his associates – men like Linacre – were disreputable in the extreme.'

'And the solicitor, Hannaway?'

She lifted her chin. 'Yes, the Hannaways father and son, they belong to the same clique. William came to loathe them, and Linacre's murder of Dolly Benson was the final straw. He wanted nothing more to do with them, but they weren't men to tolerate any sort of snub. From that moment on, they looked for some means of punishing him for his temerity in turning his back on them.'

'You thought they were threatening Rachel Savernake.'

'I'm sure of it, Jacob. Her father was once part of their fraternity. It has deep roots, going back many years. I think the Judge was their leader.'

'Until his insanity became apparent, and he took himself off to the island home of his ancestors,' Jacob muttered.

'Yet somehow Rachel antagonised them. Her arrival in London upset the apple cart.'

'How?'

'I've no idea. Whenever I questioned William, he clammed up. He obviously thought it safer for me to know as little as possible.'

'And Rachel's life was in danger?'

'It has been ever since she came to London.' Despite the warmth of her coat, she shivered violently. 'What I didn't realise was that William was also at risk.'

He blinked. 'You think these people put Barnes up to murder?'

'What other explanation makes sense?'

'Barnes may have acted in a moment of madness.'

'The crime was carefully planned. Someone else paid for the car he drove to Croydon, and for his flight to France. Barnes couldn't possibly have afforded the cost out of his own pocket.'

'Even if these people did murder Keary, and wanted to kill Rachel Savernake, why would they want to remove you?'

Her long, low sigh owed something to weariness, something to exasperation. 'Don't you see? I know too much, or at least they think so. They can't afford to take a chance.'

Clasping her hand, he said gently, 'You've undergone an ordeal. It's understandable if you —'

'I'm not making this up, Jacob.' She was on the verge of tears. 'I've moved out of the flat in Regent's Park. I've rented rooms off the beaten track in Leytonstone, hoping nobody would find me. And I'm not the only one to have taken fright. William's lover, the Italian woman, has fled.'

'You don't think she's been murdered?'

'I've no idea. She lived at William's house in Carey Street. I wanted to talk to her, but nobody has seen her since… what happened. There's a maid there, a Chinese woman. I got to know her when William brought me to his home. She tells me the Widow Bianchi took a suitcase, along with her jewels. I suppose she's left the country. She was rich in her own right; she didn't depend on William. Probably she's done a bunk out of sheer terror.'

'And the attempts on your own life?'

'Yesterday, at Leytonstone underground station, a man in the crowd tried to push me onto the live rail.'

'Did you recognise him?'

'I didn't even get a proper look at his face. If a young soldier hadn't managed to grab hold of my arm, and haul me to safety, that would've been the end of me. To any outsider, it looked like an accident, and I pretended it was. But I'm sure it was a deliberate attempt at murder.'

He breathed out. 'You've suffered a terrible tragedy.'

Her voice rose. 'I might have been mistaken, but this morning, as I strolled towards Hollow Ponds, trying to calm myself down, a car careered along the street as if out of control. I jumped out of the way, but it was a close thing. I was a couple of seconds from being mown down.' She paused. 'I look and sound like a neurotic wreck. But is it any wonder?'

'If I can help in any way...'

'Only one person who can help me now,' she said. 'Rachel Savernake.'

'I gave her your message.'

'And what did she say?'

'She didn't seem disconcerted. I've never known a woman so fearless.'

Sara looked into his eyes, as if peering through a keyhole. 'I believe you're smitten.'

'Not a bit of it.' He shifted under her gaze. 'Fascinated, yes – that I can't deny. She's unlike any woman I've ever met. More like a praying mantis, to be honest. It's as if she's inherited her father's ruthless streak.' Sara shuddered, and he said, 'What is it?'

'Nothing.'

He groaned in frustration. 'Sara, I thought you trusted me. What are you keeping back?'

Tears came to her eyes, and some moments passed before she answered.

'When I was a child, I met Judge Savernake.'

*

'You still haven't told me what you make of Flint,' Rachel said.

She and Trueman were in the dark room of the small photographic laboratory tucked in the basement of Gaunt House. Trueman whistled tunelessly, mangling an old Sousa march as he inspected his latest prints.

'Loose cannon. Don't trust him.'

'Because he's a journalist?'

'Not only that. He's young and wayward.'

'Less than twelve months younger than me.'

'You crammed a lifetime of learning into those years on the island.'

She shrugged. 'Books can't teach you everything. You've told me that often enough. Education prepares you for life, it's not a substitute for it. My experience of the world is narrower than Flint's. He's ingenuous, yes, but I rather like that.'

Trueman pointed to a photograph he'd positioned on a small wooden table. Taken from behind, it showed Jacob Flint bending over the sprawled corpse of Stanley Thurlow. From that angle, it was impossible to tell that Jacob was unconscious, and had been propped up with great care to prevent him collapsing in a heap. The picture appeared to show a murderer, admiring his handiwork.

'Don't like him too much. The time may come when you need to sacrifice him.'

'I can't remember my parents,' Sara said. 'My first memories are of my childhood in an orphans' home. It was strictly run, but we were well fed and clothed, and given the rudiments of a proper education. There were far more girls than boys, but that didn't matter. Only as I grew older did I realise something was wrong.'

'This home,' Jacob said. 'It wasn't in Oxford, by any chance?'

Her jaw dropped. 'How on earth do you know that?'

'The woman Lawrence Pardoe killed once worked at the Oxford Orphans' Home.'

Sara put her head in her hands. 'Oh God, no!'

'Sorry, sorry, I didn't mean to interrupt. Please go on. Tell me what was wrong.'

She produced a small lace handkerchief, and dabbed at her nose. 'Every now and then, one of the older girls would suddenly disappear. We'd be spun some yarn about why they'd gone without a by-your-leave. A long-lost relative had turned up, and offered them a decent home. Or a job with a good family had become available, a vacancy that needed filling without delay. I thought nothing of it until it happened to a dear friend of mine. We were very close, and she would not have left without even saying goodbye. I was told her uncle and aunt had turned up out of the blue from Australia, but I simply didn't believe it. When I protested, the matron took me to her room, and thrashed me with her cane.'

'Mrs Mundy?' She gave a slight nod. 'I've met her.'

'You have?' She blinked. 'You're very thorough, Mr Flint.'

'I told you, my name is Jacob.'

'Thank you, Jacob. It's such a relief to be able to talk to someone – at last.' She found the handkerchief again, and blew her nose. 'After being beaten, I didn't make any more fuss, and pretended to have forgotten all about my friend. From that day on, I became an actress. I kept my eyes and ears open, and over time, I gathered a few clues.'

'To the disappearance of your friend?'

'And the other girls, yes. It always seemed to happen after a meeting of the trustees. The home was run by a charity. And the man in charge was Judge Savernake.'

'I see.' It wasn't entirely true. He felt as though he were suffering from disordered vision, seeing a once familiar world indistinctly through milky lenses. 'This was shortly before the war?'

'Yes. Once or twice, the Judge and the other trustees came and talked to us orphans. To make sure we were being cared for properly, we were told. It was sheer prejudice, but I didn't like the Judge. He was supposed to be some sort of saint, but something in the way he looked at us made my flesh crawl. Sometimes, he'd invite one of us upstairs. To a meeting, he called it. It dawned on me that these were the children – they weren't always girls – who went missing immediately afterwards. At first I presumed he was breaking the news about the long-lost relation who'd come to claim them, or suchlike. Later on, I wasn't so sure.'

'Did he call you to a meeting?'

'No, thank the Lord.' Colour flowed up her throat, and across her cheeks. 'I decided he was lying, and so was Mrs Mundy, and everyone else at the home. I could never prove it, of course. And then one day the trustees met, and the Judge wasn't there. I didn't ask where he'd gone. I was just glad he hadn't turned up. I never saw him again.'

'What happened to you afterwards?'

She lowered her eyes. 'I'd rather not go into details. Suffice to say that I received what it amused the new chairman of the trustees to call a proper Oxford education.'

He bit his lip. 'I see.'

'All I will say is this. One day he called me in to a meeting. You already know his name. It was Mr Lawrence Pardoe.'

Sir Godfrey Mulhearn stood at the window of his office, staring out over London's rooftops, as if hoping that the zigzag shapes of the tiles might magically transform into a pattern making perfect sense.

Superintendent Chadwick consulted his notes, and cleared his throat.

'The local police are in charge of the investigation, naturally, sir, and…'

'Are they any bloody good?'

'We are providing appropriate assistance, sir.' Chadwick sighed heavily. 'I expect they will pass the case over to us shortly, if only to save cost for the ratepayers of Essex. Initial enquiries suggest that McAlinden knew Thurlow had arranged to meet the girl at Benfleet. Probably he'd spied on them, and become aware they used the bungalow for their trysts.'

'Long way out of London,' Sir Godfrey muttered.

'The journey is straightforward, and it's prudent to get out of town if you don't want anyone to see what you're up to. Last night, Thurlow picked the girl up in his car and drove her there.'

'Who owns the bungalow?'

'I have a man looking into that, sir.'

'I suppose there's no doubt about what happened?'

Chadwick's discipline did not permit him to shrug in the presence of an assistant commissioner, but the creasing of his strongly defined features hinted at the career policeman's disdain for the military import.

'Always an element of doubt, sir, if not necessarily reasonable doubt. At present, our working hypothesis is that McAlinden murdered Thurlow and the girl, then shot himself.'

'I take it the forensic evidence supports that conclusion?'

'We are lucky that Mr Rufus Paul was available to attend the scene. At this stage, he seems to regard it as a clear case.'

'I suppose that's a mercy.' Rufus Paul was famously definite in his conclusions. 'But the reputation of the force…'

'Thurlow was off duty,' Chadwick said, 'and we've turned up nothing to suggest that he allowed this squalid business with the girl to compromise the performance of his official duties.'

'Thank God for that.' Sir Godfrey chewed this over. 'Of course, there are degrees of moral turpitude.'

Chadwick swerved this minefield, just as in the boxing rings of his youth, he'd dodged his opponents' punches. 'Every cloud has a silver lining, you might say, sir. The *Clarion*'s editor won't be getting astride his high horse about police incompetence. Not when he's given employment to a double murderer. As for the rest of Fleet Street, they'll find more sport dancing on McAlinden's grave than grousing about misconduct within Scotland Yard. In so far as a nasty and unfortunate business can be, sir, I'd say it's all quite neat and tidy.'

Sir Godfrey puffed out his cheeks. 'We must count our blessings.'

'Absolutely, sir,' Superintendent Chadwick said.

A stiff breeze sent fallen leaves scurrying along the path as they strolled out of the garden. The sky had grown sullen, and the darkening clouds matched Jacob's mood. Sara felt guilty about her past, but Jacob regarded that as nonsense. She was a victim. Thank goodness she'd escaped the home's clutches. William Keary had given her the chance of a new life, but his circle had included Pardoe, Linacre, and the Judge. Had his former friends decided he'd let them down, and taken their revenge by inciting the demented stagehand to kill him?

Jacob had a glimmering of the truth behind Mary-Jane Hayes' murder. Suppose Pardoe had come across her in London, and taken a shine to her. As chairman of the Oxford Orphans' Home, his prime concern was to enable friends and colleagues to satisfy their exotic tastes. He'd made sure Mary-Jane, quiet and apparently biddable, was recruited with a view to succeeding Mrs Mundy, and she'd been flattered into taking the job. Jacob guessed she'd resigned after realising that the home was not all it seemed. Had Pardoe killed her because she'd rejected him, or because she'd found out too much? It didn't much matter. He'd lured her to the house in Covent Garden, strangled her, and disguised the crime as the work of a maniac.

Mrs Mundy's display of righteous indignation had been a charade designed to cover her tracks. That fur coat she'd worn to their rendezvous in Fuller's probably wasn't a fake after all, but an expensive original. The Orphans' Home provided the rich and powerful a steady supply of girls and boys to gratify the basest desires. The matron must have been rewarded generously for her long and loyal service, and above all, her discretion.

'I must get back to Leytonstone,' Sara said.

'Do you think Rachel Savernake is in danger because she knows what happened at the home?'

'To be honest with you, Jacob, I'm no longer sure what to think.'

He hadn't told Sara that he'd spent the night at Gaunt House. Trusting someone was all very well, but there were limits. The mere thought of anyone else finding out that he'd been present in Benfleet the previous evening was enough to bring him out in a cold sweat.

They reached the entrance to Russell Square Tube station. He made as if to shake her hand, but she forestalled him by planting the lightest kiss on his cheek.

'May I see you again?'

'I'd love that,' he said.

'Please don't try to find me. I expect I'll move from one place to another. But I'll be in touch soon. And thank you, for the most precious gift.'

In his confusion, he made a vague, embarrassed noise.

'You've given me hope.'

She joined the crowd queuing for tickets. He was glad she couldn't guess what he was thinking. He'd not betrayed any hint of the wild notion that had sprung into his mind.

Suppose Judge Savernake had presided over a group of decadents calling themselves the Damnation Society, who exploited children from the Oxford Orphans' Home. Perhaps Rachel Savernake was determined to keep the Judge's secret, and to remove anyone – Pardoe, Keary, and God knew who else – who stood in her way.

24

'I warned you McAlinden's boy was no good.'

Gabriel Hannaway's wheeze made his words barely audible. He'd hobbled into the office after being told of McAlinden's death. Considering his ailing father dispassionately, Vincent Hannaway wondered how many more times the old man would set foot in their chambers. Sir Eustace Leivers had confided recently over cocktails at the Gambit Club that he didn't expect Gabriel Hannaway to see out another Christmas.

'It was a chance worth taking.'

'The last client who said that to me was hanged,' Gabriel Hannaway said. 'Not even Lionel Savernake's advocacy could save him.'

Vincent groaned inwardly. That must have been more than twenty years ago. The old man was living in the past. What mattered in life was what happened next.

'I don't believe for a moment that McAlinden shot himself after finishing Thurlow and the girl. That would only make sense if he was a jealous lover. An absurd notion.'

'What if the other journalist – what's his name, Flint? – decided against going to Benfleet?'

'Why would he? He's a nosey parker, that's his job. Thurlow had already fed him enough juicy titbits to make the invitation irresistible.'

'Very well, suppose he was prevented from making the journey. If McAlinden panicked...'

'He would have sought further instructions. No, it won't do, Father. His supposed suicide is a fake.'

'What about our friend at Scotland Yard? Does he share your view?'

Vincent nodded. 'I spoke to him less than an hour ago. The whole business has left him thunderstruck. As if things weren't bad enough, the officer who broke the news to Patience Dowd reported she was having a fit of hysterics. Now he's wondering if she needs to be put out of her misery. He's very jumpy all of a sudden. He was nervous about sacrificing Thurlow, and suddenly it seems the fellow's death, and the girl's, were in vain.'

'That pair outlived their usefulness. As for the mother, she has nothing left to live for in any event.'

'Except the gin bottle.'

'Much good may it do her.' The old man dismissed Mrs Dowd with a flap of a claw. 'Perhaps Flint had the wit to take McAlinden by surprise, and do the deed.'

'Snaring McAlinden in his own trap?' Vincent snorted. 'He doesn't have the mettle. No, something happened last night that was truly exceptional.'

'*Novus actus interveniens?*' The old man coughed noisily. 'If you want my opinion, someone took Flint's place.'

'Possibly.'

Rheumy eyes considered the younger man. 'When you take

that tone with me, my boy, I know you beg to differ. What is your explanation of this wretched state of affairs?'

Vincent stabbed his blotter with his pen nib. 'McAlinden was killed by someone strong enough to subdue him, ruthless enough to shoot him at point-blank range, and subtle enough to make a good fist of creating the appearance of suicide.'

'Well?'

'There is one credible candidate.'

'Rachel Savernake's man?'

The pen nib was broken. With a furious sweep of the hand, Vincent knocked it off the desk.

'Who else?'

'I told you she'd make trouble. I never met anyone with such a vicious temper as her father. She's cut from the same cloth.'

'Perfect qualifications for a prospective daughter-in-law.' Vincent's habitually sardonic tone was edged with bitterness.

'She's blessed with more character than the grasping harlots you fool around with. Easy on the eye, too. Good cheekbones and a damned neat figure. She reminds me of someone...'

'The late Celia Savernake, presumably,' Vincent muttered.

'No, no, not her mother.' The old man shook his head. 'It's gone. My memory isn't quite what it was.'

Not just your memory, Vincent thought savagely. Containing his temper with an effort of will, he said, 'We're none of us getting any younger.'

'Which is why I want to see you settled before I go, my boy.'

'I shall never marry Rachel Savernake, Father.'

'More fool you. Your decision, of course. And I know of one other woman worthy of your affections. Someone of independent means who is no longer romantically attached.'

'The fragrant Widow Bianchi?' Vincent sneered. 'At the moment, my priority is clearing up this rotten mess. Ever since Rachel Savernake came to London, we have suffered one disaster after another. Linacre, Pardoe, Keary, now McAlinden.'

'Where will it end?' the old man asked dreamily.

Vincent banged his fist on the desk. 'I'll tell you exactly where it will end. Forget all that nonsense about wedding bells. It will end with Rachel Savernake lying cold in her grave.'

'You didn't ask Flint to question the girl's mother,' Trueman said.

Rachel buttered herself a crumpet. She and the Truemans were taking tea in the drawing room. 'Why waste his time? Mrs Dowd wouldn't tell him anything, for the very good reason that she knew next to nothing.'

'Edgar Dowd was the Judge's accountant.'

'He was never a confidant, like Gabriel Hannaway. Although his widow was bailed out of Queer Street by his old friends in return for the occasional service, it was her daughter who became valuable.'

Mrs Trueman poured herself another cup. 'What about Thurlow's wife? Would he have talked to her?'

Rachel shook her head. 'When he was misbehaving with Elaine Dowd? I doubt it.'

'What do you propose we do now?' Trueman demanded.

'A visit to Scotland Yard is called for,' Rachel said. 'But first, another crumpet?'

*

'Thank you for sparing the time to see me,' Inspector Oakes said, after a cheerful nippy had served their tea. 'Especially on such a busy day for you.'

He and Jacob were having a reunion at the Lyons Corner House on the Strand, taking tea again in the mirrored restaurant. On arriving back at Clarion House, Jacob had been told that Oakes had telephoned. When he returned the call, the detective had asked to meet, the sooner the better.

'Ironic, eh?' Jacob's smile was wan. 'My first full day as chief crime correspondent, and I'm not even writing up last night's events. It would have been challenge enough, given McAlinden's involvement, but since Elaine was one of his victims, I'm too close to the story.'

'I am sorry for your loss.'

Oakes' tone was stiff and formal, the relaxed intimacy of their early conversations a fast-fading memory. He was chain-smoking, and his eyes were bleary, as though he'd managed even less sleep than Jacob. His shirt hadn't been ironed with quite the customary rigour, and even his tie looked as if he'd tried to knot it one-handed. What was keeping him awake at night?

'Thank you.' Jacob stirred his tea rather longer than was necessary. He needed to be careful, but he must say something. 'Elaine was... good company.'

As an epitaph, it was scarcely lyrical, yet his words were heartfelt. He'd enjoyed spending time with her, and he had a lingering recollection of the warmth of her body, pressing against his. If Rachel Savernake was to be believed, Elaine had manipulated his affections. Yet somehow he couldn't bring himself to despise her duplicity. Whatever she'd done wrong, she hadn't deserved that squalid end in the silent bungalow.

'Were you very close?'

'Just good friends. Her mother seemed to think I was suitable husband material, but I never contemplated asking Elaine to marry me, and I'm sure she was only interested in having a good time.'

'Especially since she'd involved herself with someone else,' Oakes said. 'You didn't know?'

'I was vaguely aware another man had been lurking in the background, and I wondered if he was already married, but she never spoke about him, and I never asked.'

'Odd. I'd put you down as insatiably curious.'

'Some things it's better not to know. I was content to assume the affair had died a natural death.'

Oakes winced, and Jacob blushed. For a professional wordsmith, he scolded himself, his choice of phrase could be astonishingly crass.

'So you had no idea the man in question was DC Thurlow?'

'When I was told that' – Jacob caught himself before falling into a trap – 'earlier today, you could have knocked me over with a feather. I still can't take it in. Stanley, of all people.'

'Small world,' Oakes lit another cigarette. 'You knew both victims, and also their killer.'

'Yes.' Jacob felt he was tiptoeing around quicksand. 'It's not just a tragedy, it's an appalling shock. Forgive me if I seem distracted. I still haven't had a chance to absorb the news fully.'

'How well did you know McAlinden?'

'Not very,' Jacob said hastily.

'Did you think he was a pansy?' Oakes demanded.

'I didn't care. It was none of my business.' Jacob couldn't resist a retaliatory shot. 'His manner seemed peculiar at times, but I put that down to his public-school education.'

Oakes glowered. 'As it happens, he'd been arrested twice in compromising circumstances, but his father pulled strings, and he was never charged.'

A sour note in the detective's voice made Jacob look up. 'But he'd been carrying on with Elaine?'

'Or at least carrying a torch for her, yes. So it would seem.'

'You don't sound convinced.'

'My opinions don't matter. I'm here to find out what light you can shed on the tragedy.'

'I've already given a statement to one of your men. Fellow called Dobing, face like a...'

'Old Dobbin? Yes, I've read what you told him.' Oakes leaned back in his chair. 'I wondered if there was anything you might like to add. On reflection, as it were.'

Jacob opted for attack as the best form of defence. 'Only to express my astonishment about Thurlow. I don't know how good a policeman he was, but I liked him. We'd had a drink together once or twice, as you may know.'

'Yes,' Oakes said. 'I did know.'

'I'd no idea he was mixed up with Elaine. Naive of me, I suppose.'

'Perhaps that's why he sought out your company,' Oakes said harshly. 'To laugh at you behind your back.'

'Was the affair common knowledge at the Yard?'

Oakes' frown gave Jacob a jolt of satisfaction. Weary and bewildered he might be, but he'd landed a blow.

'Far from it. He took great pains to keep his... activities secret, and with good reason. He'd have been chucked out on his ear if we'd got wind of them.'

'He must have been well-regarded,' Jacob said. 'Otherwise he'd never have been offered promotion.'

'Promotion?' Oakes glared. 'What do you mean?'

'He told me he was going to be made a sergeant. To be honest, I'd not realised you held him in such high esteem.'

'As far as I was concerned,' Oakes said stiffly, 'Stanley Thurlow was a country mile away from promotion. You must have misunderstood.'

'Certainly not. He was very definite. And suitably jubilant.'

'When did he tell you this?'

Jacob knew he must tread with care. 'Only yesterday. The very last time we spoke. He rang me up to break the news, and I mentioned my own elevation. We agreed to get together for a joint celebration.'

'Which never took place?'

'And now, of course, it never will.' Jacob indulged in a lavish sigh. 'Strange that you say he wasn't earmarked for promotion. Stan may not have been a varsity man, but he'd never have got the wrong end of the stick about something like that. You don't think…?'

'I don't think what?'

'I hate to raise this,' Jacob said, with insincerity worthy of a grizzled Fleet Street veteran, 'but is it possible that he had… a hold over someone in authority at Scotland Yard?'

'What are you suggesting?' A furious colour had risen in Oakes' cheeks. Never before had Jacob seen him provoked to anger. 'Corrupt friends in high places?'

'Forgive me,' Jacob said. 'Far be it from me to suggest anything at all.'

They looked each other in the eye, both acutely conscious of derisive words hanging unspoken in the air between them.

If the cap fits…

★

Walking back to Clarion House, Jacob couldn't help congratulating himself. If Oakes' aim had been to trap him into some kind of admission, the conversation had not gone to plan. Jacob was confident he'd given as good as he'd got.

His shot about Scotland Yard had certainly hit home. Might Oakes' jumpiness be due to the fact that he'd come to a similar conclusion? If so, did Oakes have a suspect in mind?

Passing the newsroom's open door, he spotted Poyser in conference with the foreman-printer. Pop-Eye raised a hand in greeting.

'George, has anyone interviewed Mrs Dowd?'

Poyser nodded. 'Did it myself. I'm not sure it's dawned on her yet that she'll never see her daughter again. The gin bottle's offering her comfort for the time being. Don't blame you for not rushing back there.'

Heart sinking, Jacob plodded back to his room. Rather than dwell on how to comfort a woman who had lost her only child, he turned his mind back to the possibility of corruption at Scotland Yard. Oakes' shock about Thurlow's claim of imminent promotion sounded convincing. The only explanation that made sense was that Thurlow was being repaid by someone senior enough to pull the right strings.

An image sprang to his mind of the Inanity before the lights dimmed and the show began. He'd glimpsed Sir Godfrey Mulhearn in a box opposite Rachel's. Tom Betts had mocked Mulhearn's incompetence at the time the *Clarion* was hounding the Yard after Dolly Benson's murder. To Betts, Mulhearn typified what was wrong with the police hierarchy; he was a military man with a minimal grasp of the realities of detective work. During the war, he'd been a member of the band of donkeys that had led so many brave lions (including Jacob's father, blown to bits in France) to the slaughter.

But warfare was one thing, killing in cold blood was quite another. Wasn't it?

He was still debating the question when his door creaked open, and Toseland, alias Trithemius, rolled in. The unaccustomed brightness of his porcine eyes indicated that he was in a state of excitement.

'Cracked it!' He was panting. 'As a matter of fact, the cipher is damnably simple. As soon as I put my thinking cap on, it began to make sense, but I had to do a fair bit of research to paint in the details.'

'I'm grateful. What does it mean?'

'It's a note about the deaths of two people.'

'Two? Are you sure?'

'Absolutely.' Toseland tapped the side of his nose. 'Trust Trithemius.'

'With my life,' Jacob said extravagantly.

'Steady on, old boy. Let's not get carried away, specially after what happened to old McAlinden. Bad business, eh?'

'Shocking,' Jacob agreed. 'Now – the cipher?'

'Your mention of Gallows Court made me curious, so I nipped round there this afternoon.'

'You did?' Jacob couldn't picture Toseland nipping anywhere. 'And what did you find?'

'There's a place called Gaunt Chambers, and a board next to the door indicates that it's home to something called the Gambit Club. So we can account for the first six letters of the cipher. Three identical pairs of initials have simply been reversed.'

Jacob nodded. So far, so good.

'If we read the message backwards, that gives us R.I.P., and the date 29 January 1919.'

'Yes, I rather thought so.'

'In that case,' Toseland said with mock severity, 'you could have saved me a job by going to Somerset House yourself, rather than leaving all the donkey work to yours truly.'

'Sorry. You're right, of course.'

'I looked up everyone who died on that date. Took a while, but two names fitted the bill. Charles Brentano and Yvette Viviers.'

'Never heard of them.'

'The place of death given in both cases was Lincoln's Inn, so there must be a connection, and the cipher must refer to them.'

'Yes, I suppose it's the only conceivable interpretation. But as to who they are...'

'I drew a blank with the woman. French, by the sound of her. But Brentano merited an obituary in *The Times*.'

'Really?'

'Yes, came from a wealthy family. Eton and Oxford, and all that malarkey, but he didn't do anything noteworthy until war broke out. He won the DSO and was awarded the Croix de Guerre. Quite a hero, but he paid the price by being blown up in a German shelling attack. He spent the last months of the war being patched up in a military hospital.'

'Did he die of his wounds?'

'Apparently not. The death certificate gives the cause of death as heart failure.'

'Did he have any family?'

'The obituary makes no mention of either a wife or children. It struck me as rather guarded.'

'How do you mean?'

'Obituaries are often as interesting for what they leave out as for what they include. In the case of certain confirmed bachelors, sometimes their proclivities are hinted at in a subtext. More usually, they are glossed over.'

'I see.'

'The same cause of death is given for the woman, Yvette.'

'They both died of heart failure on the same day?'

'Strange coincidence, eh?' Puffing and grunting, Toseland made his way to the door. 'Hope it helps with whatever story you're working on. Anyway, I must be getting off. Feeling rather peckish after so much activity.'

'Thanks, Toseland. I'm more grateful than I can say.'

'Think nothing of it, old boy. One excitement after another these days, isn't it? First, we lose poor Betts, now McAlinden's topped himself. There's talk that he was mixed up in an eternal triangle. Incredible. I wouldn't believe a word of it if I hadn't read it in the *Clarion*.'

Jacob laughed. 'Must be true, then. Anything else of note in the obituary?'

'It was only brief. One other point might interest you. Brentano's father was a diplomat from Berlin who came over here, and fell for an English girl. She belonged to a wealthy family, the Savernakes. Her brother was Lionel Savernake, the notorious hanging judge.'

25

'Rachel Savernake wants to meet us?' Superintendent Chadwick repeated.

'This evening, yes,' Sir Godfrey Mulhearn said. 'Irregular, damned irregular, but we live in irregular times.'

'You've agreed to see her, then, sir?' For once, Chadwick's discipline slipped. A gaping mouth revealed his incredulity.

'Yes, Chadwick.' A pink tinge coloured Sir Godfrey's cheeks. 'She was most insistent, practically invited herself over here. Said she was in possession of vital information about the death of DC Thurlow.'

'What sort of information?'

'She wouldn't be drawn. I said we were satisfied that McAlinden had killed Thurlow and his girlfriend, and then put a bullet through his own brain. Simple case of jealousy. But she refused to discuss the matter further on the telephone.'

'I've expressed this view before, sir,' Chadwick said icily, 'but I don't hold with encouraging amateurs to blunder into serious detective work.'

Sir Godfrey snorted. He was acutely aware that Rachel Savernake was not the only amateur Superintendent Chadwick had in his sights.

As Toseland's lumbering footsteps echoed down the corridor, Jacob was struck by a memory. Hadn't he bumped into McAlinden coming out of this office when he'd spoken to him about his report of Shoemaker's death? What had the fellow been doing in Betts' room? He had no business there, surely. Jacob hadn't given it a thought at the time – he'd been more concerned with having a surreptitious look-see himself – but now he knew that McAlinden was a murderer. Had Oily been searching through Betts' things, looking for records of the crime correspondent's enquiries about Rachel Savernake?

Jacob surveyed the clutter surrounding him. It would be almost impossible to put your hands on anything if you didn't know where to look. For all he knew, McAlinden had turned the room upside down, and still left it tidier than he'd found it.

If there'd been anything worth taking, McAlinden would doubtless have removed it, but Jacob decided to make a further check before departing for Amwell Street. It was as good an excuse as any for delaying the dreadful moment when he came face to face with Mrs Dowd.

Ten minutes later, he was once again ready to admit defeat. After trawling through each drawer in Betts' cupboard, and glancing at every notebook he could find, he'd drawn a blank.

Lydia Betts' innocent face smiled at him from the photograph that Betts had tucked under his telephone. There was another bereaved woman Jacob would soon be meeting, at

Tom's funeral. Another stilted, hopeless conversation. Jacob groaned. He hated funerals and graveyards even more than hospitals.

As he looked at Lydia, another picture came to his mind. The bookshelf in the Betts' flat, and the one title that unquestionably belonged to Tom, Poe's *Tales of Mystery and Imagination*. Was his favourite story, like Jacob's, 'The Purloined Letter'?

Jacob pulled out the photograph, and turned it over. There was Betts' familiar, if barely decipherable, pencilled scrawl.

Charles Brentano

Vincent Hannaway

99th Division, Cumberland Fusiliers

St Quentin redoubt

What happened?

Betts' notes were hiding in plain sight, just like Poe's clue, although they gave rise to a fresh mystery rather than solving one. Charles Brentano, nephew of Judge Savernake, who had died at Gallows Court, and Vincent Hannaway, the solicitor who practised there, had been comrades in arms during the Great War.

Jacob was still wrestling with the puzzle of Tom Betts' notes when he arrived back at Edgar House. Taking a deep breath, he unlocked the front door.

He'd never thought of himself as a sensitive soul, but the moment he stepped inside, he knew something was wrong. The silence seemed not mournful but sinister. And, following his ill-starred trip to Benfleet, painfully familiar.

'Mrs Dowd?'

No answer came.

Turning the handle of the door to the kitchen, he found it locked. There was a stopper in the keyhole. He sniffed suspiciously.

'Mrs Dowd? Are you all right?'

He put his shoulder to the door, and it began to give. Heaving with all his strength, he heard wood splintering, and a final shove forced the door open.

The stench of gas almost knocked him off his feet. His eyes stung as he took in the pile of unwashed saucepans and plates by the sink, and then the sorry sight on the linoleum-covered floor.

Patience Dowd was motionless. Her head must have been in the oven for quite some time.

'Thank you so much for allowing us to meet at short notice, Sir Godfrey.'

Rachel Savernake put down her bag, and smiled at the other men in the assistant commissioner's room. Mulhearn was flanked by Chadwick and Oakes. Trueman sat next to the superintendent, closest to the window, with the moonlight shining on his face.

Sir Godfrey pointed at Trueman. 'You didn't mention that you would be accompanied by your servant.'

Rachel's voice cut the silence like a razor tearing flesh. 'I have no secrets from Trueman.'

'Even so, on a matter of delicacy...'

'Trueman is, despite his... rugged appearance, no stranger to matters of delicacy,' she said. 'Now, may we proceed?'

'Please.' Sir Godfrey made a performance of consulting his pocket watch. 'I have a dinner appointment tonight. If you don't mind keeping it concise...'

'I'll be very concise, Sir Godfrey.' Her tone was cool. 'I came here to say that DC Stanley Thurlow was taking bribes.'

'Miss Savernake!' Sir Godfrey threw a nervous glance at his colleagues. 'I really don't...'

Oakes interrupted. 'What evidence do you have for this very serious accusation?'

'Thurlow made revealing comments to Jacob Flint from the Clarion.'

'How do you know this?'

'Flint told me himself.'

'The word of a journalist,' Chadwick muttered in disgust.

'He had no reason to lie, Superintendent. I am satisfied that he told me the truth.'

Oakes said, 'He said nothing of the kind to me when I interviewed him earlier today.'

'Perhaps,' Rachel replied, 'you did not ask him the right questions.'

'Thurlow might have been romancing,' Sir Godfrey said. 'Young fellows do it all the time, Miss Savernake. Trying to impress his chum, you know.'

'I'll take your word about the behaviour of young men,' Rachel said, 'but the supporting evidence is unequivocal. Thurlow lived far beyond his means. A shiny new car, a gold pocket watch...'

'The man's dead!' Sir Godfrey barked as if he was back on the parade ground. 'He can't respond to this disgraceful slur.'

'It's rather disgraceful conduct, Sir Godfrey. And I'm afraid that he wasn't alone in behaving improperly.'

'What do you mean?' Oakes muttered.

'He told Flint he was about to be promoted to the rank of detective sergeant.'

'Inconceivable!' Sir Godfrey snapped. 'How in the blazes can you suggest...?'

'His loyalty had been bought.'

'He invented the supposed promotion. Must have.'

'No, he'd every confidence that the reward he'd been promised would be delivered.'

'Tommyrot!'

Rachel shook her head. 'One of you knows I'm right. One of you has sold not only his reputation, but also his soul.'

Once the ambulance had removed Patience Dowd's body, and a dour police constable had taken a statement from him, Jacob tossed some things into a suitcase, and trudged down Margery Street before stopping at the first hotel he came to. He couldn't contemplate the prospect of spending the night in Edgar House.

A wizened gnome occupied a glass hutch at the back of the foyer, like an example of the taxidermist's art on display in a cobwebbed museum. With every sign of reluctance, he raised the glass shutter, and gloomily confirmed that he had a single room available for the night. The room proved to be grubby, the curtains moth-eaten, and the mattress full of lumps. The mirror made Jacob resemble a deformed gargoyle, but he didn't care. The past twenty-four hours had left him numb.

The walls were thin, and he heard raised voices. The couple next door had evidently been involved in a financial transaction, and a raucous dispute was raging about the price payable and the extent and value of the services supplied. The row ended with a slapping noise, the banging of a door, and footsteps clattering down the corridor. He heard a woman weeping, but after a few minutes she departed as well, and silence reigned on the second floor.

He lay on his back, sore eyes scrutinising the ceiling. The jagged cracks in the plasterwork reminded him that the life he'd known was crumbling. The Jacob Flint who had accosted Rachel Savernake in the fog seemed a different person, innocent and carefree. Betts' death, despite its inevitability, had rattled him, and the murders of Thurlow and Elaine, followed by her mother's suicide, had left him bereft. Stan and the two women may have nursed ulterior motives in befriending him, but he'd enjoyed their company.

As for Rachel Savernake, her allure remained disturbing, her motives unfathomable. Last night, as she'd quizzed him about his dealings with the police, he'd asked if she trusted Oakes.

Her reply was as evasive as a lawyer's quibble. 'He's that rarity, a clever policeman. Sometimes, of course, one can be too clever.'

The recent alteration in Oakes' demeanour was striking. What was the matter with the fellow?

There could only be one answer. Inspector Oakes was afraid.

'Madam!' Outrage made Sir Godfrey's voice break. 'That is nothing less than an actionable slander.'

She turned to Oakes. 'What say you, Inspector?'

Pale and drawn, Oakes bowed his head. 'I'm sorry to say that you're right, Miss Savernake.'

'Would you care to enlighten your colleagues?'

Oakes took a breath. 'I've become convinced that the spate of recent... incidents is not coincidental. I believe that a group of prominent individuals have combined to defy the law. Men such as Pardoe, Linacre, and Keary, and others as yet undetected. They all came from the same social circle, but the bond between them is, I'm sure, much closer than we have realised. Their motives are as shadowy as their actions, but I suspect that nefarious activities have benefited from illicit assistance, courtesy of Scotland Yard.'

'Great heavens, man!' Sir Godfrey exclaimed. 'Have a care what you're saying.'

'I hadn't wanted to utter a word, sir. My enquiries are still in their early stages, and I freely admit that there is much I don't yet know. But Miss Savernake's outburst leaves me with no choice but to put my cards on the table. It pains me to say so, but she is right. DC Thurlow was not our only rotten apple.'

Sir Godfrey glared at him. 'Very well, man. Spit it out. Who are you suggesting...?'

'Let me save Inspector Oakes a little embarrassment,' Rachel said. 'I can read his mind. I'm sorry to say that his suspicions are directed towards you, Sir Godfrey.'

The assistant commissioner's cheeks turned an unnatural shade of purple. 'Madam, this...'

She raised a hand. 'Am I right, Inspector?'

Oakes, crimson with mortification, said nothing.

'The theory is based on diverse scraps of information, Sir Godfrey. You belong to the same moneyed, well-born class as Pardoe and Linacre. Your family banks with Pardoe's. You are an avid theatre-goer, and have often been seen in a box at the Inanity. You were even present on the night William Keary was killed.'

'It was my wife's birthday! A little celebration...'

'I won't labour the point. Suffice to say that the inspector has turned up enough material to build a circumstantial case. But it won't do.'

'What do you mean?' Oakes asked hoarsely.

Chadwick rose to his feet. 'You're not saying that Oakes himself bribed Thurlow? Damned impertinence! First you defame Sir Godfrey, and now...'

'Sit down,' Rachel snapped. 'I'm accusing the inspector of nothing more serious than a failure to see the wood for the trees.'

'What the devil are you blathering about, woman?' Chadwick demanded.

'Sir Godfrey didn't bribe Thurlow, any more than the inspector did. The rotten apple at the top of the barrel was you, Superintendent Chadwick.'

'Miss Savernake.' Sir Godfrey looked as though he might suffer a stroke at any moment. 'I sincerely hope you can substantiate that allegation. Otherwise, I must ask you to retract it and apologise. The superintendent—'

'... is one of the most experienced and well-regarded officers in this building,' Rachel yawned. 'That's precisely what blinded even Inspector Oakes to the truth. The idea that such a man would sacrifice everything he's worked for is anathema to him.'

Finding his voice, Chadwick snapped, 'That accusation is filthy and contemptible. You're a disgrace to womankind, just as your father was a disgrace to the judiciary.'

'The Judge? Twenty years ago, his savagery made you recoil, and I can't say I blame you. How disappointing that you succumbed to the overtures of his disciples.'

'Poppycock! You'll need a lawyer as brutal as your old man when I serve my writ for slander. Where's your evidence?'

'When Thurlow asked Flint who sent the anonymous note that led him to Pardoe's house, he said he wanted to pass on the information to you. Odd, given that you're a desk-bound superintendent. Surely he would report to the inspector?'

'Trivial hearsay,' Chadwick jeered. 'Is that the best you can do?'

'Thurlow told Flint about the discovery of the pawn in Pardoe's study. The inspector had instructed his men to keep that snippet of information secret, but you authorised Thurlow to leak it. You fed Flint with juicy titbits to gain his confidence.'

'Nothing to do with me. Anything else?'

'A great deal, I'm afraid. Enquiries undertaken by Levi Shoemaker before your paymasters procured his untimely demise reveal that your son and his family have moved into a new bungalow on the front at Hastings. The sea air will do your granddaughter good after her sickness. It's far less expensive than the mansion you bought for your wife and yourself in Wimbledon, but luxurious for a couple with the husband out of work and a child in constant need of medical attention. The doctors' fees alone must cost you a king's ransom.'

'Chadwick?' Sir Godfrey's eyes were popping. 'Is there any truth in this?'

'Ask Oakes,' Rachel said.

Mulhearn turned to the inspector, who nodded miserably.

'I don't know about the place in Hastings, sir, but the Wimbledon property is quite something. The neighbours are mostly high-ups in the City. I was concerned, I must admit, but the superintendent set my mind at rest. He happened to mention that he'd received a legacy after the death of his aunt. He was the residuary beneficiary, I gather.'

'Perfectly true.' Chadwick gritted his teeth. 'All open and above board. Take a look at the paperwork in Somerset House, if you doubt me.'

'Levi Shoemaker did exactly that,' Rachel said. 'You inherited the princely sum of ninety-three pounds after payment of your aunt's debts. Hardly enough to sustain the life of sybaritic self-indulgence to which you and your family have become accustomed.'

'Self-indulgence? How dare you?'

Chadwick's temper broke. He balled his fists, and took a step towards her. He'd been a heavyweight in his boxing days, but Rachel didn't flinch.

'Your days in the ring are long past,' Rachel said calmly. 'Don't embarrass yourself.'

'For God's sake, man!' Sir Godfrey said. 'Don't do anything stupid!'

'Shut up, you old windbag!' Chadwick shouted. 'Have any of you the faintest idea what it's like to work all your life, and then watch your grandchild clinging to life with pathetic desperation? Have you...?'

'We all have our crosses to bear,' Rachel said. 'Save the extenuating circumstances for your plea in mitigation at the trial.'

'You arrogant bitch! You deserve everything you get!'

Chadwick reached inside his jacket, but even as he brought out a revolver, Trueman sprang from his chair, and knocked him to the ground. Long years behind a desk had slowed the superintendent's reactions, and softened his muscles. Trueman pinioned him to the floor, and Chadwick swore wildly as Oakes snatched away the gun.

Rachel opened her bag, and fished out a pair of handcuffs. 'Forgive me, Sir Godfrey. Even in Scotland Yard, I wasn't sure you'd have these in your own room. So I came prepared.'

Juliet Brentano's Journal

4 February 1919

Expect the unexpected. It was my mother's favourite piece of advice. And this evening Henrietta brought – for once – welcome tidings along with my evening meal. So welcome that I found I'd regained my appetite.

Cliff's condition hasn't worsened. She even dares to think he may be a little better. Might there yet be hope for him?

And if so, what will he do when he finds out how Brown hurt his sister?

4 January 1919

26

Jacob overslept the next morning. As he forced his eyes open, the sombre tolling of a distant church bell told him that it was eleven o'clock. Fortunately, he didn't need to go in to work. The *Clarion* appeared six days a week, and had a sister paper, the *Sunday Clarion*. In theory, the two businesses were distinct, but journalists on the daily often wrote for the Sunday newspaper, and the British public's love of scandal and sensation on the Sabbath kept crime reporters busy. But even that taskmaster Gomersall recognised his staff needed a day – or at least a few hours – of rest.

Jacob's head was sore, and his mouth parched. He felt hungover despite not having drunk a drop of alcohol. Cramped and disagreeable as his bed was, it took an effort of will to haul himself out. He blinked at his distorted reflection in the mirror, hollow-eyed and unshaven. His bones ached. Was this what it felt like to be old?

He put on his dressing gown, and padded down the passageway to the unpleasant little bathroom at the end. A cold bath was supposed to be healthy, he reminded himself, after discovering there was no hot water.

Once he'd towelled himself dry and shaved, he lay down again on the lumpy bed, and closed his eyes. The face of Sara Delamere swam into his mind. He was beginning to understand how Sara could transform into the exotic and desirable Nefertiti. Her gamine appearance reminded him of Louise Brooks, his favourite American film star.

Sara's face somehow transformed into Elaine Dowd's. With a lurch of dismay, he realised how much he'd cared for her. Knowing that she'd deceived him made a difference, but not much. Financial necessity had driven her, as well as greed. He'd enjoyed her company. Even if she was working to instructions, surely some of her affection had been genuine?

He hated to think of her lying in a mortuary. Even to recall the moment he'd discovered her lifeless body made him feel sick. Her mother's suicide was...

Suicide? A question jolted him. Had he been mistaken in jumping to the obvious conclusion? She hadn't left a note, but then again, suicides often didn't explain themselves.

A trivial oddity had stuck in his memory. He'd found unwashed plates and pans in the kitchen, as well as a dead woman wearing a soup-stained apron. Mrs Dowd's insistence on cleanliness in her kitchen had bordered on the fanatical. Would she have left the place in such a mess when putting her head in the oven? Jacob thought that if he'd decided life had nothing more to offer, he certainly wouldn't bother about washing up. Yet Patience Dowd's priorities in life were very different to his. She cared about appearances.

Patience Dowd knew what Elaine was up to; the omniscient Rachel Savernake had been adamant about that. She'd quarrelled with her daughter, she'd told Jacob so. Was she getting cold feet about the people they were mixed up with, the likes of McAlinden and Thurlow? With her daughter dead, the landlady might have talked out of turn, perhaps to the police. Had she been silenced?

And if so, who had killed her?

Gabriel Hannaway and his son sat facing each other, at opposite ends of a Chippendale dining table. They were eating Sunday lunch at the old man's Georgian residence on the edge of Hampstead Heath. Vincent owned a luxurious flat in Chelsea, but came to dine with his father every Sunday and Tuesday. It was a family tradition.

A neatly uniformed maid with short fair hair and dimples, no more than sixteen years old, refilled their wine glasses from a bottle of Chateau Latour. Nervousness made her clumsy, and as she emptied the bottle, a few drops spilled onto the white tablecloth.

'Idiot girl!' the old man wheezed.

Blushing, the maid began to stammer an apology. Vincent caught her wrist, and the words died on her lips.

'It's all right, Beatrice.' His tone was soothing, but his stare cut into her. 'Father's not at his best today. The gout, you know. Run along, and I'll have a word with you later.'

The girl curtsied timidly. Her skinny body was shaking. Vincent dug his hard fingers into her thin wrist for an instant before releasing his grip, and allowing her to scuttle out of the room.

Gabriel Hannaway shook his head. 'She has a lot to learn.'

'I'll train her.'

The old man sniffed. 'Is that what you call it? How long before you become bored? Answer me that. At least the last child had an ounce of character.'

'Vanity caused her to get ideas above her station. I know you always have a soft spot for the plump ones, but my tastes are more eclectic.' Vincent chewed a roast potato. 'Variety's the spice of life. You know that better than most.'

'Everything's falling apart, I know that. The world's gone to pot, my boy. Paper pound notes instead of gold sovereigns, chemical mush instead of proper beer...'

When Vincent yawned loudly, the old man banged down his knife and fork, and pushed his plate away. 'I can hardly taste this rubbish. What's the cook playing at?'

'It's your illness, Father.' A mocking light came into Vincent's eyes as he savoured a parsnip. 'The vegetables are crisp, and the meat succulent, while I find the horseradish sauce satisfyingly pungent. Your taste buds, I'm afraid, are not what they were.'

'You think you know it all.' The old man clicked his false teeth, a favourite form of rebuke. 'Yet here we are, facing the worst crisis in our history. Look at the men we've lost. And now this wretched news about Chadwick...'

'Chadwick became lazy. He put far too much trust in Thurlow. What he wanted was a young fellow to do his bidding. It's a familiar pattern, when a man becomes old and complacent.'

The iguana eyes flickered. 'Which of us is complacent? All I can see is that my life's work is threatened, and you remain insouciant. I'm reminded of Dr Pangloss.'

Vincent chewed on a gravy-smeared chunk of roast beef for fully half a minute before replying. 'I'd rather seize opportunities than mourn setbacks. The deaths of Pardoe and Keary were regrettable, but at least they're no longer able to obstruct progress.'

'Get in your way, you mean,' the old man croaked.

'If you like.' Vincent shrugged. 'Rachel Savernake is behind it all, you must see that.'

The old man bowed his head. 'I misjudged her.'

'She's done me a good turn, even if it's the last thing she wanted.'

'Her father went mad, you know.'

'Dug a penknife into his own wrist in Court Number One, didn't he?' Vincent's smile was malicious. 'Of course I know. The days are gone when even to hint at that squalid episode was taboo within our fellowship.'

'You're right.' The false teeth clicked again. 'I've served the Savernakes all my life. But this is a wicked betrayal. At least the Judge fled London, and hid himself out of sight. His daughter, on the other hand...'

Vincent smiled. 'I'm convinced that she, too, teeters on the tightrope of sanity.'

'Perhaps Sir Eustace...'

Vincent made a noise of exasperation. 'Do you really think that woman would allow old Leivers to pack her off to a sanatorium? She's made of stronger stuff than Keary's wife, you know.' He paused. 'Or Mother.'

The old man said nothing. He was a portrait of defeat.

'As for that tightrope,' Vincent said, 'only one question remains. Does she need a helping hand to tip her off?'

Leaning back in his chair, he contemplated the wine-stained tablecloth. The crimson blotch resembled a bloodstain.

*

Jacob missed lunch as well as breakfast. He didn't feel hungry, but a couple of glasses of water had begun to revive him. The first thing he needed to do was to escape this godforsaken place. Should he find somewhere else, or go back to Amwell Street? The rest of his possessions were still in Edgar House, and having paid his rent until the end of January, he was entitled to stay there, even if his landlady was dead. He wasn't sure he could face it, but the only way to find out was to return to the scene of the crime. And it was a crime scene. Even if Patience Dowd had not been murdered, suicide was a felony, long acknowledged as a crime against God and Man. The landlady wouldn't be buried in consecrated ground unless someone showed she hadn't died by her own hand. But who would care?

He packed his bag, told the wizened gnome that he wouldn't be coming back – news greeted with such indifference that the man might indeed have been a stuffed exhibit – and set off for Amwell Street. On the way he passed a newspaper vendor with a placard advertising one of the *Clarion*'s competitors. What he saw made him stumble so that he almost fell under the wheels of an oncoming cab.

Scotland Yard Superintendent in Handcuffs! Conspiracy Charge Sensation!

He dug in his pocket, and brought out a few coins. It went against the grain to contribute to the opposition's coffers, but he had no choice. Leaning against a lamppost, he skimmed through the story. The report was a classic example of making bricks without straw; he'd done it enough times to applaud the skill of the enterprise.

Superintendent Chadwick had been arrested in connection with the recent death of DC Thurlow. He was suspected of complicity in the events at Benfleet – repeated in lurid detail for the benefit of readers who might have forgotten the previous day's news – but the nature of his involvement was hopelessly unclear. Sir Godfrey Mulhearn had made a brief announcement to the press using the words 'sub judice' as a fig leaf to justify his refusal to say anything meaningful.

Jacob folded the newspaper, and handed it back to the mystified vendor. He didn't want to bump into anyone he knew while carrying a rival rag. It would be less of an embarrassment to be seen brandishing a set of the saucy French postcards kept under the counter of a particular shop in Marchmont Street.

Minutes later, he was standing outside Edgar House. He'd half expected to find a police constable on guard, but the place was deserted. Presumably Scotland Yard was preoccupied with the catastrophes of Thurlow's murder and Chadwick's arrest. The gas-oven death of a distressed woman of fifty was hardly a priority.

He hurried up to his room. It was impossible to contemplate looking in the kitchen, or at the sofa on which he and Elaine had embraced. Now he was back in the building, he wasn't sure he could bear to stay overnight. Too many memories came flooding back.

As he took the rest of his clothes out of drawers, he tried to decide where to go next, but his mind kept straying to Rachel Savernake. What role had she played in the arrest of Chadwick? She wove such a tangled web, he found it impossible to believe that the superintendent's fall from grace had nothing to do with her.

A furious knocking downstairs jerked him out of his reverie. Almost without thinking, he'd locked the front door after stepping over the threshold, and was thankful he'd done so. A sudden chill touched his bones. His room overlooked an alleyway, and he hurried across the landing to peek out through the drawn curtains of an empty room at the front with a view on the street. But there was a canopy over the front door, and whoever was making such a racket wasn't visible. Should he pretend not to be there?

A thought jumped into his mind. Had Rachel sent Trueman to find him? He hated the very thought that she might mean him harm. After all, the chauffeur had saved his life at Benfleet. But their previous encounters had left him with few illusions. Rachel had guessed that he found her good looks beguiling, and she was perfectly capable of taking advantage of him. He was a means to an end, and she was quite prepared to frame him for the Benfleet murders. He found himself praying that he hadn't outlived his usefulness.

The knocking redoubled in intensity. Whoever wanted him to open up did not mean to leave without an answer. Perhaps he'd been seen letting himself into the house. If so, there was every chance the visitor would break in if he felt thwarted. The door was stoutly built, but Trueman could punch through it as if it were made of paper.

Jacob stiffened his sinews, and headed downstairs.

'This will ruin me,' Sir Godfrey Mulhearn said.

Inspector Oakes, sitting on the other side of the desk in the assistant commissioner's office, preserved a tactful silence. The old boy, he thought, was probably right.

'A corrupt police constable is one thing,' Sir Godfrey said, 'but a superintendent... the press are having a field day.'

He looked expectantly at his subordinate. Oakes cleared his throat.

'We can only hope that soon they'll have something else to distract them, sir.'

'There's talk that the Indian nationalists are plotting an outrage,' Mulhearn said hopefully. 'If we can foil them...'

His voice trailed away. They both knew that intelligence about extremist factions in the subcontinent was sketchy and unreliable. Oakes decided he must change the subject.

'Superintendent Chadwick is keeping his own counsel, sir. Seems that he's more frightened of the consequences of betraying his confederates than he is of a long stretch in prison, with or without hard labour.'

Sir Godfrey banged his fist on the desk. 'What sort of men are we dealing with, Oakes? How can these scoundrels exert such a stranglehold on someone like Chadwick, with a fine record of public service, and half a dozen commendations for bravery?'

Money had a lot to do with it, Oakes reflected, but there was certainly more to it than bribery. They had the knack of instilling fear. No, an emotion sharper even than fear. Terror.

'You refer to men, sir, but we're still not clear about the game Miss Savernake is playing.'

'What d'you mean? When she accused Chadwick, it came out of the blue.' Sir Godfrey paused awkwardly. He'd come perilously close to saying that he'd expected her to expose Oakes' villainy. 'That is, we had no idea that we were nurturing a viper in our bosom, so to speak. Chadwick is plainly up to his neck in this Benfleet business, and she's stumbled across his secret. Yet she hasn't blabbed to the press. I've said it before, and I'll say it again. Discretion and restraint in such a young filly is admirable.'

'I'm not sure Rachel Savernake has ever stumbled in her life,' Oakes said quietly. 'Everything she does, she does for a reason. I wonder about her motives.'

'If you ask me,' Sir Godfrey said, 'she's damned public-spirited.'

Oakes allowed the words to hang in the air for a few moments. 'Apparently, sir. But what other considerations are driving her on?'

'Such as?'

'Rachel Savernake poses as some kind of amateur detective. She was indirectly responsible for Linacre's death, and I feel sure she was involved with Pardoe's, though I can't prove it. The private investigator she hired was murdered, she was present when Keary was killed, and thanks to her, a well-respected senior policeman is currently languishing in a cell. All these incidents are connected; they must be.'

Sir Godfrey stared at him. 'You talked to her last night after... Chadwick was taken away. I know she blocks better than a Yorkshire batsman, but did you pick up any clues?'

Oakes gritted his teeth. 'Instinct tells me that Rachel Savernake is pursuing a mission. To destroy people who stand in her way.'

'In the way of what, though?'

Oakes shook his head. 'That's the trouble, sir. I still haven't the foggiest idea.'

The unknown caller kept pounding on the front door as Jacob fumbled with his key. He was convinced he'd find himself face to face with Trueman. When finally he opened the door, he was confronted by a squat man with sloping shoulders who was in need of a good shave. He took a step backwards, and his hesitation allowed the visitor to enter the hallway, and bang the door shut behind him.

He clenched his fists, and Jacob saw that he was wearing knuckledusters.

'Where is she?'

'Elaine?' Jacob was as flustered as a boy caught stealing from a sweetshop. 'She's dead. Murdered. And her mother has killed herself.'

The man raised his right fist. 'Don't be stupid. You know who I mean.'

Jacob felt his whole body shaking. How could he raise the alarm? It was a quiet Sunday afternoon in Clerkenwell. Even if he screamed the place down, who would hear?

'You mean... Rachel Savernake? She's not...'

The man grabbed his neck. 'I told you not to be stupid. Where is she?'

'I'm... sorry.' Jacob was finding it hard to breathe. The man was crushing his windpipe. 'Who...?'

'The Delamere woman.'

'She's not here. She's never been here in her life. She's...'

'Stop wasting my time. She's left home, but you're in touch with her. Where is she hiding?'

'I... honestly, I couldn't even guess.' He gasped as the pressure on his windpipe increased. 'I've talked to her, it's true.'

'And?' The man released his grip.

'She's frightened, she said she'd left home. I think she's moving around. I'm expecting to hear from her again, but I've no idea when.'

The knuckledusters caught him a glancing blow on the temple, and he cried out. Tears blurred his vision.

'I ought to kill you just for being a crybaby,' the man said.

Jacob could feel blood trickling down his cheek. He didn't want to die a hero.

'I'd tell you if I knew.'

Cowardice or common sense? He was struggling for breath. Fear was suffocating him.

'One last time. What's her address?'

'I haven't a clue!'

The man punched him in the ribs. 'Do I have to break every bone in your skinny body?'

'She didn't trust me enough to say.'

He coughed out the words. The blows had hurt him badly. What about internal bleeding? Was he going to die here, less than twenty-four hours after Patience Dowd?

The man gave him a long, hard stare before giving a brisk nod. 'Who would trust a weakling like you?'

Jacob cringed. He burned with humiliation, but was long past caring about his dignity. Everything in his life boiled down to this: he desperately wanted to survive.

'You're a marked man,' his assailant said. 'The minute you find out where she is, put an advertisement in the *Clarion*'s personal column. Your first name, followed by the address. Do it at once. Understand?'

Jacob made a gurgling noise. He hoped the man would take it for assent.

'Make sure you do. No delaying. Or next time, I'll break that scrawny neck of yours in two.'

The man turned on his heel, and was gone. Jacob sank to the floor. The blood had run onto his hand, and it seeped onto the floral carpet, darkening the pink pattern of a rose. But he didn't care. He was alive. For the moment, nothing else mattered.

27

'Picked on someone bigger than yourself, lad?' Gomersall demanded after the next morning's editorial meeting.

Jacob mustered a thin smile. 'Argument with a door, sir. The door won.'

'So I see.'

'It looks worse than it feels.'

'Thank heaven for that.'

Jacob winced. Studying the cut and bruising on his face in the shaving mirror that morning, he'd persuaded himself that he'd escaped lightly from his encounter with the thug and his knuckledusters. Once he'd calmed down after the intruder's departure, he'd decided he was lucky to be alive, and resolved to make the most of it. He stayed overnight in his room at Amwell Street, but after the physical and emotional pummelling of the past few days, he'd been early to bed, sleeping fitfully until his alarm clock rang. Nobody was keeping watch on Edgar House, so far as he could tell, although it occurred to him that someone skilled in the craft of surveillance might also be skilled in avoiding detection.

Gomersall, who didn't have a credulous bone in his body, gave him an old-fashioned look.

'You worry me, lad. Fighting doors is all fine and dandy, but remember what happened to Tom Betts. Let alone that young devil McAlinden. These are dangerous times for *Clarion* journalists. Given your habit of finding yourself cheek-by-jowl with violent death, there's not a life company in the land that would treat you as a good risk.'

Jacob opted for contrition rather than bluster. 'Sorry, sir. I'm learning that you need eyes in the back of your head in this job. But I won't let you down.'

Gomersall clapped him on the shoulder. 'Not saying you will, lad. But things come in threes. I don't want to find myself mourning by your graveside. Not in winter, anyhow. I don't care for funerals, and I loathe them even more when it's this bitter.'

Gomersall was right about the weather. The temperature had tumbled overnight, and Jacob had trudged to Fleet Street through a shower of sleet. As he returned from the editor's sanctum to Tom Betts' office – no, *his* office, he must look ahead, not back – he told himself to make up his mind. Last night, he'd agonised over whether to adopt Baldwin's philosophy of safety first.

The trouble was, that slogan had lost Baldwin the last election, and wrecked his career. A crime reporter needed to take risks, even if putting his life in jeopardy on a daily basis was taking devotion to duty too far. Jacob couldn't bear the prospect of simply giving up on his investigation into Rachel Savernake. It hurt more than the damage to his face. He owed it to Tom to do a Harry Lauder and keep right on to the end of the road. To do otherwise would betray not just Tom, but also Sara Delamere.

Would Sara keep her promise to contact him again? He hoped so, though he wasn't quite sure whether that was due to curiosity or desire. If she did get in touch, they'd need to take every precaution. Was it better to concoct an advertisement with fictitious information, or simply do nothing? Each time he remembered that ruffian's determination to discover her whereabouts, he couldn't help shivering. Whoever had hired him either wanted to find out something Sara knew, or to silence her because she knew too much.

Jacob chewed his lip. Rachel Savernake's man had saved him at Benfleet. He didn't want to believe her motives were impure. And Sara wanted to make sure Rachel knew about Pardoe's threats. Surely Rachel had no reason to wish her ill?

And yet. There was something wild and unpredictable about Rachel. The calm way she'd watched William Keary burn to death, and the confidence with which she'd blackmailed him to keep quiet about Benfleet, frightened him. Trueman had killed McAlinden – thank God! – and she didn't bat an eyelid. He'd never known a woman so self-possessed. It wasn't natural.

A black telephone sat quietly on his desk. His hand strayed towards it. The itch to call Gaunt House, and ask to speak to Rachel needed to be scratched. But she'd made it clear that she was the one who'd decide if and when they spoke again, and he put his hand back in his pocket. He dared not defy her.

What about ringing Scotland Yard? Inspector Oakes might be willing to spare him half an hour, even if he remained tight-lipped about exactly what had led to Chadwick's arrest.

The telephone shrilled, and Jacob jumped. Had the inspector read his mind?

He picked up the receiver, and he heard Peggy's distinctive noisy sniff.

'Lady for you.'

His heart pounded. Sara or Rachel, which of them wanted to speak to him?

'What's her name?'

'Calls herself Mrs Wenna Tilson.' He visualised Peggy pulling a face. 'Funny accent.'

Sara, he thought, it must be Sara, pretending to be someone else because she was so afraid.

'Put her through.'

'Mr Flint?'

The voice was unfamiliar. An older woman, whose burr suggested the deep south west of England.

'Sara,' he whispered, 'is that you?'

'Sorry, Mr Flint. Didn't the girl tell you? My name is Tilson. Mrs Wenna Tilson from Sancreed.'

He blinked. 'Sancreed? Never heard of it.'

'Sancreed in Cornwall. I was given your name by a very good friend of mine.' A tremulous note entered her voice. 'He told me to call you. Said it was important.'

'Who is your friend, Mrs Tilson?'

He heard the woman gulp. She sounded as though she might burst into tears. 'He died last week.'

Jacob racked his brains. The roll call of the recently deceased was alarmingly long. 'What was he called?'

He could almost picture the woman at the other end of the line squeezing the telephone in her hand. She sounded as if she was making a supreme effort of will. Unless she was as good an actress as Sara, this conversation was proving very hard for her.

'His name was Mr Leviticus Shoemaker.'

For once Jacob was speechless. The clutter surrounding him matched the confused jumble in his mind.

'Are you still there, Mr Flint?' The woman sounded timid, as if she'd committed an appalling faux pas.

'Yes, yes,' he said. 'It's just that I wasn't expecting this call.'

'I'm sorry. You must think it dreadfully rude of me, ringing you like this, out of the blue. I'm sure you're a busy man, with more important things to do than speak to a nobody like me.'

'Please, don't apologise,' he gabbled, afraid she'd hang up. 'I'm glad to hear from you.'

'I really wouldn't bother you if Levi hadn't insisted.'

'Any friend of Levi's,' he said expansively, 'is a friend of mine.'

'That's kind of you to say, sir.'

'My name's Jacob, and I'm very glad to hear from you. Was there anything in particular you wanted to tell me?'

'It's about the dictating machine,' she said.

'I don't quite understand.'

'The last time he was here, he dictated a statement. He wanted you to be the first to hear it.'

Rachel was drinking coffee with the Truemans and Martha. The housemaid had switched on the wireless, and Jack Hylton and his orchestra were playing 'The Best Things in Life are Free'. Spread out on one occasional table was a hand-drawn floor plan of a large house; folded on another was a map of London.

'Wednesday is creeping nearer,' she said. 'Soon it will be over.'

Martha was humming along with the music. 'I can't believe we've come so far.'

'I kept my promise,' Rachel said. 'Now, are our young friends ready for what they have to do?'

'Absolutely.' Martha's voice rose; she was struggling to suppress excitement. 'They're fully prepared.'

'No qualms, no second thoughts?'

'We chose them carefully.' Martha tasted her coffee. 'They won't buckle, you can trust me.'

'I trust you with my life,' Rachel said softly.

Trueman said, 'I'll collect the revolvers this afternoon. Different gunsmith, of course, but he has a good name for keeping his mouth shut.'

'Excellent.' Rachel turned to the housekeeper. 'And you've paid a visit to the chemist?'

'First thing this morning, while you were pounding away on the treadmill,' Mrs Trueman said. 'I don't know why you bother.'

'You know I like to keep fit. Ready for every eventuality.' Rachel smiled. 'You have enough to do what's necessary?'

'More than enough,' the older woman said. 'I just wondered…'

Rachel's groan was theatrical. 'You're always just wondering. If you're worried that Oakes is still a threat, let me set your mind at rest. After the Chadwick business, he's eating out of my hand.'

'But what about Jacob Flint? He might ruin everything.'

'I doubt it.' Rachel consulted her watch. 'Soon he'll be on his way to Cornwall.'

In halting sentences, Wenna Tilson told Jacob her story. She'd been governess to the children of a Penzance landowner, prior to marrying a man fifteen years her senior, who owned a grocery shop in the town. Five years ago, her husband had died, and in the summer of 1928, Levi Shoemaker had come to Cornwall for a week's holiday by the sea. The pair had struck up a conversation in Morrab Gardens, while listening to the band play selections from Romberg and Lehar. Their friendship soon ripened, and Shoemaker became a regular visitor. He talked about retiring, and purchased a house in Provence as well as funding the cost of renovating Wenna's own cottage in the Cornish countryside. There was, she said, an understanding between them. Levi wasn't getting any younger, and she thought he was ready to leave London and share the rest of his life with her. They would divide their time between Cornwall and France.

Lately, he'd been working long hours, and though he never discussed his cases, she could see that the investigation he was pursuing was causing him a good deal of worry. On a hastily arranged visit to Cornwall, a few days before his death, he'd brought a Dictaphone, and spent an afternoon locked in his study. Afterwards he said that he'd prepared a statement 'in case anything happens to me'. Distressed, she'd begged him to give up his job, and he'd said he expected to do so shortly. If the balloon went up, he might need to cross the Channel in haste, and hide away in Provence. If so, he'd send word when it was safe for her to join him there.

On Wednesday, Levi had telephoned. He was in a tearing hurry, and made her swear to tell Jacob about the dictated statement if for any reason he wasn't able to do so. It was clear that he'd rung her moments after Jacob had shinned down the fire ladder, and probably just before he lost his life. After barely a couple of minutes, the call was interrupted when Levi heard someone hammering on his door downstairs.

The next thing Wenna Tilson heard was that the man she loved was dead. A telegram from Levi's lawyer broke the news. Grief had overwhelmed her. But she needed to honour Levi's last wish.

'Will you come here, Mr Flint?' she asked. 'That is what he wanted.'

'Where is your cottage?'

'Sancreed is a hamlet a few miles west of Penzance. The middle of nowhere, Levi used to say. He loved the seclusion. So very different from the hustle and bustle of London. Or at least so I believe. I've never travelled further than Torquay myself.'

Geography wasn't Jacob's strong suit, but Sancreed sounded remote. Not only that, his experience of visits to rural hideaways was deeply discouraging. He recalled the headline in that rotten rag, the *Witness*.

Benfleet Bungalow Bloodbath!

'Will you come here, Mr Flint? I'm sure you're a busy man, but Levi wouldn't have insisted if it wasn't important.'

Would he be walking into another trap? He gazed around the room, searching for inspiration. The ghost of Tom Betts whispered in his ear: 'When in doubt, flannel.'

Jacob cleared his throat. 'Once again, Mrs Tilson, please accept my condolences on your sad loss. I only met Mr Shoemaker once, but his reputation was second to none. I'm so grateful that you've called.'

He paused, making it up as he went along. 'My diary is crammed to overflowing, but I'd like to visit Sancreed. Let me call you back later today to make arrangements.'

'That's ever so kind of you, Mr Flint.' She sounded genuine enough, but so had Stan Thurlow. To say nothing of Elaine and her mother. 'You have my number. I'm not going out again today. It's perishing cold down here.'

After he'd rung off, he set about checking Wenna Tilson's bona fides. With the help of an obliging soul at the *Cornishman*, he tracked down a five-year-old announcement of the funeral of her husband, described as a grocery merchant and supplier of comestibles. But it wasn't impossible that his caller had been hired to impersonate the woman. Sanctuary Cottage sounded idyllic – he pictured a thatched roof, and red roses circling around a brightly painted front door – but might it belong to Pardoe Properties? He begged Poyser to make enquiries of a source at the majestic building housing the Land Registry just around the corner in Lincoln's Inn Fields.

'You're wasting your time,' Pop-Eye said. 'Those new property rules don't apply to folk who buy houses in Cornwall. I suppose you could go down to Truro to try and find out.'

'Never mind,' Jacob said wearily. 'It was a very long shot.'

If only he'd asked for the name of Levi's solicitor so that he could try to check the facts. But lawyers were notoriously unwilling to discuss their clients' affairs, let alone give helpful titbits to journalists. In the end, he decided to trust to instinct. He called Wenna Tilson back, and told her that he'd catch the sleeper train. As he put the telephone down, he asked himself if he'd made a fatal blunder.

Jacob had never before travelled by sleeper, and the journey on the Great Western Railway proved surprisingly enjoyable. The train was nowhere near full to capacity, and his overnight rest was undisturbed. He had gone back to Edgar House to pack a light bag, and slipped away by the fire escape, just in case anyone was keeping watch, before hailing a taxi in Farringdon Road to take him to Paddington. As far as he could tell, nobody had followed him.

He'd arranged to call on Wenna Tilson at ten o'clock, and he occupied himself by breakfasting in a small cafe, one of the few that remained open during the winter season. Through a misty window, he watched the boats sailing in and out of the harbour, and could see the distant horizon where a slate-grey sea met the charcoal sky.

Soon he was exchanging banter with a cheerful waitress twice his age whose laugh was as loud as her bosom was formidable. Eyeing his damaged face with undisguised curiosity, she wanted to know what brought a young fellow with a Yorkshire accent so far from the Ridings. When he said he hoped to catch up with two old friends, Levi Shoemaker and Wenna Tilson, he was instantly rewarded by a shocked gasp.

'You've not heard the news, then?'

'News?' He was wide-eyed. Just as well he hadn't made the mistake of admitting he was a journalist.

'Oh dear, it's ever so sad. I was at school with Wenna's brother. Lovely lady, very popular in the town. Life can be so cruel. First she lost her husband to a heart attack, and now her gentleman friend has died. Drowned, of all things – his body was found in the Thames. Can you imagine anything more awful?'

Jacob gathered that only a censored and distorted version of the story of Levi's death had reached Penzance. The prevailing wisdom was that he must have had too much to drink one night, and fallen into the river. It was out of character, but how else could people explain his death? Nobody had a clue about the torture. Digesting his last slice of pork sausage, he congratulated himself. This time his instinct had not betrayed him. Wenna Tilson was telling the truth.

The waitress advised him where to find a taxi, and waved as he left the cafeteria. The journey to Sancreed took him along lonely, twisty country lanes that made even rural Yorkshire seem metropolitan. On the way, the driver told him about the ancient holy well and the legends surrounding it. Nowhere, Jacob thought, could be more different from Whitechapel, with its grime, its excitement, and its danger.

They pulled up outside a whitewashed stone building in its own grounds. There were no roses, and no thatch, but the lawn was well-kept, and the village church was visible through the trees. A smartly painted sign bore the name *Sanctuary Cottage*. So this was Levi Shoemaker's home from home. Anywhere less like his seedy office would be hard to imagine. The curtains were drawn at every window as a mark of respect.

Jacob bounded up the path and rang the bell. The door opened to reveal a woman of perhaps forty-five summers who mustered a wan smile of welcome. She was dressed in black from head to toe, but there was about her a touch of faded elegance, as well as dignity. Lines criss-crossed around her eyes, and pink blotches from recently shed tears coloured her cheeks, but her handshake was warm. She had a fine head of corn-coloured hair and appealing, regular features; Jacob understood what Levi Shoemaker had seen in her. His immediate impression was of a decent woman, adept at distracting her lover from the harsh realities of a private enquiry agent's professional life.

Relieving him of his hat, coat, and bag, she led him into the front room, where a log fire blazed in an inglenook. She noticed his appreciative scrutiny of the antique rosewood furniture and the deep-piled Axminster carpet.

'I could never afford such comfort on what Tilson left me. Levi was extremely generous. How did you happen to know him?'

'I was following up a lead on a story, and thought he might be able to help.' Jacob stood in front of the fire. 'I visited his office the afternoon he died.'

'The solicitor didn't tell me exactly how Levi died,' Wenna Tilson said quietly. 'Later, when his secretary called, I asked what happened, but she said there'd have to be an inquest. She was trying to be kind, but I'm stronger than people think. I buried two children and two husbands before ever I met Levi. I don't believe he drowned by accident. He was a strong swimmer. We used to go bathing together at Newlyn. Please tell me the truth. He was murdered, wasn't he?'

Jacob inclined his head. 'I'm sorry, Mrs Tilson. I don't know who was responsible for his death, but I suspect it was connected to an enquiry he'd undertaken. He told me he'd been followed, and he was planning to leave the country. I'm in his debt, because he persuaded me to leave his office by the fire escape. He must have telephoned you the moment I left. If I'd stayed ten minutes longer, I suppose I'd have been attacked and killed too. You could say that he saved my life.'

She closed her eyes, absorbing the confirmation of what she'd dreaded. 'In the Ukraine, Levi endured unspeakable horrors. He used to say that nothing could compare to that. Recently, though, something changed. He seemed to be constantly looking over his shoulder. It wasn't like him to be afraid.'

'He was a brave man.'

Wenna Tilson studied the bruise and cut on his face. 'By the look of it, so are you.'

'A minor altercation.' He waved it away. 'Something and nothing.'

'Do you think Levi's recording will cast light on who killed him?'

'With any luck,' Jacob said, 'You've listened to it?'

'No, I'm not ready to hear his voice again.' Her voice broke. 'I'm sorry, Mr Flint, I find this very difficult. Levi came here on a flying visit, the week before last, and that was when he dictated his statement. He must have realised his life was in danger. I'll leave you in peace to listen. See, the paraphernalia is over there on the sideboard.'

The door closed behind her, and Jacob took out his notepad and pencil, ready to listen to the voice of a dead man.

28

'I'm telling this story,' Levi Shoemaker said, in his careful, almost flawless English, 'without knowing how it may end. Nor do I know if anyone will ever hear me tell it. If they do, it will be because I am dead. If I meet my maker in suspicious circumstances, I trust this statement helps to bring the perpetrator to justice.

'Last autumn, I was consulted by a man giving his name as Trueman. He asked if I could undertake certain highly confidential investigations into the activities of several well-known individuals. I satisfied him of my credentials, and quoted a daily fee exceeding the highest rate I've ever charged. He did not blink at the cost.

'He gave me four names. Claude Linacre, Lawrence Pardoe, William Keary, and Vincent Hannaway. An artist, a financier, an actor-manager, and a solicitor. All were known to me by reputation, though Keary was by far the most famous. Trueman said he sought a detailed report about their personal habits and activities. Their business activities interested him only in so far as they touched on the men's private lives. He refused to explain the purpose of his enquiry, saying that he wanted me to investigate with a completely open mind.

'Trueman was businesslike and intelligent, but he displayed none of the arrogance typical of men accustomed to great wealth. Weather-beaten cheeks and calloused hands indicated years spent undertaking rough work, much of it outdoors. Plainly, he was acting on behalf of an undisclosed principal.

'When I put this to him, he said he represented Miss Rachel Savernake. I was vaguely aware of a late judge by that name, and Trueman confirmed she was his daughter. She'd recently arrived in London, and had reason to be curious about certain of her father's former acquaintances. That, he said, was all I needed to know.

'I said I was only willing to accept the instructions if I could meet my client. Ultimately, this was agreed, and I called on her at Gaunt House, a home previously owned by Crossan, the fraudster. It was not so much a domestic residence as a luxurious fortress. Even more fascinating was Rachel Savernake herself. She was astonishingly self-possessed, like those female saints whose faith was so fervent that they faced scourging and decapitation with sublime indifference.

'Although she was utterly rational, I detected a touch of fanaticism. This was a woman prepared to destroy anything – perhaps including herself – to achieve her goals.

'Whilst I was dubious about the assignment, I surrendered to intense curiosity, as well as the oldest frailty of all. Not the allure of a beautiful woman, but the prospect of comfortable retirement on the strength of what she paid me.

'First, I sought proof that she could afford the outrageous payment on account that I'd demanded. Not only was she ready for the question, she went so far as to show me her father's will. The Judge had left his estate in trust for her. She became absolutely entitled to it on her twenty-fifth birthday. The Judge had accumulated great wealth during his years at the Bar, to add to a substantial inheritance which included an island and a large if dilapidated manor house. Rachel Savernake was one of the richest women in Britain.

'Before long, I was working for her full-time, even though she also employed other agents. As she said to me, she never put all her eggs in one basket. She asked me to investigate a police constable called Thurlow, a mother and daughter by the name of Dowd, who lived in Clerkenwell, as well as three journalists on the *Clarion*, Thomas Betts, Oliver McAlinden, and Jacob Flint.

'As regards Claude Linacre, I pieced together a picture of a debauched sadist, a second-rate artist and a third-rate libertine. Making free with Rachel Savernake's chequebook, I learned sickening details of his behaviour towards young women whom he met at the Inanity, and ultimately of his affair with Dolly Benson. When she was murdered, her former lover was arrested, but my information made Linacre an obvious suspect. I told Rachel Savernake so, and said she must go to the police.

'To my surprise, she agreed without demur, promising my name wouldn't be mentioned. She was true to her word, but the buffoons at the Yard were terrified by the prospect of interviewing a minister's younger brother. Frustration presumably led her to contact Linacre. What she said to him, I do not know, but it was enough to drive him to suicide.

'Perverse as it may seem, I was reassured. Perhaps she'd gleaned information from her late father discrediting his former associates, and wanted to serve justice by having me substantiate her suspicions. I was puzzled, however, when she asked me to look into the backgrounds of Sir Godfrey

Mulhearn, Superintendent Chadwick, and Inspector Oakes. Already I'd found that DC Thurlow was conducting a clandestine relationship with the Dowd girl. Thurlow and the girl's mother had something in common. Both lived beyond their means. Stories of corruption at the Yard are rife, but I'd thought the cancer was confined to sergeants in Soho taking bribes for turning a blind eye to the local dens of vice. I never anticipated that the rottenness might have infected the hierarchy. Worryingly, however, I have now concluded that Arthur Chadwick's expenditure far outstrips his income. A modest recent legacy does not begin to explain it.

'Pardoe, Keary, and Hannaway all belong to the same clique. Pardoe's second wife was a floosie he met at the Inanity, but she died from natural causes. Keary boasts a long line of conquests, but has settled down with an Italian widow of independent means. Hannaway is a bachelor who has made more than one young woman pregnant before paying through the nose to have the unborn child disposed of.

'McAlinden relishes feasting with panthers. Flint is bright but impulsive. He, like McAlinden before him, lodges with the Dowd women. Betts was conscientious and law-abiding. He'd become intrigued by Rachel Savernake, and was making enquires about her until someone ran over him.'

Shoemaker coughed. 'Something was fishy about that accident, and although Rachel Savernake did not ask me to do so, I took it upon myself to investigate. The crucial witness vanished after giving a false name, and I suspected that Betts was injured deliberately. Had curiosity been his undoing?

'I took myself off to the newspaper reading room at the British Museum, and pored through articles Betts had published. I was struck by the disproportionate attention he'd paid to a vicious recent murder, of a criminal called Harold Coleman. His account of the death led me to his report of Coleman's original conviction for manslaughter. A bookmaker had been killed during a quarrel involving half a dozen men. The evidence identifying Coleman as the one who struck the fatal blow was questionable, and Betts implied that he'd been made a scapegoat. It wouldn't be the first time a gang has sacrificed one of its number in order to protect a more powerful rogue. When Coleman broke out of prison, Betts' articles about the escape again harked back to the dubious nature of the man's conviction.

'My next step was to investigate Coleman. A cellmate who befriended him in the Scrubs, and who had himself just been released, told me that Coleman confided in him. In a nutshell, Coleman's real name was Smith, and he deserted from the army while on leave in 1916. After that, he moved from job to job in his native Cumberland, calling himself Harold Brown. Later, he adopted the surname Coleman, earning a crust at northern racecourses through the "bucket drop". Bookmakers are threatened their business will be wrecked if they don't pay for protection, and are required to drop half a crown each into a bucket that the rogue takes around the track. Coleman set his sights higher after moving to London. He hung around the fringes of the Rotherhithe Razors gang up to the time of his arrest.

'What startled me was what he'd done before then. Specifically, a job he took just after the armistice. For a few weeks he was working – to his cellmate's amusement – as a butler in a manor house on a remote northern island.' Shoemaker paused. 'His employer was Judge Savernake.'

*

A discreet knock at the door caused Jacob to stop the machine.

'I'm forgetting my manners in my old age.' Wenna Tilson was bearing a tea tray. 'Can I offer you a drink?'

'Thanks very much.'

She looked at him. 'Are you all right?'

'Fine,' Jacob said hastily. 'It's just strange, listening to him speak, knowing that…'

'That's why I can't bear to listen. Is that cowardly, Mr Flint?'

He shook his head.

'Right, then. I'll leave you in peace.'

The moment the door closed behind her, Levi's voice filled the room again.

'How much of what the cellmate said was true, how much of it melodramatic embellishment? To me, Coleman's story was so strange that, even if embellished, it must have a kernel of truth.

'He said the Judge was wildly unpredictable. Even though a tame doctor prescribed a cocktail of drugs to keep his mind and temper in balance, he often behaved in an erratic and violent fashion. Everyone on the island of Gaunt hated him – except for his daughter, Rachel. She'd inherited his cruel streak. Whenever she was crossed, she would take out her temper on someone defenceless. Or something. Once, after she'd quarrelled with her father, Coleman witnessed her wringing the neck of a servant's pet cat.

'Another girl of similar age to Rachel lived at Savernake Hall. The Judge's illegitimate great-niece, Juliet Brentano. Her father, a soldier, was the Judge's nephew. Charles Brentano was a gambler, on close terms with the Judge. A French woman of the streets had given birth to Juliet, and mother and daughter had lived under Brentano's protection until the war broke out. At much the same time, the Judge was forced to retire from public life after attempting to slash his wrist at the Old Bailey. Brentano sent his mistress and daughter to Savernake Hall while he went off to fight in France. He became quite a hero before suffering severe wounds. He didn't return to Gaunt until some weeks after the armistice.

'Juliet was a sickly, consumptive child, though Coleman believed her ill-health was exaggerated by her mother, so as to keep her out of harm's way. Rachel resented their presence on the island, and became intensely and irrationally jealous of Juliet. To feed her father's paranoia, she pretended that Brentano had misused her, and persuaded the Judge to rid himself of both Brentano and his mistress. Coleman was paid fifty guineas to kidnap the couple, and take them to an address in London. He came back to Gaunt, but Brentano and the woman never returned. The story was given out that they'd died of the influenza. Coleman believed that the Judge's associates had murdered them. And that Rachel Savernake, not quite fifteen years old, had orchestrated their deaths.

'Coleman told his cellmate that he left Gaunt because he found the place and the people loathsome. Rachel might be young, but he described her as pure evil. Yet he seemed obsessed by the Savernakes – just as Betts seemed obsessed with Coleman. And he enjoyed dropping cryptic hints that he knew a secret about Rachel Savernake, something he could profit from, if only he could get out of jail.

'The cellmate didn't have any idea what Coleman had got up to between absconding from the Scrubs and arriving at the mortuary. The ordeal that Coleman had endured prior to his death bore some of the gang's hallmarks, although with a difference. This time, they used acid as well as razors. He surely begged to be allowed to die.

'Nobody has been arrested for Coleman's murder. Only the *Clarion*, thanks to Betts, bothered to report it. As regards Rachel's part in the deaths of Brentano and his mistress, perhaps Coleman exaggerated. Could a young girl really be so wicked? But he was right, the couple died together. At Somerset House, I found death certificates for Charles Brentano, and one Yvette Viviers. Heart failure was given as the cause of death, but many different things can cause the heart to fail.

'The place of death was given as Chancery Lane, on 29 January 1919. There was no more precise address. Both certificates were given by the country's most eminent medical practitioner, Sir Eustace Leivers. I'd discovered he was a fellow member of the chess club to which Pardoe, Keary, and Hannaway belonged. So were distinguished men from all walks of life – politicians, businessmen, a bishop, and even a trade union leader.

'The club was known as the Gambit Club, based in a building called Gaunt Chambers, at Gallows Court on the edge of Lincoln's Inn and Chancery Lane. Gaunt Chambers was home to a barristers' set founded by Lionel Savernake. The same building also houses the firm of Hannaway & Hannaway, and is the registered office of a host of businesses connected with men such as Keary and Pardoe.

'These discoveries bring me almost up to date. I am concerned that matters are coming to a head, but what happens next is impossible to guess. I have been followed more than once lately – by whom, I cannot be sure. I have no wish to suffer the same mishap as Betts. Rachel Savernake has now told me to discontinue my investigations into Lawrence Pardoe. She gave the same order forty-eight hours before Linacre died. If Pardoe also meets an untimely end,

I shall at once terminate my retainer with Miss Rachel Savernake.'

'I'm not accusing anyone of any criminal offence.' As he came to the end of his statement, Levi Shoemaker sounded as cautious as a solicitor determined to avoid any hint of defamation. 'I simply wish to state the facts of which I am aware. I leave it to others to decide what, if anything, to make of them.'

And that was all. Jacob sat quietly for a few minutes, trying to make sense of everything he'd heard. For all the old man's calm, it wasn't fanciful to detect a note of anxiety. He'd realised he was in danger. And there was little doubt in Jacob's mind that he was afraid of Rachel Savernake.

Suppose Coleman was right, and Rachel had somehow engineered, through her father, the deaths of Charles Brentano and Yvette Viviers at the hands of the Judge's friends. Having inherited a fortune, and made a new life in London, she'd be desperate to keep her secret. Had she set out to eliminate the men responsible for killing the couple?

As a man on the run, Coleman would be desperate for money. The chances were that he'd come across Tom Betts earlier in his criminal career; hence Tom's interest in writing about him.

Coleman said he knew her secret.

Had Rachel paid him to keep quiet about her past? Or arranged his death to make sure he kept his mouth shut? Taking wild gambles excited Rachel Savernake. Perhaps madness ran in the family.

Juliet Brentano's Journal

5 February 1919

A terrible storm has raged all day. The worst I can remember. It uprooted trees like a child plucking daisies. The causeway lies beneath four feet of water, and the sea is so rough that any attempt to cross Gaunt Sound by boat would be an act of suicide.

The telephone lines are down. Harold Brown is still in the village, probably drinking the pub dry. Cliff, meanwhile, is regaining his strength, though Henrietta says Rachel started coughing this morning. Now she is feverish and rambling.

Who knows what the coming days may bring?

29

Before boarding the train back to London, Jacob telephoned Clarion House. Peggy sounded pleased that nobody wanted him, not a blessed soul. So: no word from Oakes, from Sara, or from Rachel Savernake.

As the express thundered through the English countryside, he gazed out at the bare trees and sleepy meadows. Listening to a dead man's voice had left him in an unaccustomed state of melancholy. For the first time since moving to London, he felt a pang sharper than hunger. He was on his own. Sara was lovely, but she was a millionaire's former mistress. Even if she came to no harm, as he profoundly hoped, he was sure she was out of his reach.

As for Rachel Savernake, a remark of Wenna Tilson's as they exchanged farewells had stopped him in his tracks.

'The secretary told me you needed to listen to Levi's statement.'

'The secretary?'

'Yes, I told you. She rang me to ask if Levi had left any messages for anyone. Her employer needed to know.

Something to do with obtaining probate; I didn't understand the technicalities, but that's the law for you. I told her about the Dictaphone, and said Levi had asked me to call you.'

He cringed inwardly. 'You did?'

'Yes, she didn't seem surprised. Actually, she was very helpful, and even gave me the *Clarion*'s phone number, so I didn't have to look it up. She suggested I leave it until Monday morning to let you know, so I took her advice.'

Who else could be the secretary, Jacob thought, but Rachel Savernake? She must have learned of Wenna Tilson's existence, and the name of Levi's lawyer, probably from one of the other investigators at her beck and call. She left nothing to chance. She was keeping tabs on Levi even after his death.

Yet she'd made no attempt to prevent him from travelling to Cornwall. All she'd done was try to ensure that he did so at the beginning of this week, rather than earlier. It was as if she wanted him to know all about her.

Or did she simply want him out of London for a while?

Gabriel Hannaway finished his coffee – a strong Brazilian blend, imported specially at vast expense – and glared at the dimpled maid. As she hurried around the dining table with the jug, Vincent Hannaway gave her rump a playful smack.

'Where's Ewing?' the old man wheezed. 'I rang the bell for him, and he hasn't answered.'

'Beg pardon, sir,' the maid said, 'but Mr Ewing isn't here.'

'Not here?' Gabriel's leathery face crinkled in outrage. 'What do you mean he's not here? He's my butler, damn you. There's no question of his not being here.'

'Would you like me to ring again for him, sir? Then you can see for yourself.'

The iguana eyes narrowed. 'Don't you think you're being rather impudent, young lady?'

'Sorry, sir. I was only trying to help.'

'Try harder, dammit. You still haven't explained yourself.'

'I saw him put on his hat and coat half an hour ago, sir. On his way out, he was.'

'Stuff and nonsense! He wouldn't slip out without permission whilst we are dining.'

The girl was trembling. Vincent took another sip of coffee, then tweaked one of the hairs growing from his nostrils, as if in aid to thought.

'Did Ewing say where he was going, Beatrice?'

'No, sir. But five minutes later I popped outside, and his motorcycle had gone.'

'Peculiar.' He turned to his father. 'I thought he looked shifty when I was here on Sunday. You don't suppose... are you all right?'

Gabriel Hannaway's features contorted. In a faint whisper he said, 'Feeling off-colour. That's why I wanted to see Ewing. Ask him where the lobster came from.'

'It's rather warm in here.' Vincent loosened his collar. 'I like a roaring fire, but perhaps...'

'What the devil's wrong with me?' the old man wheezed. 'I feel dizzy... that damned lobster.'

The maid had left the dining room door ajar. From behind it came a low, tuneful humming. Vincent recognised the melody of a popular song.

'*You're the cream in my coffee.*'

'Who's there?' he called.

The humming stopped, and an unseen woman murmured, 'Don't blame the lobster.'

The two men looked up at the same moment, and watched the door swing open.

Rachel Savernake stepped into the room, followed by Trueman. Each of them wore gloves, each of them held a revolver; Rachel's pointed at the father, Trueman's at the son.

'Blame me,' she said.

Darkness had fallen long before a cab dropped Jacob outside the front door of Edgar House. Amwell Street was quiet, and the mist of early evening was thickening into fog. He peered through the gloom, but couldn't see anyone loitering. Yet as he fitted his key into the lock, someone hissed his name.

'Jacob!'

He opened the door, and stumbled over the threshold with his bag.

'Jacob, it's me. Sara!'

A figure emerged out of the murk. He found himself facing an elderly, hunched woman in a black bonnet and widow's weeds. She wore thick glasses and carried a large, badly scuffed handbag. He'd have sworn on the Bible that he'd never seen her in his life. But hearing was believing.

He seized her by the shoulder, pulled her inside, shut the door, and locked it.

'I'd never have recognised you!'

Shaking herself free, she straightened her bent back, and tossed the bonnet onto the floor. 'Remember, I'm an actress.'

Astonishment gave way to delight, and he laughed out loud. 'The woman of a thousand faces!'

She took off her glasses with a flourish, and the old crone metamorphosed into a young woman with a teasing smile. It was like witnessing the climax to a fairy tale.

'I didn't know if anyone was keeping watch on your house. But I've been hanging around for over an hour, ambling up and down like an old biddy with nothing better to do, and I'm sure this house isn't under observation.'

'An uninvited guest turned up here on Sunday.' He rubbed his damaged face. The bruise still felt tender. 'He wanted to find you.'

Sara groaned. 'I might have known.'

'I told them the truth. I didn't have a clue where you were.'

'And took a beating for your pains, I see.' She stroked his cheek with gentle fingertips. 'Poor boy.'

'What's happening, Sara?' he demanded. 'Who's after you?'

'They work for Vincent Hannaway.'

'Why should Hannaway want to find you?'

'Because William confided in me about the Damnation Society.'

'I haven't told you everything,' Sara said.

They were sitting chastely on the same settee he'd shared with Elaine only a few nights ago. Finally, facing the kitchen crime scene, Jacob had retrieved a bottle of Harvey's Bristol Cream from Mrs Dowd's pantry, and poured them each a glass.

'What do you know about the Damnation Society?' he asked. 'To me, it's only a name. I heard of it from a policeman, but when I asked Rachel Savernake about it, she told me it didn't exist. I'm not sure if she was telling...'

'A lie?' Sara frowned. 'The Damnation Society was founded by Judge Savernake.'

'Are you sure?' He felt a chill on his spine.

'She must be ashamed of what her father did. The society is a secret group of hedonists. Rich men with a taste for decadence. It amuses them to pretend to be pursuing the most innocent pastime imaginable. Playing chess.'

'The Gambit Club,' Jacob said slowly. 'With premises in Gallows Court.'

'That's right. The society was founded by old Judge Savernake. William belonged to it, and so did Pardoe and Claude Linacre. Alfred Linacre is a member, and the Hannaways are leading lights. Men accustomed to doing exactly as they please. To taking exotic pleasures with no constraints.'

Jacob thought aloud. 'They manage the Orphans' Home, giving the impression of philanthropy, but their interest lies in having a ready supply of young girls.'

'Not only girls,' Sara whispered. 'Boys too, I told you. A steady stream of orphans who reach the age of fourteen are taken on as servants by men like the Hannaways. A lucky few find work on the stage, as I did. Dolly Benson was the same, and Winifred Murray, the flighty piece who became Lawrence Pardoe's second wife. But members of the Damnation Society seldom marry their victims. Once they have served their purpose, they usually disappear off the face of the earth.'

Jacob recoiled. 'Vile.'

'Befriending the powerful helped William to earn a fortune. He didn't share their tastes, but he did turn a blind eye. When I begged him to go to Scotland Yard, and reveal what was going on, he asked if I wanted us both to end up at the bottom of the Thames with stone blocks chained to our ankles. Or worse.'

'You must have been terrified.'

'We both were. William admitted that even the little he'd told me put my life at risk, but he promised to make sure I was safe. If only I'd had the courage to speak out! Keeping quiet didn't save him, did it?'

'You mustn't think like that.'

'I can't help it, Jacob! But the society's tentacles stretch into the government, and even Scotland Yard.'

'Superintendent Chadwick has been arrested.'

'Yes, I saw that story on a press billboard. God alone knows what will happen next.' She laid her hand on his; her touch was cold, but he didn't care. 'I see now that it was a terrible mistake, but I felt I simply had to trust William. And now I've lost him.'

Vincent Hannaway mopped his brow, and Rachel asked, 'Pulse racing? Feeling dizzy?'

His eyes strayed from the gun to his cup. 'Was it the coffee?'

Rachel gestured with her free hand to the young maid, whose habitual nervous servility had given way to an intimidating sternness. 'You carried out your part of the bargain perfectly, Beatrice. You know what happens next.'

As Gabriel Hannaway gasped an obscenity, the maid strolled out of the room. The guns did not waver.

'Yes, it was the coffee,' Rachel said, 'mixed with potassium cyanide salts.'

'Cyanide?' Terror flared in Vincent's eyes. 'Tell me what you want, and you can have it. If you will only…'

Trueman interrupted. 'She'll have what she wants, regardless.'

'All the preparations are in place,' Rachel said. 'The telephone wires are cut. Your butler is off on his motorcycle to Soho with five hundred pounds in his wallet.'

'Five hundred pounds!' the old man shrieked.

'Yes, he's under the illusion that he's the beneficiary of a colossal mistake. He agreed to betray you for a mere one hundred. The money was left for him in an envelope. I suspect he can't believe his luck.'

Vincent opened his mouth to speak, but Rachel put a finger to his lips. 'Hush now. In a moment Beatrice will return.'

As if on cue, the maid came back into the room. She was carrying a dirty old tin can. A container of petrol.

'What's next for you?' Jacob asked.

'I've money put aside,' Sara said. 'William made me an allowance as well as paying my wages through the Inanity. Tomorrow I'll begin a new life. I'd like to stay in London, but...'

'But?'

'I must talk to Rachel Savernake. She's the only person who can bring this madness to an end.'

'What makes you believe that?'

Sara took a breath. 'I didn't tell you everything I heard when Lawrence Pardoe ranted about her. Forgive me, Jacob. I wasn't sure how much it was safe to say, for both our sakes.'

He squeezed her hand, and she didn't pull away. 'There's nothing to forgive.'

'That's kind of you.' She returned the pressure. 'Pardoe was convinced Rachel wanted to usurp men like himself and Vincent Hannaway.'

Jacob was baffled. 'Usurp them?'

'He had this fancy that she wanted to carry on where her father left off.'

'You mean – actually taking charge of the Damnation Society?'

'I don't believe it,' Sara said quickly. 'She's a woman, not a monster. I'm sure she's filled with remorse over her father, and wants to put a stop to what he created.'

'A sort of atonement?'

Sara sighed. 'Tomorrow, I hope to speak to her, once I've decided where to stay.'

'Stay here tonight,' Jacob said on impulse.

'Here?' She smiled. 'You're very kind, but you've already risked your safety for me. The bruising to your face will soon fade, but next time might be much worse.'

'I don't care. I'll stay awake all night if necessary, making sure you come to no harm.'

She raised her eyebrows. 'It's good of you, Jacob, but think of your reputation. I'm a woman with a past. And a terrible past, at that.'

'I don't care about your past,' he said. 'I care about who you are now. Who you will become. There's a spare room with a bed on the first floor, overlooking the street. Mrs Dowd kept it ready in case she took another lodger. You won't be disturbed, I swear.'

She hesitated. 'You're so generous, Jacob.'

They looked into each other's eyes. He felt himself colouring.

'Please, it's a genuine offer. No ulterior motives.'

'Thanks, Jacob. Just for tonight, then, I'll accept gratefully.' She leaned towards him, and he inhaled her lilac fragrance as she dropped a gentle kiss on his cheek.

Gabriel Hannaway bent over and retched. His son held out both arms in supplication.

'Rachel, my dear. The Damnation Society is yours for the taking. Please believe me, I never meant to stand in your way. The Judge created us, and you have every right to follow in his footsteps. You want what he wanted, don't you? Thine is the kingdom, the power and the glory.'

At a nod from Rachel, the maid opened the can of petrol. First she sprayed the dining table, then the carpet, finally the curtains. As he watched, Vincent Hannaway screwed himself up like a coiled spring. Written all over his sweaty pink face was the notion of leaping from his chair in an attempt to get away.

Rachel took aim at the wine glass standing on the table next to Vincent's dinner plate, and fired. The glass shattered with a noise like the blast of a bomb. A jagged shard caught Vincent's face. With a frantic wail, he clawed at his cheek. Blood streamed from the gash.

The old man raised his head, and croaked. 'Your father was mad, and so are you!'

Rachel smiled. 'Rest assured, the Judge's sins did not go unpunished.'

The air in the dining room reeked of petrol. From her apron, the dimpled maid produced a matchbox.

'Please,' Vincent whispered. 'You can't destroy us all.'

'Quite right,' Rachel said. 'I have the key to the door, and we'll lock you in. Our car is outside. Beatrice and the cook are coming with us. We'll be sailing down the drive as the blaze takes hold. Will you both die of smoke inhalation before the cyanide kills you? Trueman thinks so, but I'm less sure. We'd make a bet, but the inquest won't give a definitive answer. This old mausoleum will be gutted. A smouldering ruin, with precious little left for the pathologist to examine. Possibly your teeth.'

Vincent's face was reddening as the poison washed through his system. Tears trickled from the corners of his bloodshot eyes.

'You won't get away with this.'

'Actually,' Rachel said, 'I will.'

'No!'

'Scotland Yard will be tipped off about Ewing's whereabouts, and realise that his real name is Walter Busby. He's a plausible fellow, but his previous convictions include stealing from his employers and committing arson to cover his tracks.'

'What?'

'You should have checked his testimonials with as much care as Levi Shoemaker did. How will Ewing explain away the five hundred pounds in his pocket, or what Beatrice said about his vicious assaults on her in a letter she's sent to a friend from the Orphans' Home? The prosecution's case is open and shut. Ewing preyed on young women, but feared exposure. He decided to cut his losses, by taking enough money from that safe you hide behind *The Monarch of the Glen* to start a new life.'

Gabriel Hannaway clutched his throat. His hoarse words were barely audible.

'Have mercy.'

'Remind me,' Rachel said. 'When did you last show mercy?'

She and Trueman each took a step backward, their movements precisely choreographed.

'Enough conversation.' She turned to the maid. 'I kept my promise, Beatrice. The stage is yours.'

Eyes fixed on Vincent, the girl prised a match out of the little box. At the door, Rachel sang softly.

'*Even orphans with a grudge do it. Let's do it...*'

Juliet Brentano's Journal

6 February 1919

It happened very quickly, as sometimes it does. Rachel was dead within hours of succumbing to the flu.

She turned blue, Henrietta said, and started struggling to breathe. But fighting for air is fruitless when the plague has you in its clutches. Like so many others before her, she suffocated.

It would have made no difference, even had the doctor been able to reach her. What could a local medical practitioner hope to achieve, when the Spanish Lady has defeated medical science from one side of the globe to the other?

The Judge was with her when the end came, Henrietta says.

'This will turn his mind.'

'It turned years ago,' I said.

'He talks to her as if she's still alive.'

'In his eyes, she was perfect. The girl who could do no wrong. That's why she was such a wicked—'

'Oh, Juliet. We mustn't speak ill of—'

'I loathed her,' I said. 'Rachel Savernake was jealous, vain, and cruel. And she loathed me.'

Colour came to Henrietta's pale cheeks. Plain speaking does not come naturally to her, at least not in the presence of those she is supposed to serve, but she was too honest to deny the truth. Instead, she stroked my hand.

I know she's afraid. Afraid of losing her job. Afraid that in a demented fury, the Judge will turn violent. Afraid, perhaps, of me.

As for myself, I'm not afraid at all. The loss of my parents, followed so quickly by Rachel's death, has left me in a daze. But one question remains clear, insistent, demanding to be answered.

What happens next?

30

Breakfast in Edgar House was a surreal experience. Jacob and Sara sat on opposite sides of the kitchen table, passing the butter and sipping strong tea like a married couple in middle age. Outside, last night's fog still lingered, but with the stove warming the room, and the aroma of toast, Yorkshire Tea, and apricot marmalade in the air, Jacob could almost forget that a few days earlier, this had been Mrs Dowd's domain.

His eyes were tired and his joints creaky after a night spent tossing and turning, acutely conscious of Sara's presence in the house, and aching with desire for her. In a wild moment, he'd contemplated tapping on her door, and asking if she wanted company. Her remark about ulterior motives gave him hope, but he daren't risk wrecking their friendship. For all her worldly experience, those years in the Orphans' Home must have left scars.

This morning she wore a creased cream frock, and looked no older than seventeen. As she laid her bare arms on the table, he found it hard to resist the urge to caress them. How could he have failed to appreciate her loveliness that first time she'd called on him at Clarion House? Ever the actress, she'd played the part of mouse, ensuring there was no distance between them, none of the exotic grace that was Queen Nefertiti's stock-in-trade. She'd judged her performance to perfection; because he hadn't been overawed, their friendship had blossomed naturally.

Her uncomplaining bravery had won his heart. What she'd endured at the Orphans' Home would have crushed a weaker spirit. In the past few days, she'd overcome the shock and grief of witnessing her former lover's appalling death, and survived two attempts on her life. In her own quiet way, she was as formidable as Rachel Savernake.

Sara nibbled a slice of toast. 'Penny for your thoughts.'

'When can I see you again?' His eagerness was juvenile, but he couldn't help himself.

She wiped her mouth with a paper napkin, and glanced at the clock on the dresser. 'You're already late for work. Don't worry. I'll be in touch as soon as I've decided where to go next.'

'You can stay on here for the time being.'

'You're very generous.'

Honesty compelled him to say, 'With a dead woman's house. But just for a day or two...'

She smiled. 'Don't worry about me. Go now, and I'll see you very soon.'

Poyser, invariably the first senior journalist to arrive at Clarion House each morning, was munching a Cox's Orange Pippin when Jacob passed by the news desk. By way of greeting, he asked where Jacob had got to the previous day.

'I took the sleeper to Cornwall, following a lead.'

'Good luck persuading Gomersall to reimburse your expenses.' Poyser tossed his apple core towards a waste paper basket, and missed, as usual. 'Heard about this business at Hampstead?'

'What business?'

'Big house burnt down. Both occupants perished in the blaze. Thought you'd be interested.'

One of Poyser's foibles was that he liked to build suspense, but Jacob wasn't in the mood. 'Was the fire started deliberately?'

'So it seems. The Yard already has a man in custody. The identities of the deceased caught my eye, made me think of you.'

'Why?'

Poyser beamed. 'Because of your interest in Gallows Court. This father and son did business there. They were the principals of a firm of solicitors. Hannaway & Hannaway.'

Jacob gaped at him. 'Vincent Hannaway is dead? And the old man too?'

'Burnt to a crisp,' Poyser said cheerily. 'Shocking case of arson and murder. As chief crime correspondent, you can spin a few paragraphs out of the tragedy, even if there's no mystery about what happened.'

'What did happen?'

'To coin a phrase, the butler did it.'

Jacob gave an incredulous laugh. 'Be serious.'

'Not a word of a lie,' Poyser said virtuously. 'Fellow sounds like a dyed-in-the-wool rogue. History of defrauding his employers, and when the police picked him up, he was enjoying the entertainment on offer at a brothel in Gerrard Street. So the story goes, he'd hung his jacket up on the door, and the pockets were stuffed with fivers.'

'I'd better talk to Scotland Yard.'

'Good thinking, my dear fellow. By the way, what exactly was the nature of your interest in Gallows Court?'

But Jacob was already racing to his room.

'I can confirm the details we have announced.' At the other end of the telephone line, Inspector Oakes' mournful formality made him sound like an undertaker. 'Two bodies were recovered from a property in Hampstead last night, and we are treating this as a case of arson and murder. A forty-seven-year-old man is currently under arrest.'

'You're sure the bodies belong to the Hannaways?' Jacob demanded. 'If the remains are charred beyond recognition, it's possible that—'

'We're alert to the risk of mistaken identity,' the detective said coldly, 'which is why thus far we have refrained from naming the victims. The Hannaways, father and son, attended the same dentist in Harley Street, and we are consulting with him as a matter of urgency.'

'Off the record, you're confident it's them?'

Oakes' manner began to thaw. 'Off the record, very confident.'

'What on earth happened?'

'I suppose there's no harm in telling you. It'll all come out in the wash. The old man's butler was called Ewing. A presentable and hard-working fellow, by all accounts. What Gabriel Hannaway didn't know was that Ewing was an assumed name. He was born Walter Busby, and twenty-five years ago, he worked below-stairs for a landowner in Derbyshire. Busby got a housemaid into trouble, and helped himself to some of his employer's knick-knacks in order to pay for an abortionist. When he was found out, he set fire to the house. The blaze didn't do much damage, but Busby finished up in Strangeways. Following his release, he started afresh as Ewing, and went back into domestic service with the help of forged references. Two years ago, old man Hannaway took him on after his previous butler retired. We're not aware of any difficulties until last night, when the house was set ablaze. All the signs are that petrol was sprayed around in a liberal fashion, and then set on fire.'

'By Ewing?'

'Who else? A young maid and the cook were in the house, and we've found a few charred bits and pieces of servants' clothing which are probably all that is left of them.'

Jacob shivered. 'Was Ewing supposed to be on duty?'

'According to our enquiries, yes. Vincent Hannaway regularly dined with his father. Perhaps there was a confrontation between Ewing and the son. The fire brigade were called when a passing motorist spotted the flames, but by the time they had the fire under control, the house was destroyed, along with almost everything in it. Nasty way to go.'

'How did you find Ewing?'

'Anonymous phone call, a couple of hours after the fire was spotted. Chap who wouldn't give his name said that Ewing had been maligning the Hannaways, and boasting about what he might do to them. He said he'd seen Ewing throwing his money around in a pub in Soho, and picking up a prostitute.'

'Very public-spirited of him to let you know.'

He could imagine Oakes' shrug of indifference. 'People pay off scores by giving us tip-offs every day of the week. Without them, the jails would be half-empty.'

'You soon caught up with Ewing?'

345

'He was found in a raid on a brothel across the street from the pub, and was under lock and key by midnight. In his possession he had nearly five hundred pounds.'

Jacob whistled. 'Good money for a butler.'

'He gave us some bluster about a lucky streak with the horses. Surprise, surprise, he can't give us chapter and verse about which outsiders he's backed. It's a racing certainty that he stole the money from Gabriel Hannaway, and when the son became suspicious, he set the house ablaze. Old habits die hard. Only this time, he'll swing for his crime.'

A picture slid into Jacob's mind. A hooded man, mounting a scaffold on a cold grey morning.

He shivered. 'Are you sure that nobody else was involved?'

'Such as?' Oakes asked.

A name trembled on Jacob's lips. *Rachel Savernake.*

But he said nothing, and the detective rang off.

Jacob was still digesting the news of the Hannaways' deaths when his telephone shrilled. With her customary sniff of disapproval, Peggy announced that a Mrs Trueman wanted to speak to him.

His throat felt dry and rough. 'Put her through.'

The housekeeper said, 'Mr Flint? I'm ringing on behalf of Miss Savernake. She asked me to say that she wishes to offer you the chance of an exclusive story. Would you call at Gaunt House this afternoon?'

'Let me check my calendar.'

'Four o'clock sharp,' the housekeeper said. 'You know better than to let her down.'

She rang off before he could think up an impudent reply.

He rubbed his sore eyes. So much had happened over the past few days, he couldn't hope to absorb it all. The morning passed in a haze, and when the telephone rang again he was astonished to find it was already three o'clock.

'I'm busy,' he said brusquely. 'What is it?'

'Lady to see you,' Peggy said. 'Shall I tell her to go away?'

His heart skipped a beat. 'What's her name?'

'Miss Delamere.'

'I'll be there in a jiffy.'

'Not so busy now, eh?' Peggy said meanly.

Sara was waiting for him in reception. Her fur coat and scarf were as elegant as her neat hairstyle. He put his finger to his lips, not wanting Peggy to eavesdrop, and hurried her back to his room.

'You've taken over your old boss's office,' she said. 'Congratulations.'

He blushed. 'It seemed to make sense. Tom's things are still all over the place. But never mind that. Have you heard the news?'

'About the Hannaways? Isn't it incredible? I've just read the newspaper. Not yours, I'm afraid. The *Witness* had the story on its front page. Someone set fire to the old man's house, and the police have already caught him.'

'Gabriel Hannaway's butler,' Jacob said. 'Inspector Oakes tells me he has a history of this kind of crime.'

Her eyes opened very wide. 'You don't think... Rachel Savernake had anything to do with it?'

'With Rachel Savernake,' he said, 'nothing is impossible.'

Her eyes sparkled. 'I do believe you're obsessed with her.'

'Rubbish!' He had to stop himself from protesting too much. 'Frankly, she frightens me. She reminds me of those fanatics who don't care how much harm they do in pursuit of their cause.'

'I understand. The end justifies the means.'

He couldn't help saying, 'You don't seem shocked.'

'Pardoe is dead, and so are the Hannaways. All three men used and abused countless women. Deep down, I'm sure they hated us. Their existence represented a mortal danger to Rachel Savernake, as it did to me. Now they are gone, I can breathe again.'

William Keary, her former lover, was also dead, Jacob thought. To say nothing of Linacre, McAlinden, and Thurlow. Sara's trusting disposition worried him. Throughout her life, unscrupulous people had exploited it.

'Her housekeeper called me,' he said. 'Rachel Savernake has invited me to her house for four o'clock.'

'Really?' She raised her eyebrows. 'I feel rather jealous. What does she want to see you about?'

'She's offered me a scoop. That's all I know.'

'How thrilling!' Sara clapped her hands. 'To think that it took a woman to destroy the Damnation Society.'

He sighed. 'But has she destroyed it?'

'Don't you see? That must be what she's aimed to achieve, ever since she arrived in London.'

'What about the other members?'

'The survivors? They lack a leader, and without the head, the body can't function. After the Judge's mind failed, Gabriel Hannaway was in charge for years, before handing over to Vincent. William said some members wanted him to challenge Vincent for the leadership, but his heart was never in it. I'm sure the Hannaways sent that thug to Amwell Street to ask you where to find me. They knew I hated them. Now they are gone, the whole rotten edifice will crumble. All thanks to Rachel Savernake.'

Jacob nodded agreement, but his heart wasn't in it. The Damnation Society's members prized inheritance. What good was privilege if it couldn't be perpetuated by handing it on from one generation to another? Might Rachel Savernake yearn to seize control of the organisation built up by her father?

'I don't suppose,' Sara said, 'that you'd let me tag along with you, when you go to see her? I won't come into the house, if you don't want.'

He hesitated. It seemed patronising to suggest that a tea-time trip to a house in the heart of London was dangerous for her. He was letting his imagination roam too far.

'After all,' Sara said with a cheeky smile, 'if she and I are rivals for your affections, I'd like to find out more about her.'

At ten to four, a taxi deposited them in the square. The fog was closing in, as damp and cold as on the night Jacob had accosted Rachel. The night of Lawrence Pardoe's death. As he paid the driver, Jacob had a sense of coming full circle.

'Mr Flint!'

He spun round, and found himself staring at Inspector Philip Oakes.

'What brings you here?'

'I might ask you the same question. Oh, good afternoon, Miss Delamere. We met... that tragic night at the Inanity.'

Sara, extricating herself gracefully from the back of the cab, eyed the policeman with frank curiosity. 'Hello again, Inspector.'

'I received a message from Rachel Savernake's housekeeper,' Jacob explained. 'If I presented myself here at four, she would give me a scoop.'

'Really? How generous.' The inspector sounded sceptical. 'And Miss Delamere?'

'We've become friends.' Jacob couldn't help sounding defensive. Yet there was no shame in relishing the company of a beautiful actress, however lurid her past. 'I've told her about Rachel Savernake, and she was curious.'

'As a matter of interest, Inspector,' Sara said lazily, 'why are you here?'

Oakes fiddled with his tie. 'I received a message, summoning me here for four o'clock.'

'Really? I've often heard of people calling in Scotland Yard, but I never realised it was quite so easy to do.'

'Unorthodox, miss, I admit.' A faint cry distracted Oakes. 'What was that?'

He looked upward, and Jacob craned his neck. Through the gloom, he could make out a woman in a fur coat up on the roof of Gaunt House.

'Is that her?' Sara whispered.

'It's her all right, that dark hair's unmistakeable,' Oakes muttered. 'There's an enclosed swimming pool up there, and a roof garden forming a kind of balcony, but this is hardly the weather... Oh God, she isn't going to jump?'

The woman moved to the edge of the roof. Running around it was a low iron rail. She ran her hand along the rail, moving further back, and out of sight.

Clammy with dread, Jacob shouted, 'Rachel! This is Jacob Flint. Why did you want to see me?'

Even as the words left his lips, he realised his mistake. It wasn't that she wanted to see him. She wanted him to see her.

Teetering on the edge of the rooftop, far about the street, as if about to hurl herself to the ground.

Oakes pulled a whistle out of his pocket, and blew it hard. 'Miss Savernake! Don't do anything rash!'

The front door of Gaunt House opened, and Trueman came bounding down the steps, his wife stumbling in his wake. The chauffeur's face was dark with terror, the woman's wet with tears.

'What's happening, man?' Oakes demanded.

'She went up to the top floor,' Trueman hissed. 'When I followed, she locked me out. We were afraid this would happen, once...'

'Once Vincent Hannaway died?' Sara asked.

'The Judge made endless attempts to kill himself!' Mrs Trueman sobbed. 'She's never been able to get that out of her head.'

As she spoke, something she'd said on the night of the Benfleet murders sprang into Jacob's mind. *The only person capable of destroying her is... she herself.* It was almost like a prophecy. Had she feared that Rachel might commit suicide?

'We don't have time for this!' Trueman shouted. 'Where is she now?'

'She edged out of sight,' Jacob said. 'Are there steps at the back of the building?'

'A rusty old fire ladder. Absolute death trap.'

A cobbled alleyway separated Gaunt House from the building next door. Jacob took a step forward, and Oakes followed, but Trueman shouldered them aside before halting at the alley's entrance, and gazing upwards with despair scrawled over his rugged features.

'Don't do it!' he bellowed. 'Please listen to me! I'm begging you!'

In the gloom, Jacob could barely make out the figure swaying four floors above them. They heard a distant cry, and Mrs Trueman moaned.

The next Jacob knew, a muffled scream tore through the wet air, and he heard a sickening, scything thud. Trueman sprinted down the alleyway, with Oakes in hot pursuit. A police constable responding to the whistle followed close behind.

Sara gasped in astonishment as the housekeeper squealed: 'Oh God! I begged her not to do this!'

Jacob called, 'Wait here!'

He raced down the alleyway, but there was no need to run. There was nothing he could do. Inspector Oakes, the constable, and Trueman were gathered at the end of the passage. The chauffeur's shovel-like hand covered his eyes. He was making a moaning noise, like a wounded animal.

'Keep back!' Oakes shouted.

Jacob glanced over his shoulder. Sara and Mrs Trueman were staring in horror. The housemaid with the disfigured cheek joined them, panting hard. She let out a frantic shriek.

'No!'

A high brick wall separated the courtyard of Gaunt House from the public right of way. The wall was topped by black steel spikes as sharp as dagger blades.

'Fetch a sheet,' Trueman growled to the housemaid. 'For pity's sake, Martha, don't look!'

Who in their right mind, Jacob thought, would want to look?

Impaled upon the spikes was the body of a woman in an ocelot coat. Her head was hanging down, as if her neck had snapped. The lustrous black hair was unmistakable. Before turning his head away, Jacob recognised the blank, staring eyes of Rachel Savernake.

Juliet Brentano's Journal, 7 February 1919

It's long after midnight, but I can't sleep. So much has happened in such a short time. Our world has changed.

It began this afternoon. At last the causeway was passable again, and Harold Brown came back to Savernake Hall. I was talking to Henrietta in the kitchen when we heard him swaggering in.

'Hide in the pantry!' she hissed.

I scrambled out of sight just in time. I could tell from his lewd greeting that he was as drunk as a lord.

'Cliff wants to see you,' Henrietta said. 'He's better now. And he knows what you did to Martha.'

Brown swore furiously. 'He was at death's door...'

'Well, it's the girl who has died. Young Rachel.'

'What?'

'Good riddance, I say. Did she tell you to drug the Captain and Miss Yvette?'

'For God's sake!' I heard him shriek. 'Put that knife down!'

'For two pins...' she muttered.

'I'm going, you won't see me again.' His speech was slurred and jerky. I could tell he was in no state to defend himself.

I jumped out of my hiding place. 'Use the knife, Hetty. Make him suffer, like Martha suffered!'

He swore at me, but turned on his heel, and stumbled out of the kitchen.

'Cliff!' I called. 'He's escaping!'

But Cliff was still upstairs in bed. He wasn't strong enough to seize his chance of revenge. And though I wanted to chase after Brown, and pummel him with my small fists, Henrietta held me back.

Later, she came to my room. Brown had left the island, she said, and she didn't expect him to return. As for the Judge, he wanted to see me.

I refused, of course. Ever since Mother and I first came here, she made sure I kept my distance from him.

But Henrietta begged me. He was lucid for once, she said, but a broken man.

I was curious. What must be going through his diseased mind? In the end, I relented.

She led me to his study. He'd deserted his daughter's bedside, and was sitting at his desk. When he looked up, his face was wrinkled with pain. He looked one hundred years old.

'Rachel,' he said. 'How well you look, my dear. Off to bed, now? Goodnight, my sweet.'

With that, he turned back to consider the papers on his desk.

I was lost for words. Henrietta motioned me to leave with her. As soon as we were outside, she shut the door, and put a finger to her lips.

'Come with me to the kitchen.'

Cliff was waiting for us there. He looked haggard, but mustered a wan smile, and asked if I'd seen the Judge.

'His mind is wandering. He doesn't seem to have taken it in about Rachel. He called me by her name.'

Henrietta and Cliff exchanged glances.

'Why not humour him?' Cliff asked. 'What have you got to lose?'

31

'I ought to file the story,' Jacob said, half an hour later.

'The *Clarion* can wait,' Sara told him.

Two empty brandy glasses stood in front of them. He and Sara had taken refuge in a pub half a mile from Gaunt House. The cavernous snug was crammed with cheery Irishmen and decorated with chamber pots hanging from oak beams. Inspector Oakes hadn't allowed Sara to look at the corpse, but her pallor testified to the shock of watching another woman die. She'd prescribed a cognac for each of them, and he hadn't argued.

'Rachel had everything to live for,' he said, not for the first time. 'Young and beautiful and fabulously rich. Why throw everything away on a whim?'

'Was it a whim?' Sara asked gently. 'She invited you and Inspector Oakes to be her witnesses. It was like an actress's finale, an unforgettable last performance.'

His head hurt as if he'd been coshed. 'But why?'

'Guilt, remorse, who knows?'

Not wanting to give too much away, he said carefully, 'Her housekeeper once hinted to me that she had suicidal tendencies. I paid no attention at the time. But perhaps... Yet why would she feel guilty? She brought Linacre to justice, she...'

'Oh, Jacob.' Sara squeezed his cold hand. 'Don't you see? She inherited Judge Savernake's madness. And not only that.'

He looked up sharply. 'What are you talking about?'

'William spoke about her, that last night at the Inanity. He came down to the dressing room after having a conversation with her up in the private guests' lounge. He was unusually subdued, and so I asked what was wrong. All he said was that her father – a man he admired, don't forget – had scared him, and yet he found Rachel even more terrifying. Implacable, he said. Unforgiving. It made no sense to me, but now I wonder...'

'Wonder what?'

She bit her lip. 'If Rachel persuaded George Barnes to murder William.'

'You can't believe that!'

'Why not?' She crumpled up a beer mat. 'Who paid for the car he drove into a tree?'

Jacob closed his eyes. 'Would you like another brandy?'

One of the Irishmen at the bar launched into a song, tuneless and very loud. She gave a little shudder. 'Remember what Levi Shoemaker told you. As a child, Rachel incited her father to have that man Brentano and his mistress killed. Suppose she set out to eliminate – one way or another – everyone who knew the truth? Not only Pardoe, but Linacre, the Hannaways – and William. Perhaps even your colleague, Betts. Suppose Harold Coleman tried to blackmail her. She could easily have arranged for his old associates to catch up with him. Levi Shoemaker himself...'

Appalled, he gazed into her sorrowful eyes. 'How could she manage it all?'

'With enough money, you can manage anything. I can't guess the details, but I'm sure she chose her time with care. You see, today is the fiftieth anniversary of the Damnation Society's foundation.'

'What?'

'The Judge founded the association on 29 January 1880, and William told me that each year its birthday is celebrated with a ghastly ceremony.'

'A ceremony?'

'A select group of members assemble at Gallows Court. William didn't tell me the details, the celebrations were too depraved to bear description. He hinted that... each year, they would kill someone for their sport.'

Jacob felt his pulse racing. 'Charles Brentano and Yvette Viviers died on 29 January, eleven years ago.'

'The date tells us everything,' Sara whispered. 'Rachel Savernake offered them up to her father's clique for sacrifice?'

'She was only fourteen!'

'She was her father's daughter.'

'So that is why she chose today to – end it all?'

'I suppose she thought it somehow fitting.'

He let out a low groan. 'Heaven only knows the truth.'

'Frankly,' Sara said, 'we may never know the precise truth. Unless Oakes can bully her chauffeur into spilling the beans.'

Jacob thought back to the night of the murders at Benfleet, and felt his gorge rise. He was desperate for his part in the events at the bungalow to remain his secret. Although innocent of murder, he'd misled the police. Rachel was dead, but the Truemans were accomplished liars. Might he yet be at risk?

'He doesn't strike me as that sort of man.'

'What sort of man is he?' Her expression was unexpectedly fierce. 'How can we ever be sure what sort of person we're talking to? You're a journalist, you must know people are never quite what they seem. Even if they don't earn their living on the stage.'

He knew he ought to return to the office, and tell the sensational story of Rachel Savernake's suicide, but he felt too weary and deflated to string a coherent paragraph together. At least for Sara, that morning had brought good news. The Widow Bianchi was back from Milan, and had offered her temporary refuge in the house she'd shared with Keary in Carey Street.

'Is that what you want?' he asked, as they stood on the street corner, waiting for a taxi.

'Any port in a storm.' She smiled. 'It's a very luxurious port. I count myself fortunate.'

'You're sure you'll be safe?'

'Don't you see?' she asked. 'It's over. The madness has been purged. Chiara Bianchi has always been generous to me. The Continentals are so civilised. It's a big house. There's even a self-contained flat.'

'Lovely,' he said, but his heart wasn't in it. Rachel's death had left him cold and empty.

'It's large enough for two,' she said.

He stared at her. 'Are you...?'

'It's an improper suggestion, forgive me.' She permitted herself a glimmer of a smile. 'I'm older than you, a woman with a past. You're a clever young chap determined to make your own way in the world. Please forget I ever mentioned it.'

He caught hold of her hand, and only released his grip when the headlamps of a taxi cab sliced through the fog.

Sara rang the bell of the double-fronted Georgian house in Carey Street, and the door swung open. A tiny Chinese woman in a blue tunic bowed in greeting, and then stood aside to allow them to escape from the cold and the fog.

'Good evening, ma'am.'

'Thank you, Mei. This is my guest, Mr Flint. He will send for his things later. In the meantime, please show him into the sitting room.' She turned to Jacob. 'I need to make myself presentable. I won't be five minutes. The Widow Bianchi will be here shortly. In the meantime, Mei will pour you a drink to warm you up again. I recommend the Vecchia Romagna.'

Mei ushered Jacob along the spacious hallway lined with framed paintings. To his untutored eye, they looked like Old Masters: Raphael, Bellini, Titian perhaps. Before he could peer closely, the little woman directed him into an opulent rectangular room with frescoes on the walls, velvet cushions scattered across a sumptuous settee, and an intricately patterned Persian rug covering the floor. The decoration had a flavour of Italian nobility. After filling a crystal tumbler with a generous measure, the little, bird-like woman left, closing the door behind her. Jacob settled back on the settee, savouring the drink's tang. Closing his eyes, he imagined himself reclining in a Tuscan *palazzo*.

Rachel's death was such a stunning blow, he wasn't sure he could bring himself to write about it. How far he'd travelled, and so fast. The callow reporter who had lurked outside Gaunt House on the evening of Pardoe's death had grown up.

What did the future hold? Sara was utterly different from Rachel Savernake. She had a knack of conveying vulnerability, appealing to his protective instincts, yet there was no doubting her strength of mind. Even Rachel's suicide, which had turned his bones to blancmange, had caused her amazement rather than paralysing horror. For all her candour, there were surely many dark tales about the Damnation Society she was yet to tell.

A brisk tapping roused him. The door at the far end of the room opened, and a woman stepped inside. Silky black hair reached down towards her tiny waist. Slung over her shoulders was a cape of almost transparent velvet, unbuttoned to reveal an evening gown of apple-green chiffon. Tall in her high heels, wearing white glacé gloves, and carrying a silk bag embroidered with coral and pearls in one hand and with a long cigarette holder in the other, she seemed to Jacob to epitomise Continental chic. She was followed into the room by a swarthy, muscular manservant.

'*Buonasera*, Signor Flint.'

Jacob's knowledge of the Italian language was almost as limited as his experience of conversing with smart and sophisticated ladies from Milan. Did they shake hands while wearing gloves? Having no idea of what constituted the done thing, he gave a stiff little bow.

'*Buonasera*, Signora Bianchi.'

To his astonishment, the woman beamed and mimed applause. 'Bravo! You are nearly as fluent as a native!'

She was teasing him, of course, but he found himself returning her smile.

'You are very kind, Signora Bianchi.'

'Think nothing of it, Jacob.'

He goggled. In an instant, her voice had changed. The smooth Italian pronunciation had given way to straightforward English, with the faintest inflection of cockney. He couldn't be mistaken.

The Widow Bianchi was Sara Delamere.

Juliet Brentano's Journal

30 June 1919

I can scarcely believe it, but still nobody is any the wiser.

We've been lucky, yes, but boldness has its rewards. Today came the sternest test, a visit from the Judge's oldest friend. (Of course, I always refer to him as the Judge. To call him 'Father' would choke me.) The friend is his solicitor, old Gabriel Hannaway.

He was clearly shocked by the Judge's appearance and behaviour. It's barely a fortnight since the old tyrant threw himself down the stairs in his latest ham-fisted attempt to end it all, and fractured a rib. Most of the time, he's heavily sedated. I asked Henrietta if it was wise to allow Hannaway to visit, but she said he'd become suspicious if she kept putting him off. Once he saw the state the Judge was in, he'd understand in future if he was told not to come. Probably he'd be relieved.

I was introduced to him, and though he is plainly un-accustomed to talking to a girl of fourteen, he mustered a few pleasantries about how much I'd grown since he'd last seen me, on the occasion of my mother's funeral. Rachel's mother, that is. I'm sure he did not think anything was amiss.

I hate to say it, but perhaps my physical resemblance to Rachel is closer than I thought. She was shorter than me, and plumper, because she was so idle, but at this age, a girl's appearance changes rapidly. I've let my hair grow, tinted it under Henrietta's guidance, and copied her style. I shall change it again before long. We had dark eyes and high cheekbones in common, and though her complexion was pastier, and her nose beaky, such details make little impression on people. On my rare forays into the village, everyone takes it for granted that I am who I'm supposed to be. I even overheard the seamstress telling her neighbour that I've lost my puppy fat. One incredulous woman muttered that I'm turning into quite the young lady.

The years of isolation have worked to our advantage. We've had little to do with the outside world, and it's had little to do with us. I'm so grateful that my mother kept me safe from the Judge, in the days when he was capable of making a nuisance of himself. Despite her own lack of education, the way she encouraged me to read and study was her most precious gift. Of course, some books in the library aren't suitable reading for a girl of my age, or perhaps any age. But I have learned a great deal. Henrietta says I'm old beyond my years.

How much does the Judge understand? Has he deceived himself so completely that he genuinely believes Rachel is alive? Or is he pretending, well aware that the girl buried with scant ceremony as Juliet Brentano is in fact his own daughter? The funeral was excruciating, but thankfully the service was brief, and hardly anyone attended. When so many people have died of influenza, the death of a girl whom few people had met gave rise to little comment, from the senile village doctor, the doltish vicar, or anyone else in the parish.

For all the Judge's professed devotion to Rachel, he had little to do with her, even after he returned from London to live out his days on Gaunt. She was just one more prized possession, like the rare first editions in his library.

Cliff convinced me that this course offered hope for all of us. If the Judge wished to treat me as his daughter, where was the harm in humouring him? It could hardly be worse than the alternative.

He was right. What would happen if the Judge was confined to an asylum doesn't bear thinking about. As the illegitimate daughter of his nephew and a prostitute, I have no claim on him, or even to a roof over my head.

As Rachel Savernake, on the other hand, one day I might inherit a fortune.

32

'Sara! Is it really you?' Jacob's voice was hoarse with shock.

Laughing, she pulled off her white gloves, and handed them to the manservant, together with the cigarette holder. 'Yes, Jacob, you have penetrated my disguise. I've been living a double life. I found myself limited by the role of orphan made good. William was a fantasist, like so many of us in the theatre. He hankered for a beautiful foreign mistress, so I supplied the deficiency in his life. It suited me to inhabit a glamorous new personality. Sara had few inhibitions, but Chiara had none whatsoever.'

She shrugged off the cape, and the manservant folded it over his arm. 'Do I puzzle you, Jacob?'

'I don't know what to say,' he muttered.

She smiled. 'The Widow Bianchi and Sara Delamere were never seen together, of course, but that surprised nobody. A mistress and her predecessor are seldom soulmates – although each of them separately seized any chance to mention how famously they got along together in private. Meat and drink

369

to someone who loves acting. The noble art of deception, my dear Jacob.'

'I suppose so.' He yawned. 'Sorry, I told you I had a bad night.'

'Indeed.' The brightness of her smile faded. 'And now we ought to discuss what we'll do next.'

The manservant watched impassively as Jacob indicated their lavish surroundings. 'You must be a very wealthy woman, Sara. All this is yours?'

'Down to every last Leonardo, yes. At least, once the formalities are completed. William Keary bequeathed the whole of his estate to me.' Her eyes twinkled; she might have been a maiden aunt, sharing a near-the-knuckle joke. 'Without wishing to be crude, it does soften the blow. And you are right. Nobody ever admits to being rich. Let's just say I'm as comfortable as Croesus.'

Her sarcasm made him squirm. 'What I mean is, I'm just an ordinary journalist, and you're a beautiful heiress. Even if you didn't have a penny to your name, you could take your pick of men. Why would you want to share your future with me?'

'One of the things that is rather delightful about you,' Sara said, 'is that, for all your journalistic bravado, you are really quite self-effacing. Not like poor William. His ego was like Everest, utterly insurmountable. What a pity things aren't different. If we'd met when I was young, who knows what we might have achieved together?'

Her tone was as gentle as her words were harsh. She was playing a game with him. Now they'd made their final moves.

There was nothing for it but to take his leave whilst a few shreds of his dignity remained intact. Joints protesting, he tried to struggle to his feet. Each movement felt unexpectedly burdensome, and he found himself slumping helplessly onto the settee. Sara motioned to the manservant, who took a step forward.

'No, no,' Jacob said. 'I shall be all right. Honestly, I don't need a hand.'

Sara sighed. 'Oh, Jacob, you overestimate my generosity. Charm can only take you so far. You let yourself down by being so gullible.'

'Look, there's no need...'

At a gesture from her, the manservant reached inside his jacket, and pulled out a slim stiletto, its handle carved from mother-of-pearl. With a swift movement, he released a slim, shining blade, and held it to Jacob's throat.

'Gaudino comes from north-eastern Italy,' she said. 'In his home town of Maniago, his family manufactures these fearsome weapons. Every single one is hand-made, superbly crafted. Don't make any sudden movement. This is his uncle's favourite blade, and he's itching to use it. He can slice a man apart in the blink of an eye.'

'Sara,' Jacob said through gritted teeth. 'Is this some kind of joke?'

'I'm not joking,' she said softly. 'Although I admit my sense of humour can be cruel. When I said we should talk about what to do next, I meant I must explain what I intend to do with you.'

The steel blade grazed his skin, yet all he felt was a dreadful lassitude. 'The brandy was drugged?'

'Have no fear of lethal poisons unknown to science,' she said. 'You've only ingested a mild sedative. The mixture will cause no lasting damage, but your head will throb, and with your limbs like lead weights, there's no question of resistance.'

'I'm glad to hear,' Jacob said, unable to resist a croaky attempt at humour, 'there won't be any lasting damage.'

'Not from the sedative,' she said calmly. 'Otherwise, I bring bad news. Remember, this is 29 January, the Damnation Society's Golden Jubilee. By tradition, on this date in each year, we make a sacrifice to celebrate our good fortune, past, present, and future. Rachel Savernake cheated me of the chance to offer up her immortal soul, but I shall make do with you.'

'You're talking nonsense,' he said thickly. 'Stop pretending. I'm not amused.'

'Even actresses don't pretend all the time.' Sara opened her bag, and took out a small pistol. 'Every ghastly thing you've imagined about the Damnation Society is true. As for talking nonsense, don't condescend to me. Even if I only shoot to wound, your blood will ruin this lovely rug.'

'Sara,' he whispered, 'why are you doing this?'

'Because,' she said, 'nothing compares to the ultimate pleasure. The thrill of taking power over another human being's life.'

Gaudino bound his wrists and ankles with wire, and bundled him up on the settee like an oversized parcel. Twice, three times, provoked by Jacob's feeble struggles, the big man cuffed his head with a meaty paw. Throughout the ordeal, Sara told her story. Giving interviews to the press, she said, had frustrated her for years. There was so little she could confide in a journalist from *The Stage*. With Jacob, it was different.

At the time of her birth, her mother wasn't married, and she'd been sent to the Oxford Orphans' Home. Strictly speaking, she wasn't an orphan, but her mother had died when she was three. Her father was a man of wealth and influence, and as a result she'd enjoyed more privileges than the other children. Her interest in magic and Maskelyne began as escapism, and matured into an obsessive love of outrageous illusions. She resented the rules and restrictions of institutional life; performing on the stage gave her the chance to pretend.

'And I love pretending,' she said. 'More than anything. William was besotted with me. We concocted tales of his dalliances elsewhere simply to conceal the extent of his subjugation. He kept begging me to marry him, but I always said no. The prospect of cosy domesticity, even as the wife of a rich and famous man, repelled me. I could never be a conquest, or a chattel.

'It amused me to invent the elusive Widow Bianchi, and cast plucky Sara Delamere in the role of spurned lover. William's accounts of the Damnation Society entranced me. After everything I'd witnessed in the Orphans' Home, no depravity shocked me. I developed tastes which even William couldn't satisfy. And I dreamed that one day, I might not merely join the Damnation Society, but take it to fresh heights. A bold and noble ambition, don't you agree?'

Jacob had never seen her eyes sparkle with such intensity. Weak and weary as he was, he couldn't keep his mouth shut.

'Sara, it's a form of slavery. Shackling yourself to the traditions of men who are rich and cruel.'

'You don't understand,' she said. 'It's my birthright.'

'You're right. I don't understand.'

Mesmerised, he watched her stroke the gun.

'My father was Judge Savernake. I was his first-born.'

His brain was foggier than the London streets. The sedative in the brandy might have been mild, but he couldn't make sense of anything.

'You're Rachel's half-sister?'

'A quirk of the law robbed me of my inheritance. A stupid piece of paper, a marriage certificate. Something that didn't happen before I was born made all the difference to our lives. I was the Judge's flesh and blood, but that counted for nothing. She was legitimate; I was a bastard.'

Jacob mumbled, 'He treated you as an orphan. Put you in the home.'

'My mother was a prostitute who drank herself to death. He was the deadliest cross-examiner of his day. After leaving Cambridge, he founded the Damnation Society, an outlet for the energy and passion of rich young men addicted to decadence. The Society's funds were shrewdly invested. Properties were bought to accommodate members' mistresses or serve as brothels.'

'Sick,' Jacob mumbled.

'Gallows Court was at the heart of everything. The Orphans' Home supplied members with a never-ending source of... fresh blood. Every taste was catered for. My mother concealed her pregnancy until my premature birth, because otherwise she'd be disposed of, along with her unborn child. And then I was consigned to Mrs Mundy's tender mercies.'

'I'm sorry.' Jacob didn't know what else to say.

She dismissed his sympathy with a wave of the gun. 'Pity is the fruit of failure. I realised I was destined for greatness, even before I learned my father's identity.'

'How did you find out?'

'From his own lips, just before he resigned from the bench. He summoned me – yes, I lied about that, too. He was melancholy and confiding. In lucid intervals, the bitter awareness that his mind was failing tormented him. He told me he'd contemplated suicide – this was days before he slashed his wrists at the Old Bailey. Through Gabriel Hannaway, he settled some money on me. Although it seemed like riches, it was only a tiny portion of his wealth. Rachel must be his heir, he said, even though she was my junior. It was the law. He said he wished she was the bastard, not me, but he'd married her mother, not mine. At that moment I knew he did care for me, and that something was wrong with Rachel. And I hated her for standing in my way, although she was blissfully unaware of my existence.

'He fled to Gaunt, but ordered Gabriel Hannaway to make sure I came to no harm. The Hannaways had formed a dynasty, and so did others like the McAlindens and the Linacres. They were born to power and influence, in the world at large, and within the Damnation Society. Even William saw himself as a leader, with me as his consort. But second place is not for me.'

Jacob whispered, 'Why did it matter? What is so special about this... rakes' guild?'

She pouted at this naivety. 'Don't you see? Governments rise and fall, banks prosper and fail. The Damnation Society endures. The world crawled through four years of slaughter, but millions are made in a war. Pardoe and Gabriel Hannaway had a gift for making money. We can do as we please, we're beholden to no one.' Her voice rose. 'We own the future.'

'You sound like a political fanatic,' he muttered.

'Charles Brentano wanted to go into politics,' she scoffed. 'The trenches changed him, made him want to change the world. To build a land fit for heroes. He decided to betray the Society.'

'He was a member?'

'Once, he was the Judge's blue-eyed boy, audacious and dissolute. The son the old man never had. A gambler capable of winning or losing twenty thousand on the turn of a card, without so much as the blink of an eye. When he had a child by a Frenchwoman…'

'Yvette Viviers,' Jacob blurted out.

She gave him a hard look. 'You'll be a loss to journalism, Jacob. So you know how much Rachel hated Brentano's daughter?'

'All I know,' he said, 'is what Shoemaker told me.'

'It was out of the question for Brentano to marry her. Viviers was a whore who didn't even pretend to tread the boards. But she and their daughter lived under his protection in London until war was imminent. Juliet was never sent to the Orphans' Home. Brentano persuaded the Judge that she and her mother should be accommodated on Gaunt until the war ended, and the old fool agreed. Why was she permitted to live in the lap of luxury, when I was confined to the home? I had a stronger claim, I was the Judge's own child.'

Groggy and despairing, Jacob stared at her in disbelief, but she didn't notice. She was talking to herself.

'Brentano and Vincent Hannaway fought together in France, but Hannaway was guilty of cowardice in the face of the enemy. During the fiercest shelling, he panicked, and waved the white flag. Five men under his command were killed, and the rest taken prisoner. Brentano never forgave Hannaway's treachery. He came to hold the Damnation Society in contempt. Had he lived, he'd have destroyed it – yet the Judge wouldn't permit his elimination. Not until

Rachel twisted him around her little finger. She saw her chance to be rid of Juliet, and her parents. She lied through her teeth about what Brentano was supposed to have done to her, and it did the trick. The Judge agreed that Brentano and the woman must be punished. They were drugged, kidnapped and brought to London, to Gallows Court.'

'And murdered.'

'Punished as traitors.' She shrugged. 'I'll spare you the details. You'd only faint. Their daughter, the cuckoo in the nest, died of the Spanish flu, or so it was said. Who knows if Rachel poisoned her, and who cares? Good riddance to all three of them. With the Judge's brain addled, Rachel and her tiny coterie of hangers-on ruled Gaunt. The Judge lingered on for years, but even Gabriel Hannaway was kept away. Rachel and her acolytes remained in their island fortress, waiting for her father to die. On her twenty-fifth birthday, she became rich beyond the dreams of avarice, and made straight for London.

'I presumed her heart was set on seizing control of the Damnation Society. Today I realised that she was simply bent on destruction. Wiping out the past, and then wiping out herself. Pardoe, the Hannaways, and William knew that she had persuaded the Judge to kill Brentano and his mistress. So they had to die too.'

The cogs of his brain were grinding. 'And Claude Linacre?'

'Such a weakling should never have been elected to membership,' she said scornfully. 'He was easy prey for Rachel. His death sent a message to William and the others. None of them knew what to do for the best. One cannot negotiate with madness. They were in a blue funk, just like Vincent Hannaway in the trenches. That's why Pardoe murdered the Hayes woman. She left the Orphans' Home without an inkling of what was going on, but he was afraid Rachel would find her, and dared not risk any loose ends. When Thomas Betts started sniffing around, it was plain that he must be removed, but the others panicked like turkeys in December. I despaired of them. So one evening I became a crossing sweeper.'

His throat was dry. 'You were Iorweth Sear?'

'Look you, yes,' she said in a musical Welsh accent. 'William used to say I was alarmingly credible in drag. It wasn't hard to fool the rather stupid constable who took my statement. He didn't waste much time with me, perhaps he thought I was a pansy. Maurizio here drove the car that did for Betts. The Hannaways tried to scare off Rachel, but the job was bungled by a couple of amateurs. I didn't make the same mistake with Levi Shoemaker. Through William, I knew a nightclub owner who has a razor gang at his beck and call. I found them highly professional.'

Jacob's bruised face still felt tender. 'And the man who called on me at Amwell Street?'

'Another hired hand. I was pleased you kept quiet about my whereabouts. It proved that I'd landed you, hook, line, and sinker. You were quite brave, though now you look as if you're ready for a good cry.'

Jacob bit his lip, and said nothing.

'That's right, save your tears for later.' She sighed. 'William was vain enough to believe he could charm Rachel into subservience. A fatal mistake. While he and the others dithered, she eliminated them, one by one.'

'How could she cause all those deaths without implicating herself?'

'She persuaded Pardoe and Linacre that the game was up. Pardoe was dying, Linacre's brain was sodden with dope, it wasn't difficult to tip them over the edge. Then she conspired with George Barnes to murder William. As for the Hannaways, no doubt she bribed the butler. She thought their deaths spelled the end for the Society.'

'Why did she kill herself?'

Sara smiled. 'Once she'd achieved her goal, she had nothing else to live for. We shared the same father, but one crucial difference separated us. She inherited the Judge's impulse for self-destruction, and I did not.'

The wire rope bit into his wrists and ankles, and the pain brought tears to his eyes. The effect of the sedative had begun to wear off, but his head was spinning. Desperation was making him dizzy. How could he have been so deluded? An hour ago he'd yearned to share his life with this woman.

'Did you hope that by allowing me to talk, you'd improve your chances of escape?' she asked, consulting her watch. 'The opposite is the case. Whilst we conversed, Mei was making preparations. It's time for us to go to Gallows Court.'

Gaudino, who had listened in silence, stepped forward. He grasped Jacob by the shoulder, and pulled him off the settee.

'Gallows Court?' Jacob whispered.

'Where else?' she replied. 'The premises where fifty years ago today, the Society came to life. Think of it as an honour. You will become embedded in our history.'

'It may be foggy outside,' Jacob said, 'but don't you think someone might notice us?'

'Ah, Jacob. Do I detect one final flicker of bravado?' She smiled. 'Rest assured, I won't parade you down the street, like some mediaeval miscreant. Follow me.'

She strolled out of the room, and Gaudino dragged Jacob along in her wake. At the end of the hallway, she opened a door, and switched on a light. It revealed a stone staircase, and she trotted down it, taking the steps two at a time, like an excited child. Even in high heels, she kept her balance perfectly.

Gaudino pushed Jacob ahead of him. The stairs were steep, and Jacob was unable to hold onto anything to steady himself. More than once he almost lost his footing.

Sara was waiting for them at the bottom of the stairs. They were in a small rectangular space, from which a narrow passageway curved away in the direction of Lincoln's Inn. The tunnel was barely six feet high, and Gaudino had to incline his head so as not to scrape it on the roof.

'Electric lights,' Sara said, pointing to the small lamps fitted onto the brick wall of the tunnel. 'Every modern convenience, you see. This part of London is honeycombed with underground passages, as well as sewers and workings around the course of the old river Fleet. We've exploited their potential in ways beyond Bazalgette's wildest dreams.'

She set off at a brisk pace, with Gaudino dragging Jacob along in her wake. The ground was uneven but dry, although the air carried a whiff of stagnant water. Jacob half-closed his eyes, trying to drive out of his mind the pain in his shackled limbs, and his fear of what lay at the end of the tunnel. How long it took, he wasn't sure, but finally the macabre procession came to a halt in front of a padlocked steel door. Sara produced a key.

'Here we are,' she said. 'Gallows Court is above us. Shall we go in?'

The steel door opened noiselessly. She pressed a switch, flooding the room in front of them with brilliant light from half a dozen chandeliers. Jacob opened his eyes, and then closed them again. He couldn't believe what he saw.

The basement chamber was as well-equipped as the smoking room of a gentlemen's club, but twice as large and with a high ceiling. The air was fresher than in the tunnel, thanks, Jacob presumed, to some unseen but effective system of ventilation. Leather armchairs and Chesterfields provided luxurious seating, while one wall was devoted to a vast wine rack and a bar. On the facing wall hung an assortment of tapestries inspired, Jacob presumed, by erotica of the most violent and outré kind. Only a few days ago, he would have been appalled by the acts they depicted, but nothing would ever shock him again. Doors were let into the side walls, and at the far end of the room was a dais. On it stood a bizarre and intimidating figure. A larger than life-size gilded statue of a naked woman.

Gaudino pushed him into the room, and slammed the steel door behind them. Sara gestured towards their surroundings. 'Welcome to the home of the Damnation Society.'

Juliet Brentano's Journal

6 February 1920

A year has passed. I find it almost impossible to believe. Everything has changed, and yet on the surface, life on Gaunt continues much as before.

The decline in the Judge's mental state frustrates me. The best way to discover the truth about my parents' deaths would be to persuade him to tell me. Persuade him, or force him. I've tried both methods, but always in vain. And I'm not sure I could rely on anything he did say.

So learning the truth will take time, but I have time in abundance. Henrietta says I'm headstrong, but even she admits that nobody can match me for patience and persistence. My strength of will enables me to create a new life under a new name. A name that once made my flesh crawl.

I have become Rachel Savernake.

'What do you intend to do?' he whispered.

She beckoned him to follow her as the apron hid the huge gilded figure on the dais. His heart thumped as he tried to ... When he refused to move, the man servant slapped him on the cheek and shoved him forward.

'May I introduce you to Apega?'

The dazzling lights from the crystal chandelier made it difficult for him to focus. Had he fainted and bruised ... have tumbled to the ground had ... not been propping him up.

'Apega?'

'Apega married to the legendary tyrant King of Sparta. To deal with his enemies, he built a mechanical device in ...

33

Pain and fear and hopelessness numbed Jacob. Nobody knew he was here, and he had no chance of untying himself. If only Oakes had not set off with the ambulance carrying Rachel's body to the mortuary. Apart from the inspector, he could think of nobody else – certainly not a soul from the *Clarion* – who would give his current whereabouts a second thought.

'Over the past fifty years,' Sara said, 'this room has witnessed countless esoteric entertainments. Senior members compete to conjure up creative ceremonial rituals. The notion of sacrifice brings out the worst in the human imagination. The Pear of Anguish, the Wheel of Suffering, the Brazen Bull, the Judas Cradle. Ingenious means of inflicting peculiar agonies. A dishonest cook was baked in a kiln, an obese mistress boiled in a cauldron of hot fat. All for the delectation of the fellowship.'

Jacob blinked tears out of his eyes. 'Where are they?'

'Patience, Jacob. Thanks to Rachel Savernake, our numbers are depleted. But people will start arriving within the half-hour. This evening, they will elect me to reign over them.'

'What do you intend to do to me?' he whispered.

She beckoned him to follow her as she approached the huge gilded figure on the dais. His heart thumped as if about to burst. When he refused to move, the manservant slapped him on the temple, and shoved him forward.

'May I introduce you to Apega?'

The dazzling lights from the crystal chandeliers made it difficult for him to focus his eyes. Battered and bruised, he'd have tumbled to the ground had Gaudino not been propping him up.

'Apega?'

'Apega was married to the legendary tyrant king of Sparta. To deal with his enemies, he built a mechanical device in the image of his wife. Its purpose was to torment his foes. Apega the automaton bristled with sharp blades. Her loving embrace was lethal.'

Jacob saw the blades. Innumerable small but wickedly sharp points pimpled the huge naked body from head to toe.

'This was two thousand years before the automatons for which the great illusionists became famous.' Her voice was hushed in awe. 'Von Kempelen's chess-playing Turk, Frederick Ireland's bicycling Enigmarelle, John Nevil Maskelyne's Psycho. Mechanical masterpieces that I yearned to surpass. Now I've created a murderous machine that I can bring to life.'

She cleared her throat. 'Come, Apega. Jacob Flint seeks to pay tribute to you. He is a born romantic. Please rehearse how you will give yourself to each other.'

Hypnotised by sheer horror, Jacob heard the clank of unseen cogs and wheels. Apega slowly stretched out long arms, and then both jointed legs. Stepping down from the dais, the automaton began to walk forward. Its movements were stiff and jerky but purposeful. The arms reaching out for him were studded with blades. If Apega seized him, his flesh would be ripped to shreds.

'Later, when her audience arrives, she will take you in her arms, and…'

Jacob stared into the blank eyes of the automaton. 'Sara, please.'

Sara snapped her fingers. 'Wait, Apega. The time has not yet come.'

The automaton kept moving. Stride by stride, it drew closer.

'Stop, Apega!' Sara cried. 'Didn't you hear me? It's too soon. Stop at once!'

The automaton continued its advance. In its awkward, noisy way, it was heading straight for Jacob. He felt Gaudino tense by his side, and tighten his hold on Jacob's arm. Something was wrong. The illusion wasn't working. Or else it was working too well. Sara was no longer in control. The torture machine had developed a mind of its own.

'Stop!' Sara took a step back. 'Don't move another inch.'

Apega kept on moving.

'*Smettere proprio ora!*' Gaudino shouted.

The manservant released his grip, and Jacob stumbled against a leather armchair. As he fought to keep his balance, the automaton drew closer. Its arms were reaching out for him.

Sara took the pistol out of her bag and squeezed the trigger. Nothing happened.

'Maurizio!' she screamed. 'Stop her!'

Gaudino lifted the switchblade. The automaton changed direction, as if it had taken notice. With a step to the right, Apega set a new course straight towards Sara Delamere.

'Stop!'

Gaudino rushed forward, brandishing the switchblade, interposing his body between Apega and his mistress. The automaton lifted an arm and swiped the knife from his hand. Its blades sliced his sleeve, and he screamed in pain. Jacob saw a dark stain spread across the ruined cotton.

'Mei, enough!' Sara cried.

Sara hesitated for a moment before kicking off her shoes, and stumbling in the direction of the steel door at the rear of the room. The automaton lumbered after her. The door in the left hand wall was flung open, and Trueman stepped into the room.

Trueman was holding a revolver. Firing across the room, he hit one of the bottles in the rack on the opposite wall. Glass shattered, fragments flying like shrapnel. Red wine sprayed out onto the pale carpet.

'Next time,' he said, 'I shoot at the heart.'

Gaudino sank to the floor, clutching his torn arm, as the automaton halted in mid-stride.

'Mei!' Sara's face was white. 'How could you?'

The door on the right opened. Jacob caught his breath. The tiny Chinese woman appeared. She was clutching a pair of wire cutters.

Sara gazed at her in disbelief. 'Mei! What are you...?'

Her eyes switched back to Apega the automaton. The machine was jerking about as if trying to flex its muscles. As Mei cut his bonds, Jacob heard the screech of a metal plate sliding open. Apega was disgorging her secret.

Barefoot and wearing only a white cotton vest and shorts, Rachel Savernake squeezed out of the back of the machine. Her hair was in disarray, and her cheeks were flushed with exertion. Breathlessly, she hummed a ditty. Jacob recognised the refrain of 'Ain't Misbehavin''.

'The report of my death was exaggerated,' she said. 'Sorry to disappoint you, Sara. That's the trouble with illusions. They dissolve in the face of reality.'

Sara opened her mouth as if to speak, but no words came. For fully fifteen seconds, the two women and the two men were motionless, a tableau of daring and defeat. Mei's cutters snapped away at the wire. Jacob had been tied so tightly that he'd almost lost the sensation in his hands and feet. Every other part of his body hurt.

Sara put her head down, and raced for the open door. Trueman lifted his gun, and fired a warning shot which pulverised a second bottle of wine. Jacob dodged out of the way of the flying glass, but Sara fled from the room.

'Keep an eye on our friend,' Rachel said to Trueman, gesturing to Gaudino. Mei raised the wire cutters, but Rachel shook her head. 'Only as a last resort.'

Jacob rubbed his sore wrists. 'We can't let her get away!'

'Follow me.'

Rachel loped across the room, and through the door. Hobbling after her, Jacob found himself entering another brick-walled tunnel. He saw two short flights of steps. One led up to a padlocked wooden door. At the bottom of the other was the dark opening of a well. This tunnel, like the one from Carey Street, curved so that he couldn't guess where it went, but it was low and narrow, and smelled foul. Rachel strode forward, and disappeared out of sight.

He limped after her, choking as he inhaled the foetid air. After the bend, the tunnel straightened, and he heard Sara gasp as the rocky ground cut into her feet. Rachel was five yards ahead of him, breathing noisily. She was finding it hard to keep her balance. He heard her stifle a cry. The jagged stones were tearing her bare soles.

Fifty yards further on, she halted at a point where the tunnel opened out into a large circular space. When he caught up with her, they clutched each other's arms for support. Her thin, wiry frame shuddered with exhaustion. She'd been cramped up inside Apega, and he sensed her strength was ebbing.

Ahead, the tunnel split into two. One route ended in a round chamber full of strange impedimenta: spiked metal hoods and bridles, elaborate wooden contraptions with pulleys, and a large wire cage. Rachel caught his horrified expression.

'A torturer's store room,' she panted. 'Indispensable for an orgy of cruelty.'

He stared down the other limb of the tunnel. The way narrowed, and the stink wafting from it nauseated him.

'A tributary of the sewers,' Rachel said. 'She can never escape.'

Linking arms, they stumbled forward. They were moving deeper underground, as the tunnel burrowed down into the earth's bowels. There were no more electric lamps, and scarcely enough light for them to see Sara.

She still wore the Widow Bianchi's finery, and the flowing gown kept getting in the way. Her body bent into a crouch as she inched along a ledge the width of a single brick. Jacob realised that the ledge was actually the top of a high wall. This was a barricade designed to dam a sewer, a conduit culminating in a junction with the main tunnel. At the far end of the wall was a dark opening in the earth. Jacob could not see what lay beyond.

'Are you sure?' he whispered.

'The Fleet sewers form a rank labyrinth. You need gum-boots and an iron stomach to manage more than a few paces. Watch what happens.'

Sara slipped, and put out a hand to steady herself against the tunnel wall. She teetered to the left, countering the risk of falling to the right, into the depths of the sewer.

Jacob held his breath. Now the woman who had meant to kill him was risking her own life.

'And she said you had suicidal tendencies,' he breathed.

Rachel grunted. 'Like so many would-be leaders, she has devoted her life to wishful thinking.'

The stench was overpowering. Jacob felt sick, but could not keep his eyes off Sara. She concentrated as if walking a tightrope. The ledge was damp and treacherous. With each step, she paused, sucking more of the toxic air into her lungs. Jacob was conscious of Rachel beside him, and the warmth of her wiry and skimpily clad body in the cold dank air. Their bodies touched.

'Any moment now,' she whispered.

Sara caught her foot in the folds of her gown, and lost her balance. Bare feet skidding, she fell head-first, screaming and clawing at air as she plunged into the sewer. With a thud, she hit the mound of rottenness.

Grasping Jacob's hand, Rachel edged forward. Step by step, they reached the brick ledge. Below they could see the lumpy mass of waste in the sewer, bubbling, reeking and deadly as quicksand. The drop was ten feet, and Sara had landed head-first. The gown billowed on the surface of the frothy, smothering waste. Her wig had fallen off into a rocky crevice. Of Sara's loveliness, there was no sign. Nothing but the gurgling sludge of London's bowels.

Jacob turned away, and retched. Even the cauldron of boiling fat Sara had spoken of would have granted a death both quicker and less vile.

Juliet Brentano's Journal

6 February 1921

Another year gone. We live so quietly here, the Judge, Henrietta, Cliff, Martha, and me. Hardly anyone disturbs us, and we disturb no one. Every now and then, old Hannaway writes to the Judge, a brief note proposing a visit to Gaunt and enclosing a longer note written in some form of cipher.

The Judge never sees the letters. I respond on his behalf, explaining that he remains indisposed.

Caution is essential. Yet nobody has exposed me. With every day that passes, my confidence grows. The Judge's mental state is so fragile that even if he told the truth, nobody would believe him. As for Harold Brown, he won't show his face again. Not after what he did to poor Martha.

On Gaunt, I'm never at a loss for something to do, or a new skill to learn. That is why I've neglected this journal. My quest will take years, but I mean to use them well.

I've ransacked my memories of my childhood for clues, but the pictures in my mind are as faded as old sepia photographs. We lived in King's Cross, and although we didn't have much money, there was enough to get by. My father didn't live with us, and his visits were special treats. He was tall, handsome, and well-spoken, and I was in awe of him. My parents weren't married, and the boy who lived next door once teased me about that. He never made the same mistake again.

As a child, I was happier to run wild in the streets than to wear pretty dresses or play with dolls. But then I started coughing and losing weight. Just before the war broke out, a doctor said I was suffering from consumption. My father enlisted, and came to kiss me goodbye. He said he'd arranged for my mother and me to stay at Savernake Hall with his ailing uncle. I could recover in peace and quiet, Father said.

Rachel never hid her contempt for us. My mother she hated because the Judge seemed to have some affection for her. To this day, I don't know how many sacrifices Mother made to keep me from harm.

Over time, I regained my strength. I would sneak out of the Hall, and go running along the shoreline, swimming in the sound, climbing the rocky outcrops. Rachel did none of that. Perhaps her laziness explains her swift surrender to the influenza.

What I do know is that the impersonation is a success. I embarked on it recklessly, without caring about the future. From that moment on, Cliff, Henrietta, and Martha have been my partners in crime,

The truth is that I enjoy being Rachel Savernake, and imposing my tastes on her life. A girl whose reading was limited to cheap novelettes is now seldom found without her nose in a book. A girl who found learning was a chore is now determined to discover as much as possible about the world beyond Gaunt, so that she can take her place in it when the time comes.

Since the Judge had his stroke, there is no hope of extracting meaningful clues to what happened to my parents. He's ruined physically and mentally. Cliff's profoundly deaf cousin, an elderly woman named Bertha, acts as his nurse.

We make up a strange household, a handful of people rattling around in a vast old house. We've closed half the building, to make it easier to look after. But I have kept exploring those silent, musty rooms, knowing that somewhere in Savernake Hall lies the secret of my parents' fate.

Last week came the breakthrough. After endless searching, I discovered a secret cupboard in the wall of the Judge's study. It overflows with documents written in the same sort of cipher as the lawyer's notes. Among them is a copy of his last will and testament. The original is held by Hannaway. At least it is written in English, if legal gobbledegook counts as English.

In short, the Judge leaves almost everything to his beloved daughter, Rachel Savernake. She inherits on her twenty-fifth birthday. There are modest legacies to each person who is in his employment at the date of his death. In the event of his daughter's death before the age of twenty-five, the whole estate goes to the Gambit Club, of which, the will says, the Judge was 'proud to be a founding member and first President'.

The address given for the Gambit Club is that of Hannaway's legal practice. Gaunt Chambers in Gallows Court, Lincoln's Inn. The Judge practised there as a barrister. In his prime, he enjoyed playing chess. I mean to ensure that the Gambit Club never receives a penny from the estate.

From my research in the Judge's law books, it is clear that his dying in the near future would do me no good. Hannaway would control the trust imposed by the will. A new will, worded more liberally, and providing that I inherit on attaining my majority, would improve matters. Cliff, by instinct a man of action, thought it worth trying. Reluctantly, I've decided that the risk of forgery, or of trying to persuade the Judge to make the change, is too great. So much could go wrong. I mustn't draw attention to myself, or to arouse Hannaway's suspicions in any way. We must keep the Judge alive until I can inherit.

After that...

One day, I shall go to Gallows Court.

As for Cliff and Henrietta, my steadfast friends, I have the happiest news. They are to be married in April, in a quiet ceremony. Henrietta will become Mrs Trueman. And Martha and I shall be their bridesmaids.

34

'How much will you tell him?' Clifford Trueman asked.

'More than I should,' Rachel said. 'Less than he wants to know.'

'But not – about Juliet Brentano?'

'Oh no,' she said. 'Not about her.'

'If only Harold Brown hadn't seen you in the kitchen that day. He's the only person who's ever realised you aren't...'

She raised a hand. 'Enough.'

'Brown talked to Tom Betts. Suppose he let him into your secret.'

Rachel shook her head. 'Without being paid? Not him.'

'What if he told someone else about you? What if...?'

'Today is what matters.' She exhaled. 'Let tomorrow take care of itself.'

It was four o'clock, precisely twenty-four hours after her supposed suicide, and they were strolling around the roof garden of Gaunt House. On an unseasonably warm afternoon, a dipping sun streaked the blue-grey sky with orange. In the terracotta tubs, snowdrops and yellow crocuses were coming into bloom. Through the glass walls enclosing the heated swimming pool, Rachel could see Jacob in the water, on his fourth length. Seated in rattan chairs by the pool's edge, Hetty Trueman was knitting a cardigan, while Martha's head was buried in a novel, *The Way Things Are*. Wine glasses and tumblers stood on a table, alongside bottles of Merlot and Chablis, and a tankard of Guinness for Trueman.

He said, 'Martha reckons you've taken a shine to Jacob Flint.'

'Martha is a born romantic.'

'Hetty isn't, and she agrees with Martha.'

'You think he's soft, don't you?'

'He shook like a leaf at Gallows Court.'

'Forgivable, surely, in the circumstances?'

'So you are sweet on him?'

Rachel laughed. 'You're as bad as Hetty, and she enjoys matchmaking almost as much as prophesying disaster. Why does she want to marry me off to someone so credulous as to fall for my supposed half-sister? Jacob's a pleasant young man, and I've met precious few. I feel for him – what's Mr Fitzgerald's nice phrase? – a sort of tender curiosity. Leave it at that.'

She slid open the door in the glass wall. Martha was tapping bare feet to a record playing on the gramophone: the Casa Loma Orchestra, performing 'Happy Days are Here Again'. As she stepped into the warmth of the conservatory, Jacob clambered out of the pool, and picked up a fluffy white towel. Rachel slipped off her fur jacket, and poured everyone a drink.

'To just deserts,' she said, raising her glass.

Now out of the pool, Jacob savoured the tang of the wine. 'Thank you again. For saving my life, and then for putting me up here.'

'We could hardly let you stay in Edgar House or Carey Street,' Rachel said. 'Keeping company with dead women's ghosts. You're welcome to recuperate with us for a day or two, while you look for somewhere to live. A chief crime correspondent needs a place of his own, somewhere to plot his next scoop.'

He put his glass down, and towelled his wet hair. 'Gomersall is happy with my story about Sara Delamere.'

'*Tragic death of female illusionist in freak accident.* Not quite the stuff of banner headlines.' Rachel shrugged. 'A sorry epitaph for a self-styled elitist. Her final performance was relegated to page five.'

'You've taught me the value of discretion,' he said. 'I want you to feel you can place your trust in me.'

She smiled. 'Patience, Jacob. I'm not ready to bare my soul. Just as the *Clarion*'s readership isn't ready for anything quite as ludicrous as Apega the automaton.'

'You did promise to satisfy my curiosity about your supposed suicide. After all, you shared your plans with Oakes. How did you persuade him to co-operate?'

'He knew nothing about the Damnation Society, though he suspected a conspiracy between men of power and influence. His mistake was to believe poor old Sir Godfrey Mulhearn was part of it. Equally, Oakes' rapid promotion made me wonder if he was hand-in-glove with Chadwick, but the truth is simply that he's a good detective. Once I was confident we were fighting on the same side – more or less – it made sense to pool our efforts. Not that I shared everything I knew.'

'And your fall onto the railings?'

'After the Hannaways died, Oakes came to see me. I said criminals responsible for the deaths of Thomas Betts and Levi Shoemaker were manipulating you.'

The gramophone record had come to an end. Jacob took a long draught of wine. 'Ouch.'

'You asked me to be honest,' Rachel said. 'I told Oakes I needed you and Sara Delamere to believe I was dead. I said she was my half-sister, and that she'd inherited the Judge's madness. I simply needed her to reveal herself in her true colours.'

'Once Vincent Hannaway was out of the way. Her last rival for leadership of the Damnation Society.'

'Exactly.'

'But what about the Hannaways' butler? Destined for the gallows, condemned for a crime he didn't commit?'

'In his time, he's raped at least three women. One of them drowned herself and her newborn child.'

He was abashed. 'I didn't know that.'

'Some things it's better not to know,' Rachel said. 'Yesterday, when I summoned you here for four o'clock, I hoped Sara Delamere would insist on accompanying you. The Damnation Society's Golden Jubilee meant as much to her as it did to me. She meant to lure me to Gallows Court. I required time and space to catch her in flagrante. So I staged an illusion for her benefit.'

'How?'

She yawned. 'Conjurers are like detectives: their explanations are an anticlimax. The first night you stayed here, Hetty planted the seed in your mind, by letting slip that I might kill myself.'

He opened his eyes very wide. 'That was deliberate? Part of a script?'

'Sara was bound to be sceptical, and you needed to be taken in, so as to convince her I really was dead, and she had nothing else to fear.'

Jacob grunted. 'Glad to be of service.'

'Don't be grumpy, Jacob, it doesn't suit you. That morning, Martha allowed Hetty to cut her lovely hair. A sacrifice in a noble cause. When you and Sara and Oakes arrived, she pranced around up here to attract your attention, wearing a wig and a duplicate of a favourite outfit of mine. After dodging out of sight, she let out a piercing cry, and pretended to fall. I'd already arranged myself as an impaled corpse, complete with fake blood. Oakes and his men, along with the ambulance driver, lent the picture a touch of authenticity. And Hetty wailed miserably, as only Hetty can.'

Henrietta Trueman snorted. 'You think you're so clever.'

'Mmmm.'

'But Martha joined us in the alleyway…'

'She came straight down in the electric lift, slipping off the fur coat that covered her uniform, and putting on the same wig she's wearing now.'

'No wonder she was out of breath.' Jacob groaned. 'And Mei emptied the bullets from Sara's pistol?'

'Yes. She and two sisters were shipped to England eighteen months ago. The eldest of the three girls raised the alarm with the police, but Chadwick saw to it that the report went missing. Hannaway turned her execution into entertainment on 29 January last year, *pour encourager les autres*. Believe me, once Martha befriended Mei, recruiting her to our cause was simplicity itself.'

Jacob leaned back in his chair. 'I'd like to know more about Charles Brentano and Yvette Viviers.'

Rachel said carefully, 'I can assure you, I was not responsible for their deaths.'

'Sara made that story up?'

'Harold Coleman,' Rachel said quietly, 'had a lot to answer for.'

'Tell me about him.'

Trueman shifted in his chair. Abruptly, Martha put her book down, and went out through the door in the glass wall, closing it firmly behind her.

Jacob frowned. 'Sorry. Did I speak out of turn?'

'Coleman – or Brown, as we knew him then – was lower than vermin. He lusted after Martha, who was the same age as me, though much lovelier. She was protected by the presence of Charles Brentano and his mistress. In his youth, Charles ran wild. He was a gambler and a debauch, but the affair with Yvette was the making of him. He adored her, and made sure no harm came to her or their child. But then the Judge… turned against them, and Coleman seized his chance. At the Judge's bidding, he drugged the pair of them, and drove them down to London, where he handed them over to William Keary and the Hannaways.'

Her voice trembled, something unique in Jacob's experience of her. She took a gulp of wine.

'Sara told me they were punished by the Damnation Society,' he said. 'But the death certificate said heart failure.'

'Rufus Paul's euphemism of choice to explain away ritual sacrifices conducted at Gallows Court. Hannaway feared that Charles would broadcast his cowardice to the world, and bring down the Society. So he had him tortured, and then hanged, drawn, and quartered in front of Yvette's eyes. A public execution, just like the old days at Gallows Court. Except that the spectators were a select group, present by special invitation. Once Charles was dead, the members took their pleasure with Yvette before subjecting her to the same fate.'

Rachel paused, and took a moment to compose herself. 'What was left of them was cremated.'

'So,' Jacob said slowly, 'in the way that Keary and the Hannaways died, there was a touch of… poetic justice?'

Her expression was as cold and distant as the moon. 'When Harold Brown came back to Gaunt, he took advantage of the fact that Cliff was sick to assault Martha. She fought like a tiger, and tore his face with her nails. His revenge was to hurl acid at her. When Cliff began to recover, Brown fled. He changed his name to Coleman, and took up a new identity. For a long time there was no trace of him. But we never gave up the search.'

Trueman glared at Jacob. 'In the end, justice was done there, too.'

'Sara Delamere wasn't alone in employing the Rotherhithe Razors,' Rachel said. 'Their leaders are true capitalists; they serve the highest bidder. And they kept their bargain. Coleman's last few hours felt like a lifetime.'

Jacob shivered as he gazed through the glass at Martha. 'I think she is still beautiful.'

'So do we,' Rachel said softly.

'What happened to Juliet Brentano?'

Rachel looked him in the eye. 'She died a natural death.'

'I see.' Jacob had no choice but to take her word for it. 'So you spent another ten years on Gaunt, with the Judge.'

'The old man was incapable.' Hetty Trueman stood up, and refilled their glasses. 'Rachel took charge. Nobody we didn't trust was allowed anywhere near. People on the mainland reckoned it was impossible, just the three of us and an elderly nurse, looking after an old madman and his… daughter. But we got by.'

'You spent that time educating yourself, preparing for the day when the Judge died and you inherited his fortune,' Jacob said.

Rachel inclined her head. 'The Judge persisted in trying to kill himself. When we hid his pills, he tried to starve himself to death. But we refused to allow the end to come too soon. He was forced to wait until I was almost twenty-five.'

Her expression gave no clue to what was in her mind, and Jacob decided not to ask.

'Did the Judge confide in you about the Damnation Society?'

'The lucid intervals became rare,' Rachel said. 'Fortunately, he'd hoarded all his old papers, and over the years I deciphered them.'

'They were in code?'

'Members of the Society delighted in using the Playfair cipher. It became their private language for sensitive communications. They called it playing fair. The term tickled their sense of humour, just as it amused them to have a brothel and a sadist's dungeon camouflaged as a gentlemen's chess club. Fortunately, the Judge's library was a cornucopia of knowledge. I trained myself in the essentials of cryptography, and began to unlock the Society's secrets. I came across the names of Pardoe, Linacre, and Keary. Every hateful detail I read hardened my resolve to destroy them. Yet it took time and money to put my plan into practice. The Damnation Society's resources seemed infinite. I needed to inherit the Judge's estate in order to fulfil my dream.'

'So you waited.'

'And prepared. When I arrived in London, I began to communicate with Pardoe and the others. Using their own code to sow uncertainty, discord, and fear. The black pawn found close to his body served the same purpose. When the time was right, I talked to Vincent Hannaway about playing fair. He understood then that I was privy to their secrets.'

Jacob drank some more wine. Rachel's use of the cipher was surely connected with the fates of Linacre and Pardoe. But she was right. Ignorance was sometimes bliss.

'The Damnation Society was twisted and corrupt,' she said. 'Crime was legitimate, so long as it benefited pillars of the establishment. To commit a murder – the more shocking, the better – was a badge of honour. To a man like Linacre, the life of sweet, stupid Dolly Benson counted for nothing. The same was true of Mary-Jane Hayes. Pardoe took a shine to her, but that didn't stop him killing her, and cutting off her head. Dressing up such crimes as the work of a maniac was the Damnation Society's hallmark.'

'Tom Betts got on the trail. He talked to Coleman.'

'Betts was on my trail too,' Rachel said. 'I warned him to keep his nose out of my affairs. He should have taken that advice.'

An idea struck Jacob. 'It's you, isn't it?'

She gave him a cold stare. 'What do you mean?'

'You're the one giving his widow financial support?'

Rachel allowed herself a smile. 'Mrs Betts overestimates the generosity of the *Clarion*, I'm afraid. You mustn't disabuse her.'

'Of course not.' He was conscious of her leisurely scrutiny of his semi-naked body. 'Even Levi Shoemaker didn't quite realise what he was up against.'

'What he learned about Chadwick, McAlinden, Thurlow, and the Dowd women was invaluable. He even suspected that Sara Delamere and Chiara Bianchi were one and the same, but he failed to see the significance. Men of his generation underestimate women. It's a habit.'

'So you knew she posed as the Widow Bianchi?'

'Sara was a gifted actress,' Rachel said. 'But not as brilliant as she believed. Her constant comings and goings at Carey Street gave her away. Once it became clear that she would enter, and the Widow Bianchi would leave, the inference was obvious.'

'So Martha enlisted Mei's support?'

'Mei described how Sara and that animal Gaudino treated her. She and her sister had nobody to turn to. Until we came along.'

He cleared his throat. 'I've noticed it's your modus operandi. Turning servants against their masters and mistresses.'

'I see it differently,' Rachel said. 'Employers who forfeit any claim to loyalty must pay the price. Speak to Cliff and Hetty privately. After the trouble I've caused them, you may find they take the same view.'

'Get away with you,' Hetty said.

Martha came back in from the roof garden. Her eyes were red. She went over to Rachel, who clasped her hand. Nothing was said.

Jacob emptied his glass. 'What about the Orphans' Home?'

'The Oxford police are swarming over the place as we speak,' Rachel said. 'Mrs Mundy was unwise to invest her retirement fund in diamonds smuggled from Rotterdam. While she's under arrest for handling stolen goods, the police can build a case to send her to prison for the rest of her life.'

'But Leivers, Paul, and Heslop?'

'Their punishment is to live in constant fear of exposure. Waiting for the knock on the door. The same is true of Alfred Linacre, McAlinden senior, and their friends.'

'I see.'

Rachel released Martha's hand. 'The hydra has many heads, Jacob. Cut off one, and another grows.'

'Isn't that a counsel of despair?' he said boldly.

'We live in the world as it is, not as we would wish it to be. Every society conceives its own elites. What matters is that they are subject to justice. Imposed through the legal process or...'

'Extra-judicially?'

She nodded. 'Oakes balked at the prospect of throwing the Prime Minister's right-hand man into prison, to say nothing of the most popular trade union leader, our most famous doctor and forensic pathologist, and a stray bishop. The police presence in Gallows Court alerted early comers to the fact that their junket was to be disrupted, and they ran for cover.'

'So the police were out in force at Gallows Court?'

'Absolutely. What if something had gone wrong underground? Hetty feeds me so well, I might have got stuck in that absurd contraption, and then where would you be? Mei warned me to expect a tight squeeze. She's even thinner than me, but she's never spent more than ten minutes inside that monstrosity Apega. Oakes couldn't take the risk that you might actually be sacrificed.'

Jacob shivered.

'Wipe off that sad spaniel expression.' She tapped Martha's hand. 'Would you like to put on a record? We can admire Cliff and Hetty's foxtrot. And I'm in the mood for a dance myself. Come on, Jacob, Martha and I will share you.'

As Martha moved towards the gramophone, Jacob laughed. 'All right, you win.'

'She always does,' Hetty Trueman said.

Rachel Savernake stood up, and beckoned him.

'Be warned,' Jacob said. 'I've got two left feet.'

'Don't worry,' Rachel said. 'I know how to deal with inadequate men. Come on. This is my favourite song. *Let's do it.*'

Acknowledgements

This book represents a new departure for me as a novelist. I'd like to thank all those who helped and encouraged me during the writing process. I was given information and suggestions by a considerable number of people, too many to mention individually, but I'd like to thank Catherine, Jonathan, and Helena Edwards, Kate Godsmark, Ann Cleeves, Geoff Bradley, and Moira Redmond for particular help. My thanks as ever go to my agent James Wills, and I'm also grateful to Nic Cheetham, Sophie Robinson, and the team at Head of Zeus for showing faith in my writing and in this novel.